The Narrative

Deplora Boule

The Narrative is a work of satirical fiction. The characters and events portrayed in this book are creations of the author's imagination. The author confesses to having been inspired by the unprecedentedly absurd times in which we live, but nothing in this work should be construed as actually having taken place. *The Narrative* was written purely for entertainment purposes.

Book design by Logotecture

logotecture.com

ISBN-13: 978-1717160652

ISBN-10: 1717160654

...because it's long past time to point and laugh.

Chapter 1

SOMEHOW, SOMEWHERE ALONG the way, Majedah had gotten the idea that her life was pretty good. She lived in comfort with her wealthy mother. She was gifted with good health, a good brain, and exotic good looks. And at just 18, she was socially aware and perfectly situated for a dazzling future.

Thank goodness the higher minds at Lilith College had shown her the folly of her beliefs!

Majedah had spent the past four months learning the horrible truth; she was a victim! She was, first of all, a woman, but not only that—she was a woman of color!

She was so grateful for her Freshman Seminar, which had opened her eyes to the harsh reality of the world. The countless wrongs stacked up against her, both contemporary and historical, now swarmed her consciousness like angry blowflies, eating away the sheen of joy from every aspect of her daily life. She hadn't realized how badly she had been oppressed, abused, and lied to by an unfair, evil society. But at last, she had learned the Truth!

Today, home from college for holiday break, Majedah dwelt specifically on the wrongs that had been done her by her high school boyfriend. The knowledge that she thought she loved him just last summer sickened her. Now that she knew the Truth, she seethed with rage as she knocked on the front door of his home.

A tall, sandy-haired young man opened the door. His face fairly beamed when he saw her, and she accidentally smiled back before she caught herself. But he had already stepped outside, barefoot, onto the chilly front step to enfold her in an affectionate embrace. "Mandy!" he exclaimed. "It's so great to see you! How have you been?"

Majedah disengaged herself and stepped back. She looked at the ground for a moment to get her mind right and remember her rage. "Not very well, Kevin," she growled. "May I come inside for a moment?" She saw confusion on his face and felt a flush of cruel satisfaction.

"Of course. Come on in." He led the way back into the house. They passed through a small entry hall and into a modest living room. Majedah flung her coat onto the back of an armchair. "Is everything okay?" asked Kevin. "Do you want to sit down?"

"No, thank you, this will only take a minute," Majedah answered crisply. She glanced through the room towards the back of the house. "Are your parents home?"

"No, they took Scott shopping for shoes. I'm the only one home." Concern filled his robin's egg blue eyes and he looked at her intently. "What's wrong, Mandy?"

Majedah figured the best way to do this was just to say it. She lifted her adorably pointy chin, tossed her gleaming black hair over her shoulder, and looked her former boyfriend in the eye. "Kevin, just so you know, last fall I had to exercise my Constitutional right to women's health care."

"Huh, okay. So ... that's good, right? I mean, it's smart to get regular checkups and stay healthy."

She shook her head in frustration. "No, that's not what I'm saying. Last fall, I exercised my choice to procure women's health care."

"Right. ... You should go to the doctor when you need to. Even women. *Especially* women. You should absolutely have access to health care and avail yourself of it whenever you—"

"Dammit, Kevin, I had an abortion, okay?"

Kevin suddenly looked as though he had taken an MMA kick to the gut. His boring, conventionally handsome features crumpled as a red flush overtook them, and he choked out a surprised sob.

Majedah's perfect lips parted in surprise. She had learned in Freshman Seminar that men such as Kevin are repulsive, but she had also learned that men who could express vulnerability were the most attractive of all (if one *must* date a man). Then she remembered the cause of Kevin's consternation: being thwarted at his patriarchal plan to enslave her by forcing her to grow a baby for him. "God, come on, Kevin. Who cries over a clump of cells?" Disgust burned in her black eyes and sharpened her tone.

He made an effort to gather himself. "I'm sorry to get upset. After all, you're the one who had to go through that trauma."

"Trauma? It's a choice, not a *trauma*. Why are you making such a big deal out of this?" Majedah berated him. "Why can't you be more like my friends at Lilith? They threw me an amazing 'Shout Your Abortion' party, with organic dragon fruit mojitos and everything."

Bewilderment replaced sorrow on Kevin's face. "A what? With ... what?" he asked.

"Yeah, and we toasted my choice and everything. It was really nice to be surrounded by people who were supportive of me when I took charge of my own life and my own destiny."

He looked aghast again. Somehow, he was using his masculine wiles to make her feel guilty.

"Seriously, Kevin, let it go," she continued. "It was nothing and it's been taken care of." She shook her head angrily. "God, I knew it was stupid to tell you. I don't know why I even did."

"Because it was the right thing to do," he answered quickly. "And I'm glad you did, because it was my fault as much as yours, but you're the one who had to suffer the consequences. I'm so, so sorry."

"That's right, you should be sorry!" Majedah stared into the middle distance as she remembered more of what she had learned. "Except ... there's nothing to be sorry about, because it's actually great that I exercised my Constitutional right to women's health care!" *Wait, so should I thank him?* Majedah wondered. It was so challenging, getting used to how her new awareness worked!

He came to her, put his hands on her shoulders, and looked into her seal-black eyes. Majedah crossed her arms angrily across her chest. "Mandy," he said, "I just need to know you're okay. Please, let me know if you need anything."

"Ugh, I don't need anything from you!" She flung his hands away. "And don't call me 'Mandy' anymore. I use my full name now." She turned and grabbed her coat off the back of the hideous bourgeois armchair. "I have to go. I told Julia I'd pick up the vegan holiday turkey on my way home." She made her way quickly to the foyer before pausing to look back at him one last time. Kevin's brimming blue eyes, full of broken heart and regret, were trained on her.

"Thank you, Mandy—"

"Majedah!"

"Ma—Majedah. Thank you for telling me."

"Yeah, sure, whatever. Goodbye, Kevin." As she spun to leave, a glittering tree in the corner of the room twinkled at her. "Oh, yeah ... happy holidays!" she called over her shoulder. She clawed open the door and escaped into the clean winter air.

WITH THE UNPLEASANTNESS checked off her to-do list, Majedah picked up the groceries at Food Citizen and drove the electric car back to her mother's antique house on the edge of the picturesque town. There was no snow yet, but the landscaper had hung festive decorations on the specimen trees in the front yard. Majedah gathered the groceries, bounded up the steps to the deep front porch, and let herself into the house.

"Hi, Julia. I'm back," she called. She set the packages on a burnished walnut transom table and went to hang her jacket in the closet.

Her mother's voice came from a room off to one side of the flawlessly decorated center hall. "Hello, Majedah. I'm in my office."

Majedah left her boots in the front closet and walked across the thick red Persian rug, her feet sinking a good inch into the lush organic wool. She stuck her head through the doorway and smiled. "Hello."

Julia was seated behind her exquisite Regency desk, which was positioned between two enormous windows. Afternoon sun filtered through the shantung draperies to set her thick ash blond hair aglow. The damask-clad wall behind her was visible in glimpses between the numerous framed degrees of higher learning from the nation's most ivied and prestigious universities. She looked up from her computer and smiled at her daughter. Julia's blue eyes had grown pale over the years, but pride in her own intellect shone in them. "Hello, Majedah. Did you get everything okay?"

"Yes, they had everything on your list." Majedah came into the room, her feet now sinking into a blue Persian carpet. "What are you working on?"

"Oh, just setting up pricing for the new samples we're supplying to our research clients."

Julia was National President of Sales for Tissue Depot, America's premier biomedical supply distributor. She was a genius at procuring hard-to-get samples and connecting them with the most cutting-edge research facilities, enabling medical breakthroughs that would someday save humanity—all at a tidy profit.

Julia tapped on her keyboard and chuckled. "The market is so crazy these days. Look here." She pointed at the columns of numbers on the screen. "12-week specimens go for just $125 per gram, while 24-week is $450, 32-week is $600, and 48-week is almost $1,000. The bigger they are, the more you can charge by weight—just like the lobsters we get at the beach house!"

Majedah laughed and shook her head in admiration of her mother's business acumen. "You go, girl!" she cheered.

Julia sighed. "And to think, those silly girls just throw this stuff away. It costs nothing to obtain, and it's pure profit all the way." She hit the return key, sighed with satisfaction, pushed back from her desk, and tilted her head up at her daughter. "So, you say they had the vegan turkey?"

"Yes, I got the last one. I had to race another woman to get it, but she was carrying her service pig, so it was no contest."

"Good job, Majedah. We couldn't have had our dinner party without it. After all, meat is murder!"

MAJEDAH SANG TO herself as she put the groceries away in her mother's newly renovated gourmet kitchen. The reclaimed wood cabinets clicked shut with precision and the café door stainless steel refrigerator hummed with expensive efficiency. She looked forward to the tasty dinner that night, surrounded by the town's wittiest intellectuals. A feast for body and mind!

Majedah was proud of her brilliant, successful parent. Julia had more degrees than any of her friends' parents and was a pioneering scientist. More important, Julia was descended from a long line of proud, strong, feminist women. Julia's mother, Milicent, had also been raised in a good, progressive household and thus emerged with a hyphenated surname. Milicent had married well and joined her own hyphenated surname with her husband's, which the couple then passed on to Julia. Thus, Julia had provided four-fifths of Majedah's last name, and Majedah had been raised to righteously demand all teachers pronounce it properly and fully when they called attendance: *Majedah Cantalupi-Abromavich-Flügel-Van Der Hoven-Taj Mahal.*

The last fifth of Majedah's surname—Taj Mahal—had been provided by her father. Ziyad Taj Mahal had also passed to her his Middle-Eastern good looks. Now Majedah's lips tightened into a grim line as she tossed a bowl of shredded edamame cellulose with truffle oil. She was *not* proud of her father. He was one of *them*; the haters who defiled the planet and kept alive hateful things like war, toxic masculinity, rape, hate, superstition, racism, and free speech.

Julia came into the kitchen to check on the organic heirloom apple tart in a gluten-free fair-trade almond crust. Majedah rounded on her. "Mom, how could you have married my father?"

Anger descended over Julia's features to match her daughter's. "He tricked me, Majedah."

Sympathy replaced Majedah's anger. "I'm so sorry, Mom." She shook her head and growled, "Men!"

"I met your father while we were doing our residencies at the same hospital, and he told me he was Lebanese. That much was true, and then he let me assume the rest." She smiled distantly. "I couldn't wait for all the ignorant racist rednecks I had gone to high school with to learn that I had married a Muslim." She pronounced the word *Muslim* with a self-conscious Middle Eastern affect: *MOOS-lim*.

Julia paused to refill her glass with local pinot. She took a swig and continued. "When it was time for the ceremony, Ziyad told me he was Maronite and I agreed to be married in accordance with his ethnic tradition. Naturally, we traveled to Lebanon for the ceremony. Unfortunately, Arabic is one of the few languages I don't understand, so I had no idea I was actually in a Catholic church."

Both women shuddered.

"Then what happened?" asked Majedah.

"The lies kept piling up, of course," Julia said coldly. "Your father played the part of a dutiful husband and a successful pediatric neurosurgeon masterfully, and I believed him. I never thought it strange that we celebrated Christmas—everyone does, after all. It's simply traditional to get together with friends to eat good food and exchange gifts."

"When did you finally figure it out?" asked Majedah.

Pale blue fire flashed from Julia's eyes. "I first had an idea of the truth when you father said the most disgusting thing I ever heard."

Majedah gasped in horror. "What did he say?"

Julia clenched her eyes shut against the painful memory. "He said—" Her voice trembled and failed, and she gripped the soapstone countertop with her free hand, the knuckles going white. She began again, this time succeeding. "He said he thought Sarah Palin was a role model for women."

Majedah felt sick. She went to her mother and held her. "Oh god, Mom, I am so sorry."

Julia shuddered once with a spasm of revulsion, then recovered and gave her daughter a comforting pat on the back. "It's okay, sweetheart. It hurt at the time but in the long run, it's always best to know the truth."

Majedah straightened and wiped her eyes. "Yes, of course it is. And you did the right thing, throwing him out. Thank god I wasn't exposed to him any longer during my formative years."

"Yes, sweetie, you've turned out to be an amazing, strong young woman who is in charge of her own destiny, and I'm so proud of you. I just know you're going to go out there and change the world!" Julia brushed an ebony tendril fondly from her daughter's face. Her expression became wistful. "Although the next time you plan to terminate a pregnancy, let me know ahead of time so I can find a buyer."

"Okay, Mom, I promise," Majedah said ruefully.

Julia smiled and tousled her hair. "That's my girl."

Majedah smiled back and returned to her cooking. "So where is my father now? Still director of his department at Johns Hopkins?"

"Yes," said Julia frostily. She yanked open the oven door and seized the tart in mitted hands. "I can't believe they continue to employ such a deviant, let alone entrust him with the welfare of *children*." She lovingly placed the confection onto a waiting cooling rack without displacing a single crumb. "Oh, that reminds me! His holiday check for you came today. I deposited it into your account already."

Majedah's face lit up. "Oh, goody! There are some really cute boots I've had my eye on."

"Don't spend it all in one place," teased Julia. "Although it would be hard to spend it all on a pair of boots unless they were made of solid gold," she mused.

The doorbell rang as the first of the guests arrived, and the two women set family matters aside to spend the evening with their highly intelligent and morally immaculate friends.

Chapter 2

WHEN HOLIDAY BREAK was over, Majedah returned to the exclusive campus of Lilith College. Nestled into the scenic foothills near the city of Wycksburg, the elite liberal arts school had been founded as a women's college in 1881 and had remained single sex ever since. Students could study many extremely important subjects there, such as ... you know what? Never mind. It's literally impossible to satirize liberal arts colleges these days, so let's just get on with our story.

Majedah let herself into her dorm room and heaved her suitcase onto her bed. Her roommate, Bill, had already returned and was lying on the other bed, idly looking at pornography on her laptop. "Welcome back, Majedah," she greeted.

Bill was a tall, broad-shouldered young woman from a town outside of Chicago. She had thick brown hair, which she kept buzzed short in a military style, a scruffy beard, and a deep, rich voice. Bill also had a penis and sometimes at night, she would climb into Majedah's bed and stick her penis into her roommate. The first time this happened, Majedah was startled but she quickly reminded herself not to hate on Bill's identity. It wasn't like a rapey *man* was putting his penis in her, after all. In fact, it even felt nice, so Majedah held still and allowed Bill to express herself without interruption. As the rhythmic pounding went on, Majedah had the most awesome revelation—she was now a lesbian! She couldn't wait to tell her mother the good news, and she was swept away in the most amazing gurl-powered orgasm ever!

Now she greeted her roommate with a smile. "How was your break, Bill?"

"Meh, not bad," Bill answered. She kept her eyes on the screen and seemed to be massaging herself with one hand inside her sweatpants. Majedah sensed that Bill was busy, so she started unpacking. There was a whole new semester ahead of her, and she couldn't wait to learn even more!

ONE OF MAJEDAH'S favorite classes was Creative Writing. She was never happier than when she could make up an entire new reality and write about it as though it were the real world. She loved getting lost in her creations to the extent that she almost believed her imaginary world was the real one, and the real world became a distant dream.

Majedah's Creative Writing Professor, Dr. Nguyễn, asked her to stay after class one day. Majedah remained in her seat in front of the professor's desk after everyone else had filed out of the room. "What's up, Dr. Nguyễn?" she asked cheerfully.

The professor came around to the front of her desk and sat on its edge, so she could look thoughtfully at her student. "Majedah, I want you to know that you are an excellent writer. Your word choices and sentence structure are masterful. You can create new realities better than any student I can remember."

Majedah beamed. She had been raised since infancy to understand that she was gifted, highly intelligent, and generally just better than most other people, and it was nice to have this knowledge affirmed by someone as distinguished as Dr. Nguyễn.

"However, there is a problem with your writing," the professor went on in a grim voice. "A very serious problem, actually. It's such a serious problem that I fear you will never be able to succeed as a novelist."

Majedah was aghast. She had never been told she couldn't do something before. It was a very unpleasant sensation, and her mind scrambled for a way to get past it. But Dr. Nguyễn must know what she was talking about; after all, she had written a *New York Times* bestseller, and all the important critics always praised her work. Her credentials were impeccable. Majedah looked up at her pleadingly. "Please, Dr. Nguyễn! What is the problem?"

"It's your content," the esteemed author explained. "Your stories are too positive. The protagonists make sound, logical decisions. The narratives actually make sense and, worst of all, the endings are..." her lip curled with disdain as she spat out the last word, "*happy*."

Majedah was stunned. She reflected on her professor's words and began to explain herself. "But Dr. Nguyễn—my life has always been fairly good. I mean, I know I'm a woman of color and because of that, I've always been discriminated against and assaulted and oppressed. But I still managed to graduate at the top of my high school class, and I am now a student at my number one college choice. Sometimes life does work out okay, and sometimes people are happy."

"*Rubbish!*" shouted the older woman of color. "Life never makes sense! Life is messy and ugly and chaotic and miserable! No one is happy unless they are also a bad person! And it is the job of fiction to remind people that their lives are hopeless and miserable and unfair! If a reader finishes one of your books and smiles, you haven't been doing your job."

Majedah didn't know what to say. The professor whom she most admired had just pulled the rug out from under her. She had always pictured herself sitting in coffee shops in exotic locations, typing away at her bestselling novels. Now she could see her dreams slipping away. She looked up at her professor with glistening eyes, desperate to explain herself. "I'm sorry, Dr. Nguyễn. I guess I've always loved pretending that I'm creating reality when I write. I wish—" and her voice trailed off.

"You wish what, Majedah?"

"I wish that I actually *could* create reality by making it up."

Dr. Nguyễn's face broke into a smile. "Well, why didn't you just say so? You don't want to be a novelist; you want to be a journalist!"

Joyous realization flooded Majedah as her professor's words sank in. "Yes, that's it!" she exclaimed. "I'll be a journalist! I'll create reality as people *should* see it!" She leapt from the chair and hugged her professor. "Thank you so much, Dr. Nguyễn! Now I know what to do with my life!"

Chapter 3

SEVERAL YEARS PASSED as Majedah threw herself into her education with a new understanding of her destiny. She declared a Journalism major and loaded up on classes that focused on current events, civic engagement, and societal interpretation. At her academic advisor's recommendation, she also developed her skill at narrative writing with additional coursework; it turned out that a big part of journalism was the ability to put the correct pieces together, reject the pieces that didn't work, and tell the story the public needed to know.

In the spring semester of her senior year, Majedah took a class called Direct Action for Social Change. Like most science classes, it was worth a lot of credits and it included a practical lab every week. The studious young women were taught all sorts of useful skills during lab, such as: erecting shanty towns and tent cities; strategic bussing management and deployment; choosing the correct technique from options such as marching, sit-in, die-in, riot, beating, vandalism, arson, and black bloc; and effective targeting, dis-employing, and de-platforming techniques against wrong-thinking, hateful people.

Majedah enjoyed the proactive aspect of the course. She loved the rush she got from deploying to the larger university down the street and protesting in front of their frat houses.

Those horrible misogynists wouldn't let women join their organizations! Majedah waved her expensive placard the highest and yelled the loudest, earning the highest marks from her professor, Dr. Alinejad, before they all boarded the luxury bus for the ride back to their exclusive women's college.

One day, Dr. Alinejad shocked the entire lab class with a horrifying and frightening declaration: "There is an actual Nazi, employed by the college as a professor, right here on the Lilith campus!"

There were shrieks of horror and gasps of disbelief from the rapt students. One young woman broke into uncontrollable sobs, and another shook so hard that her $2,500 laptop fell right off her desk. "Tell us who, Dr. Alinejad! Tell us who!" they all cried in torment.

Rigid with righteous rage, the older woman swept the room with her glare. "Better than that ... I will show you. Come on!"

With a roar, the infuriated young women leapt to their feet and followed their professor out of the room, down the hall, and outside the building. They paused briefly to discuss the appropriate approach, settled on a quick march with raised fists and an improvised chant (*Hey hey! Ho ho! Nazi profs have got to go!*) and traversed the quad to the ~~Foreign~~ Global Studies building. Other students saw the procession and were quick to become enraged and join in.

By the time the march arrived in the lobby, it was quite large and there was a brief loss of momentum as the women had to wait for the elevator to transport them all to the third floor. Once reassembled, the group opted to go with a classic mob formation, as it was easy to fill the enclosed space and sweep obstacles and people from their path.

A brief swarm up the hall brought them to a closed office door, which bore a placard that read *Dr. Rachel Avraham, Israeli and Middle Eastern Studies.*

Dr. Alinejad held up an open hand to halt the procession. The agitated women stopped moving, although they continued to bark out the new chant they had started upon reaching the third floor: LOVE BEATS HATE! LOVE BEATS HATE! Dr. Alinejad reached down and attempted to wrench the door open, but it was locked.

Majedah, who stood closest to her beloved professor, helpfully read the small sign posted below the name placard. "Dr. Alinejad, it says her office hours ended at 2 p.m. She's gone for the day."

"Fuck!" hissed the learned professor. She turned to the crowd and hushed them with downward hand motions. "Women, please, be quiet so you can hear me."

The crowd grew silent and watched the instructor with fevered expressions, anxious to learn what to do when there was a Nazi in their midst.

Dr. Alinejad took a moment to look each young woman in the eye before speaking. "This woman—," she announced, rapping the locked door with her fist for emphasis, "is a Nazi sympathizer. She was born and raised in the Nazi regime of Israel and to this day, she vocally supports their institutionalized systemic oppression of brown people!"

"Nooooo!" wailed the crowd. Some of the women fell to the ground and writhed in sympathetic pain, some pulled hanks of hair from their scalps, and some vomited onto the floor. Majedah watched her classmates with intense compassion for their terrible pain. Thinking quickly, she raised a fist and restarted the energetic chant. "Love beats hate," she shouted. "Love beats hate!"

Soon the chant took effect and the suffering women had been reorganized into a happy, enraged mob with a single purpose. They took turns kicking the door, beating on it with their fists, and screaming, "I hate you!" into the uncaring wood. Dr. Alinejad stood by and scribbled grades onto a clipboard. One enterprising young future leader pulled a Sharpie from her pocket and scrawled a swastika onto the door. "Oh, very nice!" praised Dr. Alinejad as she made emphatic marks on the grading sheet.

At five o'clock, the lab period ended, and the group dispersed. Majedah was so jazzed from that afternoon's lesson that she was brimming with energy. She stopped by her dorm room to change into workout gear and had to run ten miles before she was able to calm herself. Even so, she barely touched her seitan on naan in the dining hall, and she could hardly concentrate on her broadcast journalism assignment in the library that evening. She finally had to admit that something was bothering her, and she packed up and went back to her room.

As a senior, Majedah had her own room, and she was grateful for the peaceful solitude in which to think. The lab class that afternoon kept replaying itself in her head, and a feeling that she was missing something important nagged at her. She tossed and turned in bed. In her mind, she watched again as the righteous students beat on a door and screamed aloud. Then she remembered the door itself, with a scrawled swastika just below the professor's name: *Dr. Rachel Avraham.* Avraham, Avraham ... *What is the significance?* Majedah wondered over and over. Her journalist senses were tingling; she was sure she was missing something important.

Suddenly, Majedah sat bolt upright in bed. "'Avraham' is a Jewish name," she exclaimed out loud. "And there is a swastika on her office door. A swastika on a Jewish professor's door is nothing less than a Hate Crime!"

She leapt from her bed and dressed quickly. She had to investigate the scene to make sure.

Majedah practically ran across campus to the darkened Global Studies building. The doors were locked for the night, and she pounded on them and yelled, "Let me in!"

At last, a pair of security guards pulled up in a utility vehicle and joined her at the doors. "What's the problem, miss?" asked the older of the two guards.

Majedah shot him a disdainful look for his sexism but decided to let it go in light of the much more serious crime that was occurring. "I must be let inside. There's a hate crime being committed inside this building at this very minute!"

The two guards looked at one another. Part of their campus security training had been the inculcation of the knowledge that Hate Crimes were the worst possible crimes that could be committed. This was clearly a very serious situation. The younger guard pulled a master key from her pocket and opened the doors. Majedah raced inside with the guards on her heels. Luckily, the elevator was on the ground floor already, so they arrived on the third floor quickly. Majedah raced down the dark hall and skidded to a stop in front of Dr. Avraham's office door. "There!" she yelled triumphantly as she pointed at the offending graffiti.

The uniformed woman trained her flashlight onto the spot Majedah indicated and both guards stepped back and gasped in shock. The older man shook his head in disbelief. "I've worked security for twenty years and I've seen some sick things, but that is by far *the worst thing I have ever seen.*" Despite her best efforts, the female guard began to sob.

A strange and powerful sensation came over Majedah. She excitedly recognized it as her gift for journalism, and she decided to follow where it led. She pulled out her phone, set it to livestream onto the Lilith College journalism site, and thrust it at the male guard. "Here, when I give the signal, hit the button and video me," she commanded. He took the. To the other guard, Majedah said, "Make sure you keep that light trained on me. Follow my lead." The uniformed woman nodded.

Majedah took a moment to flip her hair back over her shoulder and moisten her lips until they glistened enticingly. She caught the male guard's eye and nodded, he hit the button, and she went live. She looked directly into the camera and began.

"This is Majedah Cantalupi-Abromavich-Flügel-Van Der Hoven-Taj Mahal, reporting live from the campus of Lilith College. Tonight, I am breaking an exclusive story. Please prepare yourselves and make sure there aren't any children in the room, because what I am about to show you is truly shocking." She paused to allow her audience to gather itself, savoring the drama in what she instinctively knew was a powerful shot. There was a gritty realness to the sight of a courageous, beautiful young woman reporting live by the light of a first responder's torch, the only bright spot in the surrounding darkness. Majedah envisioned how the shot must look in her mind's eye, and the symbolism almost rendered her speechless. But she reminded herself that she was a professional and carried on with her report.

"I'm standing outside the academic office of Dr. Rachel Avraham, distinguished professor of Israeli and Middle Eastern Studies here at Lilith College. Dr. Avraham also happens to be Jewish, and you won't believe what someone has done to her office door." She stepped to the side with a flourish and the security guards instinctively focused light and camera on the scrawled symbol. Majedah provided the dramatic voiceover. "That's right—a swastika! The most reviled and hateful thing a human being can do to another human being." She stepped back into the shot and fixed her audience with a doleful stare. "Tonight, we are left wondering—wondering how this could have happened on a campus as famously tolerant and enlightened as Lilith, wondering what kind of racist monster could have done such a thing, and wondering what the Lilith Administration is going to do about it. Reporting live from Lilith

College, I'm Majedah Cantalupi-Abromavich-Flügel-Van Der Hoven-Taj Mahal."

The male security guard cut the transmission, and both he and his partner stood open-mouthed in awe. "That was the finest reporting I have ever seen," he gasped when he was able to speak again.

"I know," Majedah replied. She lifted her chin so that the light from the torch could better define her high, flawless cheekbones. "I could feel the power flowing through me as I reported."

"You are well on your way, girl," breathed the female guard.

"Don't ever call me that again, misogynist."

MAJEDAH WOKE THE following morning and rushed to her window. Across the quad, she could see and hear a sizable angry demonstration outside the Lilith administrative building, and a cavalcade of air-conditioned buses was bringing in more protestors by the minute.

She had done it! Her powerful reporting had drawn attention to an Injustice, and good people of righteous good will were even now assembling to demand that Something Be Done About It! With a squeal of victorious joy, Majedah fell backwards onto her bed, arms spread like wings, eyes fixed on the ceiling above, and mouth open in an enormous smile.

It was already a perfect day, and she had just woken up. But as if things weren't already great enough, Majedah's phone rang. The caller ID read, "WPDQ." Majedah recognized the name of the local broadcast news station and quickly answered the phone. "Hello?" she said in her most professional voice.

An even more professional-sounding, older female voice asked, "May I speak to Majedah Cantalupi-Abromavich-Flügel-Van Der Hoven-Taj Mahal?"

Majedah closed her eyes at the deliciousness of hearing her full name on the lips of an industry pro. "This is she," she answered.

"Outstanding. Majedah, this is Norma Troutstein, the owner and director of WPDQ News. I saw your excellent reportage regarding the hate crime on your campus. Majedah, I want you to come and work for me."

Chapter 4

A SCANT MONTH after graduation, Majedah reported for her first day of work at her first-ever job, at the headquarters of the local broadcast network, WPDQ.

Before Majedah began working, Julia took her to Cuba for a week as a graduation gift. In Havana, they lived like queens and had every whim catered to by their gracious personal tour guide. "See?" Julia had commented, "I told you the Castros knew what they were doing. It's nothing but amazing here." Then they returned to Majedah's new hometown, Wycksburg, and stayed at the only decent hotel in the area while they hunted for an apartment. Julia eventually found a home she deemed worthy of her only daughter, a two-bedroom condo in a brand-new doorman building. There was another two weeks of managing painters and carpenters, shopping for furnishings, and accepting deliveries. Finally, the day before Majedah was to begin work, Julia was satisfied that her daughter would be living at an acceptable standard. She gave Majedah a hug, wished her well in her new career, and got behind the wheel of her Lexus sedan for the two-hour drive home.

The following morning at nine o'clock sharp, Majedah walked through the doors of WPDQ and entered the small reception area. She glanced around dubiously at the industrial carpeting, dusty potted palms by the windows, and battered couch and armchair. As she resolved never to sit on either of them, she noted that at least the right publications were displayed atop the veneer coffee table. She cleared her throat and proceeded to the desk, where an ancient woman, conducting a phone conversation, met her eye and held up one finger.

"I couldn't agree more. It's a sin that we haven't had a decent podiatrist in this town until now," the woman rasped in tones achievable only by a dedicated long-term smoker. "Why, I have an absolute claw on my pinky toe, and I am simply not flexible enough to clip that beast."

Majedah listened to the receptionist's end of the conversation while she perused the framed prints on the wall behind the desk. She nodded approvingly at several certificates of recognition from the National Broadcast News Association. She recognized Norma Troutstein as well as several WPDQ reporters and anchors in glossy photographs with senators, celebrities, and even a president or two. Majedah noted WPDQ's star reporter, Gary Swanson, in a photo with the sainted past-president of color. The past-president looked young enough that Majedah guessed he wasn't a president yet when the photo was taken.

Then she noticed three Affiliate Recognition plaques from the great News 24/7, which was headquartered in midtown Manhattan. Majedah sighed with longing as she gazed at the iconic sans serif logo. *Someday*, she told herself. *Someday, I'll work at News 24/7. I'll be Lead Reporter with my own Desk. Maybe I'll even anchor my own prime time show someday!*

Visions of the power she would wield as a newscaster in the New York market fluttered Majedah's heart as she waited for the receptionist to wrap up the call. "I'm sure Gary will be thrilled to cover your grand opening, ma'am," the ancient woman was saying. She winked at Majedah as she listened for a moment before speaking again. "No, I can't say which segment they'll put the story in. That's up to Norma. Just go ahead and send the information to the email address I gave you as soon as you can, so we can get it on the schedule. ... Okay. ... Okay, sounds good. Goodbye."

She hung up and sighed heavily from the strain of discharging her receptionist duties. Then she turned her attention to Majedah, giving her a friendly but frank once-over from behind oversized glasses. "You must be the new gal," she deduced.

The receptionist's archaic usage of such sexist language stunned Majedah so that she actually took a step back from the desk. In her shock, words failed her, and the cordial smile remained frozen on her face by default.

Assuming she was just shy, the crone behind the desk continued. "You just go on down that hall there and grab the first person you see. It's not a big place, so anyone will be able to show you where you'll work." When Majedah still didn't speak, the woman's face broke into countless creases around a reassuring smile. "Don't worry, Sweetie, you'll do fine!" she encouraged.

Majedah finally found her tongue. "I'll certainly try," she declared. Still stinging from the woman's hurtful language, she turned on her heel and strode down the hall.

As it turned out, the first person Majedah saw was Norma Troutstein. The solidly built station director had her back to Majedah as she yelled an order across the open space to a pale man who stood beside an open doorway, a headset resting around his neck.

Before drawing attention to herself, Majedah glanced around, using her journalist skills to gather information. She faced a large, open, interior room that contained perhaps a dozen ugly, metal desks that looked like leftovers from a 1970's TV police drama. Several men and women, ranging in age from their mid-twenties to mid-fifties, sat and pecked at computer keyboards. There were wastebaskets overflowing with takeout containers and empty chairs that hadn't been pushed in and coats thrown on desks and all manner of clutter. Majedah swept the perimeter of the room with her keen, dark eyes. The walls were lined with ancient gray powder-coated file cabinets as tall as she. The file cabinets alternated with doorways, almost all of them open. Some revealed small offices with windows that let in natural daylight. There was also a break room, and Majedah glimpsed a coffeemaker, a refrigerator, a Formica-topped round table, and a couple chairs. The pale man to whom Norma was shouting stood against the back wall, next to an open door. This room was dark, and Majedah could see that it was filled with glowing screens and other technical equipment. The entire remaining wall was featureless, with only a single doorway. A light glowed red above it. Majedah realized that the broadcast studio must be on the other side of the wall: the place where the magic happened. A thrill ran through her and she shivered happily.

"We need to get that Board of Ed report into the next segment, okay, Brad?" Norma's voice was a blast of seasoned competence across the cluttered space.

The technician appeared to be in early middle age. His brown hair was worn short but in no particular style, and his pallor testified to long hours spent in the darkened room behind him. At the moment, his brows were knit. "So where are we supposed to find time for that?" he queried.

"Let's pull the story on the new parking meters," Norma hollered.

"Got it," the tech yelled back. "I'll have Sherry load the prompter." He spun and retreated into the glowing cave, closing the door behind him.

Before Norma could pivot to the next task, Majedah stepped up to her and tapped her shoulder.

Norma turned and recognized her newest hire. "Majedah!" she exclaimed. "At last. So good to have you aboard."

"I am so excited to be here," Majedah answered. She had only met Norma once, over a month earlier, to discuss the terms of her employment. The station manager's salt-and-pepper hair was even shorter now, cut into a low-maintenance men's style. Majedah was pretty sure Norma chose the hairstyle not to make any sort of political, gender, or orientation statement, but for rather for plain old expediency. Norma wore a white cotton blouse untucked over navy linen off-the-rack trousers. She was a study in flowing crinkly summer fabrics that floated just off her generous proportions. Her brown leather fisherman sandals displayed puffy pink toes and blue nail polish, and she had accessorized her outfit with a chunky necklace of some sort of dark wood nuggets. Majedah felt overdressed in her slim, black georgette suit, for which her mother had paid as much as she would earn this week. But Norma's smile was genuine, and Majedah recognized someone who was still in love with her profession. Smiling back, she added, "I can't wait to get started."

"Great, let's give you the nickel tour." Norma spun and began to walk around the outside of the room. "Here's Terry's office. She's our sales rep. And here's where her assistant, Raymond, sits." They passed doors and desks, framed photos of children of all ages, mugs with cute sayings and three-day-old coffee rings, sweaters hung on the backs of chairs, and potted plants. "This is my office, but I'm never in here." Norma waved at an open door and Majedah saw a desk stacked with papers and two computers, some leatherette chairs, and a wall of bright windows. "This is Gary Swanson's office," Norma said of the next door they came to. Then she walked through it and Majedah followed. "And here's Gary," Norma finished.

The room's occupant stood chivalrously as the women entered. He came from behind his desk and extended his hand. "Hello there," he intoned in his trademark rich voice. "It's great to meet the new talent. We reporters have to stick together, you know."

Majedah's mouth hung open as she shook his hand. Here, finally, she was mingling with recognizable broadcast talent in a mid-sized market! He seemed older and taller in real life than she had imagined. His blond hair apparently hung in a perfect arrangement quite naturally, and his skin had a taut, preserved quality that emphasized his fine facial structure. "Mr. Swanson, it's such an honor."

"Please, just call me Gary. You know, it seems like just yesterday that I was the new kid in the newsroom."

"Majedah, you'll report to Gary most of the time," explained Norma. "He'll show you the ropes and help you learn how we operate around here."

"That would be amazing," gushed Majedah.

"I'm sure you'll catch on in no time," said the suave star reporter.

"Okay, thanks Gary." Norma spun and walked out, and Majedah followed.

They resumed their circumnavigation of the large main room, with Norma narrating the guided tour. "This is Nancy. She's our writer. Say hi, Nancy."

A bookish blond looked up from her computer. "Hi," she said in a startled tone.

Majedah barely had time to say "Hi" in return before Norma was onto the next item. "Here's the kitchen. Rodney makes the coffee when he comes in in the morning, and there's usually cream in the fridge. Bring your own mug." They pressed on and more doors and desks passed by. "Here's the editing room. Here's Mark. He's our webmaster. And here's Loretta, our social media guru." More hi's were exchanged. At last, Norma halted behind one of the empty desks. She waved her hand over the workstation with a flourish. "Here's where you'll be sitting."

"Hooray, my own desk," Majedah enthused. She eyed the dated gray metal desk and its vinyl-covered swivel chair dubiously.

Norma made one final introduction. "And this is your cameraman, Jasper."

Jasper stood behind his desk, which faced and abutted Majedah's. "Hi, I'm Jasper," he introduced himself, as though Norma hadn't just done so. He held out his hand and leaned way over his desk.

Majedah leaned way over her own desk to shake hands. "Hi, I'm Majedah. It's nice to meet you."

"You two will be a great team. Jasper has several years' experience shooting out in the field, both for a non-profit and another news station out in Toledo," Norma told Majedah. To Jasper, she said, "Majedah, as you know, comes to us with a degree in Journalism from Lilith College, an abundance of natural talent, and a whole buttload of courage." Majedah blushed in agreement. "She's the one I told you about, who exposed the anti-Semitism on her campus," Norma added with a tone of solidarity.

"Wow, a genuine local hero," drawled Jasper.

"I'm sure anyone would have done what I did, if they had the journalistic ability to recognize an Injustice when they saw one," Majedah said modestly.

Norma chuckled. "Well, I don't know how many 'injustices' you'll be covering around town. It's mostly just local news, as you know. But I'm sure you'll be the first to spot any significant stories." She clapped her hands together and clasped them in front of her. "Okay, then, I have to go supervise an edit. Jasper can show you the rest of the operation and get you started. Let me know if you need anything."

"I will. Thanks, Norma."

The older woman strode off. Majedah watched her walk away, then turned to see Jasper eyeing her coldly.

"So, you're the Israel lover," he said in a low voice.

Majedah knew she needed to put him in his place from the start, as she planned to be the brains behind their partnership. She met his look with a haughty stare and spoke in her most authoritative tones. "Of course not. They are literally Nazis." She observed a slight softening of Jasper's aggressive posture and continued. "But I do know a story when I see one. There's something you should know, Jasper; I have a journalism degree from the most prestigious woman's college in the United States—in fact, in the whole world—and it is widely agreed upon that I also have an uncommon natural talent for spotting news. Now, I understand you have an uncommon talent for framing and capturing shots. I think this could be an exceptional professional partnership. I am looking forward to teaming up with you to uncover the countless, previously unexposed Injustices in this town and get the truth out."

Jasper visibly relaxed (though Majedah was fairly certain his thin, wiry frame was naturally strung tight, even at rest). His shoulders went back down and the tension lines around his mouth disappeared within the scraggly brown hairs of his beard. His eyes, however, remained keen. "Finally," he said, "someone who gets it."

A look of understanding passed between the two young journalists. "Oh, yes, this is going to work out quite well," Majedah breathed. "I've already lived in this town for a month, and I have spotted countless things that are being done wrong. So many people are dwelling in darkness, completely unaware that the way they live is unjust and hateful. We have so much change to make."

Jasper was grinning now. "You don't even know the half of it, sister," he said. "My girlfriend runs the vegan food cart down on State Street—"

"Oh, my god, I love vegan street food!"

"Great, then you'll love Dawn's spicy falafel! So anyway, the other day she came home and said she saw a display of hate books in a bookstore window. So, I was thinking we could—"

"Oh, Majedah!" Gary Swanson approached the pair. They stopped talking and turned to look at him, and he continued in his smooth broadcaster voice. "How'd you like to cover a grand opening?"

Chapter 5

MAJEDAH COULDN'T WAIT to get back to her condo in the gleaming new doorman building. She went right to the kitchen, placed a stem glass on the freshly oiled soapstone countertop, filled it with fair trade Chilean merlot, took a healthy swig, topped it off again, and carried the glass and the bottle into the living room. A push of a button brought to life the 72-inch plasma screen mounted on the wall, and Majedah sank into the thick, down cushions of the sofa to await her evening news debut.

When the story finally came on (a disappointing 17 minutes after the headlines), Majedah let out a squeal like an excited fifth grader. Her mouth hung open in an ecstatic grin and her eyes sparkled in the TV glow as she watched.

"This is Majedah Cantalupi-Abromavich-Flügel-Van Der Hoven-Taj Mahal, reporting live from the brand-new offices of Fussbender Superior Foot Care," said the nearly life-size Majedah on the screen.

Majedah scrutinized herself and was delighted to see that Jasper had framed the shot well indeed, with herself front and center and the balloon-festooned doorway to the foot clinic behind her. Bright midday light glanced off her vibrant hair and made her flawless pale olive skin glow. She stood at a slight angle to the camera to emphasize her slender figure, which was enhanced by the cut of her very fine clothes. Majedah noticed with slight annoyance that most of her body was covered by her own name, which she had insisted the tech spell out in full across the bottom of the screen. But she reminded herself that it was important to get her proper name out there from the start, as she planned to be the most recognizable and powerful broadcast journalist in the country one day.

On the screen, Majedah turned to a short, stocky, middle-aged woman in a white coat who was wearing an absurd party hat that said, "Grand Opening!" in metallic glitter letters beneath antennae bearing bright blue pom-poms. "Here we have the owner and chief practitioner of Fussbender Superior Foot Care, Dr. Trudy Fussbender. Dr. Fussbender, what can you tell us about your new clinic?"

In the darkened living room, Majedah watched her performance intently. She had been raised with the understanding that she was better than most people, and this excellence must naturally extend into her career, so Majedah worked hard to make sure it did. First, she used her creative writing talent to craft a comprehensive narrative to tell the story of the new podiatrist in town. Then she spent an hour online, informing herself about Dr. Fussbender's background, the town's dearth of licensed, competent foot care professionals, and podiatry in general. When she and Jasper finally drove over to Fussbender, she was armed with a list of insightful interview questions that were designed to germinate an informative discussion, as well as several pleasant banter themes to loosen up the good doctor.

On site, she had worked with Jasper to set up the best shots in the most favorable lighting. Later, back at the studio, she boldly set a precedent of sitting beside Antoine, the nerdy editor, while he cut the story together. She noted his inability to make eye contact and the nervous squeak in his voice when he spoke to her. Claiming she only wanted to learn, she asked what would happen if, say, Antoine cut the close-up of Dr. Fussbender's face (the woman had a dreadful mustache situation, after all) in favor of using a close-up of Majeda's own face as she listened to the doctor answer a question. When Antoine obliged, she clapped her hands in delight and told him how brilliant he was. The edit remained in the final cut.

Now, in her darkened living room, Majedah refilled her wine glass and watched with rapt delight as her televised self concluded, "Reporting live from downtown Wycksburg, this is Majedah Cantalupi-Abromavich-Flügel-Van Der Hoven-Taj Mahal." As the report ended and the scene cut back to the in-studio anchors, Majedah squealed again. She closed her eyes and replayed the segment in her mind. She could find nothing wrong with it.

Flush with the triumph of her first broadcast report, Majedah flicked the channel. The plasma screen filled with the perfectly preserved visage of the eminent Carol Crawford, the groundbreaking feminist news icon, long-established primetime anchor, and the face of the great News 24/7. Majedah settled in to watch and learn from the pinnacle of prime-time talk shows, *An Hour of Your Time with Carol Crawford.*

Carol's perfectly coiffed, silver-streaked blond hair did not so much as vibrate as the skilled reporter asked her interviewee a question. And what an interviewee she had scored! "Oh my god, I forgot Carol had the First Lady on tonight," Majedah breathed. Then she sneered in acknowledgement of the guest's husband's party: Republican. "Get her, Carol," Majedah urged.

On the screen, Carol Crawford focused her famous look—two-parts interrogator to one-part sympathizer—on her guest's face. "I think, Mrs. Nelson, what our viewers—especially our female viewers—what they really want to know is, what's it like to be married to a misogynist?"

"Oh, good one, Carol," cheered Majedah.

The First Lady, a polished product of private education and years of upper class social conditioning, never lost her easy poise. "Well, now, Carol, I hardly think my husband is a misogynist." She chuckled as though Carol had said something witty. "After all, he's always a perfect gentleman—"

"Well, I'm not sure what else one would call a man who doesn't believe women have the right to healthcare—"

"Burt and I believe everyone has the right to healthcare, but no one has the right to force someone else to pay for their—"

"—or the right to equal pay for equal work—"

"Yeah, get her, Carol!" Majedah pumped a fist in the air.

"Oh, dear, not that tired old canard!" Linda shook her head in ladylike mirth. "It's well known that equal work was never the basis of that claim—"

"—or the right to tampons free of charge—"

"My goodness, one wonders where you learned the concept of a 'right'. If you care to read the preamble—"

A buzzer sounded in the kitchen. "Goddammit," Majedah swore. She hit the mute on the remote, rose from the sofa, and went to answer it. She stabbed the intercom button and said, "Yes?"

The doorman's voice issued from the tiny speaker. "Floral delivery for you, Miss Cantalupi-Abromavich-Flügel-Van Der Hoven-Taj Mahal."

"Very well, send it up." Majedah released the button and sighed impatiently. She took a five-dollar bill from her wallet and went to open her front door and wait. After a minute, a young man emerged from the elevator and came down the hall. He wore a dark green polo emblazoned with the logo of a high-end local florist and carried an enormous arrangement of tropical flowers and a gift-wrapped box.

"Hi, down here," Majedah called.

He saw her and approached. "Good evening, ma'am," he said. "Would you like me to bring this inside for you?"

He seemed decent enough and the arrangement looked both heavy and unwieldy. "Yes, that would be great. Follow me." Majedah led the way to the counter that divided the kitchen from the dining area at the end of the hall. "Right here will be fine."

The deliveryman placed the items on the counter and straightened up. Recognition flickered across his face when he looked at Majedah. "Hey, you're the new news lady," he exclaimed, a goofy smile spreading across his face.

"*Reporter*, yes. I'm the new *reporter* at PDQ."

"Wow, what an honor to meet you in person. I'm a huge fan."

"Interesting, since I've only been on the air for a few hours." Majedah yawned.

"Yeah, but we have PDQ on at the flower shop and we all saw—"

"Thank you so much for the delivery. I'm actually in the middle of something right now, though."

The young man was visibly crestfallen but recovered quickly. "Oh, of course, Miss, I didn't mean to—"

If he called her "Ma'am" or "Miss" one more time, Majedah was going to have to straighten him out, and she really wasn't in the mood. She held out the folded five-dollar bill. "Here, this is for you."

"Oh, no, no tip is necessary. My pleasure."

"How kind of you." Smiling what she knew to be a devastating smile, Majedah gestured toward the open door and began to usher him out.

"Oh, of course, sorry to keep you. I'll show myself out." The lumbering oaf finally got a clue, turned, and left the apartment. Majedah followed to close the door behind him.

She went to the outrageous floral arrangement on her kitchen counter. Crimson anthurium contrasted against speckled saffron orchids, spiky birds of paradise, flaming bromeliad, and fragrant callalily. The flowers popped against glossy, dark green leaves the size of dinner plates. "God, how tacky," Majedah sniveled. She yanked the envelope from the ornate container and tore it open. The card inside read:

Congratulations on your first day at your wonderful new job. I went online and watched the report you filed for your news station. Magnificent! My dear Majedah, I am so proud of you tonight. But then, I have always been so very proud of you, every day since you were my little girl. All my love, Dad.

An alarming sentimentality rose up in her, and Majedah quickly reminded herself what her father really was. "Yeah, okay, whatever, Dad. On the other hand, you probably voted for President Nelson, so I got where I am no thanks to you." She dropped the letter onto the counter and took up the wrapped box. It was heavy and cold. Majedah tore off the paper and discovered a chilled bottle of Piper-Heidsieck Cuvée Brut. "Well, that's more like it, Dad," she sniffed. She carried the bottle into the kitchen to fetch a flute then went to sit on the sofa again.

Champagne in hand, Majedah unmuted the television. News 24/7 had gone to commercial, and she was still in a bad mood from the ignorant deliveryman and her father's presumption. Seething, she flipped to *that* channel.

The smug face of Eagle Eye News evening anchor Roy Cader appeared on her wall. Majedah growled low in her throat at the sight of him and threw back the remaining champagne in her glass. Burning eyes fixed on the television, she poured herself another.

Suddenly, the screen went hot red as a graphic eagle soared across, accompanied by an urgent rushing sound that ended with a heavily gated bird-of-prey cry. Roy Cader reappeared. "Time for an Eagle Eye News Alert," he said. "A tornado has just touched down near Tulsa, Oklahoma." He went on to give the few details that were known at that time and instructions on how to take cover.

Majedah watched him talk, her pretty face contorted into a mask of hatred. She hated everything about Roy Cader. She hated his bizarre accent that made him sound like a redneck who had been educated at a British boarding school. She hated his smug attitude and the hint of barely-suppressed mirth that always underlay his expression. She hated it that his hair and eyes were as dark as hers and his skin was four full shades darker than her own. What the hell kind of name was 'Cader', anyway? She couldn't place his ethnicity, and that infuriated her. She had heard that his mother was Cuban. Majedah hated Cubans. They looked and sounded like Hispanics, but they utterly refused to stay in their lane. They cursed the names of the brave revolutionaries who had set them free from the Injustice of capitalism, and they were responsible for Florida's electoral votes going to President Nelson in the very tight election two years earlier.

Majedah hated Eagle Eye News, with their racist nationalism dressed up as patriotism. She hated their newscasters and reporters, half of whom were females who played right into every stereotype of being an attractive, successful woman. She hated that they decided events of no or negative importance were news and reported them as such, lending them credence. She hated it that the National Broadcast News Association granted them membership and credibility. And she hated that Eagle Eye beat 24/7 handily in every time slot, every time the ratings came out.

Finally, Majedah hated the target of that night's tornado, Oklahoma. She hated the whole stupid, flat, dusty, pointless state. She hated the racist, ignorant, toothless mouth breathers who lived there and voted mindlessly for President Nelson and prevented the whole country from making Progress. Oklahoma could be blotted off the map entirely, and the country would be nothing but better for it, she fumed.

Roy Cader's expression became somehow smugger as he went on to his next story. "The Nielsen ratings have just come out for primetime news shows." The screen changed to a graphic of numbers and data. "And as you can see, Eagle Eye News has bested the next-closest competitor with over double their viewership." The visual cut back to Cader's face. The anchor had tilted his chin down so he could look up at the camera, affecting ironic puppy dog eyes. "Even this show you're watching right now, *Evening Report* with l'il ol' me, Roy Cader, is number one in our time slot again. I do thank you for your support."

The rage that had been building in Majedah could be suppressed no longer and burst forth. She let out a shriek that would have felled an ox and hurled her flute against the wall above the plasma screen. In a shower of sparkling crystal shards, she clutched her face in her shaking hands and sobbed.

Chapter 6

ON A SWELTERING late morning in August, Majedah and Jasper sat on folding lawn chairs alongside a vending cart. The sides of the cart were hand-painted with acid-trip swirls and flowers, and stick people of all colors held hands in an unbreakable chain of solidarity around the bottom. Whimsical lettering spelled out "Flora Not Fauna" in white, which popped against the colorful background. A tall, bony woman, dressed in a faded sky-blue tank top and cargo shorts that reached past her knees, labored over the hissing grill. Steam rushed past her shining face, adding a hint of body to the wisps of mouse-brown hair that had escaped her messy topknot.

Majedah took a swig of her iced cucumber water and fanned herself with a handbill. There wasn't much of a view to be had, as they were seated beneath the solitary oak on a weed-choked dirt strip at the edge of a cracked, mostly empty parking lot. Across the pavement, an under-used warehouse stood at their backs, and the grassy mounds of the Wycksburg landfill rolled away from the lot in front of them.

"This is actually my favorite part of the Transfer Station," said Jasper, as he gazed out over the manmade hillocks. "You can practically hear the earth reclaiming all the waste of mankind."

"Ha, that would make an excellent band name," said Dawn from her station at the vending cart. She rotated several kabobs on the grill with her left hand and whisked sweat from her brow with her right.

"What, All the Waste of Mankind?" asked Jasper. "Yeah, that would be an amazing band name. Heh heh."

Majedah moved her foot delicately to the side to prevent a curious beetle from clambering onto her Roger Vivier sandal. "Yes, except it would have to be All the Waste of *People*kind," she gently corrected her less-educated friends.

"Oh, right," acknowledged Jasper. "Sorry."

Dawn approached with steaming kabobs for each of them. "Here we go, today's special: Soy-Cell Skewers."

"Mm, smells great, Dawn," said Jasper with genuine enthusiasm. He reached up to receive a kabob and a kiss from his girlfriend.

"Yes, thanks, Dawn," said Majedah with feigned enthusiasm. She took her skewer and eyed it suspiciously while Dawn settled into the empty lawn chair. Jasper was right—it did smell good, anyway. Majedah had been too hung over to eat breakfast, and her stomach growled. She pulled a chunk of grilled cellulose from the wooden stick with her teeth and chewed. Dawn's masterful spicy Thai marinade and hand-grilling technique made the rubbery cube almost palatable, and Majedah was able to swallow it without gagging.

Several flies buzzed over to investigate, and Majedah waved them away with a scowl. "So, Dawn, why did you move Flora Not Fauna to this industrial parking lot? What was wrong with Memorial Park? That was right in the middle of town, and there weren't any flies."

Dawn paused in her munching to answer. "The town wouldn't renew my license."

"Those fascists! What was wrong?"

"They told me I had to wear hair nets on my armpits." She wolfed another grey-white cube. "I said, to hell with that. So, I found a spot where the Man doesn't come around to hassle honest businesswomen like myself."

"That's my girl," said Jasper, with his mouth full. Several well-chewed flecks of soy curd saw their chance to escape and fled to the cover of his scraggly beard, where they lodged and held on for dear life. "No one tells her what to do."

Dawn smiled at him around another mouthful.

Majedah looked away over the rolling landfill and listened to the distant roar of big machines as they buried the town's trash and created ever more hills. When her stomach settled down again, she held up her skewer for another bite. Unfortunately, the first thing that met her eye was a curly, mousy brown hair adorning the next cube. Majedah leapt up and ran for the stunted bushes that bordered the landfill, arriving just in time to unload the single soy cube she had eaten along with the previous night's bile.

Her friend's chatter died down behind her. "Majedah, are you okay?" came Jasper's voice.

"Yes, yes, I'm fine. Sorry, don't worry about me. I think the takeout I had last night made me sick." Majedah spit the last of the bile out of her mouth and staggered back to the cart, grabbing a napkin as she passed. Wiping her mouth, she sat back down in her chair and gulped some cool cucumber water. In a moment, she felt refreshed and turned her attention to the food cart proprietor. "So, Dawn, what's on the schedule for POPA this week?"

"In fact, we have an action planned for tomorrow morning," said the young activist proudly.

"Splendid," said Majedah. "Who, what, where, when, and why?"

They all chuckled at her corny journalism joke. "Check out that handbill I gave you," said Dawn.

"Yeah, it isn't just for fanning yourself," teased Jasper.

"I know that. Okay, let me see." Majedah picked up the half-page-sized flyer from where she had dropped it earlier and began to read. Angry, bold lettering spelled out:

The People's Organization for Perpetual Outrage invites' you to protest the lack of diversity at Skyler Memorial Library. This library that is partially funded with public money, just hired a new director. But instead of taking the opportunity to demonstrate there commitment to reflecting our town's diversity, the Skyler Memorial Library hired a white male director. Join us as we Disrupt his installation ceremony to demonstrate our extreme disappointment with the Library's blatant racism. Let's Demand Action!

There followed the next day's date, a time, and an address. "Oh, this sounds like a good one!" said Majedah. "Jasper, meet me at the station at 8:30 tomorrow morning? We can go in one car."

"Sounds like a plan." He whipped his empty wooden skewer into the bushes Majedah had recently soiled.

"What a stroke of luck to have a cameraman whose girlfriend is the Public Information Officer for the local activism organization," Majedah mused. "I don't have to do any work at all to find good stories."

"What luck for me, to have a boyfriend at the local broadcast news station," replied Dawn. "I don't have to write press releases and beg to get media coverage. I know that we're always going to be covered, and our message is always going to get out to the public."

"It wasn't always this easy," said Jasper. "Until Majedah came to PDQ, there hadn't been a decent reporter who thought your work was worth covering, Dawn."

"Oh, I remember." Dawn scowled. "But now we have Majedah." She looked at Majedah and smiled. "Good thing you showed up!"

The sound of doors banging open and engines starting rang out behind them. The threesome turned and watched employees exit the warehouse to find something for lunch. Several of the skinniest among them began to shamble across the lot towards Flora Not Fauna. "Welp, time to make some money," sighed Dawn.

Majedah stood at the same. "Thanks for lunch, Dawn. Jasper, I'll see you tomorrow at 8:30 a.m."

"You got it, Majedah."

Majedah got into her electric car and drove to the city's fashionable shopping district. She parked in front of a café called Ginger's Pantry and went inside. Twenty minutes later, with a seventeen-dollar bowl of lentil soup and a six-dollar cinnamon dolce latte in her belly, Majedah returned to her car. Her color was much improved, and revitalized energy was evident in her light step.

Majedah went home and enjoyed a restorative nap on her pillow-top king size bed. As the heat of the day began to lift, she dressed in high tech athletic apparel and went for a good, long, cleansing run in the verdant strip alongside the river that wound through town. She returned home to rinse off beneath the massaging shower head. Then, wrapped in her organic cotton waffle knit robe, Majedah poured a glass of merlot and sank into a deep, decadent, leather club chair. She gazed out over the evening city, sipped, and watched lights wink on. For an unguarded moment, she slipped into a state of contentment and gratitude.

Majedah quickly began to go over the next day's plan in her mind, and her soft lips tightened into a straight line. The narrative for the assignment was clear; once again, racist-sexist-bigot-homophobe-xenophobes were victimizing helpless, oppressed people. Majedah shook her head. *Why must they always hate?* she mourned. *Why can't they love and celebrate, like the moral majority of Americans?* She wondered dismally if her work would ever be done. Then she looked out over the darkening city, a fierce light burning in her eye. "So help me, I will not rest until every Injustice is exposed and corrected. Every Injustice in this town, in this country, and in the world!" She held up her wine glass in a solitary salute to her Great Purpose then threw back the remaining merlot.

Majedah stood purposefully and went to her open laptop. After all, dinner wasn't going to order itself!

Chapter 7

THE FOLLOWING MORNING, Majedah dressed carefully in a tailored dress and fixed her hair with extra product so it would hold its style for broadcast. She arrived at the PDQ offices at 8:30 sharp. She had barely dropped her bag on her chair when Jasper came in behind her, bearing two tall cardboard cups. "Here you go," he said, handing one to her. "Dawn made a batch of maca in goat nut milk to sell to the morning crowd. I scored us a couple before I left the apartment." He took a deep swig of his. "Mmmm, better than coffee."

"Thanks, Jasper." Majedah sniffed hers cautiously while Jasper dug through his bag for something. It seemed safe enough, so she took a swallow. The lukewarm, cloudy liquid tasted like sweetened chalk with hints of saltpeter and cumin. Majedah swallowed quickly before her throat could reject it and close up, causing an embarrassing spit-or-gag situation. She slammed the cup purposefully on her desk in a gesture that suggested getting down to business. "Okay, you ready to do this?"

Jasper met her eye. "Oh, I'm looking forward to it."

They both turned as Norma came into the large open workspace. She seemed startled then pleased to see them. "You two are here early," she observed.

"Yes, we are, Norma. We got a tip about an exciting story happening this morning, and we want to be there in plenty of time to cover it," Majedah informed her.

"Fantastic." Norma looked from Majedah to Jasper and back again. "You know, you guys remind me of a young Norma Troutstein." The old pro sighed as she recalled her distant past. "I used to come to work early with that same sparkle in my eye, eager to discover the truth and tell it to the world."

Majedah sincerely hoped that Norma had had a discernable jaw line and dressed in something other than crinkled linen camp shirts back then. *No wonder Norma wound up in production*, she thought to herself. Out loud, she said, "Yes, well, thanks to pioneers like yourself, we now know the truth. It's simply a matter of finding the right stories to show it to the world."

Norma looked dubious. "If you'll permit an old news hound to share some of the wisdom I've learned over the years, I'll give you some advice: Never assume you already know the truth."

Majedah's brow wrinkled. "But, Norma, there are some things which are simply known to be true."

"How do you know something is 'known to be true'?" queried her boss.

Majedah looked to Jasper in disbelief, then back at Norma. "Well, there's a consensus among intelligent, educated people that certain things are simply true, that's how."

Norma smiled affectionately at the young reporter. "Majedah," she said, "you may think I hired you for your education, but that's not it; there are dozens of Journalism graduates in this town every May, and I don't call each of them to offer a job. No, I hired you because, out of all the bright, hardworking students in your school, only you could see beyond the consensus among your peers and professors to spot a true story. You have a real gift, Majedah. I look forward to watching your career over the years." She almost looked misty eyed for a moment, and Majedah could hear Jasper groan under his breath. Then Norma drew a bracing sigh and barked out orders in her customary drill sergeant tones. "Okay, team, go get that story!"

As Majedah picked up her bag, strategically forgot to grab her cup of warm maca in goat nut milk, and turned to leave, she heard Norma say to herself, "Sure hope it's not those same twelve kooks that run around town protesting everything again." Majedah and Jasper glanced at one another and hurried to exit the office.

THE SKYLER MEMORIAL Library was a glass-and-steel modern structure wedged between high rises and apartment buildings that dated back to the 1960's and 70's. The library had been built on the site of a former men's club, which the City of Wycksburg had righteously de-zoned and reclaimed when more enlightened leadership came into power. As Majedah approached with her cameraman, she took in the scene. A white, vinyl banner hung across the angular portico, proclaiming 'Welcome Director Wilson!"

Halfway down the block, about a dozen protestors were assembled on the sidewalk. They varied in age from mid-20's to around 50. All were dressed casually, mostly in shorts and t-shirts. Some carried hand-lettered signs displaying clever phrases, such as *Amerikkka is Racist* and *Love Beats Hate* and *Fuck Nelson* and *This Pussy Has Teeth*. Several protestors carried pitchforks, and a glowering, bearded man carried a torch.

"Look, there's Dawn," said Jasper. He crossed the street and Majedah followed. As Jasper kissed his girlfriend hello, Majedah greeted the other protestors, most of whom she knew pretty well after covering their every exploit for the past two months. She touched knuckles with the torch-carrying, bearded man, air-kissed a pudgy young Latina's shiny cheek, and gave a *Hunger*

Games-style, three-finger kiss salute to a thirty-something Bohemian chick, who returned the gesture. Last, she received a hug from the group organizer, Stanton.

"Hey, sister, good to see you. Thanks for being here, thanks for being here." Stanton was in his late 20's. When he spoke, his words sounded quietly enthusiastic and almost musical in their delivery. He alone among the protestors was dressed neatly, in a white button-down shirt, slim necktie, belted dark trousers, and leather shoes. His hair was worn short, and he seemed cool and poised in the blossoming heat. Majedah had considered sleeping with him when she first met him, but ultimately reminded herself to stay true to her objective journalistic principles. The relationship remained professional.

"Of course I'm here, Stanton. It's my job to be here." Majedah favored the organizer with a genuine smile. "But on a personal note, let me say how proud I am to cover today's action. Thank you for doing what you're doing. You hold these bigots accountable!"

Stanton grinned and ducked his head in acknowledgement. "That we will, girl, that we will." Because of Stanton's dark complexion and prestigious occupation, Majedah took pleasure rather than offense when he called her 'girl'.

"'Scuse me, Stanton." A short, round woman with a blue bowl cut and severe bangs tugged on Stanton's sleeve until the organizer looked at her. "Which side of my sign do you think I should use first? This side?" She held up a piece of hot pink poster board on which she had painted the slogan, *Liberate Women Through Social Justice.* "Or this side?" She flipped the angry pink sign over to the reverse, on which was block-lettered, *My Vagina Itches.* She peered intently through thick glasses so as not to miss a single nuance of her leader's expression.

Stanton covered his mouth with one hand and his brow furrowed in concentration. "Hm, I think you should go with the first side, Olive," he said from behind his fingers.

"I should go with the first side?"

"Yes, go with the first side, Olive."

"Okay, Stanton."

Majedah sighed happily at the sight of the dedicated young woman. A spotty 19-year-old boy came up to Stanton next. "I got the flyers," he said. He handed a rubber-banded pack of handbills to the organizer. "I came in early and ran them this morning, before anyone else was in."

"Great, thank you, Sam." Stanton peeled a few flyers off the bundle and handed it back to the lad. "Here, hand these around. Make sure everyone has a stack to hand out."

"Yessir, Mr. Stanton." Sam moved off among the group.

Stanton handed flyers to Majedah and Jasper. Majedah looked at the handbill and saw a bespectacled, 40-ish, white male wearing a buttoned-up shirt and a necktie, printed on which was a pattern of shelves lined with books. The man looked as though he was born to be a librarian, except that the resourceful handbill designer had added a black, Hitler-style mustache to his portrait. Beneath the image was the name *Michael Wilson*. "This is our target today," explained Stanton to his followers, holding up the flyer. "And we got nothing personal against Mr. Wilson. We understand, a man's gotta make a living, he's gotta make a living. But he doesn't have to do it by taking a job that a person of color or a differently gendered person or an undocumented citizen could be doing. He needs to check his privilege, is all we're saying. That's all we're saying. ... And by 'check his privilege,' we mean he needs to go," Stanton clarified.

Majedah, Jasper, and the activists nodded and agreed vocally with words like, "Oh, yes," and "Most definitely."

"Okay then, let's get this thing going," said Stanton. He lifted a bullhorn to his mouth and issued instructions. "Folks, we're gonna march down to the library entrance in a standard mob formation. We'll go with the simple warm-up chant, *Love Beats Hate*. Once we get there, form a half-round alongside the entrance to the library. We're gonna shout down the mayor's proclamation and Wilson's remarks."

The protestors cheered their enthusiasm.

"I also have some exciting news," continued Stanton. "Olive just got back from the GOO conference…"

Gasps sounded from the assembled activists.

"GOO!"

"Wow!"

"Yes, Olive was just training with GOO—the Global Outrage Organization—where she learned some amazing new techniques," continued Stanton. "So, when we get to the site, keep your eyes on this girl. Watch this girl." He had slipped his arm around the blue-haired activist's shoulders, and pride rolled off her in waves. He raised his voice to an energizing volume. "Okay, you people ready to go fight for justice?"

"YEAH!" Fists were raised into the air.

"Okay, here we go." Using the bullhorn, Stanton began the chant: *Love Beats Hate! Love Beats Hate!* A filthy-looking college student picked up the tempo on the vegan native-American drum slung across his midsection, and the protestors joined in with their voices.

LOVE BEATS HATE! LOVE BEATS HATE!

They turned as one and began the march up the sidewalk. Jasper ran a few paces ahead then walked backwards in front of them, filming. He made sure not to move too far ahead so that the edges of the group could not be seen in the shot.

Majedah walked alongside them but just out of the shot, pumping her fist and chanting. As they approached the library entrance, she saw the white, male mayor standing next to a small podium in his navy blazer and khakis. The mostly female library staff flanked him, all white except for a nerdy-looking young man of color. Off to the side, a string trio in formal dress played classical European compositions, to the exclusion of all other global musics. Majedah began to chant louder, enjoying the dismay she saw darkening the erstwhile beaming faces of the welcoming committee.

The ignorant library staff hadn't imagined there could be anything controversial about naming a new director, so they hadn't hired any security for the event. The protestors went where they pleased, marching right up to the mayor and librarians. The ordinary, neatly dressed citizens who had already gathered retreated across the walkway and stood near the musicians, anxiously looking back at the intruders. The protestors gathered in a group and waved their signs menacingly. Stanton took to the bullhorn to modify the chant.

Check your privilege! Check your privilege! he led.

After a few false starts, the protestors picked up the new chant.

CHECK YOUR PRIVILEGE! CHECK YOUR PRIVILEGE!

They turned to chant at the oppressive librarians. Several of the librarians took up the chant as well, glancing from the mayor to the protestors and back.

Majedah motioned Jasper to the curb, where he could get a good shot of her with the library entrance behind her. She directed him to make sure the protestors were predominant in the background, switched on her microphone, and went to work.

"This is Majedah Cantalupi-Abromavich-Flügel-Van Der Hoven-Taj Mahal, reporting from the front of the Skyler Memorial Library, where a new director is being installed today. But as you can see from the crowd behind me, not everyone is happy about it." She drew a finger across her throat and Jasper stopped filming. "Let's go get a statement from Stanton," she said. Jasper nodded, and they returned to the noisy group.

At this point, the musicians who had been playing classical music had given up and simply sat in their folding chairs, staring sadly at the demonstration. Majedah tapped Stanton's shoulder and pulled him far enough from the chanting to be heard. She did a quick interview with him while Jasper filmed. "We're here with Stanton Williams, director of the People's Organization for Perpetual Outrage. Mr. Williams, what can you tell us about the demonstration behind us?"

She held the microphone in front of Stanton, and he spoke skillfully in his stern-but-reasonable voice. "We're here today to protest the lack of diversity in municipal staff that is represented by this farce of a new hire. With the filling of a position of responsibility and visibility, the Skyler Library, and indeed, the whole community, had an opportunity to show real leadership by hiring a person of color. But instead, they chose to oppress and deny the diversity of our community by hiring yet another white man."

Majedah took back the microphone. "That really is offensive," she agreed. "Mr. Williams, what do you think—"

The filthy, blond dreadlocked drummer came over and tapped Stanton on the shoulder. "Wilson's car is pulling up," he shouted.

"Oh, okay. 'Scuse me, Majedah."

"Of course."

Jasper cut the camera while Stanton returned to his group. He raised the bullhorn. "Okay everyone, signs up high. Let's stick with the *Check Your Privilege* chant for now."

The mayor took his place behind the podium. He motioned to the musicians to begin playing again. They shrugged and complied, though the chanters still drowned them out. As a van rolled to a stop at the curb, the library staff formed up alongside the politician, some of them still chanting as well. Majedah watched the mayor's face and saw resolution and dismay. She felt a momentary pang of compassion for the civil servant who had expected to be performing a happy ceremony this morning, but the feeling dispersed as quickly as it had come.

Then all eyes were on Wilson's van. But instead of a white man getting out of the driver's seat, a pretty, brunette woman in her late 30's debarked. She walked around to the library side of the van and her face registered surprise at the demonstrators. She shook her head then spotted the welcoming committee, and she gave them a thumbs-up. She turned to pull open the sliding door on the van. A platform swung out and lowered to the sidewalk a wheelchair bearing almost-Library Director Wilson. He was wearing a gray suit, a light blue shirt, and a necktie printed with lines of black illuminated text on an ivory parchment background. Beaming, his wife stood to the side and clapped for him. Everyone at the podium clapped as well, except the librarians who had joined in the chanting; they just looked confused.

The activists turned up the volume and directed their chanting at Wilson and his wife as the couple made their way up the walk to the podium. Signs shook and spittle flew. Olive broke out of the crowd to try out one of the techniques she had learned at the recent GOO conference. She planted herself in front of Wilson's wheelchair, hands open and palms in his face, blocking him. Her face was as red as her hair was blue as she screamed, CHECK YOUR PRIVILEGE!

From her vantage point, Majedah watched the dramatic moment. She saw Mrs. Wilson look at the young woman with pity. The director's wife reached a hand to touch Olive's cheek, and Majedah clearly read her lips as she said, "Oh, you poor girl." Olive snarled and spit in wrathful confusion. An uncomfortable feeling welled in Majedah; if she had had a different upbringing, she might have recognized it as shame.

Meanwhile, Wilson simply wheeled around the confounded young activist and arrived at the mayor's side. The normal, neatly dressed crowd clapped and cheered as he waved to them. An elderly senior librarian took charge and hushed her staff who had been chanting. The mayor turned on the speaker in the podium and cranked the volume. An ear-splitting shriek of feedback momentarily deafened everyone. It had the effect of a flash-bang on the protestors, who lost their place in their chanting and stood murmuring in confusion. Before Stanton could re-organize them, the mayor launched into his remarks.

"Welcome and thank you for coming, everyone. Since we have such an unexpected turnout," and he gave the protestors a look, "we will dispense with the ceremony swiftly and move indoors for the reception." He turned to the guest of honor. "Mr. Wilson, do you swear to perform the duties of Director of the Skyler Memorial Library to the best of your ability, and to uphold the statutes and values of the Town?"

He handed the microphone to Wilson, who held it close to his mouth and said loudly and deliberately, "I do." A crooked grin broke out across his face, and his wife bent to kiss him.

The mayor took back the microphone and proclaimed, "Congratulations, Director Wilson!"

The normal crowd applauded, and the string trio broke into a triumphal air. Olive, still in the middle of the walkway, turned wild-eyed to Stanton. He shouted, "Voice grenade, Olive," and signaled for her to try the new technique. The young woman fell to her knees and began to scream inarticulately at the top of her lungs. The horrid sound dragged on until she ran out of air. Then she drew another deep breath and did it again. Her fellow protestors cheered. However, the audience of normal people looked at her pityingly, covered their ears, and moved towards the entrance to the library.

Majedah turned to Jason. "Did you get all that?" she asked him.

He switched off the camera. "Yup."

"Good."

Nearby, Stanton consoled his troops. "Okay, people, we couldn't stop it this time, we couldn't stop it. Yet another white man was privileged with a job that a person of color will not have. That a person in the LGBTQWTF community will not have. That an undocumented citizen will not have…"

Stanton continued to run through the familiar litany, but Majedah's reporter senses were tingling; she knew there was a story yet to be covered. She motioned to her cameraman. "Come on, Jasper, follow me." Then Majedah strode into the library to request an interview with the new director.

Chapter 8

NORMA WAS THRILLED with Majedah's reportage about the first differently abled director-level town employee. "Your interview with Mike Wilson was inspirational," she gushed at Majedah in the next staff meeting. "I could feel people all over this town think to themselves, 'Well, if Wilson can do that, I can certainly go after my goals.' I'm putting you in for an NBNA Groundbreaker Award." She beamed across the table, and the rest of the PDQ crew clapped and hooted.

The Groundbreaker Award was given to numerous local news media across the country and Majedah knew it wouldn't capture the attention of anyone at 24/7, but at least it was a decent résumé-padder. She smiled demurely.

And so Majedah kept her nose to the grindstone, and the months began to pass. She worked hard to find and report stories around the mid-sized metro area that comprised her territory. Naturally intelligent, Majedah strove for excellence, always showing up to work on time and without a visible hangover. She was fabulous on camera, with her slender figure, exotic good looks, and high-end wardrobe.

And always, Majedah stayed hungry. Whenever contentment tried to creep into her mind, she would sternly remind herself that the world was a bigoted, horrible, hateful place, and that she must work all the harder to expose that hate. But most important, she was ever on the lookout for that all-important Story of National Significance that would catapult her name to the coastal palaces of media power.

Thus it was with teeth clenched in frustration that Majedah ventured to the working class section of town, on assignment to cover the installation of a live nativity scene and petting zoo at St. Pius X Church. She drove her tiny electric car with Jasper riding shotgun, his knees bent halfway up to his chest to accommodate his lanky frame.

When they stopped at a red light, Jasper said, "Oh, look, is that a snowflake?"

Majedah focused on the windshield and noticed several more sugar-bright crystals bouncing off the surface. They sparkled in the streetlights against the deep blue of the evening sky. "Sure looks like it," she said tightly. "And just in time for our nativity piece. How cliché."

The red sparkles turned to green when the light changed, and Majedah accelerated into the intersection. Just at that moment, a rusted, dented pickup truck with bald tires flew crossways into the intersection at a scorching rate of speed. Majedah didn't see it coming as she blithely drove into its path. The truck t-boned the tiny vehicle at 78 miles per hour, striking it squarely in the passenger compartment.

Luckily, however, the inebriated, unlicensed and uninsured driver was an undocumented citizen, so Majedah and Jasper were incapable of awareness of any problems he might cause. The truck passed harmlessly through the little car to continue careering down the side street, until it eventually struck and demolished the façade of a small, privately owned bakery.

Three blocks further down the road, Majedah pulled into a brightly lit lot and parked. She and Jasper took a moment to survey the scene before stepping out into the chill air. To the near right, under a string of white bulbs, the local scout troop was selling Christmas trees. Dead ahead was the steepled church itself. A glorious round stained-glass window above the doors glowed from within. To the side was a large, low building that housed an elementary school. On the lawn beside the school, illuminated by a single, high, LED star, was the nativity scene. A dozen young children crowded up to the fence that enclosed several animals and a moss-covered, three-walled shed. Parents huddled in long parkas, sipping steaming cider, taking pictures, and chatting with the parish priest. The snow was falling lightly now, favoring the scene with fetching seasonal atmospherics.

Majedah swiveled her head to take it all in then began to scratch angrily at the sensitive skin on her neck. "Ugh, all this superstitious patriarchal bigotry is giving me hives," she snarled.

"It really is a joke," agreed Jasper. "Pretending to be so goody two-shoes, when they're actually teaching little kids to hate Science and Love." He shook his head and looked at the cluster of people again. His expression softened. "Although it is sort of cute in a Norman Rockwell kind of way," he allowed.

Majedah had just been thinking the same thing. "Yeah, I guess you're right. Classic Christmas *kitsch*." She sighed deeply. "Okay, let's get this over with."

Majedah stood in the shimmering snowfall as she waited for Jasper to get his equipment out of the hatch. Her lip curled with loathing as she raked her gaze across the cheerful scouts in their tidy uniforms. "Just like little Hitler Youth," she muttered to herself. A small boy with plump, bright red cheeks held up a wreath for a customer to inspect. The boy's father stood behind him and Majedah's stare snagged on his form. With his hands on his son's shoulders, the man stood tall and straight, shoulders back and bareheaded, his short hair lifting in the breeze. Something about the sight of him reverberated deep in Majedah's chest. Her breath caught and her lips parted in shock as it dawned on her; he looked almost exactly like her high school boyfriend, Kevin McGuiness, although an older version of him. Majedah had the disorienting sensation of time slipping and skidding around her while she watched a significant figure from her past as he would look in his future life. *That's probably exactly what Kevin will be like someday,* she mused, *with a bunch of kids and hanging around churches and running a scout troop.* The idyllic sight threatened to hypnotize her with its wholesomeness, and she quickly added, *Barf.*

"Okay, all set," said Jasper.

Majedah snapped out of her fixation and turned to him. In his knit cap and heavy duffel coat, a gear bag slung across his body and the big camera in his hands, Jasper stood looking at her expectantly. "Oh, okay, good." Majedah reached up and slammed the hatch shut. "Let's go." As they walked across the fresh layer of snow towards the nativity scene, she breathed deeply and tried to marshal her emotions into professional mode.

The smiling, white-haired pastor stood waiting to greet them. He reached to shake Majedah's elegant gloved hand, then Jasper's, introducing himself at the same time. "Hello, hello! I'm Father Dom. Thank you so much for coming out here in the snow."

"Hello, Father Dom," Majedah replied. "Don't worry about the snow; we're professionals, and we have a job to do." She gave the elderly man her most charming smile, which made him smile back in delight.

"Tell Norma thank you for sending her prettiest reporter out here," bade Father Dom.

"Ha, ha, okay," said Majedah, deciding to let his harassing comment pass. After all, what did anyone expect from a priest? "Well, let's get to work."

"Of course, of course, right this way," said Father Dom. He turned and led the way to the snowy lawn by the makeshift petting zoo. The children noticed them and watched curiously, their attention split between the TV reporter and the animals.

Jasper set up the tripod about ten feet from the fence. Majedah stood in front of the camera while Jasper turned on the light and checked everything. He gave her a thumbs-up. Majedah looked around to find Father Dom, who was standing among the children, chin thrust forward, watching the journalists with same curiosity as they. Majedah waved him over. "Father Dom, would you come talk about the live nativity on camera?"

A grin spread across the old pastor's face. "Certainly. I'd love to." He straightened up and hustled over to her. At her side, he blinked in the glare of the light before becoming accustomed to it.

"Ready?" asked Majedah. She gave him her charming smile again, which cheered Father Dom even more.

He clapped his hands together. "Let's do this."

"Okay, here we go." She nodded to Jasper and went to work. "This is Majedah Cantalupi-Abromavich-Flügel-Van Der Hoven-Taj Mahal, and I'm here at Saint Pius the Tenth Roman Catholic Church, where a live nativity scene has just opened up for visitors." She turned to the priest and continued. "Here with me is Father Dom, the pastor of the church. Father, how long have you been bringing the animals here for the Christmas season?"

A seasoned community leader, Father Dom looked right into the camera and spoke enthusiastically. "This is actually our twenty-second year hosting the live nativity. We've been doing it so long that some of the parents who bring their children used to come here as children themselves."

"Wow, so it's become quite the Advent tradition here at Pius the Tenth," declared Majedah. To herself, she thought, *Advent? Where did I come up with that old word?* Aloud, she asked, "And what animals do you have on location this year?" She held the microphone for his answer.

The ancient skin crinkled around Father Dom's sparkling eyes. "This year, we have sheep and a donkey and some chickens, all very traditional. But then, we also have ... *a llama!*" He beckoned Jasper with a wave of his hand. "Come on, let's go see." He spun and capered off, and Jasper quickly detached the camera from the tripod, hoisted it to his shoulder, and followed. Majedah shrugged and went after them.

At the fence, Father Dom began pointing out all the animals, waving constantly at Jasper to film each one. "This is Rosy the ewe, and here's her lamb, Minty. Well, Minty's getting big now, but he's only eight months old." He leaned way over the fence to pat the sheep's head, and the children gathered around him, giggling. Father Dom laughed along with them, tousling hair and introducing more animals to the camera. "Say hello to Caspar the Llama!" he announced. Jasper brought the camera down low to film a cherub-faced little girl with a halo of black curls as she offered food pellets for Rosy to nibble from her palm.

Uncharacteristically, Majedah did not feel the need to retake control of the scene. Father Dom and Jasper were capturing plenty of heart-warming, community-relevant footage, the kind parents and grandparents all over town would tune into over and over, every time the 20-minute loop replayed on PDQ. Majedah could always record voiceover back at the studio and leave it for Antoine to cut together. The uncomplicated joy emanating from the scene before her was weaving a spell on her, despite her best efforts. She felt oddly vulnerable, perhaps due to the internal swirl of old emotions stirred up by the sighting of future-Kevin. She was certain Kevin would one day have a stable, normal life like the scout dad selling trees in the parking lot. She knew she was being ridiculous—she hadn't allowed herself to think of Kevin in so long—but she felt jealous of the woman with whom he would share that life.

She watched steam lift off the warm, fuzzy beasts and rise through the swirling snow into the benevolent light of the LED star above. She could hear children's laughter and the animated narration of Father Dom. A pretty young mom pressed a cup of hot cider into her hand; she sipped and tasted cinnamon. She removed and pocketed her gloves so she could wrap her chilly fingers around the hot paper cup. Unbidden, her feet carried her to the animal pen, where she held out her hand for a scoop of pellets. She extended a laden palm through the fence to Minty and closed her eyes as the sweet lamb tickled her skin with his soft, innocent lips. She was five years old, feeding pellets to a woolly sheep outside a long-ago church, her own father's hands on her shoulders, her mother's arm linked through his, benevolent light warming down from above. Her eyes remained closed as a tear slid from beneath her lashes, but she was smiling.

Alone in her condo that night, Majedah killed a bottle of merlot for dinner. She let the alcohol warm the spot in her chest that had been warmed earlier by the sights and sounds at Pius X. The alcohol also kept at bay her defenses against simple sentiment like she was experiencing now, but the feelings were so pleasant that she wanted to keep it going. "Just for tonight," she said as she yanked the cork from a fresh bottle. "I'll be good again tomorrow." She carried the bottle into the unlit living room, where she punched up one old Christmas children's special after another on her wall-sized TV until she fell asleep on the sofa in the wee hours of the morning.

THE MORNING'S HANGOVER displaced any warm feelings Majedah may still have harbored with waves of clammy nausea. She retched into the toilet, took a glass of water and a handful of Advil back to bed, and tried again an hour later. Feeling stronger, she dressed and descended to the street for a fresh, hot bagel and a Coke. Another hour passed, and she was behind the wheel of the electric car, her suitcase tossed on the narrow back seat, on the road to Julia's house for a pre-holiday visit. Gary Swanson was the senior-most reporter at PDQ so he got to take Christmas off. Majedah hadn't minded agreeing to work on the holiday, since it didn't actually mean anything to her. Norma had patted her on the back and told her how much she appreciated her team spirit.

"Julia, I'm here," Majedah called out when at last her feet were sinking into the familiar plush of the entryway oriental.

Her mother appeared in the doorway of her office, thin lips pulled tight in her version of a smile. "Hi, Majedah. Welcome! So good to see you." She stepped forward and the two women embraced. Majedah hugged her mother extra hard and long, until Julia exclaimed, "Well, well, okay now," and dismissively patted her on the back.

Majedah stepped away and bent to get her bag. "Hey, nice new wheels out in the driveway, Mom. Congratulations."

"Oh, the Edison Amp? Yes, thank you. It's been a wonderful year, sales-wise. There's some amazing new research going on in neogenital generation, and the market for naughty stem cells is just going wild." Julia smiled again, and this time it reached high enough to etch a small line in the outer corners of her eyes.

The two women wandered through the house to the sunroom, where they sat in cushioned rattan chairs while the housekeeper brought them coffee and sandwiches. Majedah and her mother nibbled, sipped, and caught up with one another's lives.

"Not that it's a requirement of any sort, but is there anyone special in your life these days?" asked Julia.

"No, there's not a lot in the way of eligible partners in that town." Majedah sighed. "I've met pretty much everyone who has a clue by now. Jasper, Dawn and Stanton have introduced me to all their friends. Everyone's nice and fairly woke, but I don't know … no one really stands out to me."

Julia nodded. "Well, it is rather a provincial little town, when all is said and done."

Majedah looked at her intently. "Mom, I really have to break into the New York market somehow. I just know I belong there, and that's where I'll meet people at my own level."

"Yes, Majedah, I believe that's where you belong, too. And I'm sure you'll get there. You have the talent and the drive. Keep working to build up your name and watch for every opportunity. Sooner or later, someone at one of the big stations will spot you, and they'll come looking for you."

The conversation moved on to the latest outrage from President Nelson's administration.

"I cannot believe that women still have to pay for their own tampons," hissed Majedah. "I really thought that provision would stay in the new healthcare omnibus. What is this, the Dark Ages?"

Julia shook her head angrily, blue ice in her eyes. "Exactly. These are *not* American values."

When the subject was exhausted and the sandwiches eaten, Majedah went up to her room for a nap.

She sat on her bed and flicked through messages on her phone but saw nothing of interest. She set the phone aside and glanced around the room. Julia's house was not the home she had shared with her husband when Majedah was small, and Majedah hadn't kept many mementos of her childhood. She glanced at the books on the shelving next to a window. Throughout high school, she had gradually replaced her childish books with YA novels starring empowered young women who changed the world. The tall bottom shelf housed reference books, stacks of magazines, and a few large picture books she had probably kept because of their high graphic quality. Her eyes came to rest on an exquisitely illustrated medical encyclopedia. Ziyad had given it to her on her eighth birthday, Majedah recalled, because she had told him she wanted to be a doctor like him when she grew up. It was one of the few things her father had given her that she still kept. Before she could look away again, the vague sentimental feeling from the previous evening flared within her. Majedah decided she felt this way because this was her first visit to her hometown since she started the job at PDQ. Also, the holidays were simply an overwrought time of year. Oddly warm and vulnerable, and she drifted off to a lovely afternoon nap.

When she awoke, Julia sent her to pick up a few things for supper. A refreshed and bright-eyed Majedah brushed out her gleaming ebony hair, wrapped herself in a military-style toggle coat with a vegan fur-lined hood, and drove off.

She loved Food Citizen and had missed the rambling, socially aware market; there wasn't one in the PDQ area where she lived. She wandered the aisles with a recycled plastic basket over one arm, loading it with roots, nuts, and exotic fruits. Her posture grew a little taller as she proudly reflected that the products had all been sustainably farmed, harvested in season, traded fairly, and transported to the store on vessels powered by sunshine and fresh breezes. Majedah lifted a wild-grown Galapagos prickly pear to her nose and sniffed the delicious, righteous scent before lovingly placing the fruit in her basket.

In the checkout line, she was suddenly overcome again with the disorienting feeling of time slippage. She gathered her fragmented thoughts enough to recognize the source of her befuddlement—the distantly familiar form of the tall man in front of her—when he turned to glance back at the store behind him. His gaze dropped to meet hers and he offered a neighborly smile. She was quick to recognize her high school boyfriend, as she had just been thinking of him the previous evening. Now she watched in frozen fear as his gaze remained on her and his brow knitted slightly in concentration. Finally, recognition flooded his face in the form of a broad smile. "Mandy!" he exclaimed. "Wow, what are you doing here?"

The middle-aged woman in front of him turned around and also recognized her. "Oh, my goodness, if it isn't Mandy Six-Names! How are you doing, sweetie?" A tall, solidly built woman with messy blond curls, Mrs. McGuiness shouldered her son aside and crushed Majedah in a smothering maternal hug. It was all the young woman could do not to flail in panic.

"Hi, Mrs. McGuiness," mumbled Majedah into the fabric of the woman's coat.

"Mom, I don't think she can breathe," observed Kevin.

"Oh, my goodness, I'm sorry." Mrs. McGuiness stepped back so she could look at Majedah. "Oh, you look great, Mandy, just great. All grown up!"

Majedah was helpless against the motherly effect the woman had on her, and her words came out respectfully. "Thank you, Mrs. McGuiness." Her fury at being called by her high school nickname evaporated before the woman's happy blue eyes and radiant smile.

"I hear you're a big shot reporter now, on TV and everything. I don't doubt it, with your beautiful face," gushed Mrs. McGuiness.

"And maybe her intelligence and hard work, too, Mom. I bet that had something to do with it." Kevin winked at Majedah over his mother's head, and she involuntarily smiled at him.

Mrs. McGuiness turned to her son and swatted him with her gloves. "Yes, of course it did, Kevin. I didn't mean to imply that Mandy is just a pretty face," she said in a mock-stern voice.

The twenty-something cashier finished ringing up the McGuiness's order. "That will be thirty-seven fifty-two."

Mrs. McGuiness's head snapped around. "What? For a loaf of bread and some chestnuts?"

"Those are *organic* chestnuts, Mom," Kevin explained, rolling his eyes at the absurdity of it all.

Not getting the joke, Majedah helped. "And the bread they bake here is made from rare heirloom grains, grown only on farms with humane worker policies, and baked in ovens fired by sustainably farmed blue-green algae biomass," she explained.

"Algae? On my bread?"

"No, Mom, it's not *on* the bread," said Kevin wearily. He waved frantically over his mother's head at Majedah to stop explaining.

"Humph, I only came here because I needed chestnuts," Mrs. McGuiness said, counting out bills. She glanced at Majedah and muttered "I usually shop at Grocery Barn, but they were sold out." With a huff, she handed the money to the cashier. Majedah and Kevin exchanged glances and suppressed smiles.

As the worker bagged her purchases, Mrs. McGuiness turned to her son. "Kevin, why don't you take Majedah out for coffee? You guys should catch up. You haven't seen each other since high school."

"But Mom, I drove you here." Kevin's protest, however, seemed perfunctory.

"And I can drive myself home." She turned to Majedah. "Would you mind giving Kevin a lift home after he buys you coffee?" she commanded.

Majedah had been raised by a mother who never told her to do anything or not to do anything, and she had no tools with which to counter Mrs. McGuiness's parental authority. "Sure," she heard herself say.

"Wonderful." Kevin's mother tucked her chin into her chest and beamed at Majedah again. "Oh, Mandy, it's been wonderful to see you again. Go catch up with Kevin; I can't wait to hear what you've been up to." Another smothering hug engulfed Majedah, and then she was left alone with Kevin as the smirking cashier began to ring her up.

Kevin shrugged apologetically. "Sorry about that. As you can see, she hasn't changed a bit."

"No, she certainly hasn't." Something weird happened to Majedah's face and throat, some sort of involuntary convulsion; she recognized it as laughter.

"Three fifty-seven twenty-eight," said the cashier.

"Oh, my God," exclaimed Kevin. People in the nearest two checkout lanes turned to look at him.

Blushing, Majedah handed her plastic to the expressionless worker. "It's Julia's card," she explained to Kevin.

She had forgotten how attractive (in a really boring, oppressive, outdated way, of course) Kevin's smile was. "You're still a spoiled rich girl," he teased.

"And you're still a bougie boy," she replied. She had to catch herself because she had come really close to saying "*my* bougie boy."

In the nearby coffee shop, Kevin made Majedah stand in line with him because, as he put it, there was no way he was going to be able to order whatever that was she was drinking. They scored a bistro table in the café's window, awash with winter afternoon sun. They each sipped shyly, elbows on the table, looking out at the lively holiday shoppers. Finally Kevin put down his cup, sat back, fixed Majedah with a direct look, and said, "Okay, you go first."

Holding her cup to her puckered lips, Majedah peered at him over the rim. Golden sunlight winked off her very fine black eyes, stirring memories in Kevin of hours spent enjoying the sight of those eyes. He flushed at their ensnaring power over him even now, but he held his back straight and continued to face her directly.

For her part, Majedah was secretly stunned by the impressive man Kevin had become. He must have grown an additional inch or two in college, or else his posture was even more improved;

he physically took up space and was a solid presence. She hated the idea of his toxic masculinity asserting some sort of psychological command over others and hated it even more that it seemed to be turning her on. Fascinated by Kevin's blue eyes, she forgot all about her cooling vegan half-caf doppio with almond milk and returned his gaze. The corners of her mouth kept curving up, so she began speaking in an effort to obscure her smile. "Well, as your mother said, I am a big shot reporter now, on TV and everything."

"You don't say." Kevin's neglected coffee also cooled as he leaned forward, the better to focus on her face.

"Actually, I don't." Majedah sat back in her chair, a pout plumping her lips. "I mean, I am a reporter, but 'big shot' is by no means an accurate description. And the TV I'm on is a local station in a small-to-mid-size market."

"So what? It's your first job, right? Do you know how many people would kill to be on camera at all, right out of college?"

"I guess." Majedah lifted her chin. "But I'm not letting myself get too comfortable there. I have a long-term plan."

Kevin put an elbow on the tabletop and rested his chin in his upturned hand. "Of course, you do; you're Mandy. What's the plan?"

Suddenly self-conscious, Majedah broke from his admiring gaze and glanced down at her hands, which were clasped in her lap. "You'll laugh."

"Never."

She met his eyes again, took a breath, and told him her dream. "I want to be on News 24/7 someday."

He didn't miss a beat. "And I have no doubt you will be."

She let out a sigh of relief. "Do you really think so?"

"Absolutely." His gaze never wavered, and she was once again captivated. "I know you, Mandy."

"Majedah."

"Majedah. I know you. I've never met anyone as focused as you. When you set your mind to something, you don't let go. You keep your eyes on the goal and you do what it takes to get there. I've always admired that about you."

Majedah felt a hot flush sweep from her chest to her scalp. "You have?"

"Yes. And another thing; you always aim high. You don't just go after any old goal; you set your sites on things that are really worth pursuing. You have high standards."

Majedah nodded. "It's true, I do have high standards. Which is probably why I never date anyone." She hadn't intended for that last comment to slip out; in fact, she had no idea where it came from. The blush deepened.

"Ha, lucky you."

It looked as though Kevin hadn't meant that comment to slip out, either. Majedah saw his eyes widen for a second then his cheeks went pink. She decided to save the day and steer the conversation somewhere safe. "Okay, your turn," she chirped. "What are you up to these days?"

Kevin's posture visibly relaxed. "Grad school," he reported. "Working on my Masters in Chemical Engineering."

Majedah was not particularly versed in any of the applied sciences, but she nodded for him to continue.

"I'm specializing in petrochemical engineering, actually. I also concentrate on geological analysis. I want to work in petroleum extraction beedle boddle boodle bop ..."

His words wafted off into gibberish that Majedah could neither understand nor care about. She settled for savoring the view of his robin's egg blue eyes in their nests of thick, brown lashes, bright with enthusiasm as he expounded on his studies and work plans. She leaned forward on her elbows and nodded frequently. She would have sat there happily watching his face for as long as he wanted to talk. Eventually, though, the stream of words came to an end.

"Whew, I certainly talked enough." The dopey smile returned to Kevin's face. "Anyway, that's what I've been up to."

Majedah sat back and reached for her doppio. She took a sip and scowled. "This is ice cold. Hey, what time is it?"

Kevin obligingly looked at his watch. "Yikes, it's 6:30."

"Yeah, we'd better get going. Julia will wonder where the dinner ingredients are."

They navigated the familiar roads to Kevin's neighborhood, Majedah at the wheel of the electric car, Kevin beside her with his knees up on either side of his ears so he would fit in the tiny cabin. "Are we almost there yet? I can't feel my feet," he complained.

"Make fun of it if you must, but this car makes zero emissions," Majedah stated with pride.

"Right, because they're all back at the power plant," Kevin grumbled. Majedah opened her mouth to retort but remembered that he was actually studying power generation or something and decided it would be useless to try to convince him. After all, he was one of *them*, she reminded herself.

"Seriously, I feel like I'm about to give birth here," Kevin went on. Then his house came into view and the car interior grew quiet, as the occupants both remembered the last time she had visited him here.

Majedah pulled up to the curb at the end of the neatly shoveled front walk. "Well, here you are," she prompted. She ignored the large, rebellious part of herself that didn't want him to get out.

But instead of reaching for the door handle, Kevin pushed his head back in the seat so he could look around his knee at her face. "Majedah, have you been okay since ..."

She knew what he was referring to. "Of course I have," she snapped. "Why wouldn't I be?" The vulnerability in his eyes chastened her so she hardly recognized herself, and she softened her tone. "Have you?" she asked in a small, quiet voice.

He turned away again, letting his knee obscure his face. "I am now," she heard him say. "I, um, worked through it with the youth minister when I was at Tech. I went to confession and everything. I found peace with the situation. I'm okay now." He jammed his head back against the seat so he could see her again. He had found an affectionate smile for her. "And I'm really glad you're okay, too."

"You don't have to worry about me; I am."

"That's our Mandy." Words intended to be spoken in a bracing, jocular tone accidentally came out soft and tender. Kevin's gaze had fallen to her lips, which were slightly parted in her confusion. Majedah was grateful that Kevin's cramped position and intervening knee made it physically impossible for him to lean over and kiss her, because she was pretty sure she would have kissed him back.

"Okay, well, thanks for the coffee," she blurted.

The spell broke and Kevin turned his head and began working his hand around behind his other leg in an attempt to reach the door handle. "My pleasure." His words were muffled by his jean-clad thigh. Majedah sat and waited as he worked. "Just trying to get the door here ..." he updated her. The car rocked a couple times as he lunged with his shoulder against the door, attempting to thrust his hand past his leg. "Any minute now ... okay, I can't feel my fingers ..."

"Hang on, I'll get it."

"No, no need, I'll get it..."

But Majedah had already let herself out and walked around the car. Flashing a triumphant gurl-power grin, she yanked the door handle, but nothing happened. A wave of panic washed over her. "Oh, my god, Kevin, it's locked!" She rattled the handle a couple times even though she knew it wouldn't open. "Kevin, you have to unlock it. You have to reach it somehow and unlock it!"

The car rocked savagely as the man trapped inside hurled himself into the effort. His muffled grunts came through the closed window. Majedah stood by, waiting for a click that never came. "Kevin, please!" she wailed.

The car stopped rocking as Kevin tried to say something. "I can't hear you," Majedah cried. At last she made out the words, *Come back inside.* "Oh, of course," she said as she hurried back to the open driver door. She leaned inside the car. "What is it, Kevin?"

He jammed his head back into the seat so he could see her. "Your key … use your key to unlock the door…" His voice was getting weaker and Majedah knew there was no time to lose.

"The door doesn't open with a key," she explained. Then realization dawned. "But I can use the key fob! Of course! Hang on, Kevin." She pulled the key from the ignition and marched triumphantly around to the passenger side of the car. She pointed the fob at the door and clicked.

Nothing happened.

She clicked and clicked and clicked. The door remained stubbornly locked. "What's wrong? Why won't it open?" she cried. She could hear Kevin mumbling something inside the vehicle and ran back around to the driver side. "What are you saying, Kevin?" she asked.

His head was back against the seat, his eyes closed. "Check … the … battery …" he murmured. Beads of sweat dotted his upper lip.

"Oh, right, of course." Majedah stuck the key in the ignition and turned on the electricity to the dashboard. No lights came on and the needle on the battery gauge didn't move. "Oh no, the battery needs a charge! Do you guys have a station?" she asked.

The little she could see of Kevin's face was pale and clammy, and his eyes remained closed. "No ... circulation ... can't ... hold ... on ..."

"Kevin, please, hold it together!" Majedah fought her rising panic. "What should I do?"

"My parents ... go get them ..."

Majedah leapt from the car, reflexively slamming her door behind her. She put her hand over her mouth and said, "Oops!" Then she turned and ran up the walkway.

Twenty minutes later, the burly firefighters finished cutting the door off the electric car. One of them reached in and cut the seat belt. Kevin's limp body unfurled and tumbled out onto the snow berm.

"Okay, big guy, you're okay now," said the white-helmeted captain. He stepped aside so the medics could roll Kevin onto a stretcher. They loaded him into the back of the waiting ambulance and started an IV line.

Kevin came to and saw Majedah, his parents, and his brother Scott standing outside, looking in anxiously at him. He smiled weakly and even lifted a few fingers to wave. One of the paramedics hopped out of the ambulance and closed and secured the back doors.

"He'll be okay," she reported. "He's just dehydrated and his blood flow had been restricted. We'll take him to the hospital to get him checked out but once that IV bag is done, he should be back to normal."

"Thank you so much," Mr. McGuiness said.

The medic went to the driver's seat and the ambulance rolled off. The fire trucks turned off their lights and cleared the scene as well. The neighbors on nearby lawns waved and returned to their warm houses.

A mortified Majedah looked at the McGuinesses. "I'm so sorry about that," she said. She shrugged them an *oops-forgive-me?* smile.

"That's okay, Mandy. I wouldn't know the first thing about how to work that fancy car of yours," said Mrs. McGuiness. She turned to her husband and son. "How about I give Mandy a ride home and then meet you at the hospital, John? Scott, can you go back in the house and finish supper? Hopefully we'll all be back before too long."

"Sounds good," said Mr. McGuiness.

"You got it, Mom," said Scott. He turned to Majedah. "It was almost fun seeing you again, Mandy."

"You too, Scott. Good luck with the rest of your senior year."

"Mandy," said Mr. McGuiness, "I'll call the wrecker and have your car towed to Lucas Auto, over on State Street. Unless you prefer another mechanic who handles electric cars?"

"No, Lucas is fine. Thanks, Mr. McGuiness."

Mrs. McGuiness headed for the garage. "I'll just get the car out. Be back in a minute, Mandy."

"Okay, Mrs. McGuiness." Majedah stood at the curb beside the lifeless shell of her clever car, as the McGuiness family dispersed in three different directions to set everything back to normal.

MOTHER AND DAUGHTER lingered over their late supper, talking well into the evening. Majedah told Julia what had happened to her car, and how Kevin had been entrapped until he ultimately had to be rescued by first responders. The absurdity of the scene dawned on Majedah as she finished up the tale and a grin threatened to appear on her face.

Julia, however, glowered. "That's what he gets for being so big," she said. "Imagine, eating so much food that you grow too big to be able to use today's smarter, more efficient technology." Her icy eyes narrowed with indignation.

Majedah caught her meaning. "Yes, now that you mention it; it is an obscene abuse of resources, for people to grow so big. They take up a lot of space and eat an awful lot of food. Probably takes lots of *meat*" (she wrinkled her nose) "to get that tall and muscular."

"If only there were a way to stop such big people from being born in the first place," Julia muttered into her dish of carob Patagonian ass tartufo. Majedah could practically hear the gears turning in her mother's mind and see the carboflourescent bulb flickering to life above her head. "A-ha! I've got it—big for dates."

Majedah did not have her mother's copious degrees and couldn't follow her train of thought, so she sat quietly in awe and let Julia do her thing.

Julia picked up her phone and dictated a text. "Ursula, come see me in the morning. We have to tell Chosen Children to add 'Big for Dates' to the *Why Terminate?* brochure." She punched some buttons and sent the message off to her colleague.

Majedah sensed the glow of brilliance emanating from her mother's latest epiphany and wanted to know more. "What brochure are you talking about, Julia?" she queried.

Julia seemed to remember Majedah was there. "Hang on, I'll show you." She rose and left the room. Majedah heard a drawer open and close in the office across the hall, then Julia reappeared and dropped a tri-folded brochure on the table in front of her. "Here you go. It's an informational piece Tissue Depot produces in partnership with Chosen Children, which they hand out to their women's health care clients.

"Oh, cool." Majedah picked up the printed piece to see it better. The front cover featured a photo of a model of indeterminate race. Dressed in a tastefully sexy beige peignoir, she sat in a window seat full of satin cushions and looked out at a gray sky. A single manicured fingertip was held to her chin in an attitude of contemplation. Bold serif lettering at the top read, *Why Terminate?* and in smaller italics, *Scientific facts to help you make your choice.*

"Ooh, science," murmured Majedah.

"We'll add 'Big for Dates' to the 'Reasons to Terminate' section," Julia explained.

Majedah opened the brochure and found the section. She read:

Sometimes a clump of cells has a flaw, which, if allowed to develop, will result in a drain on resources—yours and the Earth's!

There followed a bulleted list of flaws, including hereditary conditions, chromosomal disorders, privilege, deformities, and small size. "Ah, makes total sense, now that I see it in print," Majedah exclaimed. "Big people are also certainly a drain on resources."

"Exactly." Julia beamed at her bright, responsible daughter. "Just look at what Kevin did to your wonderful, Earth-friendly car."

Majedah found herself nodding along with her mother's logic. The woman's intellect was formidable. Majedah decided against mentioning that she had had a wonderful time with Kevin and had even thought about kissing him. In fact, she decided that the memory and feelings of her impromptu date didn't even belong in her own consciousness. She resolved to terminate them from her psyche at once.

Chapter 9

DAWN PUT HER lips to the top of the Lucite tube, held the lighter to the bowl, and inhaled. Smoky bubbles burbled up through the viscous, black substance. She lifted her head, clamped her lips shut to hold in the smoke, and passed the bong to Jasper. Majedah leaned with her elbows on the Formica-topped kitchen table and watched in horrified fascination as he sucked the smog up through the tar-like fluid. When he had drawn as deeply as he could, he met Majedah's eyes and offered her the bong with a nod. Majedah sat back quickly. "Oh, no thanks. I'm good."

Dawn exhaled with a sigh of pleasure. "Man, that is some good stuff," she said. "You sure don't want a hit, Majedah?"

"No, really, thank you. I can't afford to have my eyes get too veiny—looks bad on TV." She sat even further back from the table.

Jasper broke into a coughing fit, puffs of yellowish smoke emitting dragon-style from his nostrils. "Yeah—" *hack!* "good—" *cough, cough!* "stuff!" A dopey smile broke out over his face when the coughing subsided.

Majedah eyed the discolored bong as it cooled on the tabletop. "Hey, you guys want me to change out the water for you?"

"Nah, don't change it. We've been working on that potion for three months now," said Jasper. His grin widened to show most of his teeth.

"Yeah, I'm giving Jasper a high-test bong water enema for his birthday," elaborated Dawn.

"Oh," said Majedah. No further comment occurred to her.

"Yeah, there's nothing like it," Jasper said in words that were more of an exhalation than a voice. "A high like no other."

Majedah lifted her eyes from the nauseating sight of the bong to her friends' faces. She privately wished they didn't spend so much time getting stoned; the drive to find Stories of Importance and Make Change was strong in her, and she longed for professional teammates who shared her ambition and energy. "So, Dawn," she ventured, "any upcoming actions on POPO's schedule? Anything PDQ should be covering?"

Dawn's mellow expression tightened and she uttered a single, clipped syllable: "No." She stood abruptly and went to start rummaging through the cupboard, searching for snacks.

Majedah looked questioningly at Jasper. He dropped his head with a sigh and leaned forward to update Majedah. "Dawn's upset. She had to quit POPO."

"Oh no! What happened?"

"Stanton stabbed us in the back, that's what happened," Dawn growled into the cupboard.

Jasper glanced over his shoulder at his girlfriend's back then looked across the table again. "Stanton got his own GOO franchise," he explained.

"The Global Outrage Org?" Majedah wondered.

"The same," confirmed Jasper.

"He sold out," Dawn shouted into the shelves of responsibly packaged non-perishables. Her hands flung aside bags and cans, searching for just the right munchie.

Majedah thought about what that meant. "So, wait, isn't that a good thing? Doesn't he have more resources at his disposal now?"

"Well, yes—" began Jasper.

"It means he takes his marching orders from Global now," snarled Dawn. She slammed a crinkly cellophane bag of air-popped quinoa biscuits onto the table and tore it open. Then she dropped gracelessly into a chair and shoved a handful of biscuits into her mouth.

Jasper looked at her sadly. "That's the downside," he explained to Majedah. "POPO is no more; now it's just the local chapter of GOO."

"But I'm confused," Majedah said. "Isn't it better to be part of a large, powerful, well-funded global organization?"

Dawn looked furious. "No, because all they care about is their own agenda."

"Dawn has spent her entire life as an activist in this town," said Jasper. "She grew up here, and local issues are deeply important to her."

"I've spent my life trying to make this town a better place," squawked Dawn. "I kept the homeless shelter open! I got the men's club replaced with a library! I got the pet store shut down for selling animals! I fought for fair wages for municipal employees!"

Majedah still didn't get it. "But aren't those the same goals everyone wants everywhere?"

"Ha! You'd think," sneered Dawn. She rammed another fistful of quinoa crackers into her scowling mouth.

Once again, Jasper stepped in to explain. "It turns out that GOO has a more, ah, *disciplined* agenda. They work in tandem with national and global political organizations, and whatever is needed to sway an election, they provide it. For example, as you know, we've got a national election coming up in less than two years, so the DNC has put together a plan to destroy Nelson's chances at re-election. The word is that they'll run Angela Harper for president."

"Senator Harper? From California?" clarified Majedah.

"Yes, her," Jasper confirmed. "So, since Senator Harper is a woman and President Nelson is a man, the DNC is working with GOO and the national media to show how badly this country is controlled by misogyny and toxic masculinity. Once the people see the truth, a woman president will finally have a chance."

Majedah nodded thoughtfully. "So how is that a bad thing? Just sounds like good strategy to me."

"Well, it is good global strategy, maybe," said Jasper. "But it takes the focus off the local issues."

"POPO—excuse me, *GOO*— is all about vaginas and police brutality now," huffed Dawn bitterly. "Nothing local matters anymore to them. Just vaginas and police brutality."

"And neither of those things are really a problem in this town, thanks to Dawn and POPO's past work" said Jasper. "POPO actions got a majority of POC's and vagi—I mean, women—hired onto the police force years ago. And our Chosen Children clinic is one of the most active in the country." His posture straightened visibly as he listed his girlfriend's past accomplishments.

"Huh, I see," said Majedah. To herself, she thought, *I see indeed; the Important Stories are now Oppression of Women and Police Brutality. Got it.*

By now thoroughly sick of having a conversation over a cheap Formica tabletop crowned with a filthy, disgusting bong, she stood and went to get her coat off the back of the sofa. As she shrugged on the garment, she mustered a sympathetic expression and looked back to her friends. "That really is a shame. I'm surprised at Stanton for selling out like that."

"It's amazing what a six-figure salary and benefits will do to some people," said Jasper.

"Which he got for selling out the organization *I* helped build," seethed Dawn.

"Yes, that's pretty low," agreed Majedah. "Well, but I've got to head home and get to bed. Jasper, see you tomorrow. Dawn, don't feel too bad. Hopefully something good will come of it someday."

"Whatever." Dawn lit up the bowl for another hit. Majedah turned quickly for the door before she could catch sight of her friend putting her mouth on the foul bong again.

MAJEDAH SPENT A fitful night tossing and turning. Her mind tormented her with nightmarish images of her future self: middle-aged, thick of figure, and heavy of jowl, forever toiling away in her small- to midsize-market, covering Board of Ed meetings and hundredth birthday parties at the nursing home. By morning her California king bed resembled a giant bowl of linen spaghetti that had been twirled onto a human fork. Wrapped and trapped, a panicked Majedah flailed for several minutes before she was able to untangle herself from her fretful swaddling.

She needed to find a Story of National Interest to catapult her from this dead-end backwater, and she needed to do it fast.

Bleary eyed, she pulled into the lot at PDQ and parked. Under her breath she repeated the phrase *Oppression of Women and Police Brutality* to herself over and over, lest she lose her focus. It was early and the dim winter morning felt eerie and still. Majedah threw her keys into her purse and began to walk towards the entrance when something caught her eye. About twenty feet from the front door, a hedge of head-high arbor vitae concealed the massive HVAC unit that serviced the building. On this morning, Majedah noticed that a Hispanic man about her own age was half-concealed in the greenery. She pulled her cell phone from her purse to call the police but before she could dial, the man hailed her.

"Mees! Eh-huse me, Mees!" Something in his demeanor calmed Majedah's alarm. Hiding himself among the boughs, his knit hat wrung in his hands, he seemed apologetic for taking up her time. He refused to come out as though fearful of exposing himself, but rather he waved urgently for her to come to him.

Majedah's reporter senses began to tingle urgently. She looked around and saw one or two other early arrivals making their way from their cars to the building; she was safe enough. Intrigued, she walked across the lot to the mysterious stranger.

When she reached him, he ducked his head repeatedly in gratitude. "Oh, thanks you, Mees, thanks you, Mees," he fairly chanted.

"Yes? What is it?" asked Majedah. She took a quick visual inventory of the man, noting his slim size, jet-black hair, cheap fabric jacket, work pants, and worn boots. He seemed highly agitated and a sheen of sweat slicked his olive skin in spite of the chill air.

"I know you good *mujer*. I see you *Navidad* on TV. I know you good *mujer*, love Jesus. I know you help."

His thick accent made him difficult to understand, but Majedah had wisely retained several Spanish vocabulary words from her high school days. She surmised that the man had seen her reportage on the live nativity scene and mistaken her for a devout and compassionate person. Far too professional to let a misunderstanding get between her and a good story, Majedah nodded vigorously. "*Si, si*, I help. What is the problem?"

"Oh, *gracias*, Mees, thanks you, thanks you!" the man gushed. Majedah sighed impatiently and he got on with it. "My girlfren, Wanda, she wan keel my *bebé*, my *chico*."

Majedah gasped. "That's terrible! Why would she want to do such a thing?"

The informant scrambled for words. "He will born with *problema*. I tell her, I take *bebé*, I have *familia* who help. But Wanda, she say no. Doctor say my *chico* have, eh, he have, I think, *Síndrome de Maher*...?"

"Maher's Syndrome? Oh no, that's awful," said Majedah. Maher's Syndrome meant a lifetime of special needs: intense unlikeability, intractable bitterness, close-set beady eyes beneath an oversized forehead, and at best, laboring at menial work such as janitorial duties or hosting obscure talk shows on cable TV.

Maher's Syndrome ... a flaw! Something dawned on Majedah. "Wait, so he *will* have it, or he already *has* it?"

"He *will* have. He no born yet. He born two week more." The man's shining dark eyes pleaded with her.

Majedah understood what was going on now; this *macho hombre* was trying to oppress some poor woman—probably his rape victim—and deny her the Constitutional right to women's health care. Her jaw tightened and she began to shake with righteous rage. "Well, we'll just see about that," she announced.

The swarthy oppressor seemed overjoyed. "Oh, *gracias*, Mees, *gracias*! I know you help! She go Chosen Children today when open. Thanks you! *Gracias! Gracias!*" Ducking his head in repeated bows, the man faded back into the greenery.

Majedah turned and fixed her eyes on the city far across the parking lot. A breeze freighted with importance blew her gleaming hair back from her face and she lifted her chin in a heroic pose. A woman was being threatened with oppression, and the only thing standing in the way was Majedah's reporting. (Plus, it didn't hurt that the situation definitely qualified as an Oppression of Women story.)

"Yes, indeed," she declared to the distant city, "We'll see that the right thing happens today."

"I DON'T THINK this is a good idea," said Jasper. Majedah had just finished breathlessly explaining the situation to him, and he looked away from her as he spoke.

"Why on earth not?" demanded Majedah. "Don't you think women have a Constitutional Right to Women's Healthcare?"

Jasper still wouldn't meet her eyes. "I mean, I guess, but isn't this the sort of thing best left to, I don't know, 24/7 or something?"

"Yes, this is exactly the sort of thing 24/7 reports, and thank god they do. If it weren't for journalism, we wouldn't have all the freedoms Americans hold dear," Majedah pressed. "Don't you think you and I are good enough to report at the same level as 24/7?"

"I mean, this isn't that big a town, maybe the woman wants some privacy—"

Majedah threw her head back and addressed the ceiling in frustration. "Lord, deliver me from these dithering rubes."

Now Jasper looked at her. "Hey! I resent that. I am not a dithering rube."

Majedah dropped her head to rub vigorously at her eyes as she exhaled loudly. "I know you're not, Jasper. I don't mean *you*." She began to gesticulate with open hands. "It's this station, these people, it's Norma, Gary, this place, this town." She pointed an accusatory finger at the cameraman's chest. "And it's gotten to you, Jasper, and now you're afraid to step out of line. You let them intimidate you and shrink you down. You're afraid to be as good as you really are."

Jasper glared back at her, but she could see that her words had stung him. Good. A long moment crept by while they locked gazes. Then Jasper blinked. "Fine, we'll go. But if Dawn finds out I'm shooting GOO stories, so help me…"

Majedah flashed her knock-out smile at him. "Oh, thank you, Jasper! And don't worry, if Dawn asks, I'll just say I couldn't wait for you to get in and I took the night guy with me. Unless, of course, this story breaks big and you *want* her to find out."

Ten minutes later they hit the pavement outside the Chosen Children clinic. It was quarter to nine, when the doors would open. Majedah's pulse raced with the thrill of on-location reportage and the weighty responsibility of News about to be made. Her lip curled in revulsion; a handful of blue hairs from some church group was already gathered in their customary place, about twenty feet from the front walk, behind a police barricade that had become a permanent fixture. "Ugh, protestors," she snarled. "Why can't they just leave people alone to make their own decisions?"

Jasper looked at the women with scorn. "Really, man," he said.

They watched as one of the women hung a needlepoint banner on the barricade that read *Pray for Abortion to End*. Majedah snorted. "Well, I suppose we need some footage. Do your best, Jasper. Get super-tight close ups that show every mole and whisker. Try to get them while the sun is low and the light is harsh across their faces, low angles to bring out extra chins…"

"Don't worry, even us *rubes* know how to do our jobs," he said. He gave her a look, hoisted the camera to his shoulder, and went to work. Majedah watched nervously as he went right up to the women and started filming. They stopped chatting amongst themselves and eyed him nervously. One of them offered him a cup of hot tea. After a few minutes, he came back to Majedah. "Um, I guess they're not really warmed up yet.

"Okay, don't worry. Look! Here come the good guys."

From the opposite side of the building, several young women and men who looked to be students at the nearby university approached. Two of them wore hot-pink vests that had the words CLINIC ESCORT block printed on them. The others wore pink clothing of one sort or another, and there was even an art student in a vagina costume. Majedah's chest swelled with pride at the sight of the courageous, patriotic young people.

When the protestors reached the news crew, Majedah recognized one of them. "Hey, Olive, great to see you," she greeted. "I'm so glad you guys came out for this important cause."

The rotund, bespectacled young activist blinked at her. "Oh, hey, Majedah. Yeah, well, who couldn't use the work-study money? Stanton deployed us here today."

Majedah ignored a glare from Jasper. "I love your hair, Olive."

Olive had re-dyed her cropped, once-blue hair to hot pink, and had applied copious amounts of product to sculpt it into two stiff cat ears—a built-in pussyhat. "You like my new hair? Thanks." She grabbed the arm of the student in the vagina outfit. "This is my roommate, Vagida. She's a transgender woman."

A large, lavishly manicured hand protruded from a tangled mass of brown acrylic yarn to shake Majedah's. "Pleased to meet you," said the student.

"The pleasure is all mine," gushed Majedah. "I had a transgender roommate when I was a freshman at Lilith College." She waited for the customary exclamations over her academic pedigree, but Vagida's flat eyes merely looked back at her blankly. After a moment, Majedah spoke again. "Well, then, why don't you all get to work, and Jasper here will get some footage for our report."

"That's why we're here," said Olive. "Let's go, people."

"Wait, what chant should we use?" asked one of the escorts. "Professor Fluke says we should make sure to get our message out with a chant."

There was some discussion and milling about until the decision was made to go with KEEP YOUR HOSANNAHS OFF OUR VAGINAS.

The angry pink moblet advanced on the blue hairs, marching right up to the barricade with fists raised in the universal gesture for Peace and Tolerance. Some of them flipped off the older women with both hands, and one overweight young lady pulled up her pink t-shirt and shook her voluminous, pierced breasts in their direction. In response to their approach, the blue hairs joined hands and began to sing a hymn. Jasper fired up the camera and finagled himself into a spot right on the barricade, so he could capture the interaction between the two sides from a tight, dramatic angle.

With nothing to do at the moment, Majedah watched from the sidelines, anxiously biting her lip. Her keen reporter's eye recognized that the blue hairs were getting away with hiding their true, oppressive nature by pretending to be calm and gentle. She stepped into the street and walked around behind a parked car so that she was somewhat behind the church ladies, facing the pink-clad protestors. Then she scuffed through the dead leaves and debris in the gutter until she found a jagged chunk of concrete that a snowplow had chipped off the curb. She ducked back behind the parked car and peeped around it to confirm that the activists were all focused on their own interaction. Then she hurled the missile into the throng. A thrill ran through her as a red line opened up across Olive's forehead. The pink-haired activist's training kicked in, and she fell to her knees with a series of bloodcurdling screams. Jasper climbed atop a bluehair's back to get the proper footage of the bleeding, howling young woman. Majedah rubbed her hands together in satisfaction; this would be a story worthy of News 24/7 primetime. She gasped as a new possibility hit her; PDQ was a

24/7 affiliate, after all—perhaps they would air her report on their national broadcast this very evening!

It was now nine o'clock, and only Majedah noticed a young woman walking up the sidewalk towards the clinic entrance. Short and round and packed into a tight brown puffer jacket and skin-tight leggings tucked into spike-heeled boots, she resembled a cocktail meatball balancing on two toothpicks. Thick black bangs tumbled messily into the woman's dim eyes and a scowl commanded her expression. Majedah hurried to meet her.

"Hi, Wanda. I'm Majedah Cantalupi-Abromavich-Flügel-Van Der Hoven-Taj Mahal, and I'm here to make sure you get the Women's Health Services you're entitled to," greeted the reporter. The woman halted and Majedah put a reassuring hand on her shoulder.

Wanda looked surprised for a moment then her scowl deepened. "How do you know my name and my business?" she asked.

Majedah stood up straight and said, "I'm a reporter. It's my job to know things."

Wanda's expression dimmed once again. "Okay, whatever," she said. "'Scuse me, I have to go in now."

"And I'll walk with you to make sure you get where you're going," promised Majedah. She turned to face the same way as Wanda and tried to take her arm. Wanda stood still and stared at her until Majedah let go, stood back, and gestured for her to go ahead. Then Wanda proceeded with Majedah just behind her, frantically waving at Jasper to film her. The two university students who wore CLINIC ESCORT t-shirts materialized to walk on either side of Wanda, facing outward to deflect any challenges. Over by the barricade, the rest of the angry pinks cheered and applauded as she passed them (except for Olive, who was getting her forehead swabbed and bandaged by a pink-cheeked grandmother who reached across the barrier). Jasper aimed the camera in time to film Wanda's backside disappearing through the clinic door.

The pinks returned to the barricade to resume their battle against the alt-right thugs, and Majedah joined Jasper on the sidewalk to review and discuss the footage he had captured. As always, his work at the scrimmage line was outstanding. Particularly impactful was the shot of poor Olive getting knocked on the head by a rock thrown by the violent anti-woman protestors and dissolving into a full-fledged victimgasm. "Nice work, Jasper," cooed Majedah.

"Yeah, that is pretty sharp," the cameraman agreed. He grinned sheepishly. "I guess I'm glad you brought me here after all, Majedah."

She met his eyes and smiled back. "I'm glad you came, Jasper." The young reporters locked gazes, flush with the thrill of propagating journalistic justice. Self-righteousness crackled in the air between them as they reached for one another. But just before they could bump knuckles, the clinic door banged open and a furious-looking Wanda stormed out. Majedah caught Jasper's eye and nodded to signal that the camera should be running. He nodded back, hoisted his equipment, and faded unobtrusively to the edge of the scene.

Majedah planted herself in front of Wanda, forcing her to stop while disguising the action with sympathetic posture and expression. "Wanda, what happened?" she asked. "You were only in there a few minutes, and you're just as big as when you went in."

The young woman's face was red and she shook with indignation. "They wouldn't do it," she pronounced.

Majedah nearly swooned. She had found the ultimate female victim, a woman whose Constitutional right to women's health care had been denied, and she had the exclusive scoop on the story. She and her crew were capturing the dramatic moment when the oppression had just occurred. She saw Jasper filming behind and to the side of Wanda. In her mind's eye, Majedah could picture the perfect angle of the shot: concealing Wanda's identity but revealing enough detail to humanize her; and just over her shoulder, Majedah's own face, a lovely vision of compassion and justice, branding the segment as hers alone. She fought to suppress an involuntary shudder as she asked, "So they withheld vital women's health services from you?" She held out her microphone for an answer.

Wanda nodded angrily. "That's right."

"And did you explain the situation—that the fetus had been diagnosed with Maher's Syndrome?" Majedah prodded.

"How you know that?" asked Wanda.

"I told you: I'm a reporter; it's my job know things."

"Huh. Um, okay." Wanda's rage returned. "Yes, the baby has Maher's Syndrome. I don't want it. But the clinic workers told me it's too late. They say that after 32 weeks, they can't abort. It's the law or something." Majedah nodded encouragingly so Wanda would keep talking. "They said that normally they'd do it, but today some state inspector is coming any minute, so they can't. Ungh!" She shook, a spasm seeming to overtake her body, making her clench her teeth, before it passed.

Majedah took the microphone back to clarify the situation, so that Antoine would have what he needed to edit together a cohesive narrative. "So here you are, a victim of masculine oppression," (Wanda looked confused), "carrying a fetus diagnosed with a devastating defect," (Wanda nodded), "and you came here to exercise your right to women's health care. Is that correct?"

Wanda nodded vigorously. "Yes, I tole you already, that's what I tried to do."

"And you had to run a gauntlet of violent, anti-woman protestors, only to be refused service once you got inside?"

"Yes, that's right." Wanda clenched her eyes as another spasm overtook her. Then she doubled over in pain, clutching her stomach, and collapsed to the sidewalk.

Maedah was overjoyed at the young victim's dramatic reaction to the Injustice she had suffered. "Ah, I can see that this episode has been very upsetting to you…"

Suddenly, one of the blue hairs was kneeling beside Wanda, cradling her head so it wouldn't hit the pavement. "Don't worry, honey, I called an ambulance. Help is on the way."

Majedah was nonplussed. "What are you doing in my shot?" she demanded.

The grandmotherly woman looked up at her with drawn brows. "Can't you see this woman is in labor? Her contractions are three minutes apart."

"How dare you interfere with my story?" demanded Majedah.

"I'm a nurse. This woman is in distress and no one is helping her." Then the blue hair ignored Majedah and went back to stroking Wanda's hair. "Okay, that was a big one. Just breathe now." Wanda grabbed the woman's hand and clutched it.

Majedah marshaled every ounce of reporter skill in her body to salvage the narrative. "Great, so she is being forced to have a baby she didn't want," she pronounced. "Wanda, whatever will you do now?" She thrust the microphone in the young woman's face.

Panting, Wanda didn't even look up. "I guess I'll give the little brat to my boyfriend. He made such a big deal about how he wanted him. Well, he can have him." She took out her cell phone and started dialing. "Carlos? It's Wanda," she barked. "Listen, you better come to the hospital and pick up your baby in about five minutes. Ooohhhh!" Another contraction hit, and she dropped the phone.

An ambulance pulled up to the curb with lights flashing. Two paramedics jumped out and raced over, pulling a gurney between them. Majedah caught Jasper's eye and drew a finger across her throat. He stopped filming and the two of them hurried back to the car.

A TRIUMPHANT MAJEDAH and Jasper burst into the newsroom. Norma had just emerged from the kitchen with a fresh mug of coffee in her hand. "Well, well, look at you two. You look like you just caught the scoop of the week."

"Oh, it's bigger than that, even." Majedah fairly glowed.

"Wow! I can't wait to see what you got," said Norma. She rubbed her hands together in expectation.

"Is Antoine in yet?" asked Majedah.

"No, I don't think so." Norma glanced over but the editing room looked dark and empty. "I haven't seen him come in yet, anyway."

A janitor Majedah had never seen before shuffled out of the kitchen. He was in his mid-thirties and wore grease-stained workpants, a Green Day t-shirt, and an old, tan cardigan. Majedah was startled to see that he had close set, beady eyes and a permanent-looking expression of sardonic cynicism. He went over to Norma and held a full trash bag under her nose accusatorily. "I told you already, you must recycle paper. And what are sugar packets made of? Um, gee, I don't know ... could it be ... *paper*?"

Norma smiled affectionately at the obnoxious custodian. "Oh, yes, you did mention that. Sorry, sweetie."

"Don't be sorry, be better."

Majedah got a sinking feeling as she observed the man's off-putting behavior. She was quite certain that, if she were to lift his choppy brown bangs, she'd find an oversized forehead.

"Oh, you," teased Norma. She turned to Majedah and Jasper, an affectionate smile lingering on her lips. "This is my son, Daniel. He usually lives in a group home near Richmond, but it's being renovated. So, he's spending the next month with me. Since PDQ's regular janitor just got a new hip, Daniel's going to be helping us out around here while he recovers."

Majedah barely remembered to say, "Nice to meet you, Daniel." The young custodian replied with a sarcastic pleased-to-meet-you sneer. She stole a glance at Jasper. He glowered at her.

Norma clapped her hands together in a business-like manner. "Anyway, I don't want to hold you two bright, young reporters up. You've got a big story in the can, and I can't wait to see it on the evening broadcast."

Majedah looked at Jasper again. Now he offered her a smug, sadistic smile. "Yes, well, it's probably not going to be ready today," she stammered. "We, um, we still have to chase down a few more angles. It could take days, weeks, maybe months."

"Months! My goodness, sounds far-reaching," said Norma.

Majedah looked imploringly at Jasper. He seemed highly amused, and he nodded for her to continue. To Norma she said, "Yes, well, it is. I mean, we hope it is. We still have to follow up on some things, you see, so we can't say yet. Okay, well, come on, Jasper. We need to go delete—I mean, uh, *review*—what we shot this morning." She took the cameraman's arm and dragged him into the still-dark editing room.

That evening, at home in her two-bedroom condo in the shiny, new high-rise, Majedah polished off a bottle of Sangiovese dry red table wine that had been harvested and pressed by the citizens of a Roma commune. This she chased with a half-bottle of Popov vodka, which she kept under the kitchen sink for chemical-free cleaning purposes. Suddenly ravenous, she staggered seven blocks to a less fashionable neighborhood and entered a greasy spoon diner, where she perched precariously on a stool at the counter. Juices ran down her chin as she wolfed a rare bacon cheeseburger and a plate of fries with cheese and gravy. She returned home where, from the cool familiarity of her bathroom floor tiles, she accepted every social media friend request Kevin had sent her after their calamitous coffee date two weeks earlier. Then she was overtaken by a bleak oblivion interspersed with dreaming premonitions of her shapeless, gray, middle-aged self, her youth and beauty spent, and still a nobody. In the morning, she would have no recollection of the burger or the accepted friend requests, but the horror of her dreams would haunt her.

JASPER WAS ALREADY at his desk when Majedah slouched into work the following morning. He took in her hunched posture, dark sunglasses, and the quart-sized Starbucks high-test she clutched with the desperation of a drowning woman. "Rough night?"

"I look that bad, huh?" Majedah removed the glasses to reveal bloodshot eyes haunted by the intense fear of being mundane.

"You've looked better." Jasper's voice lacked the note of co-conspiratorial friendship it customarily held. He looked away from her and continued checking email on his laptop.

Majedah's towering headache and roiled stomach took a back seat to a ferocious stab of regret. She had blown the capital of Jasper's good will the previous day by insulting him and goading him to cover a Story of National Importance, which had turned out to be a complete waste of time. She had been so sure it would launch her out of this fetid backwater! But instead, she was stuck deeper than ever in the mire of mediocrity, and now she had alienated her one friend in this hellhole. She took a huge swig of coffee, forced herself to swallow, and set the cup on the edge of her desk. She opened her laptop and waited for email to load. The overhead fluorescents buzzed annoyingly. Majedah's vision dimmed around the edges and the room seemed to sway, like a large ship in high seas. She closed her eyes against it.

A rumbling noise grew louder until Majedah realized it had stopped directly beside her. Her eyes sprang open in time to see Daniel swipe her massive coffee cup into a wheeled trashcan. "Hey, I wasn't finished with that," she complained.

"You are now." He tilted the can back and rolled on implacably.

Majedah squeezed her eyes shut again and sank back in her seat. "God, get me out of here," she moaned.

"Good news, we have an assignment that will get us out of here." Jasper didn't look up from his computer as he spoke drily. "Apparently there was an accidental release of five gallons of untreated sewage down at the turd factory, and Gary insists that only PDQ's ace field team can possibly do justice to a story of this magnitude." He closed his laptop and, ignoring the whimper from his teammate, stood briskly. "Let's go."

Jasper drove them in his aging, green Ford Escape, the muffler rattling ominously beneath them. Still tight-lipped, he failed to make his customary joke about how his exhaust system was exhausted, so Majedah simply sat in miserable silence. As they rolled through the iffy neighborhood where the edge of town turned from retail to industrial, Jasper's stomach growled audibly, making Majedah jump. "I'm starving. Mind if I stop quick at J-Pat's?" he said. He was already pulling into a parking space.

"That's fine," Majedah answered. "I'll go in with you."

Jasper paused to consider the situation before getting out. "Yeah, I guess it's okay; we can see the car from inside the restaurant. I just don't want my equipment to get stolen."

Majedah waited until he was outside the car before muttering, "I'd hardly call it a *restaurant*." Then she joined him on the sidewalk for the brief walk. They pulled open a door and passed beneath a gaudy aqua sign that read "Jamaica Patty's" and featured a pigtailed, brown-skinned girl holding a crescent-shaped meat pie in front of her face like a bright yellow smile.

The stench of grease and spices assailed Majedah's delicate nose as she entered the fast food establishment. She swallowed hard twice to stave off the nausea, which was promptly replaced by a pang of hunger. When the pair reached the counter and Jasper ordered a tofu sausage breakfast patty, Majedah piped up, "Make that two."

Jasper carried the bag of food back to the car while Majedah nursed a Coke. As she stood waiting for Jasper to unlock the doors, an intense feeling overcame her, and she lifted a hand to her forehead and staggered slightly.

Jasper looked up and noticed her expression. "Majedah, what is it?"

"My reporter senses—they're tingling."

Jasper had worked alongside Majedah long enough to know that her journalistic powers were the real thing. "Hang on, Majedah, I'll get the camera." He hustled to the rear of the vehicle, stashed the food, and armed himself with his equipment. Then he went to her side. "Okay, all set. Where is it, Majedah? Where's the story?"

In a trancelike state, Majedah turned and slowly lifted a hand to point. A tall, 40-something woman of color exited the Jamaica Patty's restaurant and turned to walk away from them, up the sidewalk. "It's her," said Majedah. "Film her. Something's about to happen to her."

Jasper mounted the camera on his shoulder, flicked it on, and began to trail the woman at a distance. Majedah took a moment to smooth her hair in the Escape's side window, in case she needed to report, then she followed Jasper. The thrill of imminent News put a sparkle in her bleary eyes and a becoming flush of color in her wan cheek and lip. Majedah was fully alive and focused on the target.

The woman wore a black parka over jeans, which were tucked into a pair of leather harness boots. Above her laidback hood bounced a shoulder-length pouf of tight, dark ringlets. She walked with a languorous, hip-slung stride, her hands stuffed into her pockets against the chill. Majedah looked past Jasper to watch the woman, every nerve and fiber tight, alert for anything of significance.

Up ahead, a beat cop strolled boldly down the sidewalk towards the woman. Majedah stiffened as the phrase *Oppression of Women and Police Brutality* flashed in her mind. Her pulse pounded with expectation. She quick-stepped to just behind Jasper where she could confirm in the camera viewfinder that he was capturing the action. Unable to contain her excitement, she nonetheless issued a sternly whispered command: "Get it, Jasper." He freed one hand long enough to give her the thumbs-up sign, then continued his predatory stalk of the quarry thirty feet up the sidewalk.

The curly haired woman came to a halt as the huge, Caucasian policeman stood in front of her, blocking her passage. Majedah held her breath as the Story of National Importance began to unfold.

Perhaps, if Majedah had come from a different background or another vantage point, the scene would have looked different to her. If, for instance, she had been looking over the officer's shoulder rather than Jasper's, she would have noticed a wry smile on the Woman of Color's face. The flirtatious tilt of her head might have been more evident to Majedah.

But instead, Majedah could only see an African-American person with a vagina, confronted by a hulking white person with a penis and a gun. "Get it, Jasper," she murmured under her breath, though the cameraman needed no instruction.

A dark-skinned male teenager passed between the news crew and the News, momentarily blocking visual contact. But before Majedah could yell at him to get out of the way, there was a series of loud *pops* and he fell to the pavement. Relieved, Majedah and Jasper continued filming in time to capture the instant the News erupted into violent action. Just as Majedah had known he would, the cop screamed at the woman of color to get down. Before she could even react, he flung himself at her and wrestled her violently to the ground. And even though she was clearly down and compliant, and he had her securely pinned beneath his own body, and he had at least 100 pounds on her, the cop drew his gun.

"Oh my god, get it, Jasper! Getitgetitgetit!" Majedah squealed. She and the cameraman stepped over the teenager's body to approach the Story and try for more dramatic footage. Annoyingly, the youths who had gunned the teenager down were now between the crew and the Story, where they began to take fire from the friends of the first casualty. They returned fire, and dead teenagers began to pile up between Majedah and her salvation from news media obscurity. But she was not to be daunted! Fortified by her reporting superpowers, Majedah verily lifted Jasper over the growing heap as he continued filming. By the time they finally reached the scene of the crime, the woman of color was sheltering in a doorway and the thuggish officer was back in his car, radioing for more thugs to come to his aid.

"Are you okay?" asked a breathless Majedah. She was thrilled to see that rivulets of red ran down the woman's face from a gashed cheek and a swollen nose. "Did he do that to you?" She thrust the microphone in the victim's face for a reply.

The woman of color's posture and expression seemed odd. Majedah had expected tearful shock, perhaps even a dramatic physical reaction to the abuse. But instead, she seemed furious.

"Yes, I'm okay. Thank God I'm alive," she fumed. "I could have been killed!"

"Yes, that was close. Don't worry; we're here now. You're safe," Majedah assured her. She glanced at Jasper and saw that he was swinging the lens back and forth between the still-panting reporter and the bloodied victim. Himself out of breath, Jasper shook as he took in the action in rapid-fire shifts of perspective. Majedah released a shuddery breath. She could picture the footage in her mind's eye and she knew it was Pulitzer-level cinéma vérité.

Jasper turned the camera back to the victim as she began to rail. "When will we get these thugs off the street?" She put a hand to her face then gazed in wrath at her own blood on her fingers. "Look at this." She held her bloodied hand to the lens. (Majedah nearly swooned.) "Look at it! A woman isn't safe walking to work anymore. This has got to stop!"

The camera swung to Majedah's face, creased with concern and afflatus. "I couldn't agree more." She nodded vigorously. "This has got to stop!" She turned to look directly into the lens. Taking a deep, important breath, she stated, "It's a sad day when a woman of color isn't safe walking on the street, when the men we pay to protect us are the very ones we need to fear." Majedah paused only briefly before deciding to go with the national ID. "Reporting live for News 24/7 affiliate WPDQ, this is Majedah Cantalupi-Abromavich-Flügel-Van Der Hoven-Taj Mahal." She held the pose another second until Jasper stopped filming and gave her the thumbs up.

Chapter 10

MAJEDAH HAD BEEN wary that Jasper might be upset with her for tagging the story as an affiliate report for News 24/7, rather than just a local PDQ report. But when he lowered the camera from his shoulder and looked at her, his mouth hung open in awe. "That was incredible," he breathed.

"I know!" gushed Majedah. "Come on, let's go file it."

Leaving the bleeding woman of color in the doorway, the two young reporters raced back to Jasper's car. Within minutes, they were reviewing the footage on Majedah's laptop. Just as she had foreseen, Jasper had captured a thrilling scene. There was shaky cam and action and blood and best of all, it encompassed both the Oppressed Woman and the Police Brutality narratives in one story. She caught Jasper's eye and locked gazes with him. "I'm bypassing Norma and uploading it directly," she said.

"Absolutely," Jasper concurred. "My god, I can't believe this kind of shit still happens."

Majedah went to the News 24/7 website and logged in with her reporter ID number and the WPDQ affiliate code. When the page loaded, she clicked on the big, red *REPORT BREAKING NEWS* button at the top right. A form appeared and Majedah filled in the fields with flying fingers. She selected the dramatic footage from her laptop and a new button popped up. It read

UPLOAD. Her finger poised above the enter key, Majedah met Jasper's eyes once again. He seemed nervous but his smile was broad and proud. He swallowed loudly. "Well, here we go," he said.

"Here we go," repeated Majedah. With a high-pitched, "Whee!" she punched the key. A progress bar appeared, and the two young reporters watched it breathlessly until it changed from *UPLOADING* to *UPLOAD COMPLETE*.

"Woo hoo!" screamed Jasper.

"Woo-wheeeee!" squealed Majedah.

They bumped knuckles so hard, the rickety green Escape squeaked on its worn suspension.

As sirens approached the scene, they peeled out and headed for Majedah's well-appointed condo. She fired up the wall-sized screen and clicked to News 24/7. Then they sat side by side on the sofa to watch.

Toffee Barbeaux, the daytime anchor at News 24/7, was manning the mid-morning news desk. Behind her shoulder was a graphic of President Nelson with a clueless, open-mouthed expression on his face. The image had been snapped the previous summer in the White House Press Room, when a journalist accidentally dropped his laptop to the floor with a loud *Bang*! and President Nelson, startled, looked up. The *New York Times* reporter in the front row had snapped at the precise moment of discomposure that captured the president's stupidity, and there had been nothing any of his handlers could do to hide it. The image had been widely disseminated and was now the go-to stock photo of all the major networks. Majedah lifted her chin with pride at being a part of the industry that revealed the Truth to America.

"President Nelson met today with members of Congress in an attempt to break the current impasse regarding the national healthcare policy," reported Toffee. "While both sides seem to have reached an agreement that all health insurance should be fully subsidized by the federal government and that tampons will be provided free of charge to all women, Democrats are pushing to make the tampon provision fully inclusive. Republicans, however, are trying to limit the tampon benefit to biological women. Here with commentary on President Nelson's bigoted denial of a Constitutional right is News 24/7 contributor—" Toffee's voice was cut off mid-sentence and her image was replaced by a red screen bearing the words BREAKING NEWS. There was a dramatic rushing sound and a pulse-quickening claxon.

Toffee reappeared. She had her hand to her earpiece and she nodded several times before refocusing to look into the camera again. "We have just received an incredible report from one of our affiliate stations, WPDQ. But first, we must warn you that the footage you're about to see is graphic and upsetting."

The image cut to Jasper's gritty street-level camerawork. On the sofa, the cameraman stared raptly at the TV, while Majedah could hardly sit still.

Toffee's voice narrated the action unfolding on the screen. "Apparently, this woman of color you see here was walking up the street, minding her own business, when this large, white, male police officer stood in her way, obstructing her progress." The footage showed the officer scream at the woman to get down before setting upon her and wrestling her to the ground.

"Oh, my goodness," Toffee exclaimed. "This is just terrible. As you can see, the much larger officer has drawn his assault gun, even though the victim is helpless on the ground."

The video cut to a rear view of Majedah hurrying to the doorway in which the woman of color now huddled. Majedah began the impromptu interview and when the woman held her bloody hand to the camera, gasps from the staff in the News 24/7 studio could be heard over the audio.

On her living room sofa, Majedah closed her eyes in ecstasy; her report was a perfect home run. She opened them again in time to see herself say, "Reporting live for News 24/7 affiliate WPDQ, this is Majedah Cantalupi-Abromavich-Flügel-Van Der Hoven-Taj Mahal."

The shot cut back to Toffee Barbeaux's shocked face. "I must say," she pronounced, "in all my years of covering the news, I have never seen such a blatant example of everything that is wrong with our society and our current administration. Bravo on your groundbreaking report, Ms. Cantalupi-Abromavich-Flügel-Van Der Hoven-Taj Mahal. Bravo." She nodded once, solemnly, in tribute.

Both Majedah and Jasper's phones rang. Jasper glanced at the caller ID then answered hastily. "Hey, Dawn. ... I know, can you believe it?"

Majedah looked at her phone as well and saw *News 24/7* on the screen. *This is it*, she thought to herself.

She carried the phone into the kitchen, where she took a second to clear her throat and compose herself. Then she answered briskly, "This is Majedah."

"Hello, Ms. Majedah Cantalupi-Abromavich-Flügel-Van Der Hoven-Taj Mahal?" a prim male voice inquired. "This is Chester Chen. I'm a producer at News 24/7 in New York City. First of all, let me congratulate you on an outstanding piece of journalism. All of us here at 24/7 can't stop talking about it."

Majedah's head swam. She struggled to stay focused and sound professional. "I'm just happy to do my part, bringing the truth to the people." *Not bad*, she mentally complimented herself.

"Yes, indeed. We here at 24/7 are wondering if you're available to provide additional coverage on this developing story, since it's right in your backyard and you were the initial reporter on the scene."

"I'd be honored." Majedah's voice cracked and she reminded herself to stay cool.

"Excellent. GOO has just advised us that they are mobilizing regional assets to protest at the Wycksburg Police headquarters. Do you think you can cover the action for us?"

"Yes, I can."

"Great. We've got a satellite van en route, and it should arrive at the scene in a little over half an hour. Please be at the location to meet it. They'll take care of beaming your live report directly to us."

"I'm on my way."

Majedah barely ended the call before a squeal of excitement broke free from her perfect, pert lips. She scampered back to the living room, where she found Jasper still seated on the sofa, quarreling with his girlfriend over the phone.

"I don't think that's the case at all. ... Dawn, listen, it's a clear-cut case of police brutality. ... Because I was there! I saw it with my own two eyes. ... Well, maybe sometimes GOO is right." He looked up to see Majedah leaning over him, bouncing impatiently on the balls of her feet. He met her eyes and nodded. "... Of course I won't get taken advantage of. No one's taking advantage of me, Dawn. Sometimes things really are just as they seem. Look, I have to go, okay? I'll see you tonight. Bye, honey. ... Love you, too. Okay, bye."

Jasper's adrenaline was running at a level to match Majedah's, and he sprang to his feet. "What's up?"

"I just got a call from a producer at 24/7," Majedah told him. "They want us to meet their satellite van at the police station, to cover the GOO protest that's about to happen." She could do nothing to keep the enormous grin off her face or the squeal of happy excitement in her mouth, and Jasper looked at her disapprovingly.

"I mean, that's great and all, but please remember that a woman has just been beaten by rogue cops and maybe don't look so happy," he chided.

Majedah rolled her eyes at him. "Look, it's not my fault your girlfriend bitched you out because she's angry at GOO for stealing Stanton away." Jasper looked away and she continued. "Can't you just be glad, for once, that your work and your skill is exposing a terrible Injustice that's being done right in your home town?"

Jasper un-tensed with a sigh. "I guess so. You're right, Majedah." He met her eyes again, and this time he managed a smile of his own. "Let's go get those bastards."

"That's my Jasper," Majedah cheered. "Knuckles." She held up a fist and he bumped it with his own. Then they raced out of the condo, down the stairwell, and into Jasper's car.

THE WYCKSBURG POLICE headquarters was one of those buildings that had probably seemed modern and advanced when it was first constructed but now looked like a perfect example of where public architecture had gone off the rails. Long, bland expanses of brown glazed brick were broken up by precious few windows. No portico protected the entryway, an omission meant to indicate that there would be no waiting in the elements because the door was always open. The unintended result was a bland, soulless, institutional-looking façade. Likewise the plaza in front of the building was poured gray concrete, edged with dense yew hedges severely pruned into long boxes. Two large wooden half-barrel planters, the chief's wife's attempt to humanize the place, flanked the plaza where it met the sidewalk. Since growing season was still a couple months off, the planters were stuffed with brittle pine boughs, artificial red hibiscus blooms, and tiny American flags.

Onto this plaza streamed lines of protestors. Majedah's mouth fell open in awe; the protestors were way more numerous and professional than POPO's ragtag handful of locals. In fact, as she scanned the crowd, Majedah didn't recognize a single face. These people were dressed for the weather and for action, with high-tech parkas over black tactical trousers and heavy boots. Majedah's heart swelled at the multiple skin hues she saw. There were groups who wore matching t-shirts over their coats and others who carried custom printed signs mounted on sturdy two-by-fours and baseball bats. *Love Beats Hate* and *Impeach Nelson!* seemed to be the most common slogans. She turned to locate the source of the human tide and saw a line of buses that ran up the street for blocks. "Amazing," she breathed. Then she heard a familiar megaphonic voice and spun to see Stanton in the middle of the plaza, directing the deployment. Majedah grinned and went to greet the ambitious young activist. Jasper followed slowly, his camera on his shoulder and an overwhelmed expression on his face.

When she was a few feet away, Majedah called Stanton's name and he turned. A warm smile appeared on his face as he recognized her. He embraced her, saying, "Majedah, girl, you did it! You caught them in the act. You did it, girl, you did it!"

"I'm just glad I could be in the right place at the right time." She stepped back and took in his elegant overcoat and fine leather shoes. Then she swept her arm to indicate the enormous direct action setting up on the plaza and exclaimed, "Looks like you've really hit the big time, Stanton. Congratulations on your success."

Stanton ducked his head in a show of modesty. "Yeah, well, I guess GOO has a use for me."

"That's wonderful. Well-deserved."

Conflicted, Jasper stood back from the reunion. Two men brushed past him, and one of them had an enormous, gleaming camera on his shoulder. "Whoa," breathed Jasper. "Is that the new Chronica Pro Series?"

The man paused to glance at Jasper. "Uh, yeah." Then he moved on to rejoin his companion, who was tapping Majedah on her shoulder just as she waved Stanton off to see to his duties.

Majedah turned to see two sophisticated urbanite production specialists. Her eyes zeroed in on the embroidered News 24/7 logos on their black, high tech survival jackets. *This is it, Majedah. Don't blow it.* She straightened to her full height. "Yes?" she said.

"Ms. Cantalupi-Abromavich-Flügel-Van Der Hoven-Taj Mahal?" asked the closest man.

"Yes?" she repeated.

"Hi, I'm Ned and this is Marco. We're the News 24/7 tech team you're here to meet."

"Oh, great. Good to meet you, Ned. Marco." She presented her shearling-gloved hand for each to shake. "Please, call me Majedah."

"Sounds good, Majedah. And before we get started, may I say that everyone at 24/7 is just completely in awe of your reporting this morning," said Ned.

Marco nodded enthusiastically in agreement. "It was amazing."

Majedah smiled demurely in acknowledgement of the compliment. "I'm actually an uncommonly gifted reporter, so it just sort of comes naturally to me. I'm only glad I could capture what happened, so I could show it the world." Over Ned and Marco's shoulders she could see Jasper, standing on his tiptoes as he strained to hear the conversation.

Ned pointed to the curb, where a windowless, high roofed, black van was parked. A full-color News 24/7 logo covered most of its side, and it was crowned with an enormous satellite antenna. "Let's go over by the van and get the shot set up," he suggested.

Majedah nodded crisply. "Yes, of course." She headed for the vehicle, followed by Ned and Marco, who were trailed by Jasper. The PDQ cameraman, encumbered by his equipment and not as large or bulky as Ned and Marco, had a more difficult time navigating the boisterous crowd. By the time he arrived at the van, Majedah was already standing in an ideal spot with the protest and distant police station behind her. Marco had set up the Chronica on a sturdy tripod. Ned had already checked light settings and handed Majedah a spiffy microphone with a News 24/7 logo on it. The van door was open, and Jasper could see a third person inside, operating a battery of complex production and transmission equipment. As he watched, Ned signaled Majedah and she began reporting.

"This is Majedah Cantalupi-Abromavich-Flügel-Van Der Hoven-Taj Mahal, reporting live—"

"Hey," shouted Jasper. "Just a second, I'm not set up."

Majedah kept on talking, as though she hadn't heard him. Ned rounded angrily on him and shepherded him a few feet away. "You mind, bro? We're live." His jaw was so tight, he barely opened his mouth when he spoke.

"But I'm Majedah's cameraman. We're a team," protested Jasper.

Ned loomed over him, standing too close and blocking his view of the reporter. "You're PDQ's cameraman," he clarified. "The big boys are here now, and we're running a live, national transmission. So why don't you take your crappy little camera back to your douchey little studio and see if there's a bodega robbery or a Girl Scout meeting you can cover, m'kay?" He lingered to give Jasper a glare before returning to his post alongside Marco.

Jasper stood in confusion, watching as Majedah covered the protest swelling behind her. Chants were growing louder, and demonstrators were hoisting signs and pumping fists in the air. Jasper felt his phone vibrate and pulled it from his pocket. He saw Dawn's name on the screen and quickly sent the call to voicemail. Then he looked up again, squared his shoulders, and flicked on his camera.

As Majedah described the scene behind her, Marco filmed and Ned produced. Jasper slipped up beside Marco and began filming as well. After a second, Marco noticed him and gave him a shove. Without lowering his camera, Jasper shouldered Marco hard and stepped back into position. Marco straightened and left his camera on the tripod so he could use both arms to push Jasper. Jasper crashed into a shoal of angry-looking Melanin Matters militants. They shoved him back at Marco, who met him with raised fists. Letting his camera drop to his side, Jasper took a clumsy swing at the 24/7 man with his free hand.

Majedah saw what was happening and quickly signed off the report. Ned yelled at the staffer inside the van to cut the feed then he shouldered Marco aside and grabbed Jasper by the upper arms. Jasper was tall but not big, and Ned's hands nearly encircled his biceps. The two men stood glaring into one another's red faces, teeth bared and veins popping on foreheads and necks. "I thought I told you to fuck off," Ned reminded Jasper.

"And I told you, I'm Majedah's fucking cameraman."

"I'm pretty sure Majedah is enough of a professional to know when it's time for the real camera crew to take over," bellowed Ned. "Right, Majedah?"

All eyes were suddenly on the stunning young reporter. Majedah looked from one face to another, from her dead-end past to her glorious future, before fixing her eyes on the PDQ cameraman. "Jasper, please," she said. "It's like he says; it's a live broadcast. You just don't have the equipment..."

Jasper's face went white before flushing even redder than before. Ned released him, stepped back, folded his arms, and gave him a smug grin. Jasper shot Ned a final glare before looking back to Majedah. "Well, congratulations, Majedah. You finally got that big story you always wanted," he spat. Then he spun on his heel and waded into the crowd. Majedah watched him get absorbed by the churning human stew like a slam-dancer at a death metal show.

All around, the situation was spinning into a chaotic scene. The police chief's wife's wooden planters were pitched over and smashed, and the tiny American flags were burned in front of countless expensive, live-streaming phones. Protestors dropped their pants and crapped on sidewalks and car hoods. Bright pink, plush vaginas mingled with black-clad anarchists and violet-shirted international union tactical squads. Majedah watched the back of Jasper's head for another moment until she could no longer discern him among the throng. Then she turned as Ned approached her, holding out an earpiece.

"Could you put this in, Majedah? HQ wants you to be able to take questions from the news desk."

Majedah snapped into reporter mode. "Yes, of course." She took the device from Ned and fitted it into her ear.

Chapter 11

MAJEDAH WORKED ALL day, reporting as hard as she could. The larger and more kinetic the demonstration grew, the more energized she became, and she reported like no one had ever reported before. Then came a dizzying moment, during a break when they were all hanging out in the van and passing a joint around like old friends, when Ned handed her the phone. "It's Chester. He wants to talk to you."

Majedah composed herself and took the phone. "Yes?" she asked.

"Hey, Majedah, you're doing a great job. You're really impressing everyone back here in the New York office. And the guys in the van told us you're an absolute professional and you totally know how to handle yourself. Rosemary—that's Rosemary Jackson, our station director—she told me to get in touch with you and ask you if you'd like to work here, in our New York headquarters. We have an opening in the reporter pool. What do you say, Majedah?"

She closed her eyes and breathed in deeply through her nose, tilting her head back as she savored the heady rush of success. When she opened her eyes again, she saw the three crew members watching her expectantly. Smiling at them, she spoke into the phone, "I say ... *yes!*" The 24/7 team cheered.

After her triumphant acceptance of the position with News 24/7, she went back outside for another three-hour stint, reporting like an absolute genius. At last, darkness began to fall, and the mostly peaceful demonstrators dispersed around town to find bigots to beat and stores to loot. "Well, I guess there's nothing more to see here," said Ned.

Majedah herself was looking forward to a celebratory beverage in the solitude of her condo. "Okay then, I guess I'll head home for the evening. Goodnight, everyone. It's been amazing working with you." She started to leave before remembering that Jasper had been her ride. "I don't suppose you all can give me a lift in that thing, can you?" She indicated the van with her open hand.

Ned smiled. "Hop in."

Majedah soared across town on the wings of a dream, in the cutting-edge black 24/7 satellite van. She caught the look on the doorman's face as she stepped out of the branded vehicle, and she winked at him. She waved goodbye to her new colleagues then went up to her apartment. As she went inside and locked the door behind her, her phone rang. She saw *Norma Troutstein* on the screen, sighed, and answered. "Hey, Norma," she said.

"Majedah." Norma's usually forceful voice was oddly emotionless. "What have you done?"

"Excuse me?" asked Majedah.

"What have you done?"

"I'm not really sure what you mean, Norma." Majedah opened the fridge with her free hand and withdrew a bottle.

"24/7 called to inform me they were live broadcasting one of my reporters. I tuned in and I didn't even recognize where you were. There was so much unrest behind you, I thought you had gone to Chicago or Venezuela or something. Then I went out to the parking lot to drive home, and my car was on fire. It was on fire, and there were people I've never seen before dancing around it. A police car came to try to break it up, and they lit that on fire, too. I had to walk four miles to a safe neighborhood, where Danny could come get me."

Majedah didn't know what to say, so she remained silent.

"What have you done to my town, Majedah?" came Norma's eerie, dead voice through the phone.

Majedah almost felt regret, but then she remembered she worked for News 24/7 now, and she snapped out of her momentary intimidation. "I guess this is as good a time as any to let you know I'm leaving PDQ," she informed Norma. Holding the phone in the crook of her neck with her shoulder, she poured herself a tall, sparkling, organic Crémant d'Alsace.

There was no answer for a moment then Norma asked, "Are you going to work for 24/7?"

The irrepressible grin popped onto Majedah's face again. "I am," she announced proudly.

"So you traded my home—this town—120,000 people's home—for a fancy new job?"

Majedah bristled. "I don't think you can characterize it like that, Norma. I saw an Injustice being committed, and I did my job and reported it. It's my job to be objective and tell the truth. It's not my fault this stupid town is rotten to the core."

"*Rotten to the core?* You think Wycksburg is rotten to the core?" An incredulous edge was starting to replace the numbness of Norma's voice. Majedah decided it would be best to end the call before Norma's shock wore off.

"Look, Norma, I worked my ass off all day and I'm exhausted. So if it's all the same to you—"

"Do you even know who that woman is, that you filmed this morning?"

"What? No. Does it matter?"

"Probably not to your fancy new friends from New York. If you had cared enough to know anything about this town, though, it might have mattered to you."

The highball full of pale wine sparkled on the countertop in the halogen task lighting, taunting Majedah. She desperately wanted to drink it and relish her victory, not be bitched at by her boss. (*Ex-boss*, she corrected herself mentally.) "I think perhaps it would be best if I took a personal day tomorrow," she said.

"I think it would be best if you never came near my studio again. I think it would be best if you had never come to this town in the first place. I think—"

"Goodbye, Norma." Majedah ended the call, seized the glass off the countertop, and took six deep swallows without taking a breath. "Ah," she exhaled loudly. Then she looked ruefully at the phone in her hand. "Way to harsh my mellow, Norma," she muttered.

She tucked the phone into her armpit, topped off her glass, and carried it and the bottle into the living room. Soon she was lounging on the couch, drinking and watching the 24/7 evening report. Her incredible footage from the original incident, followed by her reportage of the growing demonstration, was shown intermittently. There were also live reports from other cities around the country, where regional GOO protests had been coordinated to amplify the message. Before Majedah got too hammered, she called her mother to tell her the good news.

"Majedah, darling, I've been seeing the news everywhere today, about how the horrible cop brutally beat that poor woman of color. I had no idea you had broken the news. Bravo, my darling. I couldn't be more proud," Julia effused.

"I bet you could, Julia. Guess what?"

"What?"

"I got a job offer from News 24/7," Majedah squealed.

"Oh, Majedah, that is such wonderful news," said Julia in the closest thing to a shriek Majedah had ever heard her use. "I am so proud. Wait until I tell everyone that my daughter is a reporter at 24/7."

Majedah grinned as she listened to her mother carry on. "Okay, Julia, I'm going to go so I can watch the coverage on 24/7. If you turn it on, you'll see my report from earlier today."

"I will do that at once, then. Congratulations, Majedah. I'm so glad you're finally going to be where you belong." Julia hung up.

Night came on in earnest and the room was dark except for light from the kitchen and television. Majedah sat and drank and watched herself on her living room wall for another half an hour. After the same clip had been repeated for the twentieth time, she decided to switch to Eagle Eye News for some gloating. After all, the footage of the initial incident was proprietary to 24/7 affiliate WPDQ, so Eagle Eye would have nothing to show. "Enjoy zero viewers, losers," she sneered, as she stabbed the remote with her index finger.

At first she thought she had put 24/7 on again by mistake, because there was Jasper's footage of the woman of color being accosted by the hateful white cop. But there was Eagle Eye's station ID on the bottom left of the screen, and she heard Roy Cader's bizarre cultured drawl as he teased the next segment over the video. "This video has been all over the internet today, as well as our competitor's broadcast news stations," he informed her.

"That's right, and how did you get it?" slurred Majedah.

On the TV, Roy Cader mentioned, "By the way, we'd like to thank WPDQ of Wycksburg for the use of their exclusive footage."

"Norma!" hissed Majedah, "how could you?"

On the screen, the cop threw the woman to the ground and flung himself on top of her for the umpteenth time that day.

"But things aren't always as they seem," Cader was saying.

Majedah's heart skipped a beat and her eyes went instantly wide. "What do you mean, Roy? Of course, they are," she insisted. But a panicky chill started working its way up the backs of her arms.

"Stay tuned for a very special guest—two guests, I should say—right after these words from our wonderful sponsors." Roy's voice and Jasper's footage disappeared, replaced by an ad for Aim True Ammo that featured trophy bucks and fat tom turkeys striding pristine natural settings.

"No, no, no! No commercials. I have to see who he has on," pleaded Majedah. She upended the bottle to refill the glass, but only a drop fell from its mouth.

The ammo commercial ended. Majedah held her breath, but a new ad began. A white-haired actor who had once portrayed action heroes in theaters across the country peddled custom installed flagpoles. "Sure to add the right note of pride and patriotism to any front yard or municipal building," he assured her.

"Come on, come on," Majedah muttered. Her eyes went from the screen to her empty glass to the screen to the glass. The commercial ended and a new one began, this time a trailer for a Christian film about a plucky pastry chef who refused to bake a cake for a satanic polygamist wedding and wound up in a court battle.

Majedah made a dash for the kitchen, yanked a fresh bottle from the fridge, uncorked it with the speed of an Indy 500 pit crew, and had returned to the couch and poured a fresh glass by the time the next Eagle Eye segment began.

Roy Cader sat smugly behind the evening news desk. Behind him was a still frame from the original footage, showing the instant the cop pounced on his victim. "Everyone's seen this video by now, and outrage mobs have been rioting—or *protesting*, as our competitors would say—in cities across America in response," he reported. "The original event that caused this uproar does look pretty bad at first; a big, burly police officer beating up on an unarmed woman, and there's the race angle, of course ... or so it seems. But here now, via satellite, to explain what was really going on are the alleged victim and abuser from the video."

The screen split, with Roy Cader on the left and the woman of color and the white police officer, seated side by side, on the right.

Majedah's mind boggled at the surreal sight. "How can this be? How can they be sitting next to each other?" she yelled at the TV.

"Some of our viewers will recognize Patty Clark, owner of the Jamaica Patty's fast food chain," said Cader. "Love those meat patties, by the way."

The woman of color smiled and nodded at Cader's plug for her restaurant chain.

"And we also have Sergeant Norris Clark of the Wycksburg PD. Patty and Norris, thanks for joining us this evening to clear the air."

"Thanks for having us," said Patty.

Roy Cader began the interview. "Tonight, half the country is on fire after dramatic video emerged of an apparent episode of police brutality. But you two have a different take on what was really happening in that video. Do you want to walk us through it?"

"Sure, we'd be happy to." Sergeant Clark's voice was deep and commanding. His graying brown hair was shorn into a severe military style and his suit jacket strained over broad shoulders and muscular arms. Officer Clark's hazel eyes looked directly into the camera and out of the screen, and Majedah quailed, certain that everyone else watching this segment was as frightened by the cop as she was.

Cader's side of the screen was replaced with Jasper's footage. Patty Clark sashayed up the sidewalk, coming to a halt as Sergeant Clark appeared in her path. The video froze. "So what is happening here?" prompted the anchorman.

Patty Clark had a rich, feminine voice. "He was coming up to me on the sidewalk, and I was saying, 'Hello, Baby,' just like that." Majedah recognized the vaguely Southern mid-Atlantic accent of a Wycksburg native, with a hint of musicality behind the words. *Immigrant parents*, she deduced.

"Sergeant Clark," said Cader, "your face seems rather grim and foreboding. Wouldn't you greet your wife with a happier expression?"

"That is my happy expression," Norris said.

Beside him, Patty turned to him and teased, "That's your only expression, baby." She smiled again, and she had a beautiful smile, a wide mouth with even white teeth and amber eyes flecked with humor.

Norris Clark turned to her and pulled the corner of his mouth up for a fleeting instant in his best effort at a smile of his own. But there was no missing the softening in his eyes as he looked at his wife.

On the sofa, Majedah was in full meltdown. *Patty and Norris Clark? Husband and wife? "Baby"?* What the hell was going on here? What was happening to her perfect story?

Back on the screen, the video began to run once more. Norris's face suddenly became ferocious as he screamed at his wife to get down, before hurling her to the sidewalk and jumping on top of her. At the sight of the footage, Majedah's panic receded.

"What about this, though?" Cader's voice inquired.

"Yeah, what about that?" Majedah yelled at the screen.

"Well, Roy, if you want to replay those last ten seconds and turn up the volume, you'll get your answer," suggested Norris.

The video replayed and this time, Majedah noticed the pesky teenager who had passed fleetingly between the camera and the action. Once he had moved out of the shot again, she could hear several loud pops.

"That sounds like gunfire," commented Roy Cader's voice.

"In fact, it was gunfire," confirmed Sergeant Clark. "Perhaps you noticed a youth pass in front of the camera a few seconds back. Once he was out of view of the camera, he was fired upon by members of a rival gang. That's what those pops you heard were."

"Oh, my goodness, how frightening. So that explains your reaction, Officer Clark."

"Yes. At that instant, my training kicked in and Patty here became an innocent civilian, whom I am sworn to protect."

"So you ordered her to get down and, when her reflexes weren't as fast as yours, you took her down and covered her with your own body to protect her?"

"That's exactly what my man did," purred Patty. She gave her husband a look that left no doubt in Majedah's mind that Sergeant Clark had been well rewarded for his gallantry.

Officer Clark maintained his rigid posture and demeanor but a flush stole over his fair face. "I would have done it for any civilian," he asserted.

"I'm sure you would have," drawled Cader. "Now let's see the rest of the video."

Patty Clark remained prone on the sidewalk beneath her husband, who drew his weapon and aimed it off camera. He did not fire, though multiple gunshots could be heard as he watched violence unfold off-screen. In another moment, it was over, and he dragged his wife to the shelter of a nearby doorway before dashing off-screen himself. The video froze again.

"At this point, most of the youths were down. One youth had fled on foot," narrated Sergeant Clark. "I could see multiple injuries, possibly some fatalities, so I returned to my vehicle to call for medical and law enforcement backup and get the first aid kit."

The left half of the television screen switched from Jasper's footage back to Roy Cader. "Wow, that is an incredible story. Patty, what on earth was going through your mind while all this was going on?"

"Well, the first thing that was going through my mind was, 'Damn, don't my man look fine today.'"

A smirk stole across Sergeant Clark's face before he quickly dispelled it.

"Obviously, that was before the shooting started," clarified Roy Cader.

"That's right." Patty's teasing smile was replaced by a grim expression, her brows drawn together and her lips pressed into a taut line. "Then all I could think was that I was going to die, right there on the sidewalk, for no good reason except these stupid punk-ass kids running wild on the street."

"Is street crime a big problem in your town?" asked Cader.

Norris replied, "Unfortunately, we do have a growing problem with gang violence. And it's not just limited to Wycksburg; it's a national problem."

"What do you recommend be done to put a stop to it?" asked Cader. "What could the police be doing better?"

Norris hesitated for a moment. "Well, we have been putting an emphasis on community policing, trying to get members of our disadvantaged communities to be more comfortable around police officers."

Patty's expression had grown more severe during the exchange and now she interrupted her husband. "Maybe we could just let the police do their jobs, Roy," she burst out. "Maybe we let them use their training and their experience to get these animals off our streets. And maybe we don't ruin their lives every time they have to shoot someone."

Norris turned to watch his wife's outburst, a stifled look of alarm on his stoic face. But he seemed to know better than to interfere.

"You think cops don't worry about what will happen to them if they have to pull the trigger? You think it doesn't keep them from doing what they have to do sometimes?" Patty went on. "You know how many officers were killed doing their job last year? 147. That's 147 sons, daughters, brothers, sisters, husbands, wives, fathers, and mothers. I bet most of them would be alive if they hadn't been second-guessing themselves at that crucial split second."

"I don't think you can generalize like that—" Norris tried in a calm voice.

But Patty was in high dudgeon. "And what about these thugs, these monsters, running around on our streets? Where the hell are their parents?" she demanded. "If I had even been rude to a police officer when I was their age, my dad would have whupped my butt, then my mom would have whupped it twice more." She looked directly into the camera. "Men out there, I'm talking to you. If you have a son, you have a responsibility to society to raise that boy right. Because he's going to grow big and strong one way or the other, and if you don't guide him the right way, he'll go the wrong way. And that hurts all of us. So why don't you be a man and show him the right way?" Her amber eyes burned into the crackling air in Majedah's living room. The young reporter couldn't look away from this forceful, focused woman of color. "Or maybe you're not really a man at all," Patty Clark concluded, lifting her chin in challenge.

Roy Cader chuckled. "So, Sergeant Clark, I assume Patty keeps the rule of law in your home?"

Norris looked briefly amused. "Let's just say that Patty didn't build up that business of hers by being a pushover."

"And how is business these days, Patty?" asked Cader.

Patty, having gotten the rant out of her system, now seemed pleased to discuss her affairs. "Business is great, Roy. We just opened our 27,058th restaurant, out in Flagstaff, Arizona. And our line of frozen prepared patties has just been picked up by Big Deal Shopping Clubs, so that has expanded our product lines by over 50 percent." Her captivating smile was back and Majedah was struck by how attractive she was for a woman who had to be at least forty-five.

Roy Cader pulled out his cell phone and pretended to dial. "Hang on a second, I just want to call my broker and pick up some stock."

Patty laughed. "Sorry, Roy, but we're a privately held family business."

Cader snapped his fingers in mock disappointment.

"Don't worry, I'll let you know if we ever make a public offering," Patty assured him.

"Thanks, Patty. And thanks to both of you for coming on the show tonight to clear up this misconception about what happened in that video."

"Thanks for the opportunity," said Norris.

"Yes, I take any chance I can get to tell the world how wonderful our men and women of law enforcement are," Patty added. "Especially this one." She nudged her husband with her shoulder and grinned.

The Clarks disappeared, and Roy Cader took up the whole screen again. "So now that we know the real story behind this so-called police brutality, maybe everyone can calm down a bit, hm? Yeah, right. ... Coming up in the next segment, has Hollywood gone too far this time? A new show is in the works, featuring children who think they're animals trapped in human bodies and letting them compete for expensive cosmetic surgeries. And you wouldn't believe what they make the kids do to win. That's up next, stay with us."

The wall-sized screen exploded in a shower of sparks, broken glass, and imported sparkling wine. With a guttural howl, Majedah flung her glass after the bottle, smashing it as well. She lurched to her feet and managed to lift one end of the heavy, recycled-steel-and-reclaimed-industrial-lumber coffee table, which she flipped over in the general direction of the TV wall.

There hadn't been any police brutality after all.

There hadn't been a Story of National Importance, involving both the crucial Oppression of Women and Police Brutality narratives.

And now there would be no job waiting for her at America's premier news station in New York City, and she certainly wouldn't be welcome back at PDQ. She looked like an idiot.

Majedah's breaths came out as a disturbing hybrid of hyperventilation and shrieking as she stormed drunkenly around the room, looking for objects to throw. But once everything had been hurled at the wall, her panicked horror had only grown. She ran to the floor-to-ceiling window and looked out over the town. Although her fashionable avenue remained untouched, fires were visible a few blocks away and occurred sporadically to the outer limits of town. Heavy, low cloud cover reflected flickering reds and oranges, which competed with the flashing blues and reds of first responder vehicles. Sirens wailed near and far as Wycksburg burned, along with Majedah's future.

Majedah took a few steps back then ran at the window and dove headfirst. The tempered shatter-proof glass did its job and repelled her.

Insensible, Majedah lay still on the thick carpet.

Chapter 12

AND SO IT came to pass that Majedah's greatest fears were realized. She became middle aged, plump, and frowzy. Obscure and unrecognized, she labored away in her mid-sized market (now her inescapable, permanent home), covering trivialities important only to a handful of town residents.

"Majedah, I told you to cover that sewage leak. Now get to work," barked Norma. Somehow she had not aged a day, though all former affection she may have had for her once-rising star reporter had long since died. She stood on a grassy bank and pointed into a swale beneath the butt end of an open 36" pipe that protruded from the incline. A rust-colored slurry trickled from the pipe's maw to feed a rivulet that ran away down the hill.

Majedah, without options or prospects, turned to obey and pick her way down to the pipe mouth. She lifted her pant legs to keep the hems from the muck and beheld her own thickened, wrinkled fingers pulling at salmon-colored, linen-polyester blend fabric. "Yuck, where did I get these hideous pants?" she wondered.

Jasper's familiar voice answered, "You got them at Dress Mart, remember? They're the only place in town that carries size 12."

"12?" Majedah turned her horrorstruck face to him. Unlike Norma, Jasper had aged; the sun gleamed off his pate, thick glasses sat astride his veined nose, and his scraggly beard was shot through with gray. But as with Norma, no glimmer of friendship warmed his eyes. They only showed resignation and inflexibility as he waited impatiently for her to get down to the leak. Majedah returned to her descent until she reached the mud puddle beneath the dripping pipe. She sank into the swampy ground up to her ankles and flies buzzed around her. Fighting off the urge to cry, she turned and looked up at Jasper.

"That's the spot. That's perfect," he said. His ancient camera was mounted atop a single pole, which he jammed into the sod. The battery must have stopped working years ago because he had a manual generator of some sort duct taped to the camera. As Majedah watched, he actually began to crank a handle to make it run. "Okay, go," he directed.

Ignoring the humid stench, Majedah swallowed past the lump in her throat and began speaking. "This is Majedah Cantalupi-Abromavich-Flügel-Van Der Hoven-Taj Mahal, reporting live from the—oh!"

With an echoing belch, the pipe emitted a burst of sludge, which spattered onto Majedah's tacky pantsuit and one side of her face.

"Dammit, stop filming Jasper. I have to clean up," she said.

Jasper never lifted his head from the camera nor stopped cranking the handle. "No, you're fine. Keep going."

Norma added, "It's not like it matters, anyway."

"Okay." The urge to cry was harder to fight off, but Majedah called on all her reporter skills and did it. "I'll start again. *Ahem* ... This is Majedah Cantalupi-Abromavich-Flügel—Oh! Oh!"

Now a steady deluge shot from the pipe. Majedah's side was thoroughly drenched and the level of muck began to rise up around her calves. Panic flared in her and she tried to pull one foot then the other free. With a soggy slurp, the rising bog claimed her shoes, but one foot was liberated. Majedah put it in front of her only to sink up to her thigh. She looked up at the crest of the bank with wild eyes. "Guys, help! I'm stuck. I can't get out of this mud, and it's starting to suck me under."

Jasper didn't reply; he only kept his eye to the viewfinder as he cranked the handle. Norma looked on impassively, without so much as unfolding her arms. "It's your own fault, you know," she advised.

Majedah was up to her waist in the sucking, clinging, small-to-mid-sized market muck. She leaned forward, clawing at it in an attempt to pull herself out. The stinking mud simply slid through her fingers, granting no purchase, inexorably pulling her downwards. "Help. Please!" Majedah began to beg, despising herself for doing so.

Over the sounds of her struggle, she heard the incongruous strains of her favorite pop anthem, "Vaginas Up!" by Rinnie Halliday. *That's odd, where is that music coming from?* she wondered.

Sisters 'round the world, unite!
Vaginas up, it's time to fight! sang Rinnie Halliday.

"OMG, I love this song," said Majedah. The filth that held her down began to melt away, though her limbs still felt heavy. She opened her eyes and recognized the pile of her living room carpet beneath her cheek.

Show the world how much we're pissed.
Vaginas up! Time to resist!

"Oh my god, it's my ringtone." Majedah sat up too fast and her head spun. Fighting off unconsciousness, she crawled to her phone. The caller ID read "News 24/7". Majedah swallowed drily, braced herself for the coup de grâce, and hit the *talk* button. "This is Majedah," she croaked.

"Majedah, good morning, it's Chester from 24/7." The producer's voice sounded crisp and civilized, a far cry from the mire of mediocrity in Majedah's dream.

"Hi, Chester." Majedah clenched her eyes in pain and said the words before he could. "I suppose you're calling to let me know 24/7 has rescinded their offer."

"Now why would we do that?"

So, he was making it as painful as possible by forcing her to describe her failure out loud. Majedah sighed and obliged. "The report that came out last night—the cop in my original report wasn't abusing that woman of color; he was protecting her. She's his wife."

"And that matters how?" Chester hadn't paused a second before posing the question.

Majedah didn't understand how he couldn't see the problem. "It wasn't really abuse and racism," she explained.

Chester chortled. "Well, it certainly looked like it to me, and to millions of people around the globe."

"But once the truth came out—"

"Majedah," interrupted Chester, "where did you see this report?"

"Last night. It was on Eagle Eye News."

"Tsk, tsk, what were you doing, watching that slum station of lies and hate?"

Majedah searched her foggy memory. "I—I had turned it on to gloat. I didn't think they'd have access to the original footage and would just look stupid, the only station not to have it. But instead, they had on the actual people from the footage."

"Majedah, who watches that station?" Chester's voice was matter-of-fact.

This time Majedah didn't need to pause to think. "Nazis, fascists, and hillbillies."

"Exactly. Real fringy types. Certainly not America's mainstream."

"Yes, but…"

"Majedah, if a tree falls in the forest and there's no one there to hear it, does it make a sound?"

"Well, I assume it does, but, hm, now that you ask…"

"I understand you graduated with a Journalism degree from Lilith College," Chester went on. "Surely you did a unit on Selective Reportage?"

Majedah sat up proudly, ignoring the answering pounding in her skull. "Of course I did. I got an A+ on the exam."

"Well, then, you know that the so-called truth can be quite subjective. And as the premier news station in America, we here at 24/7 have the very weighty and important duty of deciding what the truth actually is and then telling it to the people."

Finally, Majedah saw the light. "Yes. Yes, you do. That's why I was so excited to work for you guys."

"And we are thrilled to hire the reporter who revealed those visceral images, which underscore the tragic injustice that is the true reality here in America."

Majedah breathed deeply as warmth flooded through her icy limbs. It was going to be all right after all. She closed her eyes and smiled broadly as Chester's voice came through the phone.

"Welcome to News 24/7, Majedah," he said.

TWO WEEKS INTO her employ as an Associate Pool Reporter at News 24/7, Majedah was no less giddy as she breezed through the six-story tall lobby. She looked up to admire the sustainably harvested Amazonian kapok wood-clad walls then lingered lovingly in front of the collection of sculpture by important artists. There was, of course, a 12-foot-tall, abstract, metallic magenta vagina by Finnish artist Essi Kunz. High on a plinth was an emotional monument-style (yet provocatively amateurish) statue of a Caucasian police officer swinging a club at a cowering African-American youth by eight-year-old prodigy Ni'hira Onwuatuegwu. And of course, there was Sean Rothman's brilliant two-story tall painted bronze "Pile of Shit." Majedah was thrilled afresh every morning to walk through the 24/7 lobby and be reminded that she was, at last, where she belonged— at the very nexus of American media, culture, leadership, and thought.

As she did every morning, Majedah rode the elevator to the eighth floor. She greeted the serious young woman behind the reception desk and went down the hall, past offices and cubicles, and arrived at the Reporter Pool. In a humorous nod to the department name, the interior designer had created a large open area that was reached by descending two steps. The poured concrete floor and surrounding walls were finished with actual aqua-colored swimming pool paint. There were a dozen custom-built round desks, covered with red-and-white stripes and other bright colors to mimic various flotation devices, each with a section cut out for a chair. The lack of any privacy or personal space whatsoever represented the cutting edge of office design that fostered collaboration.

Majedah went to a red-and-white life preserver desk and hung her jacket on the back of her chair. The next desk over was bright yellow and sported a rubber ducky head on one side. There sat an intense-looking young man with a long, dark beard, onyx eyes, and a black, knitted cap. Majedah smiled in his direction and said, "Good morning, Mohammed."

Mohammed looked up dismissively and asked, "Still no hijab, Majedah?"

Majedah noted with envy that he had just the right amount of accent to sound ethnically Muslim but not enough to render his speech difficult to understand. This would be a powerful attribute as the young man climbed the on-air talent ladder. She cocked her head, smiled indulgently, and replied, "Now, Mohammed, I already explained to you that here in America, women are liberated. We do not need to cover our heads."

His look simmered. "Only a whore speaks directly to a man who is not in her immediate family." He glared at her another second before turning back to his computer.

"Oh, Mohammed!" laughed Majedah. She shook her head good naturedly as she bent to stow her shoulder bag in a bottom drawer. It was odd that Mohammed clung to religion like he did, but at least he wasn't one of those crazy Christians, like the people in that terrifying dystopian cable series she saw when she was in college. Mohammed was one of Majedah's people, after all; he was Middle Eastern, one of the most prominent victim identities there was.

She looked around to greet the other young, ambitious reporters in the Pool who, like her, dreamed of one day becoming a household name. Besides Mohammed, they were all female (including two transgendered women) and of varying skin tones. *As it should be*, thought Majedah to herself with a flush of pride. *It's so important to have dark shades of skin present in any group of people, and also as many women as possible.*

Chester passed by the reporter pool with his long, purposeful stride. "It's almost ten o'clock. Morning meeting, everyone. Let's go," he warned as he passed. Majedah had initially been startled by his height when she first met him in person; Chester was six-and-a-half feet tall with long, lanky limbs. But everything else about him was as she had expected: incisive mind, efficient manner, and fastidious dress. His short black hair was precision molded into a perfect peak that protruded off his forehead. As always, he wore a suit; today it was blue serge with a crisp white shirt and perfectly knotted pink necktie.

The young, ambitious reporters rose from their clever workstations, grabbed their morning beverages, and followed Chester. Soon they emerged into a long, rectangular conference room and took seats at the row of tables that ran down the center. Everyone plugged their phones and computers into outlets and began surfing while they waited. Majedah looked around the table at the reporters, writers, and producers. All of them were bright, right-thinking patriots who wanted America to be the best place it could be. None of them was a household name; the important on-air personalities never came to work this early, and in any case, they would be briefed in their offices by their assistants. But Majedah knew that right now, she was sitting among the next generation of media power. And she intended to be one of its leaders.

Rosemary Jackson entered the room. The station director was in her late forties, with a short, efficient hairstyle and a casual-yet-chic black outfit. She reminded Majedah of a more prestigiously pigmented, more stylish, and more correct Norma Troutstein. Rosemary went to the space reserved for her at the head of the table, put down her notes, phone, and water bottle, and got organized. She looked up to glance around the table, decided that enough staff was present, cleared her throat, and began the meeting.

"Good morning, everyone. Hope you all had a great weekend. Did everyone see this week's hilarious President Nelson impersonation on *Saturday Night Jokes!*?

"Oh, yes!"

"I never miss it!"

"That was hilarious!" came affirmations from every location in the room.

"Yes, that was a good one this week," agreed Rosemary. Then her demeanor became all business. "Couple of announcements. First of all, you may have noticed some new faces in the back of the room there." Everyone turned to look at a row of journalists arrayed five-deep across the back wall. "As you all know, we are headed into full election season, so we've added an additional forty-seven journalists to our President Nelson desk." There were several jeers and hisses at the sound of the President's name. Rosemary turned her head to spit then wiped her mouth with the back of her hand before continuing. "With the new additions, the Nelson desk is currently staffed at two hundred sixteen full-time journalists and seventy-seven interns." There were several disgruntled murmurs. Rosemary raised her hands placatingly. "I know, I know. We're working hard to get it fully staffed. We hope to have another round of hiring next week. But meanwhile, our hard-hitting investigative journalists have been doing some great work. We have an enormous bombshell that Kingston Fauler will break on the seven o'clock news hour tonight, and we are confident that this news will sink Nelson once and for all."

"Hooray!" cheered the assembled News 24/7 employees.

Rosemary cheered along with them before gesturing for everyone to settle down. "Yes, very good news, I know. Okay, moving on..." She glanced down at her notes and looked back up to continue. "We have some media assignments. Melinda?" She made eye contact with one of the executive assistants, a petite, bespectacled woman with pink hair who nodded back at her, and said, "Toffee has been invited to make an appearance on *Saturday Night Jokes!* this weekend."

Everyone around the table clapped and exclaimed at the good news, simultaneously applauding themselves for being part of the nation's most prominent network.

Rosemary looked around and picked out another assistant. "Max?"

"Present," chirped a young, bow-tied man. Everyone chuckled at his witty, self-expressive manner, and Rosemary gave him a stern smile. "Very good news out of Hollywood for your team, Max; Carol has been invited to play herself in an upcoming feature film, which will be based on the investigative journalism that broke the Great Sexism Scandal at General Investment in 2009."

Majedah cheered as loudly as the rest of the staff, thrilled to be part of America's elite cultural leadership.

Rosemary waited for the din to die down before continuing. "Yes, very good news. Great for us, and great for Hollywood. ... Let's see." She consulted her notes. "Today's preferred pronouns are as follows: Scout is going with *ze*, *zir*, *zis*; Mysty prefers *mys*, *myr*, *myz*; Candy likes *Zz* in all cases, and Ångström is using *adjutant*, *37*, and *blue*. Everyone got it?" She glowered at a few murmurs of confusion. "I sure hope so, because otherwise, you all know where the door is." The murmurs ceased.

A tech approached Rosemary, who looked at him expectantly. "The conference call is starting," he said.

"Okay, put it on speaker." As the tech scurried off, Rosemary looked around the room again. "Time for the daily DNC briefing, everyone. Please remain silent and pay attention, as there will be a new narrative announcement." A burst of excited chatter died down immediately as the conference call came over the room speakers with an initial *beep*.

Democratic National Committee chair Juan Conquista was already speaking. "...so thanks for joining us this morning, fundraisers, bundlers, agents, producers, publishers, educators, tech CEO's, members of the clergy, pollsters, bloggers, ALA, AMA, APA, AAE, ABA, AARC, NAF, NAACP, NFL, ESPN, BSA, GSA, and of course, our all-important journalists. Now, as you all know,"

Juan continued, "we fully expect our next president to be the magnificent Senator Angela Harper of California—"

His words were drowned out by a robust cheer in the conference room. Over the speakers came the sounds of cheering from the DNC room where the conference originated. Juan also cheered energetically, the sound distorted as he overloaded the volume his mic could handle. In the New York conference room, Majedah put her hands in the air and screamed with joy, doing her best to be the loudest in the room. However, the seasoned crew all around her easily produced more decibels. Majedah realized she still had much to learn.

After a full minute, the cheering died down. Juan resumed the daily briefing. "Once we nominate Angela at the convention this summer, it will be a simple matter to remind everyone that she has a vagina, while Nelson does not. After all, sexism is one of America's gravest and most prevalent sins, and the only way to fix it is to elect a vagi—I mean, a woman—as president." He paused to allow the attendees another round of cheering before continuing. "Yes, obviously, people will be overjoyed to be able to cast their historic votes, and we should have no problem. I say, 'should have,' but you never know. Since we don't want to take any chances, we're counting on you all to build the biggest, strongest narrative yet, to really get the word out about sexism. Let's tell the whole country the story of how really bad conditions are for women in America!"

The DNC Chair paused for another round of cheering. Majedah glanced around the room to confirm that the male employees were cheering this mission the loudest, as they should be. Some of them had jumped on top of the table and pulled their shirts off to wave them in the air. One punched himself repeatedly in the face while another dropped to the floor and performed a flawless 80's-style break-dance routine. Even the staid Chester Chen pumped a fist in the air. Only Mohammed kept his seat, glowering angrily around the room, but as he was Muslim, he was encouraged to keep his faith at the center of his life.

Juan Conquista began to speak again. "The good news is that the folks at our think tanks have just made this job a whole lot easier for you. Their researchers have been hard at work, and they have identified an omnipresent industry that is currently rampant with sexism and racism. It's an industry that no one really thinks about but everyone uses, and it represents a full one-twelfth of our national economy. It's an industry in a crisis of sexism, which means it's an industry that needs a woman president to take control." The 24/7 staffers glanced at one another in puzzlement, but Juan quickly solved the mystery for them. "I'm talking about HVAC, of course."

There was a collective, "Huh?" from everyone in the room and on speakerphone.

"Heating, Ventilation, and Air Conditioning," clarified Juan.

"Oh," said everyone in the room and on speakerphone.

"Our researchers have determined that fully 98.3% of HVAC technicians are men," said Juan.

Boos and hisses filled the air.

Juan had to shout to make himself heard over the din of outrage. "And not only that, not only that ... Of those men, 78.6% are *white*."

Screams and wails drowned out any additional words Juan might have said. Garments were rent and hair was yanked out of scalps. Three of the conference tables were overturned, seven employees vomited, two young men pulled down their pants to defecate, one woman began to write a novel, and three staffers of indeterminate gender began a vigorous ménage-a-trois in a corner.

After ten minutes had passed and the outrage showed no signs of calming, people began to file out of the room and go back to work, energized by their new mission. Majedah was too restless to go back to the Pool, so she let the crowd carry her along to the elevators. From the eighth floor she rode to the twentieth. She drifted down the glimmering halls of power and fame, past offices of increasing size and importance. Just before the hall became the open area off of which the network executives had their offices, she came to the door bearing a plaque with the name *Carol Crawford*. No assistants manned the desks outside, and Majedah was able to enter the chamber unimpeded.

She stepped through the doorway and drew in a breath. She was in an enormous room with European-style paneled walls, which were painted cream and ecru, except the opposite wall, which was all windows overlooking Central Park. There were sofas and armchairs of butter-soft, blush-colored leather and ornate, white, low tables, nestled into a creamy flokati rug, which overlaid pale rose wool-and-silk carpeting. An enormous white desk sat before the windows with two berry damask slipper chairs facing it. The wall to the right was covered with large, framed photos of Carol with various A-list celebrities, power brokers, and politicians. The wall to the left was empty except for a long, tufted white linen sofa and a single shelf above it. On this shelf rested not one, not two, but seven Golden Vulva Awards for Achievement in Feminist Reporting.

In a euphoric trance, Majedah went to the shelf and gazed upon the glistening organ replicas. She sighed blissfully and reached out a hand to touch one, ever so worshipfully...

"What are you doing in here?" asked a female voice.

Majedah spun to see Melinda, the pink-haired assistant from the meeting, peering at her anxiously through black-framed cats eye glasses. "I'm sorry, I just wanted to see—" Majedah began to explain.

"You can't be in here," Melinda barked.

Majedah would have taken offense, but she could see that the girl was in a panic. "Okay, don't worry, I'm leaving," she said in a soothing voice. She began to move calmly towards the door.

"You have to get out of here, now! If Carol sees that I let someone in her office, she'll kill me." Melinda's voice was rising in volume and pitch, and Majedah hurried to scoot past her, out of the office.

Just outside the door, she nearly bumped into Carol Crawford as the legendary reporter brushed past her. Majedah had a momentary flash of panic herself, but then she realized that Carol hadn't noticed her, hadn't seen her at all.

Majedah spun to retreat down the hall and promptly smacked into the Great Man himself, Richard Spinner, legendary founder and owner of News 24/7, and creator of the 24-hour incessant blather cycle. Majedah stepped back from the collision, stammering apologies.

Unlike Carol, Spinner did notice her, and he took a moment to run his gaze down her body from chest to Choos. Spinner was a large man and hadn't been much affected by the impact. He grinned at her. "No worries, kitten. We're all in a hurry around here." He gave her a wink, patted her arm reassuringly, and turned back to the battalion of suits who marched alongside him on their way to their offices.

Openmouthed, Majedah watched his retreating back. He had ramrod posture and stood a head taller than the crowd around him. His hair had retained its fullness and ash blond hue from his youth, and his powerful voice resonated as he issued commands to his staff. His torso was perhaps a bit thick and his movements a little stiff, but that was understandable for someone 75 years old.

Once Spinner passed out of sight through the double doors that led to his office, Majedah turned and, giddy from her brush with genius and power, floated down the hall toward the elevators.

Back in the Pool, the young journalists surfed hard all day, tracking down internet rumors and reaching out to contacts to find news to report on. One of the transgender women, Scout, got a solid lead about a biology professor at a downtown university who insisted on using the hate terms "male" and "female" in his lectures. Scout's request for a camera crew was granted. "Wish me luck, everyone!" ze said.

The journalists took turns hugging zir and wishing zir well. "Go get that bastard," added Mysty, clenching myz massive fist.

"You bet I will," Scout assured myr. The two make-believe women bumped fists then hugged before Scout flounced off to zir reporting duties.

As evening came on, Chester appeared at the edge of the Pool. "Hey, everyone," he said, "a bunch of us are heading the Buzz to watch Kingston drop the bombshell about President Nelson in real time. Also, Ron's buying drinks."

"Woot!" cheered all the bright young reporters.

Majedah leaned over to the desk on the other side of her from Mohammed and asked, "Who's Ron again?"

Melissa, the reporter next to her, had been in the pool the longest and knew who everyone at 24/7 was. "Vice President of Corporate Sponsor Appeasement, twentieth floor."

"Ah, thank you." Majedah nodded appreciatively. The young women took up their coats and shoulder bags and joined the group of people heading for the door.

Late season snow sifted onto heads and shoulders as the bright young reporters traversed the block and filed into the Buzz, an upscale food and drink establishment. Everyone ordered the signature "Beehive" drink, a honey-sweetened soda and small-batch local gin concoction (except Mohammed, who ordered a cherry coke and drew down his dark eyebrows at the decadent beverage choices of his colleagues). The Pool reporters huddled around the bar, chattering excitedly. The rest of the space was filled with booths and tables of media executives, city officials, and other luminaries, catching an early supper after a long day's work. An air of celebratory anticipation hovered over the crowd and at 6:59, everyone was hushed as all eyes went to the enormous television screens mounted on the walls. One of the bartenders turned the volume way up.

Kingston Fauler's grave visage appeared, his steely blue eyes drilling directly into everyone watching. "Good evening. This is the News 24/7 Seven O'Clock Report, and I'm Kingston Fauler. We begin tonight's broadcast with disturbing, exclusive News 24/7 breaking news." The screen flashed red with the familiar *Breaking News* graphic and claxon before Kingston reappeared. Now the camera was at a distance to show more of the news desk, where an energized thirty-something woman also sat.

"Joining me for exclusive News 24/7 Breaking News is 24/7 investigative reporter Sarah Markowitz," introduced Kingston. He turned to her. "Sarah, I understand your team has been tracking the multiple, unprecedented failures and scandals of the Nelson administration and tonight, you are here to break a major news story about President Nelson himself."

Sarah Merkowitz nodded before launching into her report. "That's right, Kingston, we have uncovered shocking abuse by President Nelson himself, and we have the video to prove it."

The screen cut to wide view footage of President and Linda Nelson, hosting an event in the East Room. The room was full of rambunctious children, happily eating ice cream and playing with red, white and blue spinning toys. A flashing red banner at the bottom of the screen reminded viewers that they were being shown Breaking News.

Kingston's voice came over the footage. "Sarah, can you tell us what we're seeing here?"

"Sure," answered the journalist. "This is footage from yesterday at President Nelson's annual ice cream social that he and the First Lady host for children of deployed service people. As you can see, everything looks upbeat and innocent, the President and First Lady opening up the people's White House to the children of those who sacrifice so much for our country. But our team took a closer look and found that something truly sinister was going on this whole time."

"How horrible," commented Kingston.

"Oh, you can't believe how horrible," agreed Sarah. "Take a look at this. One of our cameramen used a high-resolution hyper-distance lens and was able to pick up some shocking images. Watch."

The footage had been slowly zooming in on the table at which the president sat with an adorable little boy beside him. They were having a contest to see who could spin his toy the longest, and their dishes of ice cream remained untouched on the table before them. The camera continued to zoom in until the two treats filled the entire screen. Then the image froze.

"Tell me what we're seeing, Sarah," came Kingston's voice.

"Sure. If you take a look at these two dishes of ice cream, nothing appears to be amiss at first," explained the journalist. "But we ran the image through custom analytical and modeling software that our contributing team at MIT built exclusively for this bombshell investigation."

The image on the screen suddenly rendered in sharp relief and digitized into enhanced color cells. Overlapping green boxes appeared and outlined each sprinkle on the surface of the two ice cream servings. A green grid appeared and mapped the 3-D shape of the scoops. The image of the ice cream vanished so that there was only the 3-D rendering on a black background; then, additional green sprinkles appeared on the grid. Green numbers began flashing beneath the two dishes.

"Sarah, please explain what we're seeing. Not everyone is a rocket scientist, you know," Kingston joked self-deprecatingly.

"Yes, this can be a little confusing if you're not as educated as our investigative scientists," Sarah said. "Basically, this software captured the data, analyzed it, and projected the number of sprinkles that would also be on the backs of these scoops, out of sight of the viewers. Then the full number of sprinkles on each dish of ice cream, both visible and projected, is tallied, and you can see those numbers adding up at the bottom of the image."

"Oh, dear god," breathed Kingston. "The horror. The absolute horror."

Inside the Buzz, gasps sounded around the room as realization struck the riveted viewers.

On the television, Sarah confirmed what they all had seen. "Yes, that's right, Kingston. Our scientists project that President Nelson has 276 sprinkles on his dish of ice cream, while that poor little boy—who's already suffering enough because his mother is deployed in one of Nelson's endless wars—has only 258 sprinkles."

Furor broke out inside the Buzz. Sobs of shock and dismay interspersed with angry outbursts:

"The monster!"

"Oh my god, the poor children!"

"Deplorable!"

Kingston was back on screen, looking into the camera with an expression of righteous wrath. "If this doesn't prompt Congress to act and begin impeachment proceedings, then I don't know what will," he pronounced.

The crowd inside the Buzz reacted strongly.

"Impeach Nelson!"

"We've got him this time!"

"Impeach!"

The mood had swung from sickened outrage to energized celebration. Majedah and her colleagues hugged one another triumphantly.

"No president could survive a scandal this big!" said one.

"I sense a Pulitzer in Sarah's future," said another.

"And Nobel Science Prizes for the MIT team," declared another.

A wealthy donor somewhere in the room ordered the bartenders to open bottles of Dom Perignon and pass around flutes. In a frenzy of optimism and euphoria, Majedah and her colleagues toasted President Nelson's imminent and well-deserved downfall.

Chapter 13

ROSEMARY SWEPT INTO the conference room looking more purposeful than ever, but she set down her water bottle and shuffled through her notes in her customary manner. Then she looked up at the staff gathered around the long table and began the morning meeting.

"Good morning, everyone. Hope you all got some sleep and didn't stay up too late, celebrating our enormous scoop last night." She emphasized the word *scoop* to make sure everyone got the joke, and laughter and cheers broke out around the room. A few staffers went into a spontaneous "Love beats hate!" chant that died down again after several refrains.

Rosemary allowed the employees a moment to vent their enthusiasm before continuing. "Just a couple announcements before we go to our conference call. Let's see ... We have a new employee to introduce. Mara, can you please raise your hand?"

A tall young man standing in the back of the room raised his hand. "You meant to say, raise my hoof," he verily whinnied. Majedah noticed that he had a wonderful, thick mane of long, golden hair.

"There you are," Rosemary confirmed. She referred to her notes before sweeping the room with a stern look. "In case anyone wasn't sure, Mara is a female centaur, and Mara's pronouns are equee, equir, and equis. Everyone got it?"

Mara lifted equis chin and scanned the room from beneath lowered lashes to confirm for equirself that equee was affirmed by everyone. There were nods and murmurs of approval. Majedah joined in the supportive applause as she took a good look at Mara; now that she was paying attention, Majedah realized that what she had ignorantly presumed was a man was in fact an achingly beautiful blond woman to equis waist, at which juncture equee became a shapely, golden palomino horse. "Oh, so pretty!" Majedah exclaimed.

"Very good," concluded Rosemary. "And now, let's tune into the conference call so we can coordinate follow-up to last night's exclusive News 24/7 bombshell." A raucous round of cheering forced her to stop talking, so she simply stood and joined in with the enthusiastic staff. At last, a frantically waving tech caught her eye and she raised her hands to hush the room as the daily conference call came over the speakers.

DNC Chair Juan Conquista was mid-sentence. "... have all been airing the video, provided courtesy of News 24/7..." (The employees in the conference room gave a subdued cheer for themselves.) "... and really getting the word out through all the traditional channels. Additionally, our social media partners have generated the hashtag *#Sprinklegate*, which is to be used in conjunction with the omnidirectional hashtags *#ImpeachNelson* and *#LoveBeatsHate*." There was much nodding in agreement around the long table in midtown Manhattan, as there was around similar tables in Washington, D.C., Boston, Asheville, Miami, Nashville, Austin, Madison, Chicago, Denver, Seattle, Los Angeles, San Francisco, Portland, and other cities all across the country.

"Our tech sector has set up algorithms to ensure appropriate results across all platforms. Blither and Friendly Face have set our hashtags to perma-trend, and Goggle will auto-fill all searches to *Impeach Nelson* until further notice." There were more approving nods around the table. "Today's talking points are being emailed to all our subscribers to help everyone stay on message. Aside from that, everyone keep on doing what you're doing," Juan wrapped up the meeting. There were thousands of chirps and clicks as attendees around the country disconnected from the call.

People began to collect their phones and water bottles, but Rosemary stopped them. "One more thing before we all get back to work," she said. At that moment, an intern came into the room carrying a chocolate sheet cake. "We have a significant anniversary today," announced Rosemary. "Melissa! Where are you?"

A few seats down from Majedah, the frizzy haired Pool reporter waved bashfully. The intern brought the cake over and set it down in front of her.

"Melissa has been at News 24/7 for five years as of today. Everyone please take a moment to congratulate her and have a piece of cake," directed Rosemary.

Chairs scraped the floor as people mobbed around Melissa, taking turns congratulating her on her milestone and declining a piece of cake.

"I can't eat anything made in a facility that processes nuts," said one employee.

"I can't eat gluten," said another.

"I don't eat anything with dairy in it."

"I haven't eaten sugar in years."

"I only eat halal."

"I don't eat anything with food in it."

By the time Majedah got to Melissa, the cake was untouched. Majedah hadn't been hungover in weeks and had missed breakfast that morning, so she took a small piece. "Congratulations, Melissa," she said. "See you back in the Pool."

Melissa smiled. "See you there, Majedah."

Later, back at her desk, Majedah ate another mouthful of cake and observed Melissa as the young woman typed at her computer. She seemed content, happy even. Another Pool reporter, Ashley, stopped by and asked Melissa if she'd mind finishing up a report. Apparently, Ashley had to get uptown to a city council meeting where there would be an important vote on mandating shopping bags that were made of certified organic cotton and manufactured in fair trade mills, and she didn't have time to file the report herself.

"No problem," said Melissa agreeably. She smiled at Ashley's thanks and set to work.

Majedah chewed thoughtfully as she considered Melissa. Five years, the woman had been here, in the Pool the whole time. No upward movement and no prospect of any on the horizon.

Majedah was shaking her head as she swallowed her final bite of cake. She'd be damned if she were still sitting at her stupid, red-and-white life preserver-shaped desk in five years. "If I'm still in the Pool in five years, I'll quit journalism for good," she vowed to herself. "At the very least, in five years I'll be anchor of my own news desk. And someday, so help me, I'll anchor the Women's Desk. Carol Crawford has to retire someday. She can only get so much work done on her face." Majedah closed her eyes in a moment of reverence as she imagined herself helming the nightly broadcast of *An Hour of Your Time with Majedah Cantalupi-Abromavich-Flügel-Van Der Hoven-Taj Mahal*. Then she swiveled in her chair to throw the paper plate and plastic fork into a wastebasket before returning to her computer to search frantically for the next important story.

Although Majedah searched diligently all morning, she found no potential stories of national importance by lunchtime. The inherent sexism of the HVAC industry had never gained any traction; Sprinklegate was the largest trending story of the day, and it was amply covered by senior reporters from all the networks.

The sugar from Majedah's cake breakfast had long since burned off and her stomach was rumbling. One of the reporters from the other side of the Pool stood and stretched. "Anyone hungry?" she asked.

Majedah looked up in relief. "Me," she said.

"Me, too"

"Yeah, I could eat."

"Anyone want to walk to Food Fix?"

Soon all the Pool reporters were up and shrugging into coats and jackets. The group crammed into the elevator and emerged on the sidewalk. A three-block trek brought them to the take-out lunch vendor, and soon everyone was headed back up the Avenue to the News 24/7 tower, each carrying a black bag with white lettering that read *Food Fix* on the side. Majedah walked alongside the group, half listening to the banter and gossip, ever alert for breaking news.

As they crossed the first side street, something flickered in the corner of Majedah's eye. Way down the block, in the sunlit intersection with the next avenue—had she seen something happening? Majedah felt the prickle of goose bumps and realized her reporter senses were tingling. She turned her head to look. It was hard to make anything out because of the surging lunchtime crowds between her and the distant intersection, but was that an organized march of some sort she had seen?

Majedah glanced around at her cohorts but they walked on, chatting amongst themselves, oblivious. Then they were on the other side of the street and buildings obscured Majedah's view. She shook her head to clear it. *I want to cover major breaking news so badly, I'm starting to imagine things!* she thought to herself.

A minute later, the Pool reporters had traversed the block and began crossing a second side street. Majedah paused in the middle of the crosswalk and took a good, hard look down the street to the next avenue.

There! Marching in the sunlight with banners high and chants audible a block away, were scores of women.

Majedah ran to catch up with her coworkers. "Guys! Guys, look! There's a protest down there. A big one!"

The reporters nearest to Majedah paused. "Where?" asked one.

Majedah held her index finger high, stabbing the air urgently. "Down there. Look!" She could see the march even more clearly now. "Wow, there are pink t-shirts. It's a women's march," she practically shouted.

The other Pool reporters shielded their eyes from the sun and scrutinized the view down the street.

"I don't know, I don't see anything," said Melissa.

"Nope. Me neither," added Mysty.

"How can you not see that?" Majedah pleaded. She could plainly see a marching column of protestors as wide as the avenue, and she could hear feminine voices raised in a righteous chant.

Mohammed scanned a minute longer. "Maybe. It's hard to tell…"

A taxi honked its horn and they realized the light had changed and they were still standing in the middle of the crosswalk. They scurried to the safety of the crowded sidewalk. Majedah immediately turned right and started running before she realized no one was coming with her. "Guys," she implored, "where are you going? There's a women's march going on just one block away! We have to report on it! Nothing gets better coverage than a women's march."

Everyone kept walking and talking about eating lunch. Only Melissa answered her. "I don't know, Majedah. I don't really see a story there." With an apologetic shrug, she hurried to catch up with her colleagues.

Majedah's mouth hung open in disbelief until she clamped it shut angrily. "Fine, I'll go report on it myself," she said to no one in particular. She turned and sped across the long block to the next avenue, threading her way through the slow-moving midday pedestrians.

When she arrived at the corner, she was greeted with a glorious sight. Fifth Avenue was full of beautiful, strong, empowered women who marched, chanted, and carried placards and banners. It was a classic protest, photogenic and perfectly organized. Majedah paused to admire the rows of females with linked arms and matching t-shirts. She made out the words of the chant: *STOP HURTING WOMEN!*, over and over again.

Majedah closed her eyes, threw her head back, and uttered, "Yes!" Then she snapped into professional mode. She tossed her Food Fix bag into a nearby trashcan. She turned to the shop window behind her and used her reflection to smooth her hair and apply a fresh coat of lipstick. Then she pulled her phone from her shoulder bag and logged into the 24/7 Live Beat streaming app, which would flow her raw content, as it happened, directly onto a special section of the station website. She took another piece of equipment from her bag, a high-tech auto-report wand, and set her phone on the end of it. Then she watched the marchers until she saw a group in hot pink shirts approaching. The women were student-aged and of all pigment levels. Majedah made out the slogan on their shirts: *Women Aren't Toys*. "I've never heard of them before," she mused. "Maybe I'll break some cutting-edge feminism news today." She took one more moment to collect herself, said, "Okay, Majedah, here we go," and hopped into the line of march.

As soon as she was striding along the avenue, surrounded by thousands of uniformed, chanting, angry women, Majedah felt an instant rush of exhilaration. She observed that the WAT group appeared to be led by an intelligent-looking, tall, blond twenty-something. The woman wore her t-shirt over a black thermal fleece zipped up to cover her neck and black jeans tucked into tall boots. Beneath a pink knitted ski cap with a large pom-pom on top was a face worthy of national broadcast. *Perfect*, thought Majedah. She hurried to the young woman's side and introduced herself.

"Hello. I'm Majedah Cantalupi-Abromavich-Flügel-Van Der Hoven-Taj Mahal, a reporter with News 24/7. Do you mind if I interview you for broadcast?"

"Wow, News 24/7? That's great! Sure, we'd love it if you'd interview us," said the young activist.

"Great. Okay, let me just start recording." Majedah held the auto-report wand out in front of them until she determined that the camera was capturing a tight shot of herself and the WAT leader. Then she hit the *Stream* button on the handle and went live to the 24-7 website.

She began the report. "This is Majedah Cantalupi-Abromavich-Flügel-Van Der Hoven-Taj Mahal, reporting live for News 24/7 from mid-town Manhattan on the scene of a massive women's march. I'm here with one of the organizers of Women Aren't Toys, one of the countless groups fighting for women's rights at today's protest." She turned her head to the young marcher beside her. "Would you introduce yourself and tell us a little more about your organization?"

"Hi, sure, I'd love to," said the woman. "I'm Lily McGovern, I'm a co-organizer of the group Women Aren't Toys, and we're here today all the way from Starkville, Mississippi. Hi, Mom!" She smiled and waved into Majedah's phone.

Majedah's journalism instincts were firing on high, and she was acutely aware that she was being broadcast live on a website that reached millions of people all around the globe. She skillfully redirected the woman's comments. "Lily, what are the goals of Women Aren't Toys?"

"Women Aren't Toys is an organization that some friends and I saw a need for," explained the photogenic leader. "We realized that we were living in a culture that objectifies women and turns us into sex symbols. We felt very uncomfortable in a society where we had difficulty even going on a date with a man, knowing that half the time, he would be expecting the evening to end in a hook-up."

"Yes, I know what you mean," agreed Majedah. "Rape culture is a terrible crisis on campuses across America."

"Well, I guess, but in one way you can hardly blame the guys for thinking women want to have sex all the time. I mean, in every magazine and music video and movie and TV show, women are portrayed as these sex-crazed creatures who just follow their most base instincts and have no self-control. It's really insulting, when you think about it."

Majedah couldn't quite understand Lily's point. "Could you please clarify your remarks?" she prompted.

"Yes, okay," continued Lily. "For example, you can't even watch a sporting event without all the women present being dressed like hookers."

Majedah was back on solid ground. "Oh, I know what you mean. Cheerleading is such a primitive throwback."

Lily gave her a confused look. "Actually, I was talking about the halftime show. Singers and dancers who wear fishnet stockings and shake their butts in the camera. I mean, what kind of message is that sending to young girls—and to men?"

Majedah was having trouble following Lily's brand of feminism, so she let the young woman keep speaking in the hopes that it would become clear.

"And then you also see all these women demanding that taxpayers give them free birth control. WAT resents the implication that all women of child-bearing age are just dying to make themselves sexually availably. And if you're a guy and you pay taxes, you might even think you're entitled to use some of what you're paying for, you know?"

Lily's argument made sense to Majedah but at the same time, it contradicted what Majedah knew to be the core values of feminism. "So, you're saying..."

Lily was fired up now. "I'm saying that we have a culture problem, and that all of this leads to the objectification of women as sexual objects. And that leads to men disrespecting us, or worse, not being able to see us as human beings or take us seriously."

"Yes, exactly," Majedah enthused. She glanced at her phone to make sure it was still capturing the shot properly and noticed a message had popped up; someone from 24/7 was trying to call her. Majedah decided her women's march report was too important to abandon and ignored the message. She returned her attention to the young activist by her side. "Women not being taken seriously, but instead being seen only as objects, has been an Injustice in our patriarchal society for far too long," she reported. Lily looked unsure, so Majedah skillfully tried another angle to bring out more information. "Lily, I love your hat. Knitted pink caps are, of course, a symbol of women's rights in this country, but yours is an unusual shape. Rather than the traditional 'cat's ears' design, yours looks more like a ski hat."

"Yes, that's right, it's a ski hat. It keeps my head warm," Lily confirmed.

"Right," said Majedah. "And I notice it has a rather large pom-pom, if you will, on top. Is that meant to represent a clitoris?"

"A what?" Lily adjusted her steps to move slightly away from Majedah as they marched.

"You know, the center of female power and—goddammit, what just happened to my broadcast?" Majedah's phone had kicked her off the LiveStream app with a sharp beep. Her *Vaginas Up!* ringtone began to sound immediately. She turned to Lily apologetically. "Excuse me a minute, someone's really trying to reach me." Lily seemed just as pleased to leave her to her own devices. "This better be important," Majedah grumbled. She yanked the phone from the auto-report wand, hit the talk button, and held it to her ear. "What is it?" she snarled.

"Majedah. What the hell are you doing?" It was Chester's voice, and the usually unflappable producer sounded stern.

"What do you mean, what am I doing? I'm reporting on a major women's march!" Majedah pronounced.

Chester laughed once, a huff of disbelief. "Majedah, do you even know what that march is?"

Majedah began to feel alarmed. "I mean, I don't know exactly which one it is, but it's mostly women, and some of them are wearing pink, and it's big enough to fill Fifth Avenue. So obviously, it's—"

"It's an anti-abortion march, Majedah."

"*What?*" Majedah nearly dropped her phone in shock. "Oh, my god." She stopped dead in her tracks and several of the WAT marchers behind her bumped into her before they began to part around her like a river rushing around a stubborn stone.

A sickening wave of fear washed over Majedah along with the realization that she was surrounded by the most terrifying, dangerous, fanatical people in the country. "Okay, Majedah, don't panic," she said to herself. She glanced around, trying to figure out a discreet path out of the throng. Now that she knew who these people really were, they were revealed to her in all their true horror. Yet the implacable size and energy of the march drew her along, against her will. She found herself marching among a group of bearded men who were dressed in long black robes like medieval monks. Majedah was sure they would burn her at the stake at a moment's notice. She slowed her steps further and was surrounded by a wave of blue-haired church ladies in hideous, homemade sweaters that smelled of mothballs. Gagging, Majedah lurched to the side, floundering towards the sidewalk. Several people exclaimed in pain as her flailing knees and elbows struck them.

Then she was trapped in a phalanx of the worst of the worst: old, white men, some carrying bibles. One of them even held a huge, white cross aloft on a pole, and they were chanting something about repentance. Sweating and shaking, Majedah spun in a circle, trying to find a way out. The men closest to her stopped chanting as they reached for her with their gnarled hands. One of them said, "Are you all right, miss?" His face was only inches from hers and as he spoke, he revealed three large gaps where a normal person would have teeth. Majedah screamed as she felt herself falling.

When she came to, she was lying on the sidewalk. She could see countless feet passing by; the march continued, so she couldn't have been out long. Someone had removed his jacket and placed it beneath her head, and someone else was holding her wrist, taking her pulse. Majedah sat up with a start.

"Hooray," cheered the scary hillbillies. They had apparently abandoned their place in the march to surround her and enjoy her discomfiture.

Majedah's heart pounded as she struggled to her feet. "I'm fine, th-thank you,"

"Whoa, take it easy there. You shouldn't stand up too fast." Someone took her arm to steady her.

As soon as Majedah found her footing, she jerked her arm away. "I said I'm fine." She glanced around until she spotted an opening then she shouldered her way out of the ring of old, white men to make her escape. She could hear them yelling at her as she fled down the sidewalk.

"Miss, wait … your phone!"

She stopped and looked back to see a white-bearded man holding up her phone. "Damn it." A skittish Majedah returned to the man, snatched the device, and even managed a clipped, "Thank you." Then she was off like a rabbit, away from the crazy, scary people as fast as her shaky legs would carry her.

By the time Majedah arrived at her desk, she had caught her breath and ceased her trembling, but she still felt shaken and flustered. Melissa looked up at her. "Oh, hey, Majedah. Chester was looking for you."

"Great." Majedah stowed her bag and went off to find the gangly producer.

Chester didn't get up from his desk when she came into his tiny office. He just glanced up and spoke five words; "Rosemary wants to see you."

Majedah's heart slammed against her chest wall. "O-Okay. Where is she?"

"In her office."

"Okay. Thanks."

Chester must have felt a modicum of sympathy at her stricken expression because he offered her a brief smile and wished her luck.

Majedah was too frightened to smile back. She turned and numbly found her way to the director's office. She paused just outside the door because she could hear Rosemary on the phone.

"Yeah, I'm just waiting for her to come to my office. … Is Legal working on the situation? … Oh, good. And the web team is monitoring to make sure it hasn't metastasized? … Excellent.

Yes, I'll take care of things in my department. ... Okay, sounds good. Thanks."

Majedah heard the phone land in its cradle. She gulped, braced herself, and poked her head inside the door. "You wanted to see me?" she asked.

Rosemary's expression was unreadable. "Yes. Close the door behind you."

Majedah wondered if she looked as pale as she felt as she closed the door and turned to face whatever was coming.

"Have a seat." Rosemary indicated one of the gray fabric upholstered chairs that faced her desk. Like the chairs, the desk was standard corporate issue, unremarkable but solidly crafted and utilitarian in design. Rosemary's office was of large size but furnished to emphasize efficiency and function over status. The only nod to her personality was walls hung with large, framed, black-and-white portraiture of various types of dogs that had been taken by a fashionable photographer. Most of the wall opposite the door was a window that looked toward downtown Manhattan.

Majedah sat and faced the woman behind the desk. Rosemary got right to the point. "So, I heard you were covering the anti-women's rights beat today."

Majedah could feel her large, dark eyes well up, but she caught herself before a tear could spill over. "I can't apologize enough. It was an honest mistake—it looked like a women's rights march. When I got there, there were just rows and rows of women wearing pink shirts and hats and chanting about how they were sick of being objectified by men." Rosemary's expression remained cold, and Majedah brimmed with anxiety. "You have to believe me! I would never knowingly give the great News 24/7 platform to a bunch of toothless, anti-choice fascists."

Rosemary let her babble until she was sure the young reporter was sorry. Then she held up a hand. "Okay, okay, I believe you. For a moment there, I was afraid we had made a mistake and hired someone who didn't have an eye for news."

Majedah's chin lifted subtly at the implication. "I can assure you that I have a very keen and discerning eye for news. I'm actually an extremely gifted reporter."

Rosemary's face almost softened. "I thought so. After all, we hired you because you broke that nation-wide police abuse story, complete with devastating footage. We know you know real news when you see it."

Majedah exhaled in relief. "Thank you," she said.

Rosemary wasn't finished. "But the problem here is whether you are able to discern when something is *not* news, too. Majedah, what do we all do every morning here at 24/7?"

"Hm, um … We have a meeting?"

"Correct. We have a meeting. If something like a major march were planned, we would all be notified in the morning meeting. Then a detachment of reporters would be deployed to cover it from many angles. So, if there's something happening in New York City and it looks like it might be a big story, but you didn't hear about it in the morning meeting, it's not a big story. Understand?"

Majedah was the very picture of contrition. "Yes, Rosemary."

"Good. Because we have high hopes for you here at 24/7, Majedah. You could have a very bright future. But mistakes like this are what destroy bright futures. We need to know we can trust you with the tools to which we give you access. The LiveBeat app is an extremely sensitive tool, Majedah. We need to be able to trust the judgment of our reporters when we give them access to it. Judgment is extremely important, because LiveBeat is a live-stream app. There is no chance to edit, so a mistake like yours gets streamed right onto our branded website. And it makes us look like idiots."

"I can't tell you how sorry I am." Majedah hung her head in shame. "But it's gone now, right? It was deleted and not posted in the archives, right?"

"Yes, of course we purged it from our site," confirmed Rosemary. "But perhaps you've heard the saying, the internet is forever?"

Majedah didn't want to hear what was coming next, but she nodded. "Yes."

"Well, you should know that there are enemies of our American way of life who monitor our site and our broadcasts all the time, looking for any opportunity to hurt us." Rosemary fixed her with a serious look another moment then began to type on her keyboard. "There's something you need to see." After a moment, she turned the monitor so both of them could see it.

Majedah forced herself to look. Rosemary had opened the anti-woman, repressive website, *LifeSite.org*. A huge headline splashed across the home page:

Breakthrough! LifeMarch Receives Coverage on News 24/7!

Majedah covered her open mouth with bloodless fingers. She could feel the color drain from her face and thought she might pass out again. "Oh, my god," she whispered.

Rosemary's glare was relentless. "That's right, Majedah; oh, my god. This is one of the worst blows to 24/7's credibility in my tenure here at the station. We are News 24/7, dammit. We do not broadcast populist hate masquerading as news. We do not risk our membership in the NBNA, and we especially don't risk our reputation as the global leader in relevant, accurate, real news."

Majedah couldn't hold it back any longer. She put her face in her hands and sobbed. "I'm sorry, Rosemary. I'm so sorry."

The seasoned news director let the young journalist writhe in her torment another minute before granting relief. "The good news is that we got your feed down so quickly, it appears no one had time to download it. I clicked through to the story on this so-called website, and all they had by means of proof was a blurry screen grab and one or two recollected quotes. They can't prove we streamed or said what they say we did. Our lawyers are on the phone even as we speak, giving them a verbal cease-and-desist."

Majedah felt the tiniest glimmer of hope for the first time since stepping into the news director's office. She wiped her eyes on her sleeve and looked up. "Really?" she squeaked.

"Yes, really. We don't fuck around here."

"Oh, thank god," sniffled Majedah. She glanced at Rosemary's desk, hoping to spy a box of tissues, but there were only documents and computer equipment. She quickly blotted her runny nose on her cuff, hoping Rosemary didn't notice. Luckily, the news director was staring intently at the LifeSite homepage still displayed on the monitor. Majedah followed her gaze and saw the ugly, devastating headline again.

Then screen blanked as the webpage refreshed, and the terrible headline was gone. In its place was an absurd claim that marchers in DC and New York numbered in the hundreds of thousands.

"It's gone." Majedah blinked to make sure she hadn't imagined the update.

"Yes, thanks to our army of skilled attorneys and lucky for you, it's gone."

Majedah drew in the shaky breath of a condemned man who had just been granted a reprieve. "Is there anything I can do to help clear this up?" she asked.

"Distance yourself from it. Forget it ever happened. Don't ever do anything this stupid again."

"Yes, Rosemary. You can count on me, I swear it."

Rosemary fixed her with one final, piercing look. Majedah almost felt like Rosemary was looking directly into her brain, scanning for unacceptable thoughts. At last, the director said, "I certainly hope so. Okay, get back to work."

"Thank you, Rosemary. On my way. Thank you so much! Thank you." Majedah scampered out of the office and made for the nearest omni-gender bathroom. She locked the door behind her and spent several minutes hyperventilating and splashing her face with cold water. Then she blotted herself dry with paper towel and checked her reflection. Her eyes were clear and her cheeks flushed from the stimulating chill. She spent another minute smoothing her hair and biting her lips for more color before leaving the sanctuary and finally making her way back to the Pool.

Melissa was away from her desk and Mohammed was surfing furiously on his computer when Majedah sat down. She glanced around cautiously but no one seemed to remark upon her return. Gradually, Majedah relaxed. She had learned by now that no one in the entire building—probably in the entire city—would have been visiting a site like LifeSite, so it was highly unlikely anyone nearby was even aware of her transgression. And now, thanks to the crack legal team at 24/7, any evidence had been expunged from the internet. Majedah reminded herself to breathe normally and soon, she was back to work as though nothing had happened. By six o'clock, she at last felt it was unremarkable enough to gather her things and leave the office.

When she arrived in the quarry-tiled kitchen of her Upper West Side apartment, Majedah went to the cupboard, took out a tumbler, and placed it on the counter. She removed a bottle of hand-crafted small batch vodka from the freezer, poured two fingers into the glass, then gulped three large swallows directly from the bottle. She opened the refrigerator and removed a jar of Spanish olives. Ravenous, she fished several out of the jar and crammed them into her mouth. She put three more olives into the glass and added another two fingers of vodka to cover them. She opened a different cupboard, considered the bottle of vermouth inside, looked back at the glass of vodka and olives, and closed the cupboard. She carried the glass, the bottle of frozen vodka, and the jar of olives into the living room. She settled onto the white linen upholstered sofa, placed her refreshments on the embossed leather chest that served as a cocktail table, and clicked on the TV.

Kingston Fauler was hammering Sprinklegate with everything he had. There was a panel of seventeen media and political strategy experts seated at the table alongside him. The anchor went deftly from one to the next, exploring every possible angle, while the clever producers at 24/7 intercut the comments with looped footage of the dishes of ice cream in front of the little boy and the president. Urgent lettering at the bottom of the screen spelled out phrases such as ABUSE OF OFFICE, CONSTITUTIONAL CRISIS, and COUNTDOWN TO IMPEACHMENT.

Having spent the afternoon in a state of intense anxiety, Majedah felt drained. She clicked a button and a cheery fire sprang up in the hearth beneath the television. In the enormous windows that flanked the fireplace and television, lights in New Jersey twinkled from across the Hudson River, beyond the darkness of the park. Airplanes glimmered like shooting stars across the twilight sky. Majedah teased the last olive from the bottom of the jar, refilled the glass, settled back into the cushions, and at last began to feel at ease.

The news cycle would stay relentlessly focused, and other industries would conduct themselves appropriately to amplify the narrative. She could sense the flawlessly coordinated, invisible workings of mighty institutional machinery that ran all day and all night, incessantly, forever weaving the spell of manufactured reality on all of America. She could feel the bedrock security of a system so massive, pervasive, and entrenched that nothing could ever put a dent in it. Her foolish error of that afternoon had been disappeared as easily and completely as a speck of dust flicked from the gleaming paint of a high-speed light rail engine.

Majedah took a moment to be grateful that she was a part of this system, safe on the inside, accepted and protected, righteous and pure.

At eight o'clock, Carol Crawford's show came on. The masterful anchor got right down to business, opening with a declaration. "Tonight on *An Hour of Your Time*, we have a shocking interview. Here in the studio with me is Shania Travers, a culinary specialist who was one of the catering staff working in the White House kitchen when the controversial treats were being dished out. Shania, thank you so much for joining me this evening."

The image cut to a medium shot that showed both Carol and her guest, a thirty-something woman with multiple thick braids gathered back into a long ponytail and skin dark enough to grant unquestionable credibility to anything she might say. "My pleasure, Carol. I'm just so glad to have the opportunity to get what happened out into the open."

"Oh, this will be good," said Majedah.

"Shania, what was your responsibility while you were working in the White House kitchen that fateful day? Were you actually working with the frozen treat?"

Shania nodded enthusiastically. "I was."

"And were you scooping ice cream?" Carol conducted the interview with the incisive skill of a $900-an-hour trial attorney.

"No, in fact, I was one of the technicians charged with adding the sprinkles to the plated ice cream." Shania's voice was pleasant yet decisive, and her eye contact with Carol was direct and honest. She was an outstanding witness.

"Oh, this is so good!" squealed Majedah. She took a deep swig from her glass without breaking visual contact with the screen.

Carol leaned slightly forward in her chair, inconspicuously emphasizing the importance of her next question. "Shania, did you place the sprinkles on the president's dish of ice cream?"

"I did not, but I was standing next to the technician who did. We were sharing the same container of sprinkles. You know, I would dip my spoon in and then he—"

"—or she," interrupted Carol.

"—or she," Shania agreed.

"As you know, the worker in question has gone into protective custody, to prevent any tampering in advance of his or her crucial testimony," clarified Carol. "Congress isn't taking any chances."

"Yes, of course," agreed Shania. "So, as I was saying, we were both there, working, putting sprinkles on the ice cream dishes. All of a sudden, one of the servers came back into the kitchen and went right up to this technician, and said, and I quote, 'President Nelson asked for extra sprinkles on his ice cream. Can you set that up for him?'"

Carol reared back in her chair, her face a picture of disgust and horror. "'*Can you set that up for him?*'" she repeated.

Shania nodded emphatically. "Yes, ma'am, that's just what the server said. 'Can you set that up for him.'"

Words began flashing across the bottom of the screen. DAMNING EYEWITNESS ACCOUNT, then WITNESS SAYS NELSON INTERFERED WITH TREAT PREP, then SERVER: 'CAN YOU SET THAT UP FOR HIM?'

On her cushy linen sofa, Majedah felt nauseated. "My god, the monster! The absolute, horrible, monstrous monster!" she exclaimed. If anyone had been in the room with her, they might have noticed her words sounded rather slurred. But to Majedah, the situation could not have been clearer.

On the screen, Carol was shaking her head in disbelief. She put her hand to her ear, then the screen flashed red with the familiar BREAKING NEWS graphic and sound effects. After a few seconds, Carol's face once again filled the screen, with the red-outlined white words BREAKING NEWS at the bottom of the screen.

"This just in," reported Carol. "The House of Representatives has just voted on a special action. We go live to our Washington correspondent, Marcia Rodriguez."

The image cut to a woman with blown-out dark hair. She was wrapped in a dark overcoat with the collar popped against the chill, and she stood in the D.C. twilight with the Capitol building lit up behind her. She began to speak into her hand-held mic. "Thank you, Carol. I'm live in front of the Capitol where moments ago, the House of Representatives voted to appoint a special prosecutor to look into the Sprinklegate scandal."

Footage of the vote taking place appeared on the screen, with the caption "Earlier this evening" in the upper left corner. Marcia continued speaking over the scene. "The vote occurred mostly along party lines, but with enough Republicans crossing over to carry the motion. Representative Heimbecker was among them."

The screen changed to footage from just before the vote, showing a representative making an argument at the podium. Beneath him was the identification, *Roger Heimbecker, R-ME*. "I think it's important to get to the bottom of this," said Representative Heimbecker. "Let's have an investigative prosecutor look into the matter. I think what he or she will find is what we've been saying all along: that President Nelson may not have done the wisest thing optically, but that he was certainly within his Constitutional powers to do it."

Marcia appeared again, this time with a Congressman at her side. "Carol, I'm here with Representative Mark Offnin of the great state of Washington. Congressman, what can you tell us about this vote and what it means going forward?"

She held the mic in front of an overcoated representative who was the very image of righteousness in action. "Good evening, Carol," he said. "So, what this historic vote means is that there is enough evidence to merit a special, independent investigation of the president's decision to abuse his office to enrich himself, and possibly his illicit contacts in foreign nations as well."

"Wow, another bombshell," observed the DC reporter. "There may have been collusion with foreign governments? This definitely sounds like something that needs to be investigated."

Congressman Offnin nodded. "Indeed. So, we have taken the historic step of voting to appoint a special Super-Duper Investigative Prosecutor."

"A Super— what?"

"A Super-Duper Investigative Prosecutor. This will be someone with a long, bipartisan history of being above reproach who can take a clear-eyed deep dive into what went down. The S-DIP reports to no one and is authorized to hire anyone he or she wants to assist in the investigation, to do anything, go anywhere, look at anything, take unlimited time, spend unlimited funds, and subpoena anyone without concern about ever being questioned or, God forbid, criticized."

Marcia nodded vigorously. "Sounds like just what is needed to get to the bottom of this latest scandal from an already scandal-plagued White House and decide what charges, if any, are appropriate."

"Absolutely," concurred Representative Offnin. "If all goes as we suspect it will, impeachment proceedings should begin about a month before Election Day this November and will drag on through the rest of the year, at least."

"What a tragedy, to have this much corruption concentrated in the people's White House. I look forward to covering the proceedings here in Washington. Thank you, Congressman Offnin."

"You bet." With a nod, the representative turned and walked off to be interviewed by the next reporter in the pecking order.

Marcia looked directly into the camera. "Back to you, Carol."

From the comfort of her sofa, Majedah raised her glass to her colleagues. "We've got him now," she mumbled. Basking in the halcyon glow of her TV screen, she drank a generous toast to the good guys.

Chapter 14

IT DIDN'T TAKE long. At 11 o'clock the next morning, the staff at the illustrious News 24/7 Manhattan headquarters was gathered around the massive screen in the main conference room in anticipation of President Nelson's hastily announced Rose Garden address.

When the president at last approached the podium, there were scattered hisses and boos from around the room. Then the 24/7 employees noticed that the First Lady was beside him, and the president himself looked awful, as though he hadn't slept in days. Heavy makeup couldn't conceal the dark bags beneath his eyes, and his hair appeared to have gone several shades whiter since the ice cream social two days earlier. The watchers grew silent, wondering what President Nelson was going to say. The clicking of countless camera shutters was near deafening through the conference room speakers.

The President took a moment to glance down at his prepared remarks. He turned to his wife, who gave him a look of love and support. Then he drew a deep breath, fixed the nation with a lugubrious look, and began speaking. "My fellow, Americans," he said. "Two days ago, I made an awful, terrible mistake."

"He's going with an apology," someone called excitedly from somewhere in the conference room.

"As many of you know, my intent was only to hold a special function to honor and thank the children of our servicemen and women who are deployed for long periods of time, serving the American people."

Closer to Majedah, a tart producer sniped, "I can't believe he's trying to wrap himself in the flag right now."

"Yeah, yuck," agreed someone else.

"While performing my duties as host of this event, I am afraid I let my position of authority go to my head and in one terrible, unguarded moment, I made a deeply regrettable error in judgment."

Majedah huffed in disbelief. "An 'error in judgment'? More like a high crime!"

"I know, right?" agreed Ashley, another Pool reporter.

"Shh, I'm trying to enjoy this," snapped Carol Crawford's assistant, Max.

There were chuckles all around then the room grew silent again except for the president's broadcast.

"I want to assure everyone that I have already taken steps to repair some of the damage caused by my reckless behavior. Linda and I—" The First Lady gave her husband's arm a squeeze. "—have created a foundation, the Sweets Foundation, which will be dedicated to supplying schools in underprivileged neighborhoods with enough sprinkles for their ice cream so that young African-American and *Latino*-American children, regardless of their immigration status, will have the same quality dessert treats as the children of privilege throughout our great nation."

The First Lady began clapping her hands, glancing around at the audience of service members and staffers as she did so. A smattering of polite applause sounded from several friendly pockets, but it could barely compete with the pitiless flashes and shutter clicks raining onto the president's presser of shame.

President Nelson continued. "I also want to assure all Americans that I am deeply sorry, and that I deeply regret what I did. I have voluntarily sought out counseling from leaders of the nation's most highly recognized civil rights and ethics watchdog organizations, and I will be immersing myself in an extensive program of sensitivity training and reorientation. I want to ensure my fellow citizens that I am taking every possible precaution to make sure nothing like this ever happens again."

As the roomful of America's finest journalists watched triumphantly, the president took an extraordinary step. He looked to his wife, who nodded that he should continue. Then he came out from behind the podium, clasped his hands in front of him and looked into the 24/7 camera with tears streaming from his eyes. "What can I say? I was wrong. Please, America. Please, please, please forgive me." In the emotionless whir of clicks and flashes, the president fell to his knees, stretched his arms out in front of him, pointed his posterior to the sky, and buried his face in the grass. His sob-choked words were picked up by a directional mic aimed by a quick-thinking 24/7 reporter on the scene. "Please! Forgive me! I'm so, so sorry. Please don't hate me."

There was a moment of awed silence in the conference room. Then a cheer went up.

A group of copywriters near Majedah began to plan excitedly among themselves. "I get to write the story about the president admitting he's wrong," shouted one.

"Boo, I wanted that one."

"I'm sure there will be room for more than one," assured another. "We're not called '24/7' for nothing."

"I can do one about how the Nelsons' foundation drives obesity in minority children."

"Nice!"

"I'll do follow up with the pollsters and get the 'plummeting approval' story together."

Majedah smiled at the powerful spirit of creativity as she gathered her things. Then she streamed out of the room along with her energized, optimistic colleagues to get back to work. It was going to be a busy day!

But first, the Pool reporters headed to the Buzz for a celebratory lunch. Majedah's rooftop micro-farmed local greens salad with yak-ewe pink cheddar crumbles was only enhanced by the view of the establishment's multiple television screens; wherever she looked, the image of the weeping, prostate president filled her eyes. Before long, a bottle of gluten-free prosecco appeared at the table and the bright, young reporters toasted the never-ending war for truth.

Back at her desk, Majedah received a phone call from one of the interns. "Rosemary would like you to come to her office," said the young woman.

"Me? Are you sure?" Majedah couldn't think of anything she had done wrong.

"I'm pretty sure you're the only Majedah Cantalupi-Abromavich-Flügel-Van Der Hoven-Taj Mahal we have."

Majedah laughed nervously. "Okay, you got me. I'll be right over."

She stood shakily and smoothed her short pencil skirt over her thighs. She did a mental inventory of her outfit: tailored blouse, fashion belt, black skirt and hose with knee-high leather boots, three-inch heel. Professional enough to go live at a moment's notice. She patted her hair: blown out just that morning by one of the station stylists with time on her hands between guests. She breathed into her cupped palm and took a whiff: breath fresh from her after-lunch tooth brushing. All seemed to be in order.

Melissa had noticed Majedah's preparations. "Where are you going?" she asked.

"Rosemary's office." Majedah's voice trembled annoyingly.

Melissa gave her a smile of encouragement. "Don't be frightened," she said. "Maybe it's for something good."

It turned out to be something Majedah could never have predicted.

"Majedah, you've been requisitioned to go down to Wycksburg to interview someone," said Rosemary. The order was issued in her customary authoritative tone and with her usual direct look.

Questions began to swarm Majedah's brain. "Who am I supposed to interview?"

"Patty Clark, Founder and CEO of the Jamaica Patty's Corporation."

"Patty Clark?"

"She was the unarmed woman of color whose abuse at the hands of a white police officer you famously reported."

"Yes, of course." But Majedah was still just as baffled. "What am I interviewing her about?"

"She's holding a presser tomorrow morning outside her corporate headquarters to make a major announcement, after which she has granted one, single, exclusive interview. To us."

"Wow, how did we get so lucky?"

"Because you were specifically requested to conduct it," Rosemary revealed.

"Me?" Majedah was more baffled than ever. "Why me?"

"We didn't ask. Doesn't matter. All I know is that the call came in from the owner-operator of our Wycksburg affiliate."

"Norma Troutstein?"

"Yes, your old boss, apparently."

Majedah shook her head to clear it but remained profoundly confused. "I didn't think she'd ever want to see me again," she mumbled.

"Well, she's the one who called and said it had to be you."

"Okay." Majedah's mind was racing, trying to put it all together. Rosemary stared at her, waiting for her next question. "Well, what's the announcement Ms. Clark is going to make?" wondered Majedah.

Rosemary looked amused. "Get this: apparently, she's going to run for President of these yere yoo-nited states." The woman could affect a wicked redneck accent when she wanted to.

Majedah laughed incredulously. "What? Are you kidding? Is this some kind of joke?"

"Nope."

"I thought Angela Harper was as good as nominated by now. What chance does Patty Clark think she has?"

"Oh, she's not running for the Democratic nomination." Rosemary's grin grew wider.

"But she's a woman of color..."

"And she's challenging incumbent President Nelson for the Republican nomination."

"What?" Majedah's eyes crossed momentarily in her confusion. "She's a Republican? With no political background? And she's challenging a sitting president?"

"Yes, yes, and yes." Rosemary chuckled at Majedah's perplexion. "That's right, just let that sink in."

Majedah did, and an ugly realization blossomed. "Okay, I get it. It's a joke, a silly, absurd joke. And I'm being punished for my mistake the other day by being made to look ridiculous."

But Rosemary's expression became serious. "On the contrary, you are being entrusted with the launch of an extremely important new narrative," she explained.

"Please, Rosemary. I don't want to be confused anymore. Just explain to me what's going on and what you need me to do."

"Okay, here's the deal. Our research department did some preliminary looking into Patty Clark's background. Turns out she's pretty far to the right. I mean, way to the right; think Mussolini or Hitler."

Majedah's mouth hung open in wonder. "That far right? And we want to give her a platform?"

"Oh, yes, we very much want to give her a platform. In fact, we want to launch her campaign as far and as high as we can. We want her to become a viable-seeming alternative to President Nelson."

"But why?"

"To outflank him."

"Oh."

Rosemary nodded as she watched Majedah begin to catch on. "Let's face it, Majedah, it's Angela's turn to be president. It's far past time we had a vagina in the oval office, and America knows it. And thanks to 24/7's amazing investigative reporting, we can count on Nelson being under an investigative cloud and perhaps even on trial as we go into the final week of the election. You would think we have this one in the bag."

"Totally," agreed Majedah.

"Right, but you can't get complacent. Don't forget that this country is still full of racists and farmers and hillbillies and Nazis, and they've been known to come out and vote in big enough numbers to derail the inevitable before."

"That's true."

They both were silent for a moment, remembering the great debacle in the recent past.

"So, we need to be sure," continued Rosemary. "We need to cover our bases."

"And we think Patty Clark will get the hillbillies excited?" asked Majedah. "Are you sure it will work? I mean, after all, she has a vagina."

"Look how much those yokels loved Sarah Palin, though," Rosemary reminded her.

"True. But Patty Clark is also black." Majedah covered her mouth in shock at her own misspeak. "I mean, African-American."

Rosemary didn't seem to notice her blunder. "And look how much those yokels love that crazy black sheriff out West," she said. "Majedah, they're hypocritical, stupid people. Consistency is not their strong suit."

"True."

"If Patty Clark walks like a Nazi and talks like a Nazi, they'll vote for her in the primary. Or at least enough of them will to draw off enough support for Nelson that he will lose his base."

"But she's a joke. She won't actually be on the general election ballot," Majedah reminded her.

"She doesn't need to be. She only needs to campaign for the nomination, to run against Nelson and debate him and force him to move to the center to differentiate himself from her."

"... And turn off his base voters in the process!" said Majedah. She gave a laugh of delight. "Brilliant."

"I told you before, we don't fuck around here."

"I guess not." Majedah was ready to get to work. "So, you want me to go down there, interview her, and actually make her look good?"

"Make her look good to the far right, anyway."

A new concern niggled at Majedah. "Aren't we worried that this could make 24/7 look bad? We don't want to get kicked off the morning call or anything."

"We already ran it past Juan," Rosemary assured her. "The DNC is fully on board with this. All the teams will be briefed on tomorrow morning's call."

"Great." Possibilities began to dawn on Majedah. "I can play up the fact that Clark has a vagina, to get Republican women excited to vote for a woman. Then when Nelson gets the nomination, we may even be able to bring over some disgruntled Republican women to vote for Angela."

"Good thinking! I like it," Rosemary complimented her. "And being pro-vagina will also help explain your support for Patty Clark, so the yokels won't suspect that you have an ulterior motive."

And I can build up more vagina cred so one day, I can take over Carol's desk, thought Majedah to herself. She offered Rosemary her most professional smile. "When's my flight?"

NORMA LOOKED EXACTLY the same. She also didn't look especially pleased to see Majedah, but she stood straight with her hands jammed into the pockets of her parka and acknowledged her former employee's presence with a nod. "Majedah," she said.

Majedah had spent the night in her room at Wycksburg's best-ranked hotel (only a four-star, but Majedah was a professional and made do) bracing herself for hostility from the PDQ station boss. She lifted her chin in a defiant posture. "Norma," she answered.

They were standing in front of the Jamaica Patty's, Inc. corporate headquarters, an enormous office building fashioned of aqua and yellow poured concrete that commanded a theme park-like campus on one of the service roads that bordered Wycksburg. The grounds were meticulously cared for, with sweeping lawns (still mostly brown at the end of winter) punctuated with life-size palm tree replicas. There was even an artificial lake of Caribbean blue water, aerated by sparkling fountains and rimmed with imported white sand and more artificial palms. Norma and Majedah were among perhaps thirty reporters dispatched from various broadcast and print news organizations to cover the presser. Majedah scanned the crowd and concluded which people had been on that morning's conference call by their focused, self-consciously professional expressions, as opposed to the others who simply looked either baffled or outright amused at the preposterousness of the event.

Just in front of the entryway to the building, someone had set up a polished cherry wood podium, flanked by live potted banana plants. A cluster of branded microphones was affixed to the front of the podium and behind it hung a large sheet of Caribbean blue vinyl that was printed with the repeating words *Patty for President* and *America's CEO*.

Majedah glanced around for Jasper and spotted the PDQ camera being operated by an overweight, spotty young man whom she didn't recognize. She turned to Norma and asked, "Where's Jasper?"

Norma kept her eyes focused on the empty podium. "On assignment across town. He refused to work with you."

Majedah was surprised at how much the words stung. "Whatever," she said.

They stood side by side in the warming early spring morning, determinedly looking at the podium and not one another, silent among the hubbub of the press gaggle, waiting. After the cold silence between them had stretched into several minutes, Majedah spoke without turning her head. "I understand you requested me specifically to cover this event for 24/7, Norma."

Norma didn't turn her head either. "That's right, I did."

Majedah glanced at her former boss. "I must admit, I didn't expect that. Why did you want me to do it?"

"I didn't. She did." Norma nodded towards the doors to the office building, which were opening.

Two suited middle-aged men came out, glanced around at the crowd, and held the doors open. Next came Norris Clark, also in a suit and tie, and alongside him, Patty herself. Behind them ambled a retirement-aged couple, similar in appearance to Patty except white-haired and smaller, smiling brightly. Around them tumbled a troop of rambunctious children ranging in age from about four to 16. Several more people in various interpretations of business dress, presumably campaign executives, rounded out the delegation.

Unlike the only other time Majedah had seen Patty in person, today the restaurateur was dressed for business. She wore a black, broad shouldered, pinched waist jacket with a pencil skirt that ended well above the knee. The suit was clearly off the rack but sweet merciful heaven, the CEO was rocking it. Patty's long, stockinged legs were fitted into four-inch-heel, open-toe black platform pumps, in which the woman seemed to have no problem walking with her hip-slung stride. She made a beeline for the podium, treading with an almost predatory focus.

The crowd of reporters grew hushed and still. Patty exchanged a few words and nods with her campaign staff, turned to get a wink and a thumbs-up from her husband, then faced forward, placed a hand on each side of the podium, and began to speak.

Without preamble, without customary thanks for attending her presser, without greetings or niceties of any sort whatsoever, Patty Clark tore into her remarks. "Precisely 24 hours ago, in the Rose Garden of America's White House, the President of the United States disgraced himself and his office." She paused to allow her pronouncement to echo over the plaza and sink in.

A gasp went up from the gathered media professionals, Majedah among them. Everyone knew that President Nelson had done the first honorable thing of his presidency yesterday! Majedah glanced sidelong at Norma and was surprised to see the old news broad smiling and nodding.

Patty elaborated, enunciating each word. "We. Are. The. United. States. Of. America. The rest of the world looks to us for leadership, for strength and moral direction." Her voice was powerful and clear. "To see the spectacle of our freely elected chief executive prostrating himself on the ground, sobbing and begging, was horrifying. Not just for those of us whom he allegedly leads, but for peace-loving and vulnerable people around the world."

Patty paused again. The gaggle before the podium remained silent save for the clicks and flashes of the press reporters. But alongside the CEO, her little platoon clapped and hooted. Majedah knew that's what would show on camera.

"Do you know, I voted for him?" Patty went on. She nodded a couple times. "That's right, I voted for President Nelson. I'm a businesswoman, and I thought he'd be the best leader to help businesspeople like me. I thought he'd cut down on all the hoops I have to jump through and the graft I have to pay, just for the privilege of running my business. And I am sure he's been better than his opponent would have been, though not by much.

"But here's the thing: We are America. We are better than this. Electing someone simply because he will ruin the country slower than the other guy is not a real choice. We deserve better."

She paused again. The crowd remained silent, filming and recording, but Majedah could sense the mood shifting along with her own, from amused indulgence to anger. Nelson's opponent in the previous election would have been great for America, of course. Majedah began to deeply dislike Patty.

The brash CEO leaned back from her intense posture to look out over the podium. Her expression lightened. "When I was a young woman, still in high school, I went to work in my parents' restaurant," she related. "Back then, it was just a single storefront near the park, at the edge of the shopping district, with a deep fryer and a soda fountain. My parents worked very hard and they did okay. We had a place to live and decent clothes to wear to school and church. But I had all these new ideas. I said, 'Mama, why don't you add a couple things to the menu? Papa, why don't you ever paint this place? How about some new booths every twenty years or so?"

At her side, the older couple looked at one another and chuckled.

"I think I drove them crazy," said Patty.

The older man nodded his head vigorously. "Yes, she did," he said audibly. His accent was rich and warm, washing over the audience like a balmy Caribbean breeze.

Patty turned to give her parents a teasing smile, while Norris looked at them sympathetically. Patty's campaign organizers laughed, and Majedah even heard one or two titters from the press gaggle. She glared around at the crowd, trying to spot the dissidents.

Patty returned to her comments. "Finally, one day, my parents said, 'Patty, if you can do it so much better, why don't you just do it yourself?' And I thought to myself, 'Good question, Patty. Why don't you?'

"So, I did. My parents gave me a budget, I made my own plans, did my research, made contacts, assembled supplies, worked my butt off, got training, hired help when I needed it. The years went by, and I took my parents' wonderful little restaurant and built it into one of America's most successful businesses.

"And now, every day, I am thankful for the question my parents made me ask myself so many years ago; if I can do it so much better, why don't I?"

Patty stopped speaking and stood up straight. She drew in a deep breath, flaring her nostrils as she raked her audience with another of her focused, hawk-sharp looks. Then she leaned forward once more. "Today," she pronounced, "I think I can do a better job and I am ready to do it myself. Today, I announce my candidacy for the Republican nomination for President of the United States of America."

The cheering and applause from the campaign staffers and family all around Patty was rivaled by the cacophony of clicking shutters from the press. There were scattered claps and cheers from somewhere in the press pool; Majedah sighted one or two of the perpetrators. *Locals*, she thought to herself. She was momentarily shocked when Norma shouted out, "Run, Patty, run!"

After a moment, Patty began speaking again. "I invite everyone to visit my website, *PattyForPresident.org*, where you can find detailed information on all my positions, my campaign staff, my professional resume, and of course, how to donate to my campaign. Thank you for your attendance today." She stepped back from the podium, seemed to exhale deeply, and turned to her husband. A broad smile lit up her face as she lifted her open hands into the air beside her shoulders, a gesture that said, *Well, here we go*. He pulled her into a hearty hug. The mob of children gathered around the couple, jumping and hugging in excitement, while Patty's parents looked on with unfathomable pride.

The stunned reporters realized that the woman had ended the presser without taking any questions and began to call her name, trying to get her attention.

"Ms. Clark!"

"Ms. Clark!"

"Ms. Clark!"

Patty coolly ignored them all, turned to take her husband's arm with one hand and the small child's hand with the other, and led her contingent back towards the office building.

A tall, mustachioed man detached himself from Patty's party and went to the podium. Majedah smirked at his apparel; he wore a beige tweed blazer with honest-to-god suede elbow patches, what could only be described as "business jeans," a necktie made of string, pointy toed boots, and some sort of cowboy hat. He stepped up to the microphone array and addressed the clamoring reporters.

"At this time, I'd like to thank everyone for attending Ms. Clark's p-p-p-p. Ms. Clark's p-p-p-p-p-p-p-p-p." He gathered himself and began again. "I'd like to thank everyone for attending Ms. Clark's p-p-p-p-p-p-p-p-p-p-p."

Majedah, transfixed along with the rest of the assembled journalists, watched as the man's face contorted with effort. Her own mouth hung open and she leaned forward in an unconscious effort to assist his speech.

The man pushed his wide-brimmed hat back, wiped his forehead with his palm, and pulled the hat down on his brow again. Thus refreshed, he leaned to the microphones once more. "Thank you for attending CEO Clark's p-p-p-p-p-p-p-p-p. For attending CEO Clark's p-p-p-p-p-p-p-p-p-p-p-p."

No one in the audience made a peep or moved a muscle. Frozen, they all waited for the man to say whatever it was he was trying to say.

"Thank you for attending today's pr-pr-pr-pr-r-r-r. Today's p-p-p-pr-pr-pr-r-r-r-r-r-r-rrrrrrr. Today's pr-pr-pr-r-r-r-rrrrr-RRRRRR! Today's pr-pr-pr-prrrrrrrRRRRR! Today's presser!"

An audible murmur of relief went up from the crowd, with Majedah contributing a loud exhalation. The respite was short lived, however, as the speaker proceeded with additional remarks.

"CEO Clark is n-n-n-n-n-n. CEO Clark is n-n-n-n-n-n-nnnnn. Ms. Clark is n-n-n-n-not taking any q-q-q-q-q-q-q-q-questions to-today. Again, I'd like to refer everyone to our we-we-we-we-we-we-wwwwwwwweeee-w-website, where all information about M-M-M-M-M-Ms. Clark's p-p-p-p-p. Ms. Clark's p-p-p-p-p-p-p-p-p-p-p-p-platform and background can be found."

Majedah quickly glanced at her watch before looking back at the speaker.

"The w-w-w-w-w-w-w-w-w-w-w-w-w-w-we. We-we-we-WEEEEEEEEbsite is available to everyone, not just the m-m-m-m-m-m-m-m-m-m-m-mmmmmmmm-m-m-m-media, but to every American, to read and f-f-f-f-f. F-f-f-f-f-f-f-form their own opinions." The troublesome words out of the way, the man fixed the audience with a significant look. There was nothing to impede the force of his inspection, and Majedah involuntarily dropped her eyes when his gaze swept over her. Then he turned to follow his associates into the office building.

A voice piped up from the front of the press gaggle. "Sir, please, one moment. Sir!"

Majedah recognized the voice of an ambitious young reporter from a regional news service. As she located him in the crowd, she saw a producer next to him punch him in the arm.

But it was too late; the mustachioed man turned back to the podium. "Y-y-y-y-y-y-y-y-y-y-y-y. Y-y-y-y-y-yeeeeeeeeEEE! Y-y-y-y-y-yes? W-w-w-what is it?" he asked.

The audience of media professionals groaned. But the reporter rubbed his bruised arm and proceeded with his question. "Sir, who are you?"

"Name's Vic Waveny, son. I'm Ms. Clark's p-p-p-p-p-p-p-p-p-p. P-p-p-p-p-p-p-p-p-p-p-p-p-p-p-p-p. I'm Ms. Clark's p-p-p-p-p-p-p-p-p-p-p-p-p-p-pr-pr-pr-pr-pr-prrrrrrrr. R-r-r-r-r-rrrrrrrrrr. Ms. Clark's p-p-p-p-p-p-p-p-pr-pr-prrrrrrrRRRRRR. Ms. Clark's p-p-p-p-p-p-p-p-P-P-P-P-P-P-P-P—"

Along with the rest of the reporters, Majedah grew alarmed at Vic Waveny's facial convulsions and increasingly blue complexion. Everyone leaned forward again, silently mouthing the repetitive percussive consonant along with him.

"P-P-P-P-P-P-P-p-p-p-p-p-p. Ms. Clark's p-p-p-p-p-pr-pr-pr-PRRRRRRRRRRRRR-ess secretary." Waveny's face immediately relaxed into its ruggedly handsome resting state. He stepped back with a grin. "Whoo, that was a bad 'un," he hooted. "'K, bye y'all." With a jaunty wave, he turned and strode briskly towards the entrance to the office building.

Norma and Majedah looked at one another dazedly. "Why am I here again?" asked Majedah.

Norma's brow pulled into a line. "Hm, the, um…"

Majedah recovered first. "The interview!" she said.

Norma snapped her fingers. "Yes, that's right; the exclusive interview of Presidential Candidate Patricia Clark." She gave Majedah a stern look. "Are you prepared?"

Majedah's chin lifted. "I most certainly am," she assured her former boss.

Norma turned to the pudgy, young cameraman. "Ready, Chad?"

"You bet, Norma."

"Then let's go."

INSIDE THE JAMAICA Patty's, Inc. corporate headquarters, Majedah and her associates were shown to a bright, spacious lounge to wait. The large room was already occupied by a number of people, including Patty Clark's parents and children. Majedah counted five of the latter, ranging from a mischievous, brown-skinned, brown-eyed little boy to a willowy young woman with frizzy blond ringlets and her mother's sharp, amber eyes and wide smile.

The children's grandmother set upon Majedah almost as soon as she entered the room. "I'm sure you could use something to eat," she started in. "You're skinnier than my own girls, and they're already much too thin." The woman's gnarled fingers had already fastened onto Majedah's viscose-sleeved elbow, and the reporter had to fight the urge to yank her arm away.

Majedah reminded herself of her mission and found a smile for the old fry cook. "Aren't you kind! No, thank you, I already ate at the hotel," she demurred.

"Oh, rubbish. Today we are celebrating. I have a lovely black cake I made for the occasion." The woman had drawn

Majedah through the cavorting children and chattering adults to a kitchenette area, where an array of home-cooked foods was spread across a countertop. "Come have a little plate of food, girl," she urged.

Majedah's breakfast had in fact consisted of six Alka-Seltzer tablets dissolved in a cup of green tea with a dash of agave syrup. The makeshift meal had stayed her most pressing symptoms—a splitting headache and enough acid to dissolve a body—but nausea was still a very real possibility.

Patty's mother released Majedah's elbow in order to hoist a plate of crispy whole fish in her face. "Have some snapper, then. Protein first, then dessert, hm?"

Odors of greasy fish and too many sharp spices assaulted Majedah's delicate nostrils. She couldn't help herself and reared back in alarm, holding up a hand to defend herself from the culinary assault. "No! Thank you," she added belatedly.

There was no mistaking the hurt in the older woman's eyes, but she never lost her hospitable demeanor. "Okay, then, I understand. Our other girl, she could never tolerate fish either. Nothing from the ocean, that's our Alice."

Majedah seized on the opening. "Yes, the ocean, that's it. I'm allergic to seafood. I can't eat a bite of it." She could only hope her face wasn't noticeably green.

A nine-year-old girl with a headful of bouncing dark ringlets nudged her way between the two women and snagged a whole fish from the plate. She took a huge bite and smiled a toothy grin at Majedah, the chunk of fish visible between her teeth.

"Oh, you, move along, Jessica," laughed her grandmother. As the older woman tousled the girl's curls, Majedah spotted a fridge.

"I'll just help myself. Thanks again," she said, edging past the child and grandmother.

She pulled open the door and found a Coke, which she carried to a roomy armchair on the far side of the room from the food. But she barely had time for a sip before Vic Waveny came into the room, made eye contact with Norma, and said, "Patty's ready for you guy n-n-n-n-n-n-n-n-n-n-N-N-N-NOWWWW." He flashed a manly grin and beckoned her.

"Oh, good," said Norma. She ditched the piled-high plate she had been working through on a table and looked around for her team. Chad the cameraman was already at her side, and Majedah gathered her things and got up to join them.

Vic led them down a hall and into a conference room. Most of the furniture had been removed to create a sort of makeshift studio. One wall had been hung with the blue seamless backdrop from the press conference, with the repeating words *Patty for President* and *America's CEO* in white lettering. Two sunny yellow kid leather armchairs had been placed in front of the backdrop, with a low, round mahogany table between them. A crew—whether from PDQ or Patty's campaign, Majedah didn't know—had already set up cameras, lighting and sound.

Vic stood back and let a stylist not much older than Majedah take control. The young woman smiled pleasantly as she addressed the reporter. "Hello, Ms. Taj Mahal, I'm—"

"It's Ms. Cantalupi-Abromavich-Flügel-Van Der Hoven-Taj Mahal," Majedah corrected her, politely but firmly.

"Sorry, of course. Ms. Cantalupi-Abromavich-Flügel-Van Der Hoven-Taj Mahal, hello. I'm Pauline. Will you please come sit in this chair?" The stylist intuited that she shouldn't touch Majedah unnecessarily, and she indicated the chair with an open hand.

Majedah set her handbag out of sight behind the chair, removed her laptop, which was loaded with interview questions, and sat down. The chair was every bit as comfortable as it looked, and she sank deep into its cushioned softness. She immediately pulled herself forward and perched on the edge of the seat in a more professional position.

Pauline stood back and appraised Majedah in the studio lighting. Then she bent at the waist to take a closer look. She gave Majedah's nose a couple tentative pats with a powder puff before simply smiling. "Ms. Cantalupi-Abromavich-Flügel-Van Der Hoven-Taj Mahal, you are so lucky. Your skin is flawless. Such tiny pores! And your eyes and lips look perfect in this light."

"Thank you," Majedah acknowledged. "After all, I am a professional reporter."

"Great. Well, you're all set."

Both women turned their heads as Patty Clark's voice sounded from the doorway. "Hello, everyone. Here I am," the CEO announced herself.

Norma went right up to Patty. Majedah observed the warmth of their greeting and deduced that they were already acquainted and friendly. She struggled out of the low, soft chair and went to be introduced.

Norma glanced at Majedah. "Patty, you remember Majedah, of course," she said.

"Yes, of course I do." Up close, the CEO's eyes were bright and keen, the yellow-hazel color particularly striking. Her wide, warm smile relaxed Majedah. "How could I forget the young woman who made me a national household name?"

Majedah's keen journalist instincts told her it would be wise to cultivate friendship with this woman, the better to draw her out and make her seem like a legitimate candidate. "It's great to meet you under more normal circumstances, Ms. Clark," she said.

Patty was indignant. "'Ms. Clark.' Oh, my goodness! Call me Patty, please."

As the interview began, Majedah had a rare moment of insecurity, wondering if she was reporter enough to conduct a believable interview that would appeal to America's Nazis and hillbillies. But it turned out to be easier than she thought because Patty Clark did all the work for her. Majedah would simply bring up a current topic and the CEO would go off on it.

On the current state of national leadership, Patty's tone varied from contempt to anger. When Majedah asked her what she thought of the health care bill working through Congress, she snapped, "What the hell is Nelson doing, quibbling over whether men should get free government tampons?" she raved. "*No one* should get free government tampons! Since when is it the government's job to provide sanitary products to anyone? Show me where in the Constitution it says that."

Fighting the comfy chair's powerful gravity, Majedah looked thoughtful and nodded as though Patty's opinions were completely valid. Envious of her interviewee's firmer seat, Majedah had to look up to make eye contact. "Ms. Clark, it's interesting that you mention tampons. I'd like to remind our viewing audience that you have a vagina."

For the first time during the interview, Patty seemed perplexed. "And what does that have to do with anything?" she asked.

Now it was Majedah's turn to be perplexed. "What does that have to do with anything? Why, it's one of your most important qualifications. Americans are demanding that we finally have a historic president with a vagina."

Patty's face settled back into the pissed-off expression she had worn for most of the interview. "Who cares if I have a vagina?" she demanded. "The important thing is that right now, I'm the only candidate with balls."

"Oh!" Majedah gasped in shock at the woman's outspoken misogyny. But she also instinctively knew that a sound bite like that would be a hit with the yokels. She quickly snapped back into professional mode, making a mental note to edit out her reaction later.

AFTER THE INTERVIEW was complete, the Clarks insisted Majedah and Norma join them for a celebratory late lunch. In a comfortable private dining room in one of Wycksburg's most exclusive clubs (*exclusive for Wycksburg, anyway,* thought Majedah to herself), the brilliant young reporter sat on a curved leather sofa at a roomy round table. Norma and Vic sat on one side of her, sipping Dark n' Stormy cocktails. On Majedah's other side sat the Clarks, with Norris's arm draped over Patty's shoulders and frosty mugs of beer in front of them. The boisterous group was laughing over the story of how Majedah had mistakenly reported that Norris had brutalized Patty.

With a salving Dark 'n Stormy already in her belly and another one on the table in front of her, Majedah laughed along with them. "I'm still horrified at the mix-up," she said. "You can see how it looked bad from where I was standing."

"Sure, I can see that," agreed Norris.

"Once you got past the gang war erupting all around you," added Patty. "But whatever. Before your video went viral, the only people who knew my name were other business owners and suppliers. Now everyone knows who I am. You can't buy that kind of name recognition. And without name recognition, this campaign wouldn't have a chance." She leaned forward to hoist her mug. "Here's to the power of your reporting, Majedah."

"May it power Patty's campaign all the way to Washington D.C.," added Norma.

They clinked their glasses and toasted. Norris signaled the waiter for another round.

Majedah read through the menu several times before settling on whole grain avocado toast with beet and blood orange salad.

Once everyone had ordered, she set about learning as much of Patty Clark's background as she could. She turned to Patty and Norris with her most charming smile and asked, "So, where did you two meet?"

"Basically, Patty lured me in with her delicious food," explained Norris. "Once she had upgraded her folks' restaurant, she opened a second one herself, the one over near downtown. I was new on the job then, and the cops all knew that Jamaica Patty would give us some of those delicious spicy meat pies for free."

"You gave the cops free food?" asked Majedah.

"Oh, yes," Patty confirmed. "You've seen that neighborhood. Now picture me and maybe one or two other kids working there at night. Anything we could do to bring the cops around, we did it."

Inside, Majedah bridled at the couple's casual racism. Everyone knew that "bad neighborhood" was hate code for underprivileged societal victims. But she was a professional and she stuck to her mission; whatever she could do to gain these people's trust, she would do it. "So, let me guess," she said brightly to Norris, "pretty soon you were coming around for more than just the free food."

Norris's gaze was friendly and open as he chatted. Majedah was fascinated in spite of herself, never having had a conversation with an actual law enforcement officer before. His brown eyes softened as he recalled the past. "Well, there was this one really pretty girl who worked there, and she had the most amazing eyes and this great, big, sweet smile. So, yeah, after a while I was coming there to see her."

On Majedah's other side, Vic piped up. "And f-f-for the f-f-f-f-f-f-fr-fr-fr-fr-fRRRRRRRRRR-fr-fr-fr-fr-fRRRRRREEEEEEEEEEEEEEEE f-f-f-f-f-f-f-f-f-f. And for the fr-fr-

fr-fr-fr-FR-FREEEEEEEEEEEEEEEEEE   f-f-f-f-f-f-f-f-f-f-f-f-f-f-
f-f-f-f-f-f-f-f-f-f—"

"Jesus Christ, Vic, put your earpiece in," Patty said with a
scowl.

Vic held up a finger. "Good th-th-th-thinking." He dug into his
jacket pocket and pulled out a small device, which he inserted
into his left ear. He switched it on, took a breath, and began
again. "And for the fr-free food!"

"I mean, I suppose that would have been funny if your timing
was a little better," Norris deadpanned.

"Come on, guys, this is quality material," said press secretary.

"Keep the day job, Vic," Norma advised him. She swigged the
rest of her Dark n' Stormy and held up the empty mug for the
waiter to see.

"Wait a minute, what did he just put in his ear?" Majedah
asked.

"That's his DAF earpiece," explained Norris. "Delayed
Auditory Something-or-other. It plays his speech back to him on
a slight delay and tricks him into not stuttering."

Across the table, Vic nodded in agreement with Norris's
explanation.

"So why don't you just wear it all the time?" asked Majedah.

"I'm much funnier without it," said Vic with a grin.

Norma cracked up. Majedah had never seen people laugh
openly at a differently abled person and had no idea what to say,
so she just smiled and turned to her hosts. "Patty, were you born
here in Wycksburg?"

"Born and raised," the candidate confirmed.

"Your older sister, too? Alice, right?"

"Yes, both of us. Born in Wycksburg Hospital. Went to St.
Lucy Catholic and Wycksburg High. Visited family in Jamaica on
vacations, when we could afford it, helped our parents in the
restaurant when we were old enough."

"And what does Alice do now?" inquired Majedah.

"Drugs, mostly."

"Oh, that's too bad."

"Yeah, well, what can you do."

She seemed resigned to the situation, so Majedah moved on. "Patty, I understand you took Norris's last name when you married him. What was your name before that?"

Norris huffed out a chuckle as Patty answered. "It was also Clarke, but with an 'e' at the end."

"That's a great name," declared Majedah. "Why didn't you hyphenate your last name?"

"Are you kidding?" asked Patty. "Clarke-Clark? Everyone would think I talked like Vic."

Vic snarfed his beer and everyone else laughed—everyone but Majedah. She couldn't believe the insensitivity of these people, laughing at a man's disablility. She remembered to play along and produced a rueful chuckle, but to herself she vowed that brutes such as these must never be anywhere near the levers of power.

Chapter 15

THE PRODUCERS AT News 24/7 cut Majedah's interview with Patty Clark into five segments. By running a different segment each day, they managed to keep the interview alive for a week. Patty's profile was raised markedly, and Majedah's name recognition rose along with it.

Two days after the first segment aired, the 24/7 broadcast team gathered for the morning meeting, where they heard updates about Patty Clark's candidacy. First, the social media team reported that Patty's soundbite—"I'm the only candidate with balls"—was the number one .gif shared on the Internet. "We didn't even have to write an algorithm to make it happen," wondered the Silicon Valley wiz on the call. "People just keep sharing it on their own."

This prompted a round of bawdy laughter from everyone in the conference room and on the call. "How crude," they all exclaimed. "So *not* presidential."

Next, the financing team reported that they were creating new, ostensibly right-wing non-profits daily and funneling money through them to help fund Patty's campaign. So far, they had already added 10.2 million dollars to her war chest.

Then the pollsters reported their preliminary numbers; Patty had debuted with support from 36 percent of eligible

Republican primary voters, versus 62 percent who intended to vote for Nelson. The campaign was off to a brilliant start.

When the call ended, Rosemary caught Majedah's eye across the expanse of conference table and said in a loud voice, "Kudos to our humble Pool reporter, Majedah, for the amazing job she did with this interview. Congratulations, Majedah. You made a Wycksburg fry cook look like a viable presidential candidate to the nation's wingnuts!" She clapped, and everyone joined in to cheer and applaud the gifted young journalist. Majedah acknowledged their adulation with a serene nod.

In her Upper West Side apartment the following evening, Majedah dined on a market bowl of thinly sliced rare soy steak, golden avocado, mango chutney, and scallions on a bed of ancient Ulu grains. She paused to sip her chilled Brooklyn distillery vodka and turn on the television. In the mood to gloat, she flipped to Eagle Eye News and sure enough, Roy Cader was crowing about having presidential candidate Patty Clark on his show right after the break.

"Playing catch-up, Cader?" smirked Majedah. "Sorry, only one journalist was granted the exclusive announcement interview." She shoveled food into her mouth until the commercials ended and the segment began.

Roy Cader seemed genuinely excited to introduce his guest. "Joining Eagle Eye News tonight via satellite from her newly opened campaign headquarters in Wycksburg, Virginia, is Ms. Patty Clark. Ms. Clark, it's great to have you with us again."

The screen split between Roy and Patty. The candidate looked earthy and attractive in a soft, camel jersey sweater with a neckline just low enough to tease a hint of the swell of her breasts.

"Ha, what a throwback," snickered Majedah. "No self-respecting woman looks *feminine* anymore, Patty."

But Patty's appearance seemed to be charming Roy Cader as she smiled and said, "Thanks, Roy. It's good to be back on Eagle Eye."

"Patty, the last time we spoke, a hapless competitor of Eagle Eye News had mistakenly broadcast that you were in trouble with the police, but nothing could have been further from the truth."

Majedah simmered. "Go to hell, Cader," she shouted at the smug anchor.

"Yes, Roy, that's true," confirmed Patty. "But it all turned out well, because when I decided to make this run for office—"

"This *historic* run for office," Roy corrected her.

Patty giggled. "Okay, Roy, this *historic* run for office."

"We can never forget to remind everyone how *historic* your candidacy is," lectured Roy.

Majedah hated it when Cader spoke like this, because it always sounded like he was mocking her and everyone she knew. She narrowed her eyes at the screen, teeth bared, as the obnoxious anchor prattled on in his bizarre British hillbilly accent.

"You're a woman, the first woman to run for the Republican nomination, and the first African-American woman to run for either party's nomination. These things are very important, I'm told."

On the right side of the screen, Patty was laughing. "Oh, yes, very important," she said. "My physical characteristics—very important."

Once again, Majedah began to deeply dislike her.

"But anyway, by the time I decided to run," Patty went on, "my name already sounded familiar to people, which allowed me to make great headway in gaining ground quickly."

"And indeed, you have been gaining a great deal of ground quite quickly," said Roy. "In fact, a new Eagle Eye poll has just come out, and it has you at 42 percent against President

Nelson's 56 percent among likely Republican primary voters. That's simply amazing, given that you've just sort of come out of nowhere with your campaign."

"What can I say? My message is resonating. I knew I couldn't possibly be the only American thinking these things," said Patty.

"You're not, not by a long shot," agreed Roy. "But tonight, we're hearing from White House attorneys who assure us that you can't possibly succeed with your campaign to unseat President Nelson for the Republican nomination because of a serious technical issue. Namely, you're not on any primary ballots and it's too late for you to get onto any primary ballots. Some states have already held their primaries, in fact."

"Yes, this is an obstacle, to be sure," Patty concurred. "And we can't do anything about the handful of states that have already had their primaries." Her expression, however, was anything but defeated. "But I didn't get where I am today by giving up and doing what I'm told. I'm a successful businesswoman precisely because I don't give up. When people tell me I can't do something, I have to prove them wrong.

"I have lawyers, too, Roy," Patty continued. "And my lawyers have been studying the situation on a state-by-state basis to see what can be done. If there's a loophole, they've found it and put together a plan to get me on the ballot. And in states where they can't get me on the ballot, we're going to be running a robust and sophisticated write-in campaign."

Her glass of vodka suspended halfway between the tabletop and her mouth, Majedah laughed incredulously at the screen.

Even Roy seemed unconvinced. "While I wish you the best, Patty, this seems unlikely to succeed. No one has ever done anything like this and succeeded before," he said.

"That's because you're talking about politicians," Patty explained. "Politicians don't know how to actually get anything done."

"But you do, I assume?" queried Roy.

"Obviously, I do. I've run a business since I was a teenager. I've gotten things done that you can't imagine. I've gone up against zoning laws, import-export statutes, health food fads, busybody dietary boards, FDA regulations, banking executives, competitors, litigators ... You wouldn't believe what I've had to go through, around, under, and over to make my business succeed. But I have always succeeded. And I will succeed at the polls, too."

Majedah shook her head. "Good luck with that, Patty," she said. Then she allowed her glass of vodka to complete the journey to her lips, where it was met with great enthusiasm.

THE POOL REPORTERS were hard at work, surfing the Internet for rumors and theories to develop into new narrative threads. At one point, Muhammed got up and left his desk to skulk off in the direction of the all-gender-inclusive facilities. Once he was out of sight, Melissa turned to her neighbor and said, "Hey, Majedah, are you auditioning for the Islamophobia Desk?"

Majedah had been reading a treatise about feminist feminism, but her attention was immediately riveted on Melissa's question. "I hadn't heard about that," she said cautiously. "Is there an opening?"

"That's what I heard," said the frizzy haired journalist. "The topic has always been covered by the Racism Desk up until now, but one of the researchers found an old video of Nelson claiming that a man-made disaster had been caused by an Islamist terrorist. He actually used that racist word, *Islamist*. So they're starting up a new narrative, that President Nelson is Islamophobic and incites Islamophobia. They think it's so important that they're breaking out a whole new desk to highlight incidents around the country up until the election."

Majedah nodded thoughtfully. "Makes sense," she said.

"Yeah," Melissa agreed. "And I figured that, because of your Middle Eastern background, you might be going for the seat."

"Of course I'm going for the seat," snapped Majedah. To herself, she thought, *It may not be the Women's Desk, but it is an upward move. And once I show them I can run my own desk, I'll be that much more obvious a choice for the Women's Desk … as soon as Carol slips up.*

"Right, I should have known you are," Melissa said apologetically. "So, you probably already told Rosemary and everything."

"I was just going to do that after I finish this research," Majedah informed her.

"Oh, okay. Well, don't forget; the interview panel is tomorrow at noon."

"I know," Majedah said.

"Right, of course. Okay then, good luck." Melissa looked around then leaned closer and whispered. "I don't think Mohammed is very nice. I hope you get it, Majedah."

Majedah favored her Pool-mate with a real smile. "Thanks, Melissa. I hope so, too." Then she heard her phone buzz, indicating a new email to her personal account. She swiveled back to her desk to see who had sent it.

As providence had it, the email was from her father, Ziyad Taj Mahal. It read:

Hi, Majedah. Guess what? I'm in NYC for a couple days at a conference, and I am free for dinner this evening. I'd love to see you and catch up if you are available. Sorry about the short notice. What do you say? Love, Dad

"What a great opportunity to brush up on my Middle Eastern roots," murmured Majedah to herself. She typed, *Sure, Dad, what time?* and hit Reply.

Then she returned to her laptop and opened a new search window. There was still time to do some opposition research on the competition before she met her father for dinner.

AT SEVEN THAT evening, Majedah stood in front of a high-end Lebanese restaurant in lower Manhattan, watching her father approach her on the sidewalk. Ziyad Taj Mahal was about the same height as Majedah, five-and-a-half feet tall. He stood erect with his slim shoulders back as he ambled up the sidewalk at a comfortable pace. He was clean shaven, and his hair was still mostly black, with just the right amount of grey at the temples. His intelligent eyes crinkled with pleasure as he approached his daughter.

"Majedah, how lovely you look," he exclaimed. His arms were already out for a hug, and Majedah stepped into them primly.

"Hello, Dad." She copied her father as he kissed first one cheek and then the other, and she made a mental note of the ethnic greeting ritual.

Inside the restaurant, Majedah and Ziyad shared a linen-draped table that was lit by an oil lamp. Majedah gazed at the ruby glints from the tiny flame as it glowed through her glass of Shiraz. Ziyad removed his reading glasses when a platter of baba ghannouj hit the table. He tore off a chunk of man'oushe and slathered it with the eggplant dip. He took a bite and gestured at his daughter with the half-eaten mezza. "Have some, Majedah," he suggested.

Majedah smiled sweetly. "After you, Dad." She sipped her wine and watched him load up another piece of flatbread.

"That was a great idea you had, to come here for dinner." Ziyad paused to wash down his appetizer with a swallow of wine before refilling both their glasses. "I was going to take you to Bistro Tek. Everyone says I simply *must* eat there while I'm in

New York. But this is great. I haven't had good Lebanese food in ages."

Majedah nodded and tipped her glass to her lips. At another gesture from her father, she placed a piece of the flatbread on her plate and added a dollop of dip. "Is this baba ghannouj as good as Teta used to make?" she asked, working hard to get the accent right on the foreign words.

Her father glanced up at her, surprised, then decided to be pleased at her interest in her heritage. "Almost," he said. He polished off the last piece on his plate and gazed longingly at the uneaten portion in front of his daughter before forcing his eyes back up. "But tell me, how do you like your job at 24/7? Impressive, especially for so soon out of college, I might add." He saluted her with his glass.

Majedah grinned modestly. "Thanks, Dad." She clinked her glass to his, and father and daughter toasted. Majedah took a healthy swig before answering. "It's really fun and exciting. But I'm still just a pool reporter, so there's nothing much to tell you at this point."

Ziyad smiled at her expectantly. "Okay, then, how about the apartment? Do you like it? Are you happy there?"

"Yes, Dad, it's beautiful. Thanks so much."

"Of course, sweetie. I know a humble pool reporter can't afford Manhattan rents, so I'm happy to help out until you make it big." He waited for her to elaborate, but as she simply swirled her wine around in her glass, he tried again. "Seeing anyone special? Anyone I should know about?" He grinned hopefully.

"Sorry to disappoint, but I haven't really been seeing anyone since I dated Kevin back in high school."

"Kevin! He was a good kid. How's he doing? You ever hear from him?"

Of course, he likes Kevin. Majedah had already grown tired of trying to have a conversation with her fascist father, but she reminded herself of her mission. "Every now and then. He's fine, working as a petro-something-or-other. But look, Dad, I'd really rather hear about how the family is doing back in Lebanon. What are they up to? What's life like for them?"

Ziyad gave her a curious look again. "You and I haven't had a chance to catch up face-to-face in a few years, and you want to hear about your relatives in Lebanon whom you haven't seen since you were a child? How come?"

Majedah avoided his eyes by looking around the room. "I don't know. I've just been thinking about them lately."

After a beat, Ziyad decided to humor her and shrugged. As she had hoped, the wine and ethnic food had gotten him into a mood to muse on his family origins. "Okay. Well, let's see. ... Your Aunt Maryam has been going crazy lately." A grin tugged at the corners of his mouth. "Her neighbor's goats keep getting into her yard, and they trash all her date trees."

Majedah smiled as she refilled her glass and held up the empty bottle for a waiter to see. "Goats, huh? That's hilarious." Majedah pictured the fuzzy, long-legged critters bounding around in a grassy backyard like she had seen in a video one time. "What funny pets people have over there."

"Pets? No, the neighbor keeps them for milk and meat, the usual. ... Oh, speaking of goat, this looks great!" Ziyad rubbed his hands together and licked his lips as a waiter placed a huge platter of fragrant roasted meat in front of him. He sliced off a chunk with a surgeon's precision and popped it into his mouth.

Majedah watched his plate in horror as red juice oozed from the wound. She didn't even acknowledge the waiter when he placed a dish of fattoush in front of her.

"Mm," groaned Ziyad. "Melts in your mouth. You should try a bite, Majedah." He held up a dripping hunk of flesh speared on the tines of his fork.

Majedah swallowed her gorge and plastered a smile onto her face. "No, thanks, Dad. It looks great, but you know I don't eat meat." She put just the right emphasis on the last sentence so that a listener could infer that he shouldn't, either.

"Still? Okay, your choice. But you're missing out." Ziyad stuffed the meat into his mouth and chewed rapturously, his eyes rolling up to his forehead in pleasure like Bill Cosby in an old Jell-O commercial.

Majedah picked up a fork and valiantly pushed the vegetables around on her plate. The new bottle of wine appeared, and she eagerly held up her glass for a refill. Then she mentally toasted herself, for the lengths she was willing to go to perfect her craft.

MAJEDAH ADJUSTED HER hijab, took a deep breath, and proceeded through the door into the small studio. The first thing she saw was Mohammed's eyes narrowing in rage, and she knew the head scarf had been the right decision.

She took a moment to glance around the small studio. There was a gleaming new desk, already perfectly lit in an enchanting glow. Behind it sat a spiffy new set with tasteful Middle Eastern wall hangings mounted behind a cutting-edge monitor. Majedah let her gaze linger over the desk lovingly. She could easily imagine herself seated behind it, weaving a new narrative for America as she reported on the countless acts of Islamophobic violence and bigotry that had been inspired by Burt Nelson's presidency.

She heard someone clear his throat and turned to see a long table with five people seated behind it. At one end was Rosemary, her expression steely as always. Then there were three people Majedah didn't recognize, but she assumed they were the executives in charge of the new desk.

And last, there was the Great Man himself, Richard Spinner. The station founder and CEO looked directly at her. Majedah's heavily kohled eyes went wide and she gasped in astonishment at unexpectedly being in the man's presence. She could feel his aura of power warming her like the glow from the sun lamp he obviously used.

But Majedah was a professional and she quickly recovered her poise. "Good morning, everyone," she called out. She went to Mohammed and took his hands, then kissed him on both cheeks. He reared back, choked out the word, "Whore!" and spat on the ground, but Majedah had already breezed over to Rosemary.

As Majedah reached for the News Director, Rosemary shot her down with a withering glare and the command, "Don't touch me." Majedah lifted her hands, palms facing out, to indicate she would not. She settled for shaking hands across the table as she introduced herself to the remaining bigwigs.

When she got to Richard Spinner, he held onto her hand and probed her face with his watery blue eyes. "Majedah," he repeated her name back to her. "Excellent work, launching the Patty Clark narrative."

Her hand still in his, Majedah felt herself blushing. She couldn't believe such an important, powerful man even knew who she was, let alone was familiar with her work. "Th-thank you so much, Mr. Spinner," she stammered. "It's an honor to work at 24/7."

"I'm looking forward to seeing what you've got," he said. He held her hand one beat longer before letting go.

Rosemary started talking. "Okay, everyone's here. Let's get this audition started."

A female producer appeared and placed two stools in front of the table, indicating that Majedah and Mohammed should sit.

Rosemary continued, "First, there will be a brief interview in the form of questions from the panel—"

"Would anyone like a date?" Majedah stood in front of the table, proffering a small bronze platter of the dried fruits.

"No, Majedah, no one wants a date," said Rosemary.

"I do," Spinner's gravelly voice sounded from the other end of the table. "How about Saturday night?" He winked at Majedah and guffawed, and two of the executives laughed sycophantically. The third executive, the one with a thick black beard, scowled but reached for the snacks, so Rosemary paused her remarks to let everyone help themselves.

Majedah left the platter on the table and returned to her seat, and Rosemary started again. "As I was saying, first there will be questions from the panel, then both candidates can go back to the Pool while we talk amongst ourselves and make our decision."

The reporters nodded to show they understood, and the interview began.

The bearded executive led off the questioning. "Majedah," he said, "tell us about your personal connection to Islam."

Majedah felt panic rising in her throat as she was struck by the similarities between the executive and her rival, Mohammed; both men had long beards, heavy brows perpetually drawn together in disapproval, and embroidered skullcaps. She suddenly realized her error in focusing on ethnicity over Islam during her interview prep, but it was too late to remedy that now. She gamely reminded herself that she was brilliant and surely able to ad lib in this situation. Then she flashed a devastating smile and launched into her answer. "To me, Islam is the purest form of spirituality when one chooses to worship the lord." She noticed her questioner's brows pull even closer together so that they almost touched. "I mean *Allah*, of course. When one chooses to worship—" The man's face darkened, and she corrected herself again. "—to *glorify* Allah, there is just no better choice than Islam—"

"There is no other *choice* at all, because Islam is the one true religion and Allah is the one true God," roared the executive.

"Of course, I know that, I was just—"

"Mohammed, same question." The executive dismissed her.

Mohammed faced the man confidently. "I undertook my first Hajj at the age of 20," he began.

Majedah groaned to herself in frustration as the panel leaned forward, the better to hear the tale of Mohammed's spiritual journey.

"Allah had blessed me as a mustati at that time, and I knew I must go." His gaze seemed far away as he recalled the event. "I have never experienced anything like being surrounded by a mass of humanity, all gathered for the same purpose, the glorification of the Prophet, (peace be upon him)."

Frustrated, Majedah noticed that the executives were all nodding along with Mohammed's account. Even Spinner seemed riveted, his eyes fixed on the devout Pool reporter.

Mohammed went on with his story. "And when I finally completed my pilgrimage, as I slit the throat of my very first goat and watched its lifeblood stream away in bright red rivulets, a feeling of the greatest peace and completeness came over me." He looked at the ground for a moment, a thoughtful smile curving his mouth. Majedah realized she had never seen Mohammed smile before; it was a disturbing sight.

At last, he looked up again and concluded with, "I have since been fortunate enough to return every year—"

"You make the Hajj every year?" The original questioner's eyes were wide with admiration.

"Yes, I do. Allah has blessed me bountifully."

The members of the panel murmured excitedly to one another and jotted down notes.

Majedah could feel the position slipping away from her. She was a competitive person and used to winning when she went after something, and this position would be no exception if she could help it. It was time to play her trump card. She stood and in her most assertive voice said, "Excuse me! Excuse me, everyone, but need I remind you that, unlike Mohammed, *I* have a vagina?"

The murmuring stopped as her comment sank in. She could see several of the panelists whisper into one another's ears and begin to nod. A glance at Mohammed's rage-reddened face told her that her gambit had worked, and the tide was turning in her favor. She smiled smugly at him.

Spinner leaned forward across the table and looked down the line of executives. Everyone except the bearded executive nodded and gave a thumbs-up sign. The executive shook his head furiously, but Spinner overruled him with a glare and a few sharply whispered words.

Rosemary stood and began to make an announcement. "So, in light of the superior qualifications one of our applicants has demonstrated, we won't need to discuss this matter further. Congratulations to the new Islamophobia Desk anchor, Ms.—"

Her words were cut off by the nasal tones of an imam whining out the call to prayer. Heads swiveled as everyone sought the source. Mohammed leaped off his stool and pulled his phone from his pocket. The droning got louder as soon as the phone was out in the open, and he switched off the alarm. He placed the phone on his seat, reached into his jacket, and pulled out a folded bit of brocade. Unfolded, it revealed itself to be a prayer rug, which Mohammed spread on the floor. As he removed his shoes, fell to his knees, and raised his posterior in devotion, a chorus of approving *oh*'s and *ah*'s rose from the seated panelists.

Majedah shuddered with rage. Mohammed loudly recited the salat while the executives looking on approvingly, nodding vigorously at one another and shaking hands. At a signal from Spinner, Rosemary turned to the candidates and proclaimed,

"As I was saying, congratulations to the new Islamophobia News Desk Anchor … Mr. Mohammed Al Kaboom!"

The executives all rose to their feet and began to applaud.

Over the noise, Majedah shouted, "Are you kidding me?"

The applause continued as if she hadn't said anything, so she yelled even louder. "This guy is the biggest phony ever! He's not even Middle Eastern, like I am. He was born in Mill Valley! His real name is James Walker Lang, and he's a graduate of Marin County Progressive Prep!"

She must have been trapped in a waking nightmare, because everyone seemed to have forgotten she was there at all. Her unheeded words were drowned out by rapturous applause as Mohammed sat up and bowed down again, lost in his recitations. Only Spinner kept his seat, probing a nostril with a thick finger as he observed the young Muslim on the floor and the executives' adulation of him, an expression of corporate shrewdness on his jowly face.

"Ugh, forget it!" Majedah whipped the lovely new scarf from her head and flung it to the floor. She spun on her heel and stormed from the room.

Chapter 16

SPRING FINALLY SHOVED winter aside in typical brusque New Yorker fashion. Majedah marked her first springtime in the big northeastern city by noting she no longer needed a heavy coat as she made her way from the News 24/7 offices to the liquor store to her Upper West Side co-op.

Evening found Majedah in her living room, seated on the sofa with a glass of wine in her hand. The sliding doors to the balcony were closed against street noise as well as the warm evening breeze, as she voraciously absorbed broadcast news media. She set her drink down and shoved empty take-out containers out of the way to place her bare foot on the table so she could touch up her pedicure while keeping an eye on Kingston Fauler's evening news report.

"Good evening. I'm Kingston Fauler and this is News 24/7 Seven O'Clock Report. Our top story tonight: fallout from Sprinklegate continues as Congress moves to begin impeachment hearings for President Nelson. We go now to our Washington correspondent, Maria Rodriguez. Maria, what's going on in the nation's capitol tonight?"

The screen split to show the 24/7 reporter on location in front of the Capitol building. She began her report. "Kingston, the House of Representatives was packed today as Congresswoman

Rwanda King of Louisiana introduced a resolution to impeach President Nelson." There followed footage of the congresswoman introducing her resolution before Maria returned to wrap up her report by noting that, while impeachment looked likely, it would be followed by a lengthy Senate trial before Nelson could be convicted and removed from office.

"Ha, ha, we've got him now," Majedah cheered at the screen.

Kingston concluded the segment by noting, "Of course, even if the motion to impeach fails, this puts President Nelson in a terrible position as far as his re-election prospects are concerned. Historically speaking, no president has ever been in such a difficult position and come back to win re-election."

He turned to face in a different direction as the broadcast shifted cameras to the new angle. "As if President Nelson's troubles weren't already bad enough, new video has emerged tonight that has women's groups up in arms. President Nelson gave a commencement address at his Alma Mater, Fale University, this afternoon, and his comments are drawing outrage. We just want to warn our viewers, it can be difficult to watch."

The screen switched to a shot of President Nelson attempting to deliver remarks from behind a podium as protestors mobbed the front of the dais, chanting loudly in an attempt to drown him out. Several of the more patriotic professors on the dais joined in the chant from their seats. Majedah recognized the ubiquitous LOVE BEATS HATE chant, and she pumped her fist and chanted along with it.

Suddenly, three female students jumped up onto the dais and approached the president. They pulled off their graduation gowns to reveal an assortment of pierced, painted, and unrestrained breasts, which they waggled angrily at the president.

President Nelson seemed confounded and momentarily stopped speaking. Two secret service agents stepped forward from behind the seated dignitaries. Noticing them, the president said, "Oh, good. Would you please remove these young ladies from the dais?" The live microphone picked up every word.

Majedah's face went ashen as the force of the words' sheer violence struck her.

Kingston was back on the screen. "In case you couldn't hear him clearly, Nelson said, 'Would you please remove these young ladies from the dais.'" His mouth pruned in disgust as he enunciated each word, and he paused to let the full horror sink in to the viewing audience. Then he collected himself and continued, "Here via satellite to comment on the president's shame is presumptive Democratic Presidential Nominee—and, let's face it, presumptive Next President of the United States—Senator Angela Harper. Angela, thank you so much for joining us tonight."

The screen split to show the California legislator alongside the anchor. "Thank you for having me, Kingston," said Angela.

Majedah exhaled in relief as the woman's strong, commanding voice salved the pain from what she had just heard the president say. She took a moment to admire the senator's flawless cosmetic work, Hollywood-perfect makeup, and precisely coifed 'do. At 93, the Senator doubtless no longer had the chestnut hair of her youth, but the most highly skilled colorists and stylists in the entire country had long since leapt to her support, and she was never less than immaculately turned out. The result was a woman who looked no older than 79.

"Angela, what was your reaction when you heard the president's comment at the Fale commencement address?" prompted Kingston.

The senator's expression went as fierce as it's possible to look with an immobilized forehead. "Kingston, I felt like it was 1950 all over again, and women were still in chains and treated as mere property, or chattel, for men to control and abuse." Her faded blue eyes burned into the camera. "I haven't been this frightened or outraged by a president's words since President Clemson's infamous 'internal humidor' comment, back in the 1990's."

Kingston nodded along with every word. "I quite agree, Senator."

"When will this war on women end, Kingston?" demanded Senator Harper. "When will women ever be regarded as equal members of our society? When will we be free of this institutionalized misogyny? When will women ever be able to feel safe from repression and abuse, in these Sexist States of America?"

Kingston shook his head sadly. "Maybe when we finally have a woman in the White House, that's all I can think of," he said. "Senator, thank you for being with us to discuss this crisis tonight. Thank you for your strong voice and courageous leadership in these very frightening times."

"Of course, Kingston."

The seasoned anchor filled the screen again. "I couldn't agree more with what the Senator just had to say. In fact, I owe America an apology." As Kingston gazed directly into the camera, his eyes welled up. He gulped and spoke. "I am deeply, deeply ashamed to be a white cis-het man." Majedah watched with satisfaction as Kingston's face crumpled with regret. He looked upward imploringly and cried out, "Why? Why could I not have been born a woman? Why am I trapped in this repulsive, hateful form? Why-y-y-y," he concluded in broken sobs. He leaned forward and began to bash his forehead against the desktop, repeating his heart-wrenching question between strikes.

Bam! "Why?"

Whap! "Why?"

Whack! "Why?"

The station went to commercial, and Majedah changed the channel to see what the despicable Roy Cader was reporting over at Eagle Eye News.

The smug anchor had a guest of his own.

"Mr. Waveny, it looks as though your candidate is going to the Republican National Convention after all. I must say, we're all shocked here at Eagle Eye News—in a good way, of course."

On his half of the split screen, Vic Waveny laughed. "Th-thank you, Roy, I think." He was hatless today, his shaggy gray-brown hair parted at the side and combed into submission. Today he was wearing normal business attire, a jacket over a dress shirt and a corny stars-and-stripes necktie.

"Mr. Waveny," continued Cader, "as I'm sure you already know, a new Eagle Eye/Naugapissus poll released today shows Ms. Clark has garnered support from almost an equal number of likely Republican voters as President Nelson—45% to 47%. It's almost starting to seem like President Nelson—an incumbent, sitting president—could actually lose his party's nomination."

"Yessir, we're in a f-f-fine position as of now." Vic grinned. "We're looking forward to the convention."

"You're welcome, Patty," Majedah sneered. She helped herself to a gulp of wine.

"In all of modern time, I don't think a sitting president has ever gone into the convention in such a weak position," Roy added. As he spoke, Eagle Eye News dedicated the entire screen to a rerun of the footage of President Nelson prostrating himself on the White House lawn as he apologized for Sprinklegate.

Majedah shouted at the screen, "Suck it, Nelson!" and broke into a diabolical cackle. To herself, she remarked, "My god, we're really doing it."

It was working! The amazing, incisive, righteous media, of which she was an important part, had built a narrative so strong that it was overwhelming the voice of the people and bringing down an American president. Soon, they would install the historic first president with a historic vagina in the White House, and Majedah and her cohorts would be the messengers of a new Era of Goodness and Light.

As the realization struck, the rush of power Majedah felt was dizzying. She closed her eyes and drew in a sharp breath through her nose as ecstasy washed through her. It was the most intense high she had ever felt.

And like all addicts, even in the very throes of her euphoria, her need for more—ever more!—grew.

THE FOLLOWING MORNING meeting at the illustrious News 24/7 Manhattan headquarters heaped more good news onto everyone's plates. All the 24/7 Staffers listened intently as Juan Conquista introduced that morning's presenter to the nation-wide phone conference attendees.

"As we move closer to this summer's national political conventions, we are in an amazing position," Juan reminded everyone. "If we keep doing what we're doing, Senator Harper's win over Nelson will be the most lopsided victory in American history. Here with an important announcement is the CEO of the Sexism Prevention Institute for Equal Rights, Florence Houlihan."

"Good morning, everyone," said the head of SPInstER.

The journalists in the conference room were far too sophisticated to applaud every time a person of national prominence spoke in the daily briefing. Even so, one or two fangirl squeals sounded around the room, and Mara gave an excited whinny.

"This Tuesday, we're going to need all hands on deck," advised the chief executive of the women's group. Her aged voice cracked with the force of her principled words. "We have organized a nationwide protest for Women's Rights, in reaction to President Nelson's despicable comments at Fale University. Everyone please plan on donning your best vaginery and joining us in the nearest city that has a Progressive administration for the Million Muff March!"

The excitement in the conference room had grown too great to be contained, and spontaneous whoops erupted. Majedah hooted and cheered as loud as anyone. Here would be her chance to distinguish herself as the most obvious choice for the next anchor of the Women's Desk, when the fateful day arrived that Carol Crawford would be ousted.

After the phone conference ended, Rosemary instructed the staff on procedures for the event. "The Million Muff March begins at the southeast corner of Central Park and ends at a rally in front of the Fale Club on East 47th Street. All reporters are authorized to use the 24/7 Live Beat streaming app if a cameraperson is not avail—"

Her words were cut off by a scream from across the table. Every head turned to see the source. It was Mara; the lovely golden palomino centauress was trembling with traumatic stress as though from a dreadful act of violence.

"What's the matter, Mara?" asked Rosemary.

"You said 'rape'," neighed Mara.

"When did I say that?"

But the centauress was too distressed to answer. The women on either side of equee comforted equee and gave equee supportive hugs.

Several seats away, Scout, Mysty, and Candy glared at Mara. "Equee really overdoes it with the victim routine," Mysty muttered.

"Some people really go too far," agreed Scout.

A subdued hubbub buzzed the air until it was determined that the word 'rape' was contained in the word 'cameraperson'.

Once the source of Mara's distress had been identified, Rosemary's face went ashen. "Mara—and all women present, of any biological status and species—I am so sorry. It was never my intention to hurt any of you with hate speech." All the women in the room looked at her dubiously, so she quickly added, "Unlike Burt Nelson."

"Ah," said all the women in relief, and there was a smattering of applause.

Her virtue adequately signaled, Rosemary was allowed to continue. "As I was saying, all reporters should feel free to use our proprietary Live Beat app to stream your reports if a camera operator is unavail—"

Mara shrieked and flung herself onto the floor, where she curled into the fetal position. The nearest women quickly went to her aid, petting her soothingly.

"What's wrong now?" asked Rosemary.

One of the female staffers held her ear to Mara's lips, then stood up from her knees. "You used the word, 'operator.' The middle syllable is 'rate,' which sounds too much like 'rape'."

From the floor, Mara whinnied in distress.

"Okay, scratch that. Let's try again," pleaded Rosemary. "I am sure everyone knows what I mean; if no one can work the camera for you, use the streaming app and your wand. Is that okay, Mara?"

The centauress sat up weakly and nodded. "Thank you," she nickered. Someone placed a warming blanket over her withers and another person brought her a pail of water. Her color already looked better. Everyone breathed a sigh of relief.

With the dire situation now stabilized, Rosemary continued the meeting. "The usual rules apply for covering a direct action. You all should know them by heart, but here's a refresher: Always focus on the protestors. Always frame your shot to maximize crowd size. Always crop your shot so that the edge of the crowd is not visible. Never allow opposition protestors any coverage whatsoever."

Melissa raised her hand.

"Yes, Melissa. Question?" Rosemary acknowledged her.

"Hi, yes. What opposition protestors are we expecting?"

The woman seated beside her spoke up from beneath her burka. "Yes, are there actually people who disagree with women's rights?" she asked. Her voice was marked by disbelief.

Rosemary's expression became stern. "Believe it or not, even in this day and age, yes; there are people who are against women having equal rights." She glanced down at her tablet to retrieve some information before continuing. "Our opposition research shows that Patty Clark's novelty candidacy is giving rise to a populist movement of far-right radicals who reject traditional Progressive American values. These despicable people insist that marriage is the unique right of one man and one woman. They say that only men have penises, and only women have vaginas. They think children are best raised by their *biological* parents." With each word, her audience became more horrified. "They also hold fast to archaic ideas like people only being entitled to what they themselves have earned, as if everyone can just go out there and *earn* things. They are totally ignorant of the massive privilege they enjoy, simply by being in a position to pay taxes in the first place." She looked up again before concluding in a dire voice with, "They call themselves the 'Norms'."

Wails of consternation sounded from around the room.

Majedah felt faint for a moment, but then anger rose in her and she rallied. She would never give a second of airtime to those troglodytes.

Rosemary had moved on to the next topic. "Finally, I'd like to introduce the new, er, face in the crowd." She gestured towards the burka'ed woman seated at the table. As you all know, Mohammed has been promoted to anchor of the Islamophobia

Desk, so he no longer attends these staff meetings. From now on, his new assistant will be here to represent him. Everyone, please say hello to A'shadieeyah."

Everyone said, "Hi, A'shadieeeyeeyee," until the lengthy name petered out into uncertainty. Across the table from Majedah, the newcomer most likely smiled beneath her burka.

Majeda's mouth said hi, too, but her powerful mind was already focused on Saturday's march. She would follow the rules of reportage perfectly and do everything in her power to promote the narrative that the Million Muff March represented the overwhelming majority of American opinion.

And in the process, she would create a narrative of her own; that she, Majedah Cantalupi-Abromavich-Flügel-Van Der Hoven-Taj Mahal, was the very face of the Women's Rights Movement. She would weave this second narrative with such consummate skill and subtlety that everyone at 24/7, from the lowly doormat Melissa all the way up to the great founder, Richard Spinner himself, would instinctively know that she was a perfect fit as anchor of the Women's Desk. And one day, when Carol Crawford finally slipped up, Majedah would be crowned as the new anchor without a moment's thought or hesitation.

MAJEDAH EYED HERSELF critically in the triple-view mirror. She stood on a small raised platform as a young designer pinned the folds of her garment into a more pleasing shape. Loud club music filled the air from the workroom behind the counter, where Majedah could glimpse several other people cutting fabric or hunching over sewing machines. The walls of both the showroom and the workroom were hung with Broadway-ready costumes for every kind of stage production, from *Cats, Too!* to the latest presidential assassination porn in the park.

Majedah looked in the mirror and regarded her own face, protruding out of a round hole in the fabric of her garment. She sucked in her cheeks and lifted her chin so that the light played over the angles of her made-for-TV visage, exaggerating the contours of her very fine bone structure. She pouted to plump the fullness of her lips and admired the effect in the dramatic contrast of the down-lighting.

The designer added a final pin and stood up beside her. "There," he said.

Two sets of eyes appraised the seven-foot-tall plush vagina in the mirrored triptych. The costume was crafted of peachy pink velvet surrounded by a mantle of glossy, black, silken fringe. Majedah turned to the right and the left. "Mika, you're a genius," she said.

"That's not even the half of it." The designer grinned impishly and told her, "Now, raise your hands out at your sides."

Majedah did as she was bidden and drew in a breath as the clever design revealed itself. The fleshy folds parted to reveal a striking gradient of color that varied from peach to ruby red. In the center was Majedah's own slender form, sheathed in a column of black satin that cleverly mimicked the unseeable and unknowable depths of womanhood. Majedah squealed and clapped her hands in delight. "Oh, Mika, it's brilliant! I love it!"

"Oh, I just knew you would!" The designer stood and bounced on the balls of his feet, his hands clasped to his chest in celebration. They both watched the mirror ecstatically as Majedah spread her arms and closed them again, and the labial folds opened and closed with them.

Another young man emerged from the workroom to admire Majedah's outfit. "Mika, you've outdone yourself," he said.

"I know, Brad."

"Majedah, you'll be the best-dressed lady part at the march," said Brad.

"That's the plan," purred Majedah. She turned to admire herself from a new angle.

To Mika, Brad said, "You just about ready to wrap it up for the night? It's nearly eight, and we have an 8:15 reservation."

"Almost, sugar. Just one last thing to pin in place, and we are free to go."

"I bet I know what's missing," said Majedah expectantly.

"I bet you do," said Mika. He winked and went behind the counter to rummage through a carton of accessories. He found what he was looking for and returned to his client. With a flourish, he held a pink pom-pom the size of a volleyball against the fringe and velvet just above Majedah's head. "Ta-da!" he said.

Majedah eyed the accessory with a dour expression. "I don't know, Mika, I'm just not feeling it."

"What do you mean, Majedah? It's the perfect hue to match the fleshtones, and it's prominent without being too flashy."

Majedah gave it another look but her expression didn't change. "I don't know, it's just too pedestrian. I feel like everyone's going to have the exact same one. Maybe I *want* it to be flashy, you know? The clitoris is the center of a woman's power, after all. It should stand out."

Mika's buoyant mood transformed abruptly to one of intense annoyance. "Well, *one* of us graduated from the Theatrical Academy of London with a degree in costume design, and one of us didn't," he sneered.

"And one of us actually has a clitoris and one of us does not," Majedah shot back.

A brief staring match ensued until Mika backed down. "Fine," he snipped. "Have it your way. Parade down Fifth Avenue with a great, vulgar clitoris on your otherwise flawless gown. See if I care." He went to fetch the carton of accessories from the workroom and dropped it at her feet with a bang. "See anything you like?" he asked saucily.

"Can you go through it for me?" asked Majedah. "I can't bend down in this thing."

"Sure thing, your highness," the designer muttered under his breath. Majedah didn't hear him over the pulsing music from the back room.

Mika held up first one accessory then another. Each time, Majedah shook her head. "Too plain. ... Too small. ... Ugh, what is that color?" Soon the box was empty, and Brad was standing nearby, tapping his foot and looking at his watch.

"Well, Majedah, it looks like you'll just have to pick one of these," prompted Mika.

"But none of them will do," Majedah protested. She glanced around the shop. "I just know you must have *something* here for me." Then a flash of light momentarily blinded her, and she turned to look for its source.

There, in a corner of the back room, next to a ceiling-mounted speaker, a dust-covered, hot pink disco ball lazily spun on a short length of string. "That's it," Majedah shouted, pointing.

Mika followed her finger with his gaze. "Oh, no," he said. "No way. That is beyond garish. I would never hear the end of it from the Guild."

"It's the disco ball or nothing," Majedah said.

"Then it's nothing. I won't have my good name sullied like that." Mika crossed his arms and turned his face away.

"Okay, have it your way." Majedah began to remove an arm from a sleeve, moving carefully to avoid the pins. As though speaking to herself, she said, "I'm sure Steve still has time to put something together for me. I'll have to remember to ask him what contact info he wants me to use in the credits."

Mika clenched his fists at his sides. "Damn it, Majedah, you are such a bitch," he whined. But Majedah could tell he was relenting when he brought up a practical consideration. "Besides, it's not like we can just *sew* a metallic disco ball onto something," he said.

Majedah gave herself one last admiring appraisal in the mirror. "You'll think of something," she said breezily. "Didn't you say you had a degree from the Theater School of England or something?"

"*The Theatrical Academy of London*," Mika hissed. Majedah held out a slender wrist and he reached to carefully pull the costume off first one arm and then the other. "Perhaps a hot glue gun," he mused as he worked.

Majedah flashed herself a victorious grin in the mirror, secure in the knowledge that her vagina costume would be the most magnificent one in the march.

Chapter 17

THE DAY OF the Million Muff March dawned fair and flawless. Majedah and her fellow credentialed media professionals gathered in a large fenced area reserved for them, while the marchers organized into divisions that filled a vast swath of Central Park, as far as the eye could see. Majedah thrilled to the vision of an endless sea of demonstrators.

She accepted a complimentary non-GMO wild-harvested soy cream macchiato from a server at the One World Roasters kiosk. The drink arrived in a custom-printed pink paper cup with the both the One World Roasters ("Official Sponsor") and Million Muff March logos imprinted on it. Majedah nodded her thanks.

"Just happy to do our part," said the gender-fluid server. (Majedah strongly suspected the server was female, based on their height and overall build, but then again, they also had a pronounced Adam's apple. Majedah knew people could get realistic Adam's apples added to their throats nowadays, and she was dying to know if this one was genuine. But she knew better than to ask.)

"Love your costume, by the way," said the server.

"Thank you. I had it custom made."

The server looked at her outfit with admiration. "I thought so. You don't see a clitoris like that every day."

Majedah carried the beverage to an enormous white tent with the News 24/7 station logo on the flaps. In the cavernous space beneath the canopy were sofas, coffee tables, a craft services table, and two hair-and-make up stations. Majedah spotted a gaggle of reporters and production assistants and glided towards them. As she moved through the crowd, she noticed countless positive reactions to her stunning outfit from the corner of her eye. "Hello, everyone," she greeted her associates when she arrived among them.

Melissa saw her first and her mouth dropped open. "Wow, Majedah, you look magnificent," she breathed.

Melissa was wearing one of the more common off-the-rack vagina costumes. Majedah flashed the plain reporter an indulgent smile. "Thanks, Melissa. It's a custom design."

"I knew it. I just love your clitoris. It's so sparkly." Melissa's hand reached up towards Majedah's crown jewel.

Majedah smacked it away. "Please don't touch it. I don't want fingerprints gumming it up."

"Of course not. I'm sorry," apologized the Pool-reporter-for-life.

The rest of the reporters, producers, and assistants gathered around to ooh and aah, and Majedah found kind words for the cookie-cutter costumes that half of them wore. She was touched to see that even Mohammed's new assistant wore a simple, pink, plush lady part over her black burka. "Wow, A'shadieeyah, you look great," she complimented the Muslimette.

"No, she does not. She looks like a whore!" Mohammed had come out of nowhere to berate his assistant, who bore his criticism wordlessly. "Only a whore would wear such a thing," repeated the angry anchor. He approached A'shadieeyah and, in a quick, ruthless motion, circumcised the pink pompom from the costume. "There, that is better. Now you may be seen in public."

Beneath her burka, A'shadieeyah presumably nodded in agreement.

"Great, looks like everyone's here." Rosemary strode into the middle of the group with her usual forceful stride. In a nod to the event, she wore a muted raspberry blouse with her black dress slacks. "Let's go over assignments," she said. "Mysty, where are you?"

"Right here." At six-foot-three and 270 pounds, Mysty hadn't been able to find a vagina costume to fit myr. But mys had more than made up for it by dressing in a Pepto-Bismol-pink cocktail dress with magenta fringe at the neckline, sleeves, and hem. Myz feet were sheathed in size 14 magenta go-go boots that reached to myz knees.

"Mysty, you have your wand?" asked Rosemary

"It's in my pocket," the ostensible woman confirmed.

"So that's what that is," Melissa said to herself.

"Great," said Rosemary. "We're going to have you do a live stream via the LiveBeat app. You're going to capture the color, the spirit, and the pageantry of the event."

"You got it," said Mysty. Mys turned to Scout and clasped zis hands in myz. "Yay, I get to be with the people," mys said.

"You're going to have too much fun," ze said.

"Let's see now." Rosemary consulted her tablet. "Majedah, where are you?"

Majedah stepped from behind Mysty to emerge before the news director in all her rosy velveteen glory. She angled one hand out at the wrist in a model pose to give a subtle glimpse of the ensemble's colorful inner folds. At that moment, a happy sunbeam chanced to gleam off her remarkable clitoris and flash in Rosemary's eye.

"Wow," the dazzled director said. "Majedah, you look fantastic. Tell you what." She turned to scan the depths of the tent until she saw who she was looking for. She inserted her index finger and pinky into the corners of her mouth and gave an ear-splitting whistle. "Carter," she yelled.

Over by the craft services table, a big, corn-fed cameraman looked up and pointed at himself with an inquiring expression. Rosemary nodded and waved him over.

"Majedah, I'm going to assign Carter to you. You guys should shoot formal reportage so we have some hard journalistic footage for Carol to run on her show tonight. Okay?"

Majedah met the executive's eye. "It would be my honor, Rosemary," she said.

"Good. It would be a shame to waste that outfit." Rosemary gave Majedah one more admiring look before returning her attention to her tablet. "Okay, who's next?" she said.

Standing nearby in zis cheap, Chinese vagina costume, Scout stamped zis foot in a fit of envy. Majedah pretended not to notice and smiled serenely, giving no outward sign of her inner excitement.

The custom outfit had been worth every penny; Majedah was going to be a featured reporter on An Hour of Your Time that evening. She would be News 24/7's face of the biggest women's story of the year. She took Carter's elbow and led him away, so they could set up in just the right spot from which to report.

Twenty minutes later, Majedah stood on the southwest corner of 59th Street and Fifth Avenue. Behind her, the Million Muff March was just about to step off from the park and begin its flow down Fifth.

"How do I look, Carter?" asked an anxious Majedah for the third time.

For the third time, the sturdy cameraman looked into his viewfinder and gave a thumbs-up sign.

"Are you far enough back? Can you see enough of my costume?" Majedah fretted.

"Yes, Majedah."

"But is my face prominent enough? Maybe you should get closer."

Carter raised his eyes from the camera to meet hers. "Your face is clear, Majedah," he said in a placating tone. "You look beautiful."

"Excuse me?" Majedah's nervousness transformed to anger on a dime. "Could you be any more sexist?"

Carter rolled his eyes to the heavens and sighed. "*Great.* You look great." He returned his attention to the camera, repeating a mantra under his breath: "It's better than working on Uncle Larry's hog farm. It's better than working on Uncle Larry's hog farm. ..."

A whistle blew behind Majedah and the march sallied forth in all its splendor.

"Oh! They started," Majedah said. "Carter, quick! Start shooting."

The cameraman hit the Record button and said, "You're on in five, four..." He silently indicated the rest of the countdown with his fingers, and Majedah swung into action, doing what she was born to do.

"This is Majedah Cantalupi-Abromavich-Flügel-Van Der Hoven-Taj Mahal, reporting live from the Million Muff March in New York City. Behind me is Central Park, and you can see the first divisions are just starting off on the march down Fifth Avenue. Leading the demonstration here today is Celeste Roberts, the Regional Director for SPInstER. National Director Florence Houlihan is, of course, directing the larger sister demonstration in Washington, D.C. today."

Maria Rodriguez would no doubt be covering that march—and all the big names that were headlining it—for the station. The tiniest note of envy had crept into Majedah's voice, and she reminded herself that she needed to be a consummate professional today. To psychologically re-set herself, she straightened her posture and tossed her head to get her bangs out of her eyes. As she did so, she felt the heavy disco ball shift ever so slightly from its position right above her head. "Shit! The hot glue is giving out," she exclaimed.

Carter lifted his head from the camera. "What?" he asked.

"My clitoris! It's falling off!" Majedah wailed.

"What? Oh." Carter gave the disco ball a critical look. "No, it's not. It looks fine." The morning sun reflected off it, shooting blinding rays into his eyes. "Argh," he said, turning away and covering his eyes with his hands.

"Well, it slipped a little. I felt it." Majedah insisted.

"It looks fine, Majedah. Can we just get on with the report?"

Majedah moved her head from side to side then patted the accessory with one hand; the disco ball stayed put. "Okay, I guess it's settled now."

The pink flow of marchers had already reached her position on the sidewalk and begun streaming past on their way down the avenue.

"Oh no! They're already passing us. Go, Carter!"

Carter bent over his camera again. "In five, four..."

"Just go! Start shooting."

Carter gave her a thumbs-up sign and she began the report again.

"This is Majedah Cantalupi-Abromavich-Flügel-Van Der Hoven-Taj Mahal, reporting for News 24/7 from the Million Muff March in New York City. Behind me you can see the very first division, the regional chapter of the venerable women's rights organization, SPInstER."

As if on cue, the pink-shirted marchers noticed the media attention and began cheering and waving. Majedah waved back at them. "You go, girls! I love you!" she shouted. She blew them a kiss then turned back to her report. "And these women are not alone today. Many other civil rights organizations are joining in to help protest the President's hateful, misogynistic remarks this week at Fale University. There are representatives from GOO—that's the Global Outrage Organization, of course— as well as women's healthcare provider Chosen Children, Fast Food Workers International, Temperature Justice Now!, and many, many others. And in a touching show of solidarity, New York's own Mayor, Sandra Neehsta, is at the head of the march as well. The protest will proceed down Fifth Avenue and end in a rally in front of the Fale Club, where University President Bernie Bridges is expected to address the demonstrators' concerns about the university's invitation to President Nelson to speak there.

"Meanwhile, SPInstER is also organizing sister marches and rallies across the nation. The biggest demonstration will be in Washington, D.C., of course, where the protestors will pressure President Nelson to step down."

Majedah stopped speaking and held her position for several seconds until Carter gave her the signal that he had stopped shooting. "That was perfect," he said. "Great intro for the report."

"Excellent. Okay, let's get going so we can follow the march down to the rally point," instructed Majedah.

"Right. I can snag some b-roll along the way." Carter folded the tripod legs together and hoisted the camera to his shoulder.

"And I'll find some participants to interview, too. There's nothing like getting the voice of the people." Majedah spread the fingers of one hand over her breastbone as she spoke, and the sun glinted off her shining clitoris like a searing beam of truth.

Most of the trip to the rally point consisted of Majedah marching along with the demonstrators, clapping, pumping her fist, and chanting, while Carter filmed the proceedings. Every now and then, Majedah signaled him and they would conduct an impromptu interview.

"What's your name and where are you from?" Majedah asked a pair of suburbanites. The women were dressed in expensive boots and pink jeans, topped with pink t-shirts that read Moms Allied Against Men. Their fashionable shoulder-length hair was stiff with temporary pink color for the event. Majedah held the mic up as Carter walked backwards in front of the group, filming as they marched.

"I'm Sara and this is my best friend, Mindy," said one of the soccer moms. "We're from Larchmont and we're here to support all the women who were hurt by the President's hateful words this week."

"Whoooo!" said Mindy as she shook a clenched fist in front of the camera.

"Whoooo!" echoed Sara and Majedah.

"I couldn't help but notice your adorable jeans," said Majedah. "Are those the Marcus Puhtsee special edition jeans?"

"You know it," Mindy affirmed. She spun to display her pink denim-clad buns while Carter got a good shot for the footage. Each back pocket had decorative stitching that bore the designer's name, three MMMs in a row, and an abstract line drawing of a stylized vulva.

"Oh, my god, those are so cute," Majedah squealed. Then she looked down and asked, "And who do we have here?"

Carter swung the camera down to pan along the row of children marching with their mothers as Sara gave their names. "This is Sophia, Emma, Zoë, and Kaden." The footage showed three pre-teen girls, their hair plaited into thick braids interwoven with pink and magenta ribbons and feathers. The last child, someone's nine-year-old younger brother, was likewise dressed in a pink shirt, and several fuschia ornaments were affixed to his shoulder-length, brown hair. He looked about as happy as a cat who had been forced into a tiny sweater for someone's holiday card photo.

Majedah stooped slightly to hold the mic in front of the children. "How does it feel to have moms who brought you to this historic event, girls?" she asked.

The middle girl, clearly the most empowered, immediately shoved the others aside, stepped close to the mic, and started talking. "I think it's great to be here, and I think it's really important for women of all ages to speak out against systemic patriarchal misogyny," she carefully regurgitated.

"Wonderful," Majedah bubbled. "Good for you! So precocious." She held the mic in front of the boy. "And what about you?"

"Please kill me now."

Majedah stood and turned to the camera. "Production note: edit that last bit out."

"Majedah," called a familiar voice.

The courageous newswoman raised her head and looked around until she saw someone waving. "Oh, my god. Stanton!" She abandoned the indoctrinated children and ran back to the next group of demonstrators.

Her old acquaintance from her Wycksburg days marched proudly alongside the massive banner that read *GOO 4 Women.* "Majedah! Hey, girl!" Smiling broadly, Stanton broke ranks and quick-stepped towards her.

As she reached him, Majedah spread her arms to hug him, opening her artfully crafted costume to reveal all its crimson glory. Stanton froze mid-step, a look of horror on his face, but then the seven-foot-tall velveteen vulva was upon him, engulfing him in fuzzy folds of affection. "Stanton! It's so good to see you," Majedah sang.

Stanton recovered himself and returned her enthusiastic greeting. Then he asked, "How's 24/7 treating you? You doing good, girl?"

"Yeah, I love working here," Majedah said.

"I can see that, I can see that." Stanton discreetly glanced at her costume once more. "That's some outfit you got on there, girl. Look at you, all dressed up like the belle of the ball, nice spangly clitoris an' everything." He shook his head and whistled in admiration.

"Oh, thanks," said Majedah. "It's a custom design by the same designers that did the costumes for *Stalin! The Musical.*" She fell into step alongside her fellow traveler.

"Damn, that's great, that's great. 'Scuse me a second." Stanton squeezed her arm then he spun to waive a fist in the air and chant along with his contingent:

HEY HEY! HO HO!
MISOGYNISTS HAVE GOT TO GO!

Majedah waved at Carter to make sure he was capturing images of the valiant young civil rights leader in action. When Stanton faced front again, Majedah said, "Hey, how about a little interview for 24/7? This is for An Hour of Your Time tonight." Majedah dropped the name of the broadcast in a perfectly casual voice and watched Stanton's face light up.

"Oh, that would be great, that would be great. Yes, ma'am, please and thank you. Just give me one second." He tightened the knot on his hot pink necktie and pulled at the hem of his jacket. Then he squared his shoulders and nodded.

"Sir, what is your name and what group do you represent?" Majedah asked.

"I'm Stanton Michaels, and I am the Northeast Regional Director for the Global Outrage Organization."

"And why is your organization participating in today's march?" asked Majedah.

A perplexed look crossed Stanton's face. "Well, hell, I never really thought about it. Do we need a 'why'? I mean, it's a march. We're a protest organization. This is what we do; we march."

Majedah nodded along with his answer before taking back the mic. "Of course. That only makes sense. And what do you hope to accomplish with your participation here today?"

"What do we hope to accomplish? Majedah, girl, you're killing me." Stanton gave his forehead a quick swipe with a handkerchief, which he then stowed back in his pocket. "Well, we hope to make some noise and, uh, get to the end of the march."

"The rally," Majedah offered helpfully.

"Yes, the rally. And, uh, you know, it's great that you're interviewing me and getting our message out for the people to see."

"That's what we do at News 24/7; we tell the news," said Majedah.

"Yes, you do, and very well, too. Very well. Now, uh, here's some more news for you." Stanton raised a clenched fist and joined back into the chant.

HEY HEY! HO HO!
MISOGYNISTS HAVE GOT TO GO!

Carter recorded several rounds of the catchy phrase before he and Majedah moved on to capture more sights and sounds of the big day.

All too soon, they arrived at the rally point. A platform had been erected in the middle of the street, and it was surrounded by a massive crowd that filled the entire intersection and at least a block down each connecting street. One speaker after another took turns working up the crowd. At one point, a tired old used-up hag who had once been a Manhattanite pop star performed a lipsynch of one of her biggest hits from decades before Majedah was born. Majedah admired the frowzy woman's professional precision as she mouthed each word and strutted the stage in a fishnet cat suit, flanked by a pair of bare-chested male dancers in tight, pink leatherette pants.

Carter leaned over and asked, "Who is that woman? Isn't that Virginia?" Then he added, "I heard Rinnie Halliday is performing at the DC rally."

"She is? Dammit! Why can't she perform at this rally?" Majedah wailed. "Oh well, Virginia is a huge star in her own right. She was a great pioneer of women's rights. She was one of America's first female idols to promote her genitalia as part of her repertoire. So brave." Majedah began to dance and cheer the pop star of years past. There was a brief ripping sound and her sparkling clitoris shifted down to just above her eyes. "Oh no! Not again," Majedah cried. "Dammit!" She tested the dangling accessory with her hand; it had come to rest in its new positon, but its adhesion to the costume felt tenuous. "Ugh, it's really loose. I'm going to have to hold still for the rest of the event."

Luckily, at that point, Fale University president Bernie Bridges was brought onto the stage. The event organizers had exercised their Constitutional right to petition him by dressing him in a black leather singlet that snugly covered his nether parts and ran straps across his chest that offered up his saggy moobs for discipline. Two enormous buzz-cut female escorts led him to the microphone and removed the red ball gag from his mouth.

"Thank you, th-thank you," he groveled to his captors. Then he blinked at the mob in front of him and began speaking into the microphone. "Good afternoon. I'm Bernie Bridges, President of Fale University, and I use the he/him pronouns."

Raucous booing erupted from the crowd. Protestors hurled water bottles and tampons at the speaker, but the plucky academic forged ahead with his remarks.

"I have read the list of demands your organization presented to me, and I am pleased to announce that Fale University will comply with every single one." He waited as the crowd cheered his announcement. "In addition, we will take the extra step of firing every single male employee from the university. From faculty to security to food service to administration to IT to custodial staff, Fale will become a toxic masculinity-free campus." He paused for dramatic effect before closing with a triumphant declaration; "Effective immediately!"

The pink mob roared its approval. President Bridges smiled weakly before one of his escorts popped the ball gag back into his mouth. The other huge female flung him over her shoulder like a sack of fair trade rice, and the threesome departed the stage.

Celeste Roberts took to the stage again to deliver her closing remarks. But before she could speak, the unmistakable sounds of disruption came from nearby. Majedah turned to look and Carter swung his camera.

A large group of counter-protestors had forced its way into the intersection and was disrupting the gyno-centric gathering with a chant of its own. Majedah strained to make out the words:

WE LOVE MEN
WE NEED MEN
WE WANT MEN

"What the hell?" she wondered aloud. Her reporter instincts were humming like a high-tension wire in a hurricane, and she began to force her way through the crowd to get a better look, holding her clitoris in place with one hand and shoving people aside with the other. Carter followed behind her.

When she got close enough to get a good look, Majedah saw that the counter-protest was made up of women, but the completely oppressed, wife-and-mother variety. They changed up their chant to a riff on an old anti-war song from the hippie era:

MEN, HUH! WHAT ARE THEY GOOD FOR?
HUSBANDS-BROTHERS-FATHERS-SONS!

The women weren't unattractive; they seemed healthy, clean, and nicely dressed, and very few of them were obese. The usual demonstration scent of body odor, unwashed clothes, patchouli, and dirty hair was missing. Many of the women carried hand-lettered signs that bore slogans such as *Up With Men* and *Stop Oppressing My Son* and *Adam's Rib and Proud Of It!*

Majedah spotted the 24/7 camera in her peripheral vision, and she spun and smacked it aside. "What are you doing, you moron?"

Carter's irritated face appeared from behind the viewfinder. "What? I'm doing my job."

Majedah gestured in his face with her hand. "Do not film the counter-protestors, remember?"

"Oh yeah, that's right." Carter was duly chastened. "Sorry. I'll delete it as soon as I get back to the station."

"You're damn right, you will." Majedah clenched her eyes shut and shook her head to try to clear it. By now, her reporter instincts were screaming through every nerve ending in her body: *There's a big story here. Cover it!* But she stood firm and said aloud, "No." Her loyalty lay with her employer, News 24/7. She was well on the way to achieving her ultimate dream, and she wasn't going to derail herself now with an act of insubordination. To both Carter and herself, she said, "If we don't cover it, it didn't happen, okay? Everyone knows the country agrees with the principles behind the Million Muff March. Those sexists over there aren't a story."

"You're right, Majedah." Carter covered his lens and slung the camera back over his shoulder. "Okay, then, looks like we're done here. I'm going to head back to the station. See you there."

"Yeah, bye." Once he was out of sight in the pressing crowd and any danger of accidentally covering the wrong thing was gone, Majedah turned to watch the counter-protestors. In spite of herself, she was compelled to witness their ignorance and hate. It was like being unable to look away from video after video of abused animals on the internet.

The Million Muffs were doing their best to repel the invasion, but the counter-marchers had formed into a wedge shape. And they had brought something diabolical with them that the Muffs didn't have: men.

The men appeared mostly as unremarkable as the women, in their tidy polo shirts and khakis. But they had locked arms and arranged themselves as an outer shield that served both to protect the women within and to force the group into the midst of the angry protestors.

On the stage, Celeste Roberts was becoming hysterical. Her panicked outbursts were picked up by the microphones and broadcast over multiple speakers. "Oh my god, they're penetrating us! They're forcing themselves on us! Help us, someone! We're being assaulted! Rape! Rape!"

The hateful scrum pressed forward, gradually parting the mass of pink-clad humanity and forcing its loathsome wrongthink on them. Majedah held her breath, wondering where it would end. She thought of the children and young women who had come here today, still innocent and unaware that ugly thoughts such as the counter-protestors were spewing even existed, and she wept for the cerebral defilement they were enduring. "This is horrible," she cried. "Someone, help us!"

At last, there was forceful movement among the Muffs in the direction of the haters. Majedah made out the black t-shirts of the Fast Food Workers International and GOO marchers. They were biological males and, being a force for good, they virtuously used their physical strength to halt the incursion. A cheer went up from thousands of Muffs as the brave freedom fighters opposed the intruders. The LOVE BEATS HATE placards the heroes carried had been presciently fastened to two-by-fours and baseball bats, and these they used to defend the noble Muffs from the suburbanites. As wood cracked down on skulls full of hate, Majedah joined in the joyful and righteous chanting:

LOVE BEATS HATE!
LOVE BEATS HATE!
LOVE BEATS HATE!

With a thrill, she noticed that the tide was turning, and the bloodied bigots were being ejected from the area. The crowd around her began to whoop in victory, high-fiving and bumping fists. Majedah turned to touch knuckles with the person next to her—and came face to face with her first (and so far, only) love, Kevin.

"Mandy?" he said in disbelief.

"Kevin?" Majedah said in even greater disbelief. "I never thought I'd see you, of all people, at the Million Muff March."

"Yeah, me neither," he said in a downcast tone. Then he seemed to notice her costume for the first time and an amused grin stole over his face. "Wow, that's quite the get-up you're wearing," he said.

"Yes, it is. It's a very expensive custom design, and I don't need your snark, thank you very much," Majedah snapped.

"Who's this?" The young woman next to Kevin conspicuously took his arm and gave Majedah a critical up-and-down look.

Majedah returned the favor. The woman had a tidy blond ponytail, which had been spray-dyed temporarily pink for the occasion—a sure sign of her superficial commitment to women's rights. She wore an off-the-shoulder, sheer floral designer blouse, layered over a black satin camisole and pink jeans.

"This is Majedah," Kevin said in a voice pitched with nervousness. "Majedah, this is Andy."

"Ah, Majedah. The old high school flame," said the perky demonstrator.

Majedah's seal-black eyes were locked with hers. "Yep, that's me. And you must be the current flame." She put the slightest emphasis on the word *current* and watched Andy's nostrils flare as the barb hit its mark.

"If by 'current,' you mean 'future wife,' then yes, that's me," retorted Andy.

"How heteronormative of you," purred Majedah. "Congratulations." She smiled as Andy's eyes widened then narrowed. "Perhaps next year, you can march with the breeders over there," added the journalist.

Kevin turned to face his companion, subtly inserting himself partway between the two women. "Andy," he said in a bid to change the subject. "Majedah is a reporter with News 24/7. Isn't that cool?"

"You don't say," Andy sneered. "And here, I thought she was just a giant cunt."

"Oh, dear," said Kevin. "This is not what I expected."

"You're right." Majedah's voice dripped with sarcasm. "I should've just gotten the same off-the-rack weekend warrior Marcus Puhtsee jeans as every other poser here."

"Poser? How dare you?"

"Please. I can see the crease down the front from yesterday when they were still folded on the shelf at Barney's."

"Ooh!" Andy's lack of a coherent reply told Majedah she had hit the mark once more.

An increasingly stressed Kevin tried again. "So, Majedah, when can we look for your report on TV?" He strove comically for a conversational tone.

Andy rounded on him. "Who cares about her stupid report? Why aren't you telling *her* when she can see *my* doctoral thesis published?"

"Oh, an academic," said Majedah. The reverence she would ordinarily have felt for this revelation evaporated in the heat of her (surprising, to her) wrath. "What's your thesis on?"

Feeling more sure of herself, Andy lifted her chin. "It's called *Labial Labeling and Genitalia as Identity: On a More Discrete Understanding of Gyno-Centric Self-Determination*. She gave Majedah a superior look. "And I think I've just found the perfect case study."

Majedah glanced at Kevin. He brushed his hair back with a sweaty palm as his eyes darted back and forth between the two women, and he gave a nervous laugh. Despite her best efforts, Majedah felt a pang of sympathy for the man who had once been everything to her. "Kevin, what are you doing with her?" she asked. His eyes met hers and in his momentarily unguarded face, she read the truth: He had no idea.

"What is he doing with *me*? More like what the fuck was he ever doing with *you*?" Andy squawked. "Who dresses like a giant vagina, anyway?"

"Who comes to the Million Muff March and *doesn't*?" Majeda shot back.

Andy's eyes shot flames and daggers at her. "Are you questioning my commitment to Women's Rights?" she said in a dangerous tone of voice.

"No. I'm pointing out your lack of commitment," said Majedah.

"Now, ladies," tried a panicked Kevin. But Andy brushed past him, placed a palm on Majedah's breastbone, and shoved.

Majedah stepped back half a pace to absorb the blow. "Oh, yeah? Come at me, bitch," she shouted. She curled her fingers into talons and raised her hands to her shoulders. Her fantastic costume flared open, revealing layered folds of hot female color. At the same moment, sunlight gleamed off the magenta disco ball and sent searing rays into Andy's eyes. The poser's hands went up defensively as Majedah's full feminine glory momentarily blinded her.

Kevin put a hand over his mouth. "Oh, my goodness, Majedah!" he exclaimed. He looked as though he didn't know whether to laugh or scream.

Andy recovered and hurled herself at Majedah, knocking both of them into the nearest fellow protestors. Majedah swung back, her open hand making contact with Andy's cheek with a satisfying slap. Then there was a loud ripping sound and Majedah's long-suffering clitoris finally tore free from its moorings, swung down on the single silken strand of black fringe to which it was still attached, and bashed the reporter in her perfectly proportioned nose.

"Augh," yelled Majedah. She covered her nose with her hands as blood flowed through her fingers, spattering down the front of her beautiful costume. The renegade clitoris finally liberated itself entirely and clattered away among the feet of the surging crowd.

"Majedah! Are you okay?" Kevin stood before her, his hand on hers, trying to assess her injury.

"Is *she* okay? She just punched me in the face, and you're worried about *her*?" Andy screamed at Kevin. Majedah was delighted to see a red handprint materializing on the woman's cheek.

"I mean, she's gushing blood, Andy." He stopped in confusion, squinting at her cheek. "Are you okay, babe?"

"Don't you *babe* me," Andy barked. "Come on, let's get out of here." She spun and began lunging through the crowd. Torn, Kevin watched her leave then turned his attention back to his bleeding first love. His hands fluttered in the air on either side of Majedah's face, searching for a way to aid her.

"It's okay. Just go, Kevin," she said.

"Yeah, you're right, I should go." But still he lingered.

Majedah's eyes widened from behind her cupped hands. "Go!" she commanded.

With a nod, Kevin was off.

Majedah was left standing alone in the crowd, watching her only ever real boyfriend follow a miserable bitch, away from her, forever. She couldn't believe a shrew like Andy was going to get to marry Kevin. An empty cavern threatened to yawn open in her soul. Also, her nose really hurt, and she didn't have a tissue to clean up her face. With no other option, Majedah used the hem of her sleeve to wipe her nose, inadvertently smearing blood and snot across her cheek.

"Looking good, Majedah," said a voice.

Majedah realized that a small utility vehicle had appeared several feet in front of her. No larger than a golf cart, it was sheathed in bulletproof glass to protect the occupants. The passenger seat was occupied by a technician who had his shoulder-mounted camera trained on Majedah's face. The speaker, who was also the driver, was none other than the Eagle Eye News primetime desk anchor.

"Cader!" hissed Majedah.

The obnoxious anchor sat up straighter and grinned. "Thank you for providing excellent source material for our 'covering the coverage' segment tonight," he said.

"You wouldn't dare run that," Majedah seethed. "What about professional courtesy?"

"I believe professional courtesy is reserved for professionals," retorted Cader in his upper-class drawl.

The conversation was interrupted by the sound of people screaming. Both journalists swiveled their heads to find the source. Thirty yards away, where the righteous protestors had nearly vanquished the hateful counter-protestors, a massive disturbance rippled through the crowd.

"Oh my god—Norms!" gasped Majedah.

Cader forgot all about her. He began to maneuver the newsmobile through the panicked throng, towards the action, while his cameraman filmed.

Majedah watched them go, and the pink tide began to recede past her as virtuous women of all ages and chromosomal arrangements fled the incursion. They shouted warning as they ran by:

"Norms!"

"It's an invasion!"

"Run!"

But Majedah's reporter instincts kept her rooted to the spot; she *had* to see what was happening.

She didn't have to wait long. Hot on the heels of the fleeing Muffs were men: big, bold, brash, stinky men. And not only that, they were outfitted in the same manner as their protesting sisters, not in vaginas, but in full-body tubes of flesh-colored velveteen. Their mischievous faces leered from round holes cut into the bulbous heads of their costumes, and huge beige balls bounced with each running step they took.

Majedah's tingling reporter senses gave way to sheer horror as she watched the apocalyptic scene unfold around her. With whoops and jeers, the rampaging phalli routed the screaming vulvae, thrusting at them mercilessly. Terror held Majedah in place more firmly than professionalism had. "Oh my god, this is the worst thing I've ever seen," she wailed. "It's a holocaust! It's a tragedy! It's a mass rape!"

Dizzy and lightheaded, she held her hand to her forehead as the light began to flicker out. Through fluttering eyelids, she beheld a thing of nightmares; a seven-foot-tall penis was running directly at her. "No!" screamed Majedah. She raised her hands defensively, inadvertently spreading the wings of her glorious womanhood gown. It was as a red flag to a bull.

"Baby, we were made for each other!" yelled the charging John Thomas. When it was a few yards away, it leapt headfirst towards her and plunged into the crimson folds of her costume. Majedah felt the sensation of being knocked off her feet before losing consciousness.

Chapter 18

MAJEDAH DIDN'T KNOW if her head was pounding because of the assault she had suffered the previous day at the Million Muff March or because of the five martinis she had downed once she returned to her apartment that evening.

She had showered and retired to the sofa to drink and watch the news coverage. Carol Crawford's show mostly featured Maria Rodriguez's footage from the Washington, D.C. demonstration. And Majedah had to admit, Maria looked fantastic. She had opted for a funky deep raspberry scoop-neck t-shirt atop black jeans that were tucked into a divine pair of high, black boots. Her shiny, black hair spilled pin-straight over her shoulders from beneath a pink pussy hat. Maria had footage of Senator Harper speaking and Rinnie Halliday doing a live performance of "Vaginas Up!" Majedah stiffened with envy and poured vodka directly into her glass. Her own reportage had been relegated to the end of the C-block and consisted almost entirely of b-roll. Majedah herself got zero facetime on-screen.

She had also cautiously flipped to Eagle Eye News and was relieved to see that Cader's footage of her at her low point hadn't made it onto the broadcast. Instead, Eagle Eye seemed intent on humanizing the terroristic counter-protestors by showing scenes of injured Norms, their heads having been split open and limbs shattered by well-deserved beatings. Disgusted, Majedah had changed the channel back to the virtuous people on her own station, the glorious News 24/7.

Now, the following morning, at her ridiculous desk in the Pool, she struggled to focus on her computer screen as she sat through a webcast of mandatory sensitivity training. Her phone buzzed and she glanced at the screen; it was a message from Kevin. She tapped the screen to read it.

Hey, I'm still in town until tomorrow morning. Can we meet for coffee or something?

Coffee with Kevin sounded like heaven, but Majedah quickly quelled her unruly and inappropriate emotions. She typed, *I don't think that's a good idea.* She paused, then, with a catty expression, added, *What would Andy say?* and hit send. When she replaced her phone on her desk, a dull pain blossomed in her chest to match the throb in her head. Ignoring it, Majedah redoubled her efforts to pay attention to the important instruction on her computer.

"Words are the bread and butter of our business, here in the news media," explained a somber African-American woman on the screen. "But words can also cause grievous injury and even death. When you are speaking or typing an email to your colleagues, it's critical that you evaluate every word you use. Look at each word from all conceivable angles and every point of view."

Majedah nodded in understanding as she watched.

"For example," continued the virtual instructor, "if you are a privileged white male, try to evaluate your words from the point of view of a Mexican-American female. How would you feel about those words if you were in her shoes?"

"I can do that," murmured Majedah.

"This does *not*, however, give you license to assume you can understand an oppressed person's experience," cautioned the instructor. "So, whatever you do, don't think for a moment that you can understand how someone else is affected by your bigoted word choices."

"Huh?" Majedah's brows knitted together as her head throbbed painfully in an attempt to follow the important training.

Chester appeared and strode into the midst of the Pool. Today he wore a custom-tailored suit of pale pink Oxford cloth, in solidarity with the ongoing coverage of the previous day's march. "Guess what I have, everyone!" he intoned loudly. One of his long, thin arms was raised to wave a fan of tickets in the air at a height of around eight feet.

"What you got there?" asked Scout from zis rainbow-striped floaty-shaped desk.

"Just tickets to the hottest comedy show in town," Chester said.

"Oh my god!" shrieked Mysty. "Amelia Kaufahrt?"

Chester splayed the tickets across his chest with a flourish. "The same," he said.

Exclamations broke out from a dozen Pool reporters.

Melissa squealed above the din, "How did you get those?"

"Amelia's PR company sent them to the station, and I managed to secure them."

"When is it?" asked another junior journalist.

"Tonight at eight," answered Chester. "We're going to meet up in the lobby at 6:30 so we can all share cabs down to the club and get good seats. Now, show of hands—who's coming?"

Majedah raised her hand instantly, along with Melissa, Scout, Mysty, and a few of the other Pool reporters. Chester counted off respondents with his long index finger, checked the tickets again, and said, "Great, all set and with two to spare. Okay, see you all at 6:30." He sashayed out of the Pool.

When 6:30 at last rolled around, Majedah and her coworkers chatted exuberantly in the lobby as they waited for stragglers to show up.

"I'm so excited," Scout bubbled. "I've never seen Amelia Kaufahrt live before!"

"Me either," chirped Candy, an assistant associate producer.

Majedah liked Candy, a transgendered female who used one pronoun—Zz—in all cases. This made it super easy to remember which pronoun to use, and thus avoid messing up and risking disciplinary action from Human Resources. Majedah's thoughts were interrupted when she realized she heard someone saying her name. She turned towards the sound and saw the back of a tall man who was speaking with a guard over at the security desk. "Do you have Ms. Cantalupi-Abromavich-Flügel-Van Der Hoven-Taj Mahal's number? asked the guard. "We can try to ring her up for you. Is she expecting you?"

"No, she's not expecting me." The man's familiar voice sounded optimistic, though. "I was just hoping she was still here, in case she had time for a drink with an old friend."

Majedah crossed the lobby, dodging employees both leaving for the day and showing up for the evening. "Hang on, let me look up her work number," the visitor said. Just as he pulled his phone out, she arrived behind him.

"Kevin?"

He spun at the sound of her voice and a smile lit his face at the sight of her. "Hey, Majedah. I was just looking for you."

Majedah firmly suppressed a smile of her own. "Does Andy know you're here?" she asked.

Kevin's smile flickered briefly then relit even brighter. "I don't know, and I don't care," he said. "She left town last night, and I haven't heard from her since."

Majedah felt a triumphant thrill, but to Kevin she said, "Oh, no. I'm so sorry."

"Well, I'm not. Look, I apologize for showing up at your work like this, but I just wanted to tell you how glad I am that I ran into you yesterday. I almost feel like it was fate or something, because out of—what, 40,000 people? 50,000?—you just happened to be standing next to me."

"That was an amazing coincidence," agreed Majedah.

"Coincidence, fate, tomato, to-mah-to," said Kevin. "I'm just glad you were there. It kind of saved me from making a big mistake." His face was flushed with the kind of revelatory joy a condemned man experiences when his sentence is overturned. "Anyway, I wanted to buy you dinner to say thanks. Or at least a drink."

"You smell like you've already had a drink," observed Majedah.

"Just a small one, to get my courage up." Kevin held up a nearly touching index finger and thumb to indicate how small the drink had been.

Meanwhile, Chester, having finished assembling his party, led the group to where the pair stood talking. "Majedah," he interrupted them, "does your handsome friend want to join us? We still have one ticket."

Before Majedah could answer, Kevin asked, "Where are we going?"

"To see Amelia Kaufahrt at the Laugh House," said Chester.

"Sure, why not? Thanks," said Kevin.

"Sure thing. Okay, let's hit the road, people," said Chester, waving his hands in the air like a conductor. He spun and headed for the door, a full head taller than the next tallest person, followed by a colorful collection of Pool reporters, junior staffers, Kevin, and a flustered Majedah.

At the club, Majedah ordered fem-friendly pink martinis and chatted loudly with her coworkers about the trendiest topics she could think of. She was irked that Kevin had weaseled his way into joining them, as she would have preferred to appear indifferent to him. She settled for showing off her urban sophisticate lifestyle while conspicuously ignoring him. From the corner of his eye, Kevin watched her flit from one person to another, gossiping and exclaiming and laughing with her head thrown back, black eyes sparkling.

Meanwhile, Majedah kept a discreet eye on Kevin as well. She observed him obliquely as he polished off a second bourbon and coke and ordered another. He seemed completely comfortable talking to Chester (an impressive feat for the small-minded bigot Majedah knew people like him were), listening with interest as the gangly producer described his Chinese immigrant parents and lamented that he couldn't seem to find the right guy.

When the show began, Kevin claimed the seat next to Majedah, which her co-workers helpfully left vacant for him. Foiled again in her attempt to appear aloof, Majedah looked away at the stage, as if the drunken warm-up comic's performance was riveting. Nonetheless, she could feel Kevin's gaze on her face.

"City life must be agreeing with you," he commented. "You look so pretty."

"I didn't before?" Majedah asked absentmindedly, her eyes fixed on the front of the room.

"I didn't mean it like that," Kevin rushed to correct himself. "I mean, you were always pretty."

Majedah favored him with a quick glance and a smile. "I know, silly," she said.

Before he could answer, the audience broke into unenthusiastic applause as the comic left the stage. A middle-aged man in t-shirt, jacket and jeans took his place at the microphone. "Thank god that's over, huh?" he said, earning the heartiest laughter so far. "Welcome, welcome to the Laugh House, friends," he greeted. "Tonight, we're thrilled to bring you one of the hottest comics in the country today. We were supremely lucky to engage her on one of her rare free nights, between wrapping up her *Disgusting Woman* tour and guest-hosting *Saturday Night Jokes!* Ladies and gentlemen and everything in-between, please give a loud New York homecoming welcome to … Amelia Kaufahrt!

The crowd went wild, screaming and whistling. The 24/7 employees were among the loudest, and Majedah stood up out of her seat, so vigorously did she signal her enthusiasm. Kevin remained seated, clapping politely as though he were at a golf tournament or a piano recital.

Up on the stage, the club manager stood aside and clapped as the famous comedienne took the stage. She strode out confidently, smiled at the audience, and pumped a fist in the air.

Candy exclaimed, "Oh, my god, she's so beautiful!"

"I know!" squealed Mysty.

Amelia Kaufahrt had thick, blond hair that cascaded to her shoulders in carefully formed curls. She had tiny, sparkly blue eyes, thin lips, and a pert, turned-up nose, and her full figure was crammed into a skin-tight, strapless, pink latex jumpsuit.

Majedah heard Kevin snicker. "What's so funny?" she asked.

"She looks like Miss Piggy." He chortled to himself.

Majedah was shocked by Kevin's irreverence. "Well, Miss Piggy is beautiful," she informed him.

He looked at her, trying to make out if she was serious. In the gloom of the club, he couldn't gauge her expression. He let it pass and turned back to the stage.

Amelia Kaufahrt stood grinning, the mic in one hand and her other hand resting on the mic stand, as the audience's boisterous welcome began winding down. She nodded a few times as one or two fans called out her name, but she said nothing. Finally, her prolonged silence caught on and the crowd answered with silence of their own. Once the room became quiet, the celebrated comic dragged it out even further, reveling in the hush and the dramatic spotlight until the level of anticipation became nearly unbearable. Then she raised the microphone to her lips and said, "You know what?"

"What?" answered the audience, as one.

Amelia Kaufahrt paused once more, recapturing everyone's rapt attention before lobbing the first joke of her routine. Speaking one word at a time and pausing for a full second between them, she said,

"I" (titters from the audience)

"hate" (one or two subdued "whoop"s)

"President" (anticipatory ooh's and aah's)

"Nelson."

The entire club erupted into hysterical laughter and applause. Majedah laughed so hard, she was afraid she might vomit. Tears streamed down her cheeks as she turned to Kevin. She was shocked to see him sitting quietly, a confused expression on his face. "Wait, was that a joke?" he asked her.

Majedah could barely control her laughter enough to answer him. "Yes, duh," she said breathlessly. "Wasn't that hilarious?"

Kevin looked at her as though she had spoken in aboriginal Australian.

On stage, Amelia Kaufahrt cranked up the humor. "No, but really, fuck him, folks, right?" Cheers and raucous laughter filled the air. "Fuck him," she repeated.

Majedah clutched her stomach and laughed and laughed. She shoved Kevin's shoulder, but he continued to look from the stage to her and back in apparent bewilderment.

"And speaking of this year's Republican candidates," went on the comedienne. "Or should I say, Nazi Party candidates—am I right?"

Scout was writhing on the floor at Majedah and Kevin's feet, and Candy was slumped in Zz seat, weak and shaking with laughter.

"Speaking of candidates," continued the comic genius, "what's with Patty Clark and all those kids of hers? She has more kids than I have hemorrhoids!"

A fresh frenzy of laughter wracked the room. Dizzy from lack of oxygen, Majedah dropped her head onto Kevin's shoulder and slapped his upper arm three times. But not only was he still not laughing, his lip was curled in distaste. "What was that? Was that a joke?" he asked Majedah. "That's disgusting."

"Well, she did just finish her *Disgusting Woman* tour," panted Majedah. She was confounded by Kevin's serious demeanor in a club full of people in the throes of explosive mirth. "I don't understand how you're not laughing," she accused.

"Get this, get this," said Amelia Kaufahrt's amplified voice. "My vagina? It smells like an open sewer." A roar of hilarity washed over the comedienne as she nodded in mock solemnity at the audience. "Scout's honor," she added.

Majedah was holding her middle and rocking with laughter when Kevin's hand closed around hers. "This sucks," he said. "Come on, we're getting out of here.

Weak and dizzy, Majedah grabbed her purse with her other hand and allowed Kevin to lead her out of the club and into the calm, cool evening. He almost seemed angry, and Majedah had to trot to keep up with his long, quick strides. They had put three blocks between them and the club before she finally dug in her heels and stopped. "Kevin, please, slow down," she insisted. "I can't keep up with you."

He halted and finally seemed to see her. "Sorry," he said. "I just had to get out of there."

"Why? What was wrong? Didn't you think Amelia Kaufahrt was funny?"

"No, I didn't." He was practically yelling. "I thought she was disgusting, and I don't understand why all those people were carrying on like that. It was like being in an insane asylum."

Majedah gasped. Kevin looked into her wide, shocked eyes and asked, "You didn't think she was funny, did you?"

"I absolutely thought she was funny. Amelia Kaufahrt is the hottest comic in the country right now. She just came off a tour where she performed in every important city in the country, and she's about to start filming a major motion picture."

"So what?" He searched her face, looking for something he could connect to. "Do you, Majedah, think the things she just said in that club were actually *funny*?"

"I'm not sure what you mean."

"When she expressed hatred for the president, then talked about her personal hygiene disorders, did you really, truly—" He noticed her earnest expression as she tried to understand his point and shook his head. "Oh, never mind. I'm sorry, Majedah, I just didn't get it. I hope I didn't embarrass you in front of your work friends." He turned and began walking again.

After a second's pause, Majedah caught up to him. The bellyful of pink martinis had rendered her mood mercurial, and her amusement gave way to sudden annoyance. "So, what, are you just too noble and virtuous to find Amelia Kaufahrt's humor funny?" she demanded. "Like, you're just cleaner and purer and holier-than-thou?" Kevin was doing his best to ignore her, and she hooked her hand into the crook of his arm to slow him. "Now you answer me! Do you think you're better than everyone in that club?"

Kevin halted abruptly and locked gazes with her. "No," he said, "but I thought you were."

Majedah caught her breath at his unexpected answer. Quickly, she regained her composure. "You're drunk," she accused.

"Eh, so are you," answered Kevin. His robin's egg blue eyes were trained on her own, and Majedah could feel her carefully mustered indignation collapsing.

The couple had come to rest by a pocket park that occupied an odd triangular island alongside a busy avenue. They stood facing one another beneath a canopy of leafy dogwood, through which the eerie light from a street lamp was sifted and dappled. Groups of young professionals passed around them on the sidewalk, talking energetically on their way to an evening's diversions. In the deeper shadow alongside a tall bank of rhododendron, a grizzled street person ransacked a trashcan for discarded treasures. Nearby, an old man with a great white mustache glowered at the vagrant while he waited for his leashed papillon to do its business.

Majedah noticed none of these things. Her vodka-fogged mind could only focus on one thing: the man in front of her. He was searching her face again with those eyes of his, bright enough to appear blue even in the surreal urban evening light. The spring breeze riffled his thick, sandy hair so that it stood up straight, daring her to plunge her fingers into it. Her hand still rested on his arm from when she had stopped him, and she felt the tension in his bicep through the fabric of his shirt. She realized her mouth was hanging open and she primly pressed her lips together. She tried to swallow but her throat felt so tight.

When Kevin spoke again, his voice was soft. "I don't understand what you're doing with those people, Majedah," he said. "The Majedah I know is happy and positive. She looks at something awful and always finds something good. She doesn't stop trying until she makes it right." He gave a soft laugh. "Remember senior year, when you used to make me lunch every day?"

"That was because I couldn't stand to watch you eat all that crap you kept buying in the cafeteria. You were the most unhealthy eater I ever saw." A faint memory of a different time came to Majedah, bringing with it a barely remembered feeling of well-being and something else, too; something she couldn't quite put her finger on, but she recalled was most pleasant.

Happiness? Without even realizing she was grinning, she said, "God, I used to get up at five in the morning, so I could make fresh hummus from scratch for you. And I'd dice peppers and shred kale..."

"And I hated those nasty pocket sandwiches you brought me," Kevin said.

"What?"

"But I ate them all, every day," he went on. "Because you made them for me. It was so important to you to make sure I was eating right. I wouldn't have missed your nasty sandwiches for the world." He smiled warmly. "That's the Majedah I know."

"But that was high school, Kevin. I'm different now."

"Different how?"

"I'm smarter. I went to college and learned a lot of important things I didn't know before."

Kevin laughed once, softly, an exhalation through his nose that did nothing to diminish his affectionate gaze. "I went to college, too, Majedah. I learned all about petrochemical engineering. But the really important things—the life things—I learned from the people who are important to me. People like you. Anyway, I wanted to take you out tonight because I wanted to tell you something, Majedah."

Should I stop him? Majedah wondered fleetingly.

Shut up and let him talk, her ego responded.

Kevin seemed determined to speak. "When I saw you at that march yesterday, it made something clear to me."

Majedah had to interrupt to ask something she'd been wondering since the previous day. "What were you even doing at that march, Kevin? That was the last place I'd have expected to run into you."

He glanced away at the old man walking his tiny dog, and she saw the muscles of his jaw tense up. "I was trying to be a good boyfriend, or fiancé, or whatever. I was trying to be supportive. Andy wanted to go; it was really important to her. And I thought, you know, since we're going to spend the rest of our lives together, I should try to take an interest in the things she cares about."

Majedah was shaking her head. "But Kevin, how did you even wind up with a feminist in the first place? I know you—you're a conservative guy. Why did you think that would work?"

He met her eyes again. "What else am I going to do, Majedah?" His question sounded plaintive. "All women are like that now. I've resigned myself to a life with a wife who has different values than me. It's just what I have to do unless I want to be alone forever."

"Not that I approve of your outdated misogyny or anything, but surely you should be able to find one of those backwards, self-loathing women who think the same way you do?" Majedah asked supportively.

Kevin shook his head sadly. "Nope. No matter who I meet, all women have bought into this feminism thing." He noticed Majedah's eyes narrow slightly and quickly clarified, "And that's okay! That's fine. I can live with a woman who has her own belief system."

"How very open minded of you." Majedah had intended to huff indignantly, but he was still looking at her with those eyes of his, and her words came out unexpectedly mild.

Several paces away, the papillon had produced a grape-sized turd, which its elderly owner bagged and deposited into the trash can. The homeless woman who had been rummaging there stepped back with a rusty screech. "Hey! I am working here," she chastised him in an accent that sounded like old Transylvania.

"Ah, too bad. Get a real job," the old guy bleated back. He stooped to pick up the small, fluffy dog, which he tucked under his arm. Glaring at the street woman, he skulked around her and headed away up the street, shaking his head and muttering.

In turn, she shook her fist at him. "I curse you, you old devil! And I curse your dirty little dog, too!"

Majedah had turned to watch the interaction when Kevin spoke again. "Anyway, what's the use of being drunk if we can't say what we're thinking? Majedah, what I wanted to tell you..." He reached for her, and the feel of his large hands firmly encircling her slender biceps thrilled her. Instantly pliant, she could only look up into his face while he spoke. And lubricated with liquor, he was speaking straight from his heart, she was sure. With her head buzzing (or was that the street light above?), Majedah fancied she could stare into Kevin's eyes and peer directly into his very soul. The connection was so intense, it took her breath away. Her lips parted ever so slightly as she stood perfectly still, looking into Kevin's soul and lapping up his emotional confession.

"When I saw you yesterday, in your crazy costume, and you got into it with Andy, uh, I don't know how to explain it, but ... you ruined her for me," he said. Words were gushing out of him now, and Majedah stood silent, listening with every fiber of her being. "I thought I was going to marry that girl," he said. "I had bought her a ring and bit the bullet and got my head around it, and everything. I was resolved.

"And then you were there, and you ... you're funny! And crazy, and beautiful, too, and I just thought about how different you are from Andy. She's so serious and humorless. I realized I had never even seen her smile. Can you believe that? And all of a sudden, I couldn't stand the thought of marrying her. I wanted to stay with you in that crowd, Mandy. I felt like I had rediscovered something, something crucial."

Kevin's monologue brimmed with intensity and slurred words, and Majedah was as rapt as she had ever been. She knew he was all wrong for her, and she had no intention of letting it go any further than this drunken moment of revelation. And yet, somehow, she couldn't get enough of him, of his spellbinding words and mesmerizing eyes. "Go on," she said.

"Since yesterday, I've been thinking about my life since you and I were together, and about other girls I've dated, and when I'm being honest with myself, none of them compares to you. It's always been you, Mandy. I wanted to take you out tonight because I wanted to tell you that I think I—"

"Oh, my god, it's the TV star!" rasped a loud voice next to Majedah's ear. The sour stench of cheap liquor and unbrushed teeth washed over the couple. Grimacing, they broke contact and stepped apart.

"I know you. I see you on the TV when I pass the store," screeched the old homeless woman. Now that she was close by and in the glow of the streetlight, she was revealed to be wearing a soiled men's dress shirt, trousers, and brown leather boots. She had wrapped an embroidered scarf around her head like a babushka, from which tendrils of wild gray hair had escaped to drift about her greasy face. Her chapped lips were spread wide in a gap-toothed grin, but it was her fevered eyes that now held Majedah captive. Kevin took Majedah's arm in a protective gesture, but she continued to stare back at the old woman.

"You have bright future, do you not?" asked the hag. "A very bright future indeed. You are young, you are beautiful, and you are on the TV." She squinted into Majedah's eyes as though scrying the future, and her expression changed abruptly from ecstatic to grave. "But maybe not so bright future as you think."

Majedah felt a stab of panic. "What do you mean?" she demanded.

The woman's heavy brows drew together above the protruding bridge of her nose as she scrutinized her subject. "You and your friends on the TV," she said. "You journalists. You think you are all so clever. You think you speak 'truth to power,' as you like to say. You all think you will be next journalist to bring down the powerful, like in the Watergate." She raised her hands to shoulder height, waggling her fingers as though channeling divine prophesy. Majedah gasped. "But the days when journalists bring down presidents are over," proclaimed the hag. "These are the days when presidents bring down journalists!" Then she broke into a manic cackle.

Majedah began to tremble with fear. Kevin, seeing her state, intervened. "That's enough out of you, now," he said sharply to the hag.

The old woman seemed to have finished her performance and became suddenly businesslike. "Thank you. That will be twenty dollars."

"What?" asked Kevin. "For what?"

"Just give her the money, Kevin," ordered a shaken Majedah.

He looked at her oddly, but he pulled a few bills from his pocket, peeled off a twenty, and handed it to the hag. "Here. Now go away."

"Thank you, young man. God bless you and your girlfriend."

Girlfriend? Majedah bristled. She turned to her companion. "Goodnight, Kevin. It was fun seeing you again." Before he could answer, she had spun 180 degrees and hurried away up the sidewalk.

"Majedah," Kevin called after her. "Mandy!"

It was the hardest thing she had done all year, but Majedah didn't turn back. She doubled her speed and kept walking, forcing herself to think of her future.

There was no place for a man like Kevin in her future.

Before the strange hag had interrupted them, Majedah was pretty sure he had been about to blurt out that he loved her. She didn't want to know that. To a man like Kevin, love would require her complete surrender to him; that she make a home with him and spend the best hours of her days with him; that she place him above all else and let him do the same for her; that she be cherished and cared for, and probably have babies someday, too; cute, pudgy, silly babies...

Majedah shook her head savagely to clear it of such anachronistic notions. "This is Majedah Cantalupi-Abromavich-Flügel-Van Der Hoven-Taj Mahal," she recited out loud, "reporter at News 24-7, New York City." She skirted a couple that was making out right on the sidewalk and descended the subway steps at a run. "Someday to be Anchor of the Women's Desk at News 24-7 World Headquarters in midtown Manhattan!" She swiped her MetroCard and passed through the turnstile. The incantation was clearing her head, and she continued with greater force. "Someday to be the first woman ever to win ten Golden Vulva Awards for Feminist Reporting!" The hissing train at the platform chimed a warning that it was about to shut its doors, and she dashed across the platform. "The most famous, powerful, and historic woman journalist ever!" she declared, as she flew into the car at the last possible second. The doors closed behind her and she breathed a huge sigh of relief. She had narrowly escaped a fatal derailment.

Safely alone in her condo, Majedah turned off her phone so Kevin couldn't tempt her. She showered and dressed in organic linen pajamas and brought a glass and a bottle to bed to watch the late news cycle. But no amount of comforting, Progressive reporting could purge her mind of the memory of Kevin's impossibly blue eyes, focused on her and only her, as if she were the sole thing in the world he could see. No amount of vodka could make her forget the feel of his strong hands on her arms, holding her still as he confessed his feelings for her. With a grunt, she turned off the TV and curled onto her side.

But no matter how tightly she clenched her eyes shut, she could still see Kevin. Just like a controlling, aggressive man, he shoved aside her customary bedtime fantasies of professional success and manspread himself into all the space in her mind and heart. Drunk and drowsy, Majedah was helpless against the assault. She saw herself with him, loved, cared for, and happy. She was horrified to realize that she was even aroused, so thoroughly had his manipulative behavior invaded her body and soul. She groaned with self-loathing and spent the long hours of the night chasing elusive sleep. Only as dawn's first glow infused the sky outside her floor-to-ceiling window did she fall into a stupor.

Chapter 19

A HUNGOVER AND dejected Majedah skulked into the News 24/7 office the next day. She was so distracted in the morning meeting that she barely remembered to cheer when it was announced that Patty Clark would be challenging President Nelson at the Republican National Convention. Apparently, New Hampshire and Colorado had thrown all their delegates to a baked Libertarian candidate while Utah had gone for a Principled Conservative who had come out of nowhere. Thus, no candidate had garnered the minimum required number of delegates. The Republican presidential candidate would need to be selected at the upcoming convention.

For the first time since coming to New York, Majedah was unprofessional enough to check her phone under the conference table. There were two more missed calls from Kevin, bringing the total since the previous night to six. There was also a text:

> *On my way to the airport. I wish you had taken my calls, but I understand why you didn't. I hope I didn't come on too strong last night but I don't regret anything I said. Anyway, it was so good to see you. I'll be in touch soon. Love, K.*

Majedah sighed dreamily before catching herself. She turned the phone off and commanded her mind to eradicate all traces of loneliness and longing. With her cravings for male company banished to somewhere in the back of her head, she tried to pay attention to the rest of the meeting.

She spent the workday at her desk with her chin propped in one hand, surfing the internet and getting no work done. Kevin's specter haunted her, and while she refused to dwell on him, she couldn't concentrate on anything else, either.

"You poor thing, you look like you just lost your best friend," said Mysty. The busty transgender woman had been passing by and paused to look with sympathy on myr fellow Pool reporter. "Everything okay, sweetie?" mys asked.

"Huh? Oh, yeah, sure. It's nothing," Majedah assured myr.

"Okay, if you say so." Mysty gave her a skeptical smile. "But I still think you should come out for drinks after work with us."

Majedah welcomed the invitation to distract herself. Kevin's visit had left her lonely and vulnerable, and the thought of spending the evening alone in her apartment was daunting. "That would be great. Where are we going?"

"Just to the Buzz. We'll scoop you up on the way out the door."

By eight o'clock, Majedah was starting on her fourth pink martini and feeling much more like herself. She sat at a high table near the bar, along with Mysty, Scout, Melissa, Chester, and Ångström, the transgender male camera operator who sometimes hung around with them. Majedah was always a little nervous when Ångström joined them; she had finally mastered all of Scout, Mysty, and Candy's preferred pronouns, but Ångström's were more obscure, and she was afraid she'd mess them up and get called a bigot.

Melissa choked on a swallow of wine and set her glass down quickly. "Oh my god, look who just walked in. It's Spinner!"

The young professionals turned to look, along with everyone else in the bar, which was, after all, a broadcast media industry establishment. An awed hush spread over the place, so that only the multiple wall-mounted televisions (which were always tuned to News 24/7) were heard.

"Whoa," said Scout.

"What's he doing here?" wondered Ångström. Blue recent hormone therapy had given 37 a voice like an adolescent frog as well as three or four blond whiskers on blue chin, which adjutant stroked thoughtfully.

Chatting loudly with a retinue of suits, the Great Man proceeded towards the dining tables. He cast a sidelong glance at his employees, and he inclined his head in a nod as he passed.

"Amazing—he recognized us," observed Chester. He raised a hand in greeting, but the Great Man had already passed by.

Majedah's seat faced the back of the restaurant, and as she nibbled on her kale leaves seasoned with Himalayan salt crystals, she observed Richard Spinner take a seat at a table with the suits. For the briefest of moments, Majedah imagined his eyes had met hers across the bustling expanse of the restaurant. She smiled reflexively and looked down at her kale, flushing. *Don't be ridiculous*, she told herself. Then she redirected her attention to her companions. They were all looking up at the enormous screen on the wall beside their table. "Who's Carol have on tonight?" asked Majedah.

"Young adult author Judi Picklebloom," said Chester.

All the real and imagined females at the table said, "Aw!" in unison.

"I loved her books when I was a kid," cooed Melissa.

"Me too," said Scout. "I still have all my copies of everything she ever wrote."

"That is so cool," exclaimed Ångström in blue cracking, amphibious voice, momentarily forgetting that adjutant was supposed to be a manly man.

"Shh! I want to hear this," commanded Mysty.

On the screen, Carol had just finished greeting her guest with a polite hug where the women touched cheeks. Then they sat on the white leather sofa facing one another. The soft light on the rosy-hued set flattered their crepey skin and added a glow that one associated with youth.

"Judi, we are so excited to have America's best-loved tween author on the show tonight," declared Carol. Majedah studied her poised delivery; Carol Crawford did not gush, no matter how squeal-worthy her guest was.

"Thank you so much, Carol." Judi Picklebloom smiled broadly, her glossed lips sliding over pronounced and immaculately bleached teeth. She did such an effective job smiling authentically that creases crinkled the skin at the corners of her brown eyes.

Mysty hissed in horror. "Girl, time to get some work done," she advised the televised author.

"It's not her fault," Chester said. "Carol designed her studio lighting herself. See how there's a shadow just under Judi's nose, but not under Carol's?"

Everyone at the table squinted at the screen, then exclaimed at once.

"Yes, I do see that," said Mysty.

"What does it mean?" asked Melissa.

"That's because there are all kinds of fill lights aimed at the precise spot where Carol sits on that sofa," explained Chester. "If she doesn't sit in that precise spot—if she accidentally sits an inch to the right or the left—she immediately looks ten years older."

"Whoa," said Scout.

"And she doesn't have a similar lighting set-up for her guests?" wondered Majedah.

"Would you?" asked Chester. "Especially if your job depended on you somehow staying young-looking forever?"

"And what better way to trick everyone into thinking you look young than to make everyone near you look old?" Majedah guessed.

Chester nodded archly. "Exactly. The light on the guest's side of the sofa is ever-so-slightly harsher, and there's no fill…"

"…so every imperfection stands out in relief," Majedah finished for him.

"That is how it's done," acknowledged Chester. Majedah tucked the information away in her memory for later use.

On screen, Carol began to draw her guest out. "Judi, tell us about your new tween romance series that's launching this week." Her brows descended slightly in concentration as she asked her first question.

"How does she do that?" wondered Melissa.

"What, move her brows?" asked Chester.

"Yeah."

"It's a very expensive and proprietary technique known as CAPBT: Computer-Aided Precision Botox Targeting. It smooths the forehead while preserving just enough sub-muscular function to simulate emotion."

"Whoa," said Scout admiringly. "I suppose it's too expensive for most of us."

"Let's just say that it takes a Carol Crawford-sized paycheck to be able to afford it," Chester confirmed.

Judi Picklebloom was holding up a hardcover book in front of her. "Sure, Carol. It's a new series for young women who are ready to leave their childhoods behind and embrace the full meaning of womanhood. The series is called *Beginner's* … well, I can't say it on TV, but you can show the book cover."

The cover of Judi Picklebloom's newest book filled the screen. The author's name in large, all-cap lettering covered the top third of it. There were small words across the bottom that read *Book One: Freshman Orientation*. The title of the series covered the entire middle of the cover with bold, swashy letters that spelled out *BEGINNER'S F*CK*. The space where a *U* might have been was instead filled with a barely-opened pink rosebud.

Carol's voice talked over the image. "Oh, my goodness, isn't that pretty," she chuckled. "I love the flower; it sort of classes up that last word and makes it suitable for tween readers. So clever!"

The women returned to the screen. Judi gave a cultured laugh and lightly tossed her chin-length curls. "Thank you," she said. "Our cover designer is a genius. And you know, Carol, embracing one's sexuality is such an important part of feminism for today's young women. So, I saw a real need for this series. It tells authentic and relatable stories while also answering questions and concerns tweens might have about becoming sexually active."

"A sort of how-to, wrapped up in a young adult romance," clarified Carol.

"Exactly," agreed Judi.

Around the table, besotted sighs sounded. "I wish she had written that when I was ten," said Melissa.

"What a really genius idea," agreed Mysty.

"Tell us about the first book in the series," Carol prompted her guest.

"So, it's called *Freshman Orientation*, and it's the story of a young woman named Britney whose parents have moved to the suburbs of Chicago from a more rural area in Illinois. And right away—at freshman orientation, in fact—she meets an adorable boy named Miguel. They totally hit it off and it's clear they belong together. But Sandra has some obstacles to overcome before she can be with Miguel."

"Such as?" pried Carol.

"Such as, first of all, she has been raised in a very oppressive, conservative church, and she has all this guilt holding her back."

"Oh, dear. That's so sad when that happens."

"I know." Judi nodded, her dark eyes shining with compassion for the fictitious character. "And not only that, Miguel is a Dreamer."

"So, his family is undocumented?" Carol clarified.

"Yes, exactly. And that presents another problem for poor Britney."

"Well, if you say she comes from a conservative family, I can guess what that might be." Carol's exquisitely preserved forehead tightened with ladylike contempt.

Judi nodded again. "Yes, unfortunately, Britney has internalized racism from her upbringing, and she has to overcome that as well so that she can ultimately lose her virginity to Miguel."

Carol's face warmed with an estrogenic smile. "Sounds like all is well by the end of the book?"

"Well, there are some difficult, painful struggles along the way," said Judi. "But I can promise my audience that the book has a happy ending."

Carol began to wrap up the segment. "So, if anyone out there has a daughter or granddaughter or niece who'll be entering high school soon, this sounds like a great gift for them."

"And this is a great time to get the book, because beach season is just starting," Judi added.

"That sounds amazing, Judi. Thank you so much for being my guest on *An Hour of Your Time* tonight."

"My pleasure, Carol. Thank you so much for having me."

Majedah watched closely as the women faced each other and smiled their goodbyes. Carol's smile had a made-for-TV charm, but Judi's smile actually reached her eyes—which made her look twenty years older than Carol, even though Majedah knew the opposite had to be true. She gazed at Carol Crawford's visage with profound respect, thinking, *The woman is a genius.*

Carol looked directly into the camera. "Thank you so much for joining me tonight, dear viewers. Starting tomorrow, I'll be on vacation for a while, getting some much-needed spa time so I can be rested and ready for the upcoming election season. I miss you all already, and I can't wait to see you again when I return, refreshed and rejuvenated and ready to report." A Rinnie Halliday ballad swelled to play the show off the air for the evening.

Across the table from Majedah, Chester snorted.

"What?" she asked.

"'Spa time,'" he said, shaking his head.

Majedah leaned forward onto the table, a wicked smile on her face. "What's she really doing?" she asked. All the junior journalists at the table went silent, waiting to see what Chester would say.

"What do you think?" he shot back.

"Getting more work done?" ventured Mysty.

Majedah shot an incredulous look at myr. "She can't be! How many procedures can a woman have before her skin is simply stretched too tight and thin?"

But Chester nodded affirmatively. "Oh, she is, alright. Her surgeon approved her for one more round."

"How do you know all this?" asked a shocked Majedah.

"Because the woman is stupid enough to talk on speaker phone," explained Chester. "She thinks she's safe because she closes her office door, but let me tell you, the walls have ears in that building."

"Noted," said Majedah. "So, her doctor really thinks he can pull it off again, huh?"

"Well, my sources say that she had to do some persuading. Namely, a combination of shrieking at the man while possessing an eight-figure bank account," explained Chester. "And now, she's off to the 'spa' once more. Although if I were her I'd invest in some higher necklines, or she'll have to start waxing her chest, if you know what I mean." He bent his head to lap delicately from a saucer of milk that a waiter had just placed in front of him.

Majedah sat quietly as the new information sank in. Carol Crawford had to be on borrowed time by now. Even if her surgeon was the best and somehow managed to work with the paltry scrap of skin Carol still had on her face, at her age, it wouldn't hold up for long. The time was drawing ever closer when Majedah would be able to make her move.

She polished off her martini and noted that her head was spinning nicely. She hadn't slept well the night before, but this new development would hopefully be enough to drive Kevin from her mind. Maybe she could get some rest tonight. She wanted to be fresh in the morning, so she wouldn't miss any opportunities to impress anyone in a decision-making capacity. "Be right back," she told her companions. Then she took her purse and headed for the women's room at the back of the restaurant, in preparation for the trip home.

As she passed the table full of suits, she could hear the roar of their high-powered discourse, punctuated by raucous laughter. She chanced a glance in their direction and spied Richard Spinner sitting back in triumph as everyone pounded the table at whatever he had just said. Raw power rolled off him in waves, and Majedah flushed as his eyes noted her passage near the table. She smiled nervously and moved quickly to the short hallway where the restrooms were located.

The door to each of the ostentatiously gender-neutral restrooms was locked, indicating an occupant within. Majedah leaned against the wall to wait. Then she drew in a sharp breath as the Great Man himself appeared at the end of the short hallway. He spied her and began speaking immediately in a familiar tone. "Well, well, if it isn't our star Pool reporter, Ms. Cantalupi-Abromavich-Flügel-Van Der Hoven-Taj Mahal."

Majedah felt light-headed, hearing her full name trip off the tongue of the media mogul. "You—you know who I am?" she stammered.

"Of course, I do. You're the one who made that fry cook into a real presidential candidate—in enough people's eyes, anyway." He gave two short laughs: *Huh! Huh!*

"Yes, I was fortunate enough to be granted that interview," Majedah agreed cautiously.

"And you auditioned for the Islamophobia desk," the billionaire stated. He stood before her in the empty hall, his presence filling the space. Majedah felt pinned to the wall by his direct stare.

"Y-yes, that was me," she admitted. Her cheeks burned as she thought about her poor performance and humiliation at the audition. "But I didn't get the position."

Spinner waved her concerns away. "Ah, don't worry about that. You're better off not getting it. As soon as the election is over, that desk is going away."

"Going away?"

"Yeah, it'll have served its purpose by then."

A wave of satisfaction warmed Majedah. She failed to keep the cattiness from her voice as she asked, "But what will happen to Mohammed?"

"Al Kaboom? Oh, I don't know, we'll find a use for him somewhere." Spinner's jovial tone was having a relaxing effect on Majedah, loosening her up in his presence. He nodded at her with his chin. "So don't worry about it; I'm sure there's a bright future for you at 24/7." He winked.

"Oh! Thank you, Mr. Spinner," Majedah said. "I certainly hope so."

"Listen, I gotta take a piss, but where you going? You heading home after this?" he asked.

"Yes, I was going home in a minute."

"Where you live? Wait, let me guess … Brooklyn?"

Majedah giggled fetchingly. "No, but good guess. I live on the Upper West Side."

"Wow, nice. Tell you what. I was just leaving, too. I got a car out back, let me give you a lift home."

Majedah couldn't believe her good fortune. "Oh, that's very nice of you, Mr. Spinner. Are you sure you don't mind?"

"Why would I mind? Durante's driving."

"Oh, okay then. Yes, thank you, that would be great."

"Good, glad that's settled. I'm just gonna take a piss, then you meet me outside that back door there. You see that door at the other end of the hall?"

"Yes, I see it."

"Okay, so the car is out there. See you in a minute."

In the back of the limo, Spinner poured champagne and dangled tantalizing fruit. "You hear about Carol's 'spa' vacation?" he asked as he passed her a glass.

Majedah took a gulp while she framed her answer. She decided to play innocent and said, "Yes. How wonderful for her."

Huh! Huh! laughed the cable news founder. "'Spa,' my ass." He topped Majedah's glass off. "She's trying to freshen up, if you know what I mean. But her days in prime time are numbered. We'll need to find a new feminist anchor soon."

The enormity of (maybe) being on the cusp of realizing her life's dream was overwhelming. Majedah could only mumble,

"Uh huh.'" She took another swallow of the exquisite Krug Private Curée.

The limo had traveled several midtown blocks and come to rest in front of a glitzy skyscraper. Majedah looked out the window, confused. "Where are we? This isn't my building."

"I just gotta pick something up from my place. It'll just take a minute." Spinner put his glass in a holder and made to open his door, then stopped and turned to her as though something had just occurred to him. "Hey, you wanna come up and see the penthouse? The view is spectacular. You gotta see this."

"The penthouse?" squeaked Majedah.

The Great Man moved up against her on the seat and grasped her wrist in his cologne-scented hand. "How'd you like to find out why they call me 'Dick?'" he growled. Then Majedah's hand was in his lap and his meaty lips were covering half her face.

In a perfect tawdry storm, Majedah's unaddressed longing for intimacy met up with her oh-so-strokable ego as well as a heady rush from having power over a man of Spinner's stature, by virtue of his desire for her. Breathless, she opened her mouth to receive his vigorous tongue thrusts while she manipulated him through his worsted trousers. All of her trials and embarrassments and frustrated strivings would soon be a thing of the past, she realized. With affection on offer from a man who could have any woman and with her goal in sight, Majedah proceeded enthusiastically and joyfully past the liveried doorman, into the elevator, and up to the Great Man's penthouse.

And he hadn't lied, she realized; the view from up there *was* spectacular.

Chapter 20

FROM THE LUXURY of her butter-soft first-class seat, Majedah Googled "contested convention." Carter, the cameraman who had filmed her at the Million Muff March, and Candy, the transgender female assistant associate producer, were tucked away in coach class, and Majedah was able to read in peace. By the time the plane landed in Nashville, she felt adequately informed to cover the Republican National Convention.

It was not the gig she had wanted, of course; Maria Rodriguez had buttoned that one up. 24/7's Washington correspondent would wing her way out to Seattle to cover the Democratic National Convention almost as soon as Majedah returned to New York. In fact, Senator Harper's official nomination would be so historic and empowering that most of 24/7's heavy hitters would be on hand as well. Daytime anchor Toffee Barbeaux would handle direct interviews with power players and celebrities, since Carol Crawford was still out of commission, while Maria would cover the overall convention scene. Chester was among a small army of producers and technicians also going, and Rosemary herself would oversee operations to ensure broadcast perfection. The Democratic National Convention would be News 24/7's most impressive production to date.

Majedah's job was important too, she told herself as she unpacked in her hotel room. President Nelson would go into the election as the weakest incumbent in American history. The forecasters at 24/7 predicted there would be at least three rounds of balloting before he would even secure enough delegates for the nomination—a complete humiliation for a sitting president. Reporting it might not be as prestigious as announcing Senator Harper's historic nomination, but it would be satisfying in its own way, Majedah assured herself. She dressed carefully in a tightly fitted sleeveless red dress, fixed her hair and makeup, and left the room to meet her team in the lobby.

"Are we going to have to talk to anyone at this thing?" worried Candy. The three 24/7 employees were riding in the car from the hotel to CroniBank Arena, where the convention was being held, and Majedah could see the fear on the assistant associate producer's face.

"If we have to, I'll handle it," Majedah said in as soothing a voice as she could. She made a renewed effort to conceal her own anxiety at spending the next few days surrounded by thousands of hostile hillbillies and Nazis.

Carter cleared his throat self-consciously. "Well," he said, "my mom emailed me that my Aunt Gloria will be one of the delegates from Tennessee, I'm ashamed to say. But while Aunt Gloria isn't exactly enlightened, she's not all that bad either."

"Is that supposed to make me feel better?" Candy snapped at him. "Because it doesn't." Zz exhaled in sorrowful angst and began to rummage frantically through Zz purse.

"I'm sorry," said Carter. "I was just trying to—"

"Just stop trying, okay?" Candy found what Zz was looking for and pulled a family-size jar of Xanax from Zz bag. Zz popped the lid and shook half a dozen tablets into Zz hand.

Majedah observed her sole producer with a watchful eye. "Are you going to be able to do your job okay, if you take all of those?" she asked pointedly.

Candy looked up from Zz pharmaceuticals to meet Majedah's stern eye. A simpering smile broke out on Zz face. "You're right, Majedah," Zz agreed. Zz carefully shook a single tablet out of Zz hand and back into the jar. "There!" Zz said. Zz quickly popped the remaining pills into Zz mouth and took a swig from Zz water bottle.

Majedah shook her head indulgently. She had noted Candy's deference to her, an unspoken acknowledgement that Majedah was the leader of the team. Well, good, because she took her role seriously, even when she was on as unpleasant an assignment as this one. "Don't worry, you guys," she said in an empowering voice. "With a little luck, we won't even have to leave our booth in the convention hall. It's not like there will be anyone there anyone's ever heard of, who we'd need to talk to. Everyone who's anyone will be at the *real* convention next week," she added wistfully.

The car neared the arena, and the very air seemed to grow dark. Mobs of people were running to and fro, throwing bricks and bottles. On one side of the vehicle, black smoke blossomed from several blazing cars. On the other side, groups of thugs surrounded individuals and beat them with two-by-fours or kicked them in the head with steel-toed boots when they fell. Screams and yowls rent the air. Fists pumped, sirens wailed, flames kindled, glass shattered, and blood flowed deep and red.

Then the car reached the gate to the parking lot, and the intrepid journalists saw sights that would strike terror into the staunchest of hearts.

First, a phalanx of law enforcement officers signaled to the car to stop. Majedah, Candy, and Carter clung to one another and trembled in the backseat as the driver lowered his window and produced a press pass.

"I can't believe, in this day and age, we have to show our papers to the jackboots," moaned Candy.

Majedah hushed Zz, watching the interaction anxiously. After a moment, the officers waved them on. "Thanks," said the driver in a perfectly normal-sounding tone of voice. He raised his window and drove on serenely.

"Good job, Mike," Majedah complimented him.

"What, showing our press pass to security?" asked the driver. His eyes glanced at Majedah in the rearview mirror before he returned his attention to the road.

Majedah gasped in terror at the next sight that met her eyes: Americans. Wherever she looked, there were SUVs with popped hatches, pickup trucks with dropped tailgates, and even a vast section of RVs with dining flies erected alongside them. In and among these Gaia-raping vehicles were thousands and thousands of people. They wore dresses, polo shirts, button-downs, and jackets with khakis, shorts, or skirts. Some wore red, white and blue cowboy boots over jeans. Some had printed hats or t-shirts or signs. Majedah noted that most of these read *Patty for Prez* or *America's CEO*. She only saw small pockets of business-attired people with *Re-Elect President Nelson: Principled Leadership for America* placards. American flags flew. Hick music played and voices rang with optimism. Smoke filled the air here, too, but instead of burning trash it smelled like grilled brats and corn on the cob. Majedah gagged on the scent of charred animal flesh. Candy was clinging to her now, and she returned the embrace. She could feel the assistant associate producer quaking in terror as Zz stuttered out a single syllable:

"N-N-Norms."

The driver slowed the car for a group of nuns who were crossing the road, carrying great bowls of macaroni salad and cut up watermelon. A bolt of fear shot through Majedah. "Don't stop!" she ordered. The driver's eyes were in the rearview again. "Go, go, go!" shrieked Majedah.

"Um, they're probably fine," Carter said gently.

Majedah watched distrustfully as the last nun quickstepped out of the car's path and they rolled on. She let go of Candy, cleared her throat, and sat up straight. "Yes, you're right, Carter." To Candy, she said, "We should be safe enough." The car rolled up to an entrance and came to a stop. Majedah gathered herself, took a deep breath, and said, "Come on, team, we've got a job to do." Then she opened the door and stepped outside.

A friendly young blond woman met them at the curb and introduced herself as Susan. She led them inside the convention center, into an elevator, and along the upper balcony. After a short walk, she showed the 24/7 team their booth in Media Row. The premier broadcast company's illustrious name had secured them an excellent location near the center of the balcony. A changeable-type board alongside the booth entrance spelled out *NEWS 24-7*. The booth was about 20 feet wide and 12 feet deep. It was furnished with a sofa and a low table, a desk, a stylist bench with a well-lit mirror, and several chairs. The back of the booth was open to a sweeping view of the entire convention hall: audience, floor, and stage. Two tall interview chairs were arranged just in front of the view, with two more stowed against a wall. There was a mini-fridge stocked with assorted waters and a basket of fruit and packaged snacks on the table.

The sophisticated New York media professionals fanned out into their booth. Candy went to the desk and began unpacking computer equipment while Carter started setting up a camera on a tripod facing the tall chairs.

"The main feed is available via closed circuit, and we'll be forwarding b-roll to your headquarters throughout the event," their helpful escort explained in her country twang. "If you need anything else—additional power strips, cables, or even more snacks—just visit the hospitality booth on level three or call the number on that card there, by the snack basket. If you get real hungry, there's also a list of pre-cleared caterers who deliver, and there are several concessions on level one. We even have a J-Pat's." The woman's emphasis on that final bit of information, as well as her broad smile, broadcast her fondness for the fast Caribbean food.

The only team member who didn't have anything constructive to do at the moment, Majedah listened to the woman's spiel. "Great, thanks so much," she said when Susan had finished. She honored the venue worker with one of her dazzling smiles; after all, one never knew when one might need something from the facility staff.

Susan dimpled back. "Okay, then. Welcome! We hope you have a wonderful convention." She turned and headed briskly for the elevator to find and assist her next charge.

Majedah wandered deeper into the booth, dumped her makeup bag onto the stylist bench, and primped her hair in the mirror. Then she dropped onto the sofa and leaned forward to finger the snacks on the low table, wrinkling her nose in disapproval. She sat back again and watched her teammates bustle at their stations and get their equipment online. She crossed one leg over the other and bounced her foot for a few seconds then stood and went to lean over the railing behind the chairs.

The building had originally been built as a massive concert venue, and it lent itself seamlessly to such a staged and slickly produced event as a political convention. At the far end of the vast space from Majedah, a massive platform stretched a hundred feet wide. The wily Republicans had also built a stage set that transparently intended to patronize all segments of American society. Each end of the stage was populated with enormous mock-ups that acted as wings from which politicians and performers could enter and exit. Ranging upwards from ten feet tall, the structures were scaled down replicas of various iconic American buildings; there was a barn, several silos, a spaceship-like Silicon Valley headquarters, a skyscraper, a wind turbine, a minaret, a bell tower, a cable-stayed bridge, a farmhouse, a power plant, the national Capitol, and tallest at over 50 feet, the Freedom Tower. A thirty-five-foot-tall LED screen ran behind the entire length of the stage. It currently displayed a titanic American flag billowing aloft among rosy-hued clouds. A smaller screen above each side of the stage showed a close-up of the speaker currently at the podium and displayed his name in a blue chyron at the bottom. It was the afternoon of the first day of the convention, and Majedah didn't expect any big names. The speaker on the stage at that moment was some first-term congressman from Mississippi she had never heard of.

Majedah blew her bangs out of her eyes and surveyed the floor of the arena. It had been divided up into sections, one for each state's delegates. Right now, it was only half-filled, and attendees wandered from place to place. According to the schedule, in a few hours the floor would be packed and organized as roll was called and each state's delegates officially cast their ballots for a candidate. Majedah was already not looking forward to the tedious formality since there wouldn't be a clear winner yet. She thought longingly of her elegant Upper West Side apartment, then lifted her face to scan the rows of seats. "Huh, that's odd," she muttered to herself. Even at this uneventful early time, and even with President Nelson being wildly unpopular and under investigation, the stadium was nearly full. What's more, there seemed to be positive energy emanating from the audience. People cheered and waved and held up home-made signs and passed beach balls around. Majedah squinted down to get a better look at some of the audience members. "Ugh, Norms." She wrinkled her nose.

The unimportant congressman from the inconsequential state droned on, the Norms cheered, and Majedah grew bored. "I'm going to go see who our neighbors are," she informed Candy and Carter. They looked up, nodded, and went back to work. Majedah passed back through the booth and stepped into the corridor. She turned and went in the direction of the stage, stopping after only a few paces at the entrance to the next booth. The placard read *MSDNC*. Majedah peeped into the space.

CFL bulbs sent flickering, Soviet-style light down on the booth's occupants, rendering their skin tones in sickening hues. Seated cross-legged on the floor, one of the station's producers drew great colorful crayon loops on a wall, a strand of drool trailing from his mouth into his lap. A news director skipped past him, grinning maniacally and swinging a butterfly net at imaginary insects. Nearby, a male news anchor was seated at the stylist table. Although he was smiling serenely, his arms were pre-emptively immobilized in a strait jacket. A humming stylist of indeterminate gender combed and spritzed the anchor's short hair. "You like?" asked the stylist, meeting the anchor's blank eyes in the mirror.

"Oh, yes, yes. Pretty, pretty!" the anchor sang, nodding vigorously.

Majedah's eyes were drawn to a commotion over by the far wall; a white-coated doctor and an orderly were attempting to calm MSDNC's primetime anchor. Her howls were piteous. "Can't you see? It's the Fifth Reich! Don't you see how much danger we're all in?" she cried. Her hands flailed about her head as though fending off a swarm of killer bees, and her wild eyes flicked all about.

The muscular orderly seized hold of one of the anchor's arms. On her other side, the doctor soothed, "There, there. We're safe here, don't worry. They can't get us here." He deftly pinioned the terrified anchor's arm and plunged a hypodermic needle into the scrawny bicep.

"Aah! Arrgh!" shrieked the hysterical journalist.

"Shh, don't be frightened. Settle down now," encouraged the doctor. He gently stroked the anchor's short hair, and the unhappy woman began to quiet down as the medication went to work.

Majedah shuddered at the sad scene and backed away before anyone noticed her. She turned, passed the 24/7 booth, and went to see who occupied the prime real estate on their other side.

This booth was massive, taking up at least three times the footprint of 24/7's space. Majedah finally reached an entrance and peeked around the corner.

Inside, there was a swanky party in full swing. Craft tables overflowed with chafing dishes and platters of finger foods, sandwiches, fruit, and pastries. Majedah noticed there was real china, utensils, and linen, and off to one side she heard the *whoosh* of an espresso machine. An entire wall was lined with monitors and equipment, tended by a bank of technicians. Three stylist benches were in full operation, lights glowing and hairdryers humming as grinning fashion experts groomed the talent. Stylish, professional-looking people chatted in two separate conversation areas, where chairs and sofas were grouped around coffee tables covered in glossy magazines, swag bags, laptops, snacks, mugs, and tumblers. A row of chairs fronted a vast, sweeping view of the arena; beyond, the massive stage was dead center. Against a side wall, a bow-tied young man with an ironic beard manned a full bar. Majedah watched as he wielded a chrome shaker then strained syrupy thick vodka into a martini glass. She licked her lips and smacked a couple times.

The bartender handed the glass to a stunning blond woman, who sipped it daintily and nodded her appreciation. Then the woman looked around and her blue eyes unexpectedly met Majedah's black ones. Her coral lips slid over white teeth in a welcoming smile as she waved for Majedah to join her. The 24/7 anchor glanced around to make sure the woman meant her. Her gaze lit once more on the frosty stemware in the stranger's hand and she shrugged and stepped into the booth.

"Hi, I'm Gretel Hanson. It's a pleasure to meet you," said the woman as Majedah joined her. She had long, blond hair that tumbled over her shoulders in shiny waves, and her skin looked as dewy and fresh as a peach. She wore a classy sheath dress in a sky-blue shade that matched her eyes, and the expression on her honest, mid-western face was open and welcoming.

Majedah nodded at her host. "Hi, thanks. I'm—"

"I know who you are. It's so nice of you to visit us. Please, order yourself something to drink." Gretel gestured gracefully at the bar.

"Thanks, I don't mind if I do." Majedah turned to the bow-tied bartender. He was watching her with sharp gray eyes, a sardonic smirk visible through his lumberjack-esque beard. "I'll have a pink martini, please," she ordered.

"Of course you will," he replied. Before Majedah could decipher his remark, he set to work pouring and shaking.

She glanced around the well-appointed news booth. "You people certainly went all out," she observed. Contemporary country music was playing somewhere and the volume from numerous high-energy conversations made it necessary for her to raise her voice. She almost felt like she was at a nightclub. She accepted her beverage with a nod and took a swallow (it was excellent) while her new friend answered.

Gretel had a contagious, open mouthed smile. "Yeah, well, it's not every day you get to cover history being made," she said.

"Wait—you really think Clark has a chance?" Majedah was stunned.

"You don't?" Gretel's smile closed and pulled to the side as she gave Majedah a wry look.

The 24/7 reporter stared off into the distance. "I guess I never actually considered..." she began.

"Come on!" Gretel's grin was back in full force. "You especially should be thrilled, after all the brilliant work you did in that interview. You practically launched Clark's campaign yourself." Her expression dimmed. "Too bad Clark's a Republican, or you'd be up for a Golden Vulva this year, for sure."

The excellent pink martini had lowered Majedah's guard, and Gretel's comment zinged her like an electric shock. *She's right! Clark has a vagina—and a high melanin level, even!—and I really did do a brilliant job interviewing her. It's not fair that I can't win a Golden Vulva just because she's not from the right party.* "Oh, god," Majedah moaned aloud. The strain of trying to reconcile this epiphany with her core beliefs was intense, and beads of sweat broke out on her forehead.

Gretel looked concerned. "Are you okay, Majedah?" she asked.

"Yes, I'm fine, I just...must've eaten something funky this morning."

"Oh, no. I hope you're not getting food poisoning at such an important time."

"I'm sure I'll be fine. ... Well, better kill some germs." Majedah winked and took a gulp of her pink martini to buy time. A sense of unease had overcome her, and she needed to establish context for the conversation. It occurred to her that she hadn't entered the booth through the main entry and therefore hadn't seen the name of the network with whom she was partying. She looked around for a logo. Across the booth, a tech stepped away from a monitor, stretched, then turned to face the room. On the left chest of his red polo, Majedah could just make out the silhouette of a soaring eagle. "Oh, my god," she breathed.

"Majedah, my dear, what a pleasant surprise," spoke a bizarrely cultured voice at her elbow.

With a sinking feeling, Majedah faced its source. She fought to control her features and put on an expression she hoped was commanding and professional. "Cader," she fairly spat.

In person, Roy Cader was no taller than herself, although he had a large head which showed up well on camera. His skin possessed the preternatural texture and tautness of an over-40 television star. There was just enough grey interspersed in his hair to show that it was naturally dark and thick, and his bespoke suit lent him smooth sophistication. And seen up close, his customary smugness made Majedah want to slap him.

"We're so glad you saw fit to join us," he drawled. "I haven't seen you since, my goodness, was it that Battle of the Body Parts back in New York?"

Majedah's mind flashed back to her humiliating state at their last meeting, with her heart aching and blood, tears, and snot smeared across her cheek. Cader's grin told her he was remembering it, too. She desperately wanted to ask him what he had done with that footage, but she would never give him the satisfaction. Instead, she smiled tightly. "Yes, wasn't that a magnificent event? Thousands and thousands of strong, empowered women, marching against misogyny and hate ... the misogyny and hate of the Nelson administration!" she finished righteously.

Cader snorted a laugh. "Yes, well, that's certainly one interpretation of it. At any rate, his goose is cooked."

"You really believe that?" It made Majedah uncomfortable that everyone here seemed to know something she didn't.

"You don't?" Cader's arch look made her clench her teeth until her jaw ached. "This is a fascinating point in history, don't you think?" he opined. "The first time in over a century a sitting president won't be re-nominated at his own party's convention."

"But—but that's impossible," Majedah protested. "What other choice do they have?"

"I don't understand what you mean," said Gretel.

Majedah looked at her incredulously. "What, you think they're going to hand Clark the nomination?"

"Absolutely," averred Gretel.

Now it was Majedah's turn to snort out a harsh laugh. "We're talking about the actual Nazi party here," she reminded her competitors. "There is no way Republicans will ever nominate a woman or an African American, and certainly not an African-American woman."

With a twinge of regret, Majedah noted that Gretel seemed taken aback. "I must admit, I'm surprised to hear you say that," Gretel commented. "I thought you would be as excited as we are."

But Cader became smugger if anything. "Told you," he said to Gretel.

She in turn looked into Majedah's face as if searching for confirmation of something. Bewilderment appeared in her eyes as she glanced from Majedah to Cader. "Excuse me, please," she said.

As Majedah watched Gretel retreat through the boisterous throng, she felt oddly bereft.

"Right now, you're thinking you could almost be friends with her, if only she didn't work for us," Cader deduced.

Majedah gave him a wrathful look but couldn't think of a retort.

"Do you want to know what I'm thinking?" teased the despicable anchor.

"Not particularly," Majedah sneered.

"I'm thinking about how funny it's going to be, watching you people try to come up with a new narrative to go after Presidential Candidate Patty Clark."

In truth, the very possibility completely unnerved Majedah. It was a terrifying and impossible prospect, like trying to comprehend what lay beyond the universe. She fought back a spell of vertigo and settled for retorting, "You're a racist idiot, Cader." He looked as though he could barely suppress laughter at her outburst. "And what the hell kind of name is Cader, anyway?" she added.

"Wouldn't you love to know; then you'd know which box to file me away in," he drawled.

"Oh!" huffed Majedah. She threw back the last of her pink martini, slammed the glass on the bar while ignoring the bartender's smirk, glared at Cader, and flounced out of the booth.

IN THE END, it only took two rounds of balloting before Patty Clark secured the Republican Party nomination for President of the United States. At 6:37 p.m. on day two of the convention, the Chairman of the Republican National Committee, Helmut Strombopoulos, made the astonishing announcement from the stage. Then some Mormon band that no one had ever heard of launched into an alternative rock version of "America the Beautiful."

The shell-shocked News 24/7 team cowered together, trembling with fear, as the roar inside the arena flooded their booth. It was the most terrifying sound they had ever heard, a sort of mass exultation comprised of thousands upon thousands of voices, each rejoicing as though being heard for the very first time.

As the three teammates sat shaking on the sofa, their arms around one another, there was a muffled *Whoompf!* from next door. "Wh-what was that?" Majedah asked.

"I don't know, and I don't want to know," squeaked Candy.

"Carter, go and see what it was," Majedah commanded.

"Why do I have to go?" resisted the cameraman. "It's because I'm a white cis het male, isn't it?"

"That's reason enough for you to have to go," said Majedah. "You've got some serious privilege to burn off. But also, because you're *from* this god-forsaken state, so it's partly your fault."

"What? Fine, whatever." Carter stood, squared his shoulders, and marched to the doorway. He peeked cautiously to both sides then stepped out of sight. He was back within two minutes with a report. "It was the MSDNC crew." His face was twisted with anguish. He removed his trucker hat and held it solemnly to his chest. Then he hung his head so his bushy brown beard covered half the hat while he explained, "The shock was too much for them; they spontaneously combusted."

Candy let out a high-pitched wail of sorrow.

"Oh, god," groaned Majedah. "Those poor people."

The somber mood was disrupted by the intensifying sounds of celebration from the Eagle Eye booth on the other side. "Ugh, what is wrong with those people?" raged Majedah. "Don't they know something horrible has happened?"

Candy was openly crying, great gasping spasms of fear and sorrow. "What is happening to this country?" Zz sobbed, momentarily forgetting to use Zz ladylike voice. "I don't understand this country at all anymore."

"Nothing makes sense," Carter murmured, barely audible above the din.

Majedah agreed with her colleagues, but she said nothing. She looked at Candy, trembling and whimpering beside her on the rented couch. Then she looked at Carter; the slump-shouldered cameraman was the very image of dejection and sorrow.

Fury erupted within Majedah. "I can't believe they did this," she said. When she saw both Candy and Carter stop sniveling to look at her, she repeated, "I can't believe they did this to us. This was supposed to be our victory. Ours! We're the ones who worked night and day to destroy President Nelson, to bring him and his whole administration down. We decided what to report, and we reported the shit out of it. We lectured, we organized marches, we wrote anthems, we set trends, we protested, and for what?" She looked wildly from Candy to Carter, her eyes ablaze with fervor. "For them to steal it from us, that's what!"

Carter seemed mystified. "Who's 'them'?" he wondered aloud.

"The Norms!" Majedah hollered. "The despicable Nazis screaming in this arena at this very minute. They took out Nelson before we got to take our final victory at the polls in November." She stabbed the fingers of both hands into her hair, clenching and pulling. "Those backstabbing bastards," she screamed.

A fresh wave of revelry sounded from the Eagle Eye mega-booth next door, the noise incongruously washing over the traumatized journalists. "Now what are they getting all riled up about? Have they no decency?" Majedah leapt to her feet, fists clenched at her sides. "That does it," she declared. "I'm going over there to straighten them out."

"Be careful, Majedah," Candy implored her. Majedah could see the whites of Zz eyes all the way around the iris.

"The time for caution is past." Majedah stormed out into the passageway and immediately stopped short. The cause of the celebratory din stood a dozen feet away: Patty Clark herself. Her eyes were alight and triumph radiated from her. The Eagle Eye team had poured out of their booth to stand in a semicircle around the candidate, applauding and shouting congratulations.

"You did it, Ms. Clark!"

"Bravo!"

"Onward to Washington, D.C.!"

Patty Clark stood tall and proud in her five-inch heels and waved at the exuberant media with one hand; the other held that of her husband, Norris. He was watching her with an expression of fierce pride. Behind them stood a small retinue, among whom Majedah recognized the campaign press secretary, Vic Waveny, today attired in western wear. As usual, a swarm of children accompanied the couple, some staying close to their parents and some weaving through the gathering of jubilant adults.

Majedah observed the scene with her keen reporter eyes, noting every small detail. She watched as Roy Cader confidently approached the nominee, microphone in hand. "What do you say, Ms. Clark? A victory interview for your friends at Eagle Eye news?"

Patty Clark smiled fetchingly at the anchor. "Hm, I don't know, Roy," she teased. The right-wing reporters all laughed at her coy routine, and Patty crossed her arms and turned her chin up and away as though snubbing them. But then her eye lit on Majedah, and the familiar wide smile spread across her face. "Majedah, baby, how are you?" she said. In three long-legged strides, the CEO had reached her and enfolded her in an affectionate hug. A stunned Majedah returned the embrace. Her reporter instincts were firing on high alert, admonishing her to be smart and professional and figure out a way to use this turn of events to her advantage.

"Congratulations, Patty." Majedah conjured genuine-sounding enthusiasm. "What an absolute thrill and triumph."

"Aw, you're so sweet, Majedah." Patty Clark released her and straightened up. She turned to look at the swarm of children. "I don't know, kids. I think Majedah was really brave to come onto enemy territory like this, just to cover our convention. I think I should give my first statement to her, don't you?"

The children cheered in unison.

Majedah allowed her jaw to drop as if she were in awe of the remarkable opportunity she was being given. "Thank you so much, Patty. Please, come into the News 24/7 booth." She stood aside and pointed the way. Patty breezed past her, followed by Norris, who gave Majedah a hug and a social kiss on the cheek, Vic, who punched Majedah in the arm and shouted, "H-h-h-hhey, Madge," several other adults, and a pack of kids. As the crowd finished passing by, Majedah paused a moment to savor her rival's shocked look of betrayal. "In your face, Cader," she sneered. Then she followed the historic candidate into the booth.

Candy and Carter were in such an advanced state of shock and terror, they performed their duties in a daze. Majedah stood by while Candy showed Patty Clark to one of the interview chairs. Norris sat in a chair facing his wife and watched the assistant associate producer affix her microphone. As Candy leaned over the candidate to clip a cord to the back of her shirt, Zz cropped blouse pulled up from the waistband of Zz low-rider jeans. A deep, wooly cleft was revealed betwixt two stubbly mounds, a sight that would have done any plumber proud. Nestled into its apex was a tiny scarlet satin triangle edged in black lace, with the words "Sexy Bitch" printed in gold metallic script. Norris spied the thong and his head turtled back in horror, his eyes widened, and a grimace pulled the corners of his mouth down to his chin. Patty caught his eye and winked, and Norris suddenly had to stifle a spasm of laughter.

Majedah realized that these hateful people were snickering at Candy's personal expression. It took her entire reserve of professionalism to maintain her composure. *Hold it together, Majedah,* she told herself. *Just get the interview for now. Your time will come, and you will put these horrible bigots in their place. And it will be spectacular and triumphant.*

A large bowl clattered off the low table and onto the floor as the children fought over the packaged snacks. Norris focused a laser glare on them and commanded, "Hey! Knock it off, kids. People will think we never feed you."

"Whoa, now there are eight kids," Majedah remarked. "I thought you guys only had five."

"That's right. And five is plenty," said Patty as she sat still in her chair, waiting for Carter to finish adjusting her lighting.

Norris shot her a flirtatious smile. "I don't know, Patty. We haven't had a baby in the house in a long time."

"Five is plenty," she reiterated, giving Norris a hard look. Then she turned to Majedah. "The other three are my sister's kids."

Majedah pulled up Clark family information from her memory bank. "Oh, Alice, right? Is she here tonight?"

"Nope." Patty looked straight ahead. "Back in rehab."

"Oh." Majedah didn't know what to say. She lamely remarked, "Well, it's nice for the kids to spend time with their cousins, I'm sure."

Patty gave a sad chuckle. "Would be nicer for them to spend time with their mother."

"Well, they'll be able to soon, when she gets home," said Norris.

"That's true," Patty agreed.

"And who knows?" her husband expounded. "Maybe she'll stay straight for a whole month this time."

Patty cracked up and Norris laughed along with her.

Majedah watched their familiar, comfortable interaction. The empty, lonely place she always carried within her flared painfully. She quickly reminded herself that she was romantically involved with the Great Man himself, Richard Spinner. He even let her call him "Dick." In fact, he seemed to like it when she called him that. She glanced away from the Clarks. Vic Waveny was leaning over the back of the sofa to pluck a bag of chips from the hands of nine-year-old Jessica. "Hey!" she squawked. She immediately stood on the sofa cushions and reached for him. He removed a dove gray cowboy hat from his head and wielded it like a shield to fend her off while using his other hand to empty the bag into his mouth. "Uncle Vic!" squealed Jessica.

"Get him!" yelled a slightly older boy.

The children were on their feet, leaping off the back of the sofa to pile onto the press secretary. "T-t-t-take it e-e-e-e-ee-eeee—" he began. He fought valiantly but there were too many of them. With a hoarse cry, he collapsed, taking the pile of children with him, out of view behind the sofa.

Patty craned her neck to see what happened. "You kids cut it out now, you hear me?" she hollered.

Norris stood. "I got this. You just do your interview, babe. I'll take the kids and Uncle Vic for a walk or something."

"Thank you, baby." Patty lifted her face to her husband's kiss. He went and rounded up the laughing children and shepherded them out, followed by a small secret service detail.

With the sudden decrease in noise level, Majedah heard her phone buzzing in her bag. She fished it out and saw Chester's name on the screen. She quickly answered. "Hey, Chester, what's up? I'm about to interview Patty Clark."

There was a brief pause. "What? Whoa. How'd you get that?" wondered the producer.

"She asked me to do it."

"Wow, well, … hm. Ordinarily I'd say, 'nice get, Majedah.' I mean, objectively, this should be a big deal, 24/7 scoring the first candid comments from a technically historic presidential candidate."

"I know, isn't it?" Majedah smiled to herself.

"I guess it's just the repugnance of the candidate that taints the whole thing."

"Well, what did you expect? You guys sent me out here to cover this—" Majedah glanced at Patty, who had gotten out of her seat to lean over the railing and raise her hands in a victorious gesture. The crowd in the arena roared its approval. "—this right-wing rally," Majedah finished. "Whom else should I interview that's a bigger name?" She hoped she didn't sound as peevish as she felt.

"No, you're doing the right thing. Like it or not, Patty Clark is news now. We need to know what we're up against," Chester allowed. "But anyway, the reason I called is that Kingston's going to lead off Carol's hour with a live report from the Republican convention, starring you. As soon as you're done with Ms. Clark, let your team know and get set up."

Majedah was instantly buoyed by the good news. Carol was still out as her "spa" vacation stretched mysteriously on, and her show had temporarily become an extension of Kingston Fauler's seven o'clock news hour, rounded out with extensive panels of political experts and pundits. And tonight, Majedah would be the first female journalist to speak in that weighty timeslot. Millions of people would see her face, live, reporting on the historic African-American candidate with a vagina.

Too bad the woman was a heartless Nazi who would ultimately need to be destroyed (though Majedah looked forward to performing that public service herself, simultaneously sealing her own position as the most powerful journalist in the business). But for now, Majedah would take the high-profile appearance on the primetime show she one day planned to anchor. *One step at a time*, she reminded herself. She spoke a brief sentence into the phone; "I'll be ready." Then she hung up.

Majedah went to sit in the chair facing Patty Clark, Candy affixed her microphone, and she began to interview the Republican Party's unlikely and historic candidate for President of the United States of America.

Chapter 21

THE ATMOSPHERE IN the morning conference was subdued as the media professionals talked amongst themselves, waiting for the ten o'clock call to begin.

"I mean, as a woman of color myself, I want to say I'm thrilled to have a candidate who looks like me to vote for," declared Mysty. "But I just *can't.*"

Mara snorted at the far end of the table. "At least you have a candidate who looks like you at all," equee whinnied. "I doubt I ever will." Equee stamped equis hoof petulantly.

Seated side by side, Mysty and Scout rolled their* eyes at one another.

(*Author's note: Please accept my heartfelt apologies if I have offended anyone with this particular plural pronoun choice. As of this writing, a standard protocol has yet to be developed for pronouning groups that contain people and/or otherkin of varying personal pronoun preferences, so I am falling back on imperial English. I am deeply ashamed and will work to do better.)

Majedah listened idly to the conversation rather than joining in. Since her affair with Spinner had begun, she noticed a subtle difference in the way her colleagues seemed to treat her. She still worked alongside the other Pool reporters and joined them at The Buzz for the occasional pink martini, but emotionally she was held at arm's length. The comfortable familiarity with which her comrades addressed one another was replaced by a self-conscious formality when they spoke to her.

The situation was compounded when Majedah returned from the Republican National Convention that morning. Her profile was definitely elevated by her high-level interview and subsequent live report two nights earlier. But still, it was impossible to separate her journalistic success, pushing the Patty Clark narrative, from the stink attached to its subject. Majedah felt herself being pigeonholed, ghettoized as a right-wing specialist; maybe even—god forbid!—a suspected sympathizer. Patty Clark's apparent fondness for her was a diabolical curse, a means to score the highest-value interviews, but for the wrong people. And Majedah's own network seemed all too happy to assign her to the task. Yes, it was a critical task, but it was also distinctly distasteful, much like every town needs a sewage treatment plant but no one wants to shake hands with the turd wrangler. Majedah observed the knuckles of her right hand turn blue-white in her lap as she clenched her fist around her phone. Hatred for Patty Clark welled within her, and she thirsted for the day when she would destroy her. Then everyone at 24/7 who was now standoffish and holier-than-thou would be falling at her feet, begging for her patronage.

Then the conference call connected, and Juan Conquista's voice filled the room. "Good morning, everyone. It's great to have the sordid spectacle of the GOP convention behind us. We had a little bit of a surprise there, I'll admit. Didn't see that one coming. But let me assure everyone that our think tanks are polling and strategizing and focus-grouping and devising new narratives. When the time comes, we'll all know how to deal with 'CEO Clark,' as she likes to be called." He changed his voice to affect a decent imitation of Patty Clark. "'If Angie Harper gets to be called *Senator* Harper, I should have an equally important-sounding title,' I believe was her exact quote. Thank you so much, Ms. Cantalupi-Abromavich-Flügel-Van Der Hoven-Taj Mahal, for broadcasting her demand live to the entire country."

Everyone looked at Majedah and laughed. Majedah laughed along with them, even as she flushed red and insisted to herself that they were all laughing together at Patty.

"That certainly was uppity of her, I must say," continued Juan's voice from the ceiling speakers. "Unfortunately, now certain people will refer to her as 'Chief Executive' when they address her, and Senator Harper will be outranked. Touché, *CEO Clark*, touché.

"But don't worry about it another minute, people. As I said, we're working on it and we'll have new talking points for everyone soon. We have three months until Election Day, plenty of time to bury this bitch."

More righteous laughter interrupted the DNC Chair's opening monologue. He let it play out for a minute, then retook control. "Anyway, let's talk about some good news now. Something we're all looking forward to so much: next week's Democratic National Convention!"

Juan paused for explosive cheering of earsplitting volume, in which he himself joined, his rowdy cries distorting through the overloaded phone speaker. Majedah cheered along with everyone else, even though she felt like Cinderella watching her stepsisters dress for a ball everyone except her would be attending.

ONE WEEK LATER, Majedah sat in her darkened living room and watched the final night of the Democratic National Convention. The only light came from her wall-mounted TV screen and from the city itself, which winked and glowed outside the floor-to-ceiling windows.

Majedah was watching News 24/7's coverage of the historic event. Everyone who was anyone was in Seattle, covering the event. (Majedah imagined the 24/7 media booth would make the Eagle Eye space at the Republican convention look meager by comparison.) Richard Spinner was in Singapore, wining and dining Asian media moguls. Julia was furious with Majedah for interviewing Patty Clark the previous week and wasn't speaking to her. (Ziyad had called to congratulate her. Kevin had called too, his voice warm with admiration as he offered to come to New York to take her out for a celebratory dinner. Majedah had declined.) And so, Majedah was alone.

The other Pool reporters, also stranded in New York City, had invited Majedah to come to The Buzz with them for a DNC viewing party, but it was obviously a courtesy invitation. Majedah told them she already had plans.

In fact, she did have plans: to watch the convention alone in her living room and get hammered. She had already accomplished the hammered part and was working to keep her eyes open long enough to see the candidate make her historic acceptance speech.

At nine p.m., Rinnie Halliday took the stage. She wore a scandalously low-cut red latex corset with a white spandex micro-skirt that resembled a wide belt more than a skirt, blue fishnet stockings, and scarlet thigh-high vinyl boots with five-inch spike heels. She performed her huge feminist hit *Vaginas Up!* with a new verse written specifically for the occasion:

Time for us to make history
Time to end misogyny
Only a woman can clean this mess
Time for a vagina in the oval office

As the final chord sounded and the song ended, Rinnie struck a pose, legs spread and feet planted wide apart, and threw her hands up in the air. Her doughy breasts burst from the constraint of the corset and bounced free. The nipples were covered by sparkly red pasties; one read PRESIDENT and the other HARPER.

In the convention center in Seattle, the delegates and well-wishers went wild. On her sofa in Manhattan, Majedah laughed with delight at the pop star's cleverness. She raised her glass in salute and took a gulp of room-temperature vodka.

Rinnie and her band all turned to look stage left and began to clap. Amid the applause, Senator Angela Harper wobbled out onto the stage. She wore a custom-made tunic pantsuit in the trademark style she had pioneered. The knee-length coat was of quilted fabric, similar to the padding inside moving vans and freight elevators, cut in an A-line style that flared loosely over the candidate's considerable hips. Beneath this she wore a pair of man-tailored trousers that concealed her thick ankles and just kissed the tops of her whimsical candy-apple red but otherwise sensible flats. She took her time making her entrance, pausing frequently to wave and catch her breath. The approval of the audience was a steady roar. The candidate eventually reached Rinnie, and the pop tart leaned over to give her a hug, which she returned. Then the musicians left the stage, the lighting focused on the senator, and she took her place behind the podium to give her acceptance speech. The podium was lit internally so that it glowed red. A circular seal decorated the front panel; it featured a stylized eagle encircled with the words "Presumptive President of the United States of America."

Senator Harper swiveled her head to take in the massive sea of supporters, an enormous smile on her face. Her hair had been coifed and straightened and spritzed and processed to perfection; now it wreathed her face with steely dignity.

She waved and said, "Thank you" a dozen times before the hall quieted enough for her to speak. Then the historic candidate began to make her remarks.

Passed out on the sofa, Majedah heard none of Candidate Harper's speech. This actually wasn't a big deal because there weren't any new or compelling ideas in the forty-seven-minute address. Nevertheless, in the morning, Majedah was disappointed to have missed the novelty of warmed-over Marxism being mouthed by the presumptive first female President of the United States. While she imbibed a breakfast of a liter of Coke and a handful of Advil tablets, Majedah watched a rebroadcast of the entire thing so that she would be up to speed when she arrived at work.

"DICK, CAN I ask you something?" Majedah spoke just loud enough to be heard over the prattle of 24/7's *Sunday Morning Savants* show, which played on the wall-mounted TV that faced Spinner's cherry frame California King bed.

The mogul was rustling through a stack of newspapers. "Uh oh, this sounds serious," he said in his gruff, staccato syllables. "I suppose you want to know if we're going steady, right? *Huh! Huh!*" He raked an oversized page noisily to the side and began skimming the next one.

Majedah chuckled. "No, nothing like that."

"Oh, thank goodness." Spinner folded the paper in half and held it closer so he could zero in on something. "So, what is it, kitten?"

"Well, it will probably sound crazy or really stupid or something, so I want to say up front that I'm asking this in all seriousness."

Spinner glanced momentarily from the paper to his bedmate to confirm her earnest expression. "Okay, shoot."

Majedah paused briefly as though afraid to utter such a thought before coming out with it. "How are we going to keep using the War on Women narrative, now that both candidates are women? I mean, it doesn't really make sense anymore, does it?"

"Easy: Patty Clark isn't a real woman."

Majedah wanted to let it go at that; he was a Great Man, after all. But she was of higher intelligence than the average person, and her acute mind was not satisfied. She persisted. "I absolutely understand what you mean by that. She believes in anti-woman policies like the federal government not paying for women's health rights and stuff. But remember how stupid most people are in this country. Less-informed women will just look and see that both candidates have a vagina and be happy voting for either. And then the ones who get told what to do by their husbands will wind up voting for Clark."

Spinner snorted. "Don't be ridiculous. Republicans aren't going to vote for her. She's black! *Huh! Huh!*"

Majedah cleared her throat delicately. "See, that's another thing I'm worried about. America's righteous Progressives have spent decades educating everyone about how oppressed African-Americans are and making Caucasian-Americans feel guilty about it, and part of me is concerned that this could backfire now, because some people might reflexively vote for Clark because of her skin color." Spinner snorted so loudly he had to send a finger probing into one nostril to attend to whatever had been dislodged. Majedah hurried to say, "I know, I know— she's not a real African-American, either. And you and I and all *educated* people know that, but I can't stop worrying about all the uneducated blacks and women."

"Majedah, my dear, you can already go onto any social media platform and see celebrities by the score, educating the public.

Remember what Juan said in the last 10 o'clock meeting? The new hashtag is #votewithyourbrain."

"Yes, I know, I saw that. Rinnie Halliday did a great video where she explained that voting with your lady parts is so yesterday. Now we need people to think about each candidate's policy positions. But, see, this is where it gets tricky; once you have to explain your position in more than one hashtag, people lose interest. WarOnWomen worked great when there was only one woman in the race. BlackLivesUberAlles was an awesome tag when there wasn't an actual African-American in the race. But now we have to say, 'Vote for policies that help you, such as universal free health care, a guaranteed income, ending racism, and the government providing free tampons for all women.' ... You see what I'm saying? That's a mouthful, and it contains a lot of ideas. It might not work on all the stupid women and black people."

Spinner grunted agreement. "I do know what you mean, and it's possible that Clark's physical appearance will throw a few people off. But never fear, we will prevail." He rolled a booger thoughtfully between his thumb and forefinger as he gazed at the distant TV screen. "Remember, there are two parts to every election: motivating the good voters and suppressing the bad voters. Clark's vagina and melanin may confuse some of our good voters into not voting properly, but it's a double-edged sword; how many Nazi hillbillies are going to vote for her, huh?"

Majedah wasn't comforted. "I was at their convention, Dick. They love her. I saw it with my own two eyes."

"Huh, well, maybe some do. But where there's a will, there's a way." Inspiration struck him and he snapped his fingers, sending the booger off like a BB in the direction of the en-suite bath. "I've got it! The Jesus Freaks! They'll never vote for a Catholic. They hate 'em! *Huh! Huh!*"

Majedah gasped with relief. "My god, Dick, that's right! No Republican has ever won without the support of the Evangelicals, and she'll never get that."

"That's right, my dear. Just like when they ran that Mormon guy; not gonna happen. *Huh! Huh!*"

Majedah leaned over and kissed his cheek. "You're a genius, Dick," she said.

"Keep that up, and I'll take another one of my fun pills," Spinner said in a sensual growl. He reached over to his bedside table, shook a blue pill out of a bottle, and swallowed it with some water from the glass that rested there. He turned back to Majedah with a wicked grin. "Hey, how about a little foreplay?"

"What did you have in mind?" purred Majedah.

"Let's do the dirtiest, nastiest, filthiest thing I can think of."

"Ooh, sounds kinky."

He leaned in close and whispered in her ear, "Let's watch the bimbos on Eagle Eye News try to pimp that fry cook to the rednecks."

Majedah stiffened with disgust. "Ugh, I hate them," she said.

"That's why it's fun to watch them go about their stupid business," Spinner whispered. "There's nothing more arousing than watching your enemies striving, whoring, slutting their stuff … and failing." He aimed the remote, winked at Majedah, and hit the channel changer. Then he froze, gobsmacked, rheumy blue eyes locked on the screen. "What the fuck is this?" he uttered.

Majedah's mouth hung open as she took in the live coverage. "Who … who's she speaking to?"

On the screen, Patty Clark was in mid-address, flush with inspiration and energy. She stood on an open stage in the middle of a packed arena, comfortable and confident, a wireless mic in one hand, and an enormous audience all around her.

Majedah scanned the cheering throng, reflexively processed the demographics, and scowled. "How can this be?" she wondered aloud. "All those little fascists cheering her on are young! And quite a few of them appear to be African-American and Hispanic. That isn't a Republican crowd, that's our demo! Where did she get them?"

Beside her, Spinner said nothing. He clenched his jaw and watched in silence as the unsettling scene unfolded on the screen.

Patty Clark was grinning her wide smile and nodding, looking up at the distant heights of the roaring audience, glittering stage lights reflected in her eyes. She raised the mic and said, "That's right." She nodded once more and repeated herself. "That's right. Because who knows more about freedom than the students of Freedom University?"

"Oh no!" wailed Majedah. "It's the Evangelicals."

On the TV, Patty spoke in a firm, inspired voice. "Let's talk about that most fundamental American Freedom of all … the freedom to worship as you see fit."

HHHAAAAAHHHH!!! roared the students.

"The freedom to say, 'God bless America' and 'Merry Christmas' and 'In Jesus' name, amen!'"

HHHAAAAAAAAAAAAAHHHH!!!

"I think I'm going to be sick," said Majedah. She turned dazed eyes to her bedmate, searching desperately for the answer that would make everything all right.

But Spinner didn't look at her. He appeared to be in shock and unable to break his visual connection to the screen as he digested what he was seeing. At last he said, in a voice robbed of all its customary force, "I certainly didn't see that coming."

Chapter 22

AS AUTUMN CAME on, an almost surreal uncertainty plagued the Forces for Good across the country. There was a vague sense of confusion in every mainstream sector, as once-reliable identity-based tactics failed to have an effect. Precious time slipped past as the frightening Republican candidate campaigned with energy and enthusiasm, gained ground, and—worst of all—appeared to be having a great time. The optimism and vigor she projected was deeply disturbing to all right-thinking people, and the offices and halls of the great News 24/7 headquarters were uncharacteristically hushed. Everyone was ready for some good news.

Relief arrived at last, a mere three weeks before the election, with the announcement of the triumphant return of premium feminist anchorwoman Carol Crawford.

Carol's spa vacation had stretched on throughout the summer and into the fall. Chester let slip that it had included an unplanned stint in an ultra-exclusive and secretive facial rehab facility. But now, at last, America's best-loved and most-trusted feminist spokesperson would be returning to tell women everywhere what to think.

As if this wasn't exciting enough, on her triumphant first show back, Carol would have the entire hour with the historic presumptive first-ever woman president, Angela Harper. Right here, in the venerable studios of News 24/7's midtown Manhattan headquarters! As if someone had flipped a switch, the cloying despondency was replaced with elation.

On the day of the much-anticipated show, Majedah, Chester, Melissa, and Scout, returning from a coffee run, stepped into the elevator from the lobby of the 24/7 skyscraper. The doors had closed behind them when, with a shock, the troupe realized they were sharing a ride with Carol Crawford herself. It was the first time the famous anchorwoman had set foot in the offices since she left for her extended vacation. She was accompanied by her assistant, Max, and two of the station's stylists. Carol wore a pair of Marcus Puhtsee Platinum Label jeans cropped at the ankle to display a pair of one-off sample boots so unique that another such pair had never been made. Her stick-thin torso was wrapped in a soft, drapey suede jacket topped with a fluffy, natural alpaca wool scarf. Even before her pre-show visit with the stylists, her wavy ash-blond hair fell into perfect shape, thanks to an extravagantly expensive haircut.

But most fascinating was Carol's face. Majedah and her companions couldn't look at anything else. Carol's skin had an uncanny quality of perfection to it; it glowed, it shimmered, it shone majestically. It was strung so tight, it hummed. The surface was as smooth and even as porcelain, with pores so small as to be nonexistent. Artful implants shaped ideal contours. A smattering of carefully cultivated wrinkles appeared precisely where they should on a woman of a certain age, arrayed in discrete, tasteful fans at the corners of her eyes and in two perfectly formed dimples that framed her mouth. Her teeth were newly bleached, her lips were freshly plumped, and her jaw and neck were drawn high and tight.

As the junior journalists focused their awed attention on her, Carol finished speaking to Max and turned the full glory of her restored visage upon them. They gasped in unison at the sight. Melissa especially seemed impressed out of her senses. "Ms. Crawford, my god," she breathed, "you look so … beautiful …" The daft girl's hand began to lift of its own accord, fingers splayed, reaching to touch the celebrated journalist's face. Majedah noticed it just in time and slapped the errant appendage back to its owner's side.

"Melissa, what are you doing?" she hissed into her friend's ear. The action drew Carol Crawford's attention, and Majedah trembled to realize the anchor's elegantly shaped eyes were focused on her. She commanded herself not to be intimidated by the older, established woman. She straightened and lifted her chin.

Carol Crawford's mouth pulled to one side ever so slightly (circumscribed in its movement by lack of facial flexibility) in a superior smirk. She tilted her head back to address her entourage and said, "So that's what the old man's tapping these days. Not exactly up to his usual standard, if you ask me."

Carol's toadies dutifully snickered as Majedah's companions drew in their breath. She could hear Chester murmur, "Carol, oh no!" as the full weight of the broadside struck. Majedah flushed red, but she acknowledged the comment with an arched brow and a crafty smile of her own. Then the doors opened, and she and her colleagues disembarked, leaving Carol and her attendants to ascend to the higher levels.

Chester immediately faced the young journalist, aghast, and said, "Majedah, you poor thing. I can't believe she said that to you. That was really too much."

Majedah was serenely composed. "It didn't bother me a bit," she asserted. "In fact, it was the highest compliment she could have paid me."

Chester voiced the confusion they all felt. "How do you figure that?" he asked.

Majedah looked him dead in the eye. "Carol Crawford just confirmed that she sees me as a threat." She tossed her gleaming black hair over her shoulder, spun on her heel, and led the way to the Pool.

Half an hour later, when her colleagues had all settled into their afternoon work, Majedah slipped from her desk and took the elevator up to the executive level. She glided down the hall towards Carol Crawford's office. A crowd of admirers thronged the open doorway, their backs to Majedah, cooing and drooling at their returned idol. As she passed Carol's assistant's desk, Majedah grabbed the smallest of the countless floral arrangements sent by wishers well. Ten feet further on, she upended the container into a wastebasket. Then she reached into the emptied vessel and removed the small, pin-topped florist's frog. She slipped the frog into her jacket pocket, dropped the empty vase into the wastebasket atop the flowers, and kept moving.

She rounded the corner at a brisk pace. As she passed an unattended mailroom cart, she swiped a box cutter without breaking stride. She put the box cutter into her other pocket and headed for the elevator.

Majedah rode down to the main production level and navigated the halls until she reached the staging area outside the studio used exclusively for *An Hour of Your Time with Carol Crawford*. Hearing voices, she paused to linger over a table covered with printouts, as though reviewing the schedule for the evening. Several high-level producers and suits whom she didn't know emerged from the studio, jabbering about that night's broadcast.

"It keeps hitting me that we're going to have a President of the United States right here in our studio."

"I know what you mean. It's surreal."

"Well, let's make sure she doesn't get inundated while she's here."

"I think the secret service people will keep all the lower level employees away from her."

"Good, because I definitely want a selfie with her."

"Who doesn't?"

They laughed together as they vanished down a hall, and Majedah went quickly to the studio doorway. She paused to gaze dreamily into the room and ascertain that it was empty. Then she stepped inside.

Similar to Carol's face, the anchor's set had undergone a 14-million-dollar renovation in anticipation of her return. Corinthian columns, masterfully painted to mimic rose quartz, framed a flamingo-pink matte satin tufted semi-circular sofa. Behind that stood floor-to-ceiling white wooden shelving lined with books tastefully bound in shades of blush, taupe, and cream, and in front was a low round table topped with mounds of high-end blooms in even more shades of trendy gyno-pink. Two large flat screens were mounted on the bookshelves behind the sofa for displaying graphics on the occasions when Carol would be covering hard news.

Majedah drifted deeper into the room and breathed in the aura of power and influence. In this sacred space, feminist narratives would be crafted and dispersed into millions of households nationwide, inspiring women (and, increasingly, enlightened men) to go out into their communities and work change. From this very spot would flow the wisdom, courage, vision, and leadership for the people at last to demand that hetero cis-gender Christian-bigot men and the women who enabled them—Norms—get what was coming to them.

Majedah meandered behind the sofa and trailed her hand along its back, letting her fingers glide over the heavy satin. She halted and looked up at the meticulously configured lighting, imagining herself sitting in the host seat when the soft, rosy glow lit up. She glanced down at the sofa and spotted an X of white fabric tape on the seat cushion. With one last glance at the door to make sure she was alone, Majedah leaned over and quickly peeled up two-thirds of the X. She pulled out the box cutter and made a three-inch slit in the fabric, then returned the tool to her pocket. She reached her tapered fingers into the opening and plucked at the cushion foam until she had created a small divot. Into this space she nestled the florist's frog. She pulled the upholstery back over the frog and secured it by replacing the white tape X. She stuffed the bits of foam into her pocket where the frog had been and surveyed the site. The seat looked exactly as it had before she altered it.

Satisfied, a smiling Majedah made her way out of the studio, down the hall, and back to elevator.

SENATOR HARPER'S ARRIVAL at News 24/7's headquarters was met with a greeting worthy of royalty. A convoy of shiny black SUV's pulled up to the reserved curb space in front of the building, and nearly a hundred staffers and supporters disembarked. A dozen Secret Service agents surrounded the central vehicle, creating a bubble of safe space, while one of them opened the door and held out an arm for the Senator to take. Richard Spinner himself, flanked by a handful of his closest executives, stood on the sidewalk to greet her.

Packed inside the cavernous lobby, the entire staff of the premier media broadcast company pressed against the glass to watch the Senator's approach. When she had hobbled to within ten feet of the doors, everyone scurried to their positions, creating a long passageway through the lobby that was lined with trembling adorers.

Senator Harper passed through the doors to an ear-splitting cheer that echoed around the cathedral-high ceiling and bounced off the important artworks that dotted the space. Her face creased with a beaming smile as she waved to acknowledge the crowd. Then she began to proceed through the human walls that lined the way. She smiled at as many individuals as she could, and the 24/7 professionals each expressed their support in his, her, xyr, equis, zis, myz, Zz, or blue own way. Candy, Scout, and Mysty, in matching frilly pink frocks, curtsied deeply; A'shadieeyah ululated her excitement; Mohammed Al-Kaboom glowered approvingly; Mara pranced and whinnied; and Chester squealed like a girl, clapped, and wiped at cascading tears. Everyone shrieked and shook and reached their hands towards the divine politician who would deliver them from darkness to a world of light, and urine puddled around more than one pair of vegan footwear.

As Senator Harper approached Majedah, the bold journalist forced herself through the underlings in front of her just in time to plant herself in front of the candidate. The Presumptive First Woman President of the United States noticed her and broke stride. Majedah quickly held out her hand and said, "Majedah Cantalupi-Abromavich-Flügel-Van Der Hoven-Taj Mahal, journalist. It's an honor to meet you, Madam."

Senator Harper reflexively took her hand in a practiced gesture and said, "So good to meet you. Thank you for everything you do." Then she moved on, leaving Majedah to cradle her right hand in her left as an electric thrill ran up and down her arm.

The Senator and her entourage were escorted to the studio level, where half the floor had been sectioned off for their use. Luxurious furnishings, lavish spreads, and uniformed wait staff had been pre-positioned to help the VIPs refresh while the Senator prepared for the hour-long special.

Meanwhile, all 24/7 staff who were not directly involved in the broadcast converged in the massive, lower level conference room for a viewing party. Eight-foot-wide screens had been placed around the room, interspersed with tall loudspeakers so no one would miss a single word while the interview occurred. Champagne and delicacies were passed freely, and the atmosphere was jubilant.

Rosemary stood on a chair and gave a shrill whistle to get everyone's attention. Then she shouted, "Juan Conquista just Tweeted that Nielsen announced that 50 million U.S. households are tuned to News 24/7 right now, and two billion people around the world are live-streaming us!" A deafening whoop shook the room, and Rosemary yelled along with it, "We are *not* fucking around!"

Then the lights dimmed, the screens glowed, and the audio feed blared from the loudspeakers. Everyone hushed and turned to watch. Majedah snagged a fresh flute of Armand de Brignac, positioned herself in front of a screen, folded her arms across her chest, and smiled inscrutably.

A commercial for Summer's Eve douches concluded, the screen went black for one beat, then the show began. Video clips faded in and out, showing Carol Crawford interviewing incredibly important people, appearing in exotic locations, clutching a helmet to her head as a third world concrete building collapsed behind her, and finally, laughing as a small monkey climbed from her arms to her head. All the while, consequential-sounding music played. The shifting images resolved to an aerial nighttime view of lower Manhattan's Freedom Tower surrounded by countless city lights. With percussive typewriter-strike sound effects, one white letter at a time appeared to spell out AN HOUR OF YOUR TIME. A glittering swirl of pinkish light danced across the bottom of the title with a sound of rushing wind, leaving the cursive words *with Carol Crawford* in its wake.

Everyone in the conference room cheered and clapped as the opening credits faded and Carol herself appeared on the screen.

The renowned feminist anchor stood in the foreground of her new set. She looked polished and poised in a tailored peach-colored suit. Her hair had been immaculately coiffed, and her slender feet were encased in a pair of golden fabric open-toed pumps. Her hands were clasped in front of her, her mouth formed a warm smile, and her eyes were locked on the camera as she re-opened her show after a three-month hiatus. "Welcome, everyone, welcome to *An Hour of Your Time*. I'm your host, Carol Crawford, and I cannot tell you how good it feels to be back here, in my studio—my home—bringing you the most important news stories of the day. And I am thrilled to be able to host a very special show tonight, where we will spend the entire hour getting to know the woman who will finally shatter that old glass ceiling to become the first woman president of the United States of America. Viewers everywhere, please join me in welcoming, from the great state of California, Senator Angela Harper." The corners of her eyes crinkled elegantly as she clapped and turned to greet her guest. Senator Harper had also been polished and buffed for the occasion, and she wore a brand new custom tunic-pantsuit in salmon-hued quilted fabric. The two women embraced, then held one another by the elbows to exchange pleasantries.

At the senator's entrance, the conference room once again burst into cheering and applause. Chester was close enough to Majedah that she could hear him talking with a new employee, and she stepped closer to listen. "Carol's okay walking around on the front of the set because the camera is far enough away that you can't see details on her face," the lofty producer explained.

The young man beside him had brown hair styled fashionably short with a longish forelock, and he wore glasses, a cardigan over a collared tartan shirt, and jeans. Majedah recognized him as a new writer named Dylan.

On screen, the women parted to circumnavigate the low table. As they reached the sofa, Chester spoke again. "Now, see, she's going to sit in the exact spot where her lighting is set up, and only then do we switch to the close-up camera."

The new writer asked, "So what happens if she doesn't sit in the precise spot?"

"Lighting disaster. One inch to the left or the right adds ten years. Two inches adds twenty, and so on."

Impressed, Dylan exclaimed, "Oh, my."

They watched as Carol glanced down at the cushion, sighted her target, then turned and began lowering her backside to the seat.

"See? She's aligning her ass with the spot," said Chester.

Dylan covered his mouth with his extended fingers and scrunched up his shoulders. "Oh, my god, you're right," he marveled.

Majedah held her breath as she watched the famous anchor drop to her seat. As soon as the woman's cheeks hit the sofa, the main camera switched to close-up, just in time to catch her expression. Carol's eyes went wide, and her mouth formed an O of confusion and pain. She half-lifted off her seat and landed again four inches to the side. A collective gasp sounded throughout the conference room as the station's premier anchorwoman suddenly appeared as an aged hag. Realizing her mistake, Carol immediately adjusted her posture, keeping her bottom safe from pain while contorting her body at a steep angle towards her guest so that her face was thrust back into the magic spot where the clock turned back.

"Why is she sitting like that?" someone behind Majedah wondered. "She looks so uncomfortable." Majedah shrugged innocently.

Ever professional, Carol forced herself to smile cordially. But even with the lighting wizardry, Majedah could see that the woman's neck was stippled with pull-lines, and the skin on her face was stretched to the breaking point. Every expression the woman made was a harrowing risk.

But the venerable anchor hadn't gotten where she was by losing her head every time there was a problem. She read her first cue from the off-screen teleprompter and began, "Senator Harper—actually, what the heck, let me be the first to say it—*President* Harper, thank you for gracing our studio with your presence tonight."

"Oh, you know it's my pleasure and my honor to be here," the senator gushed. Her lighting was also designed to be flattering, in accordance with her importance, and she looked fabulous for a woman her age. "And may I say, I love the gorgeous new set. I hope you didn't go to all this trouble just for me," she joked.

"Oh, it was no trouble," Carol bantered. She tilted her head coquettishly away from the senator as she spoke, pulling the skin on the side of her face even tighter. As she fluttered her lashes, the strain was too much and a small, red rip appeared just above her left eyebrow.

Another gasp resounded from the viewers in the conference room. "She's got a cut on her forehead," called out Scout, pointing at the screen in alarm.

Chester's mouth hung open in fascinated horror. "My god," he breathed, "she has no idea her forehead is tearing open, because it's so full of Botox she can't feel a thing."

Unaware, Carol soldiered on. "President Harper, tell us, what will be the first thing you do once you're sworn in as President Harper?" she asked.

Angela Harper's ancient eyes didn't detect the tear on Carol's forehead, and she proceeded with the interview as though nothing were amiss. "The very first thing I will do is something that has always been near and dear to my heart," she proclaimed loftily. "As soon as I finish taking the oath of office, I will march right into the Oval Office and sign an executive order that finally, once and for all, provides free healthcare for everyone!"

Carol Crawford clasped her hands just beneath her chin and beamed at her guest. "Oh, President Harper, that is the most gracious, presidential, and good thing I've ever heard anyone say."

The interview was momentarily interrupted by the off-camera sounds of the studio staff clapping and cheering. Then Carol took control again. "Tell everyone watching tonight; what would free healthcare for everyone mean? What would Harpercare look like?"

"Well, first of all, my free healthcare executive order would benefit the children, of course," almost-President Harper began to explain. "From the moment they're born, actually." The camera cut to a shot of Carol Crawford nodding intelligently before cutting back to Angela Harper's face as the nonagenarian went on. "For example, studies show that, when babies are born, they're already in a hospital, so this is the ideal time to administer the first comprehensive schedule of vaccinations."

"Of course! What a clever idea, to get it all done at once," Carol expounded. "What vaccinations would a newborn expect to receive in the hospital?"

"Oh, we would mandate all the important ones, of course. You know ... we'd vaccinate against HIV and HPV, because you want to do those before the child becomes sexually active. And for male babies, we would also vaccinate against toxic masculinity."

Carol lifted her brows slightly in surprise, a herculean effort that she made to look natural. "Oh? I didn't know a vaccine had been developed against toxic masculinity."

"Well, it's more of a procedure, actually," Angela Harper explained. "It just takes a second, a little snip-snip, and the baby will safely grow into a good, feminist man."

"That sounds simply wonderful," Carol proclaimed. "Imagine, a world without toxic masculinity! President Harper, you are a gift to the earth and all her peoples." Still sitting in her stressful posture to keep her butt off the prickly frog and her face in the sweet spot, she lifted her chin and half-closed her eyes to express the joy she felt.

An eerie creak sounded below the women's conversation; it reminded Majedah of a tree she once heard groaning in a windstorm, just before it snapped.

"Oh, I'm just getting started, sister," said the senator. "We've got a lot of work to do, cleaning up Nelson's mess."

Carol called out, "Amen, sister!" and smiled broadly. The smile was the last straw; her poor, overtaxed skin, stretched beyond its limits, gave way at last. A rift opened up from the corner of her mouth all the way to her ear. With a report like a pistol, the skin snapped up and away like a shade rolling up.

As the camera operator fainted, the camera remained focused on Carol's Halloween-horror face, which now resembled a plastic model used to teach anatomy to high school students. "What? What is it? What just happened?" Carol chattered, her fully exposed teeth, gums, and tongue flapping in the open air.

Senator Harper was caught by a fast-acting secret service agent just before she hit the floor. Three more agents rushed to hustle the semi-conscious politician outside to a waiting black SUV that spirited her out of the public eye.

In the packed conference room, sobs and shrieks of horror rent the air, vomit spewed, and unconscious bodies rained to the high-traffic carpeting. Someone pulled the Trigger Alarm and a loud bell started clanging as hidden panels slid open and trauma counselors flooded into the room. Mara couldn't stop rearing and plunging hysterically, until someone finally tied a shirt over equis eyes and patted equis neck soothingly.

After a full ten seconds of unobstructed footage of Carol's ruined face beamed live to every corner of the globe, someone in the control room who wasn't too sick finally flipped a switch and took the station to commercial.

Amid all the chaos, Majedah stood, calm and unruffled, a victorious smile on her face as she lifted the flute to her mouth to sip the sweet, sweet taste of celebratory champagne.

Chapter 23

AS THEY WAITED for the ten o'clock meeting to begin, the crowd in the conference room was noisy and unruly. No one could stop talking about Carol Crawford's facial implosion the previous evening, and even the black eye it had given the 24/7 brand could not suppress the sensational aspect of the event. At last, Rosemary had to stick her thumb and index finger in her mouth and give one of her ear-splitting whistles.

"Okay, enough! Let's get this meeting going," barked the veteran News Director. The room quieted while she forged ahead. "Couple personnel announcements before Juan starts the call. First of all, no. No decision has been made regarding a replacement for Carol."

"Oh, gee, sorry, Mara," sneered Scout.

Mysty, sitting cross-armed beside zir, cocked myz head obnoxiously and said, "As if."

Across the table from them, Mara narrowed equis eyes and snorted angrily.

Rosemary talked over the drama and drowned it out. "For now, the eight o'clock prime time hour will continue to be an hour-long panel of experts, hosted and moderated by our experienced anchors and reporters. Luckily, this format makes sense as we move into the final weeks before the election, when we'd be doing political analysis no matter whose name is on the show.

"Also, be advised that Ångström has requested a pronoun change. Ångström now wishes to go by the pronouns nut, 24, and gander. Please make sure you use the correct pronouns going forward … or you'll be hearing from HR." She paused to glare around the room at each employee individually, which took about five minutes. Then it was ten o'clock and Juan's voice came over the speakers.

"Good morning, everyone. Wow, what a show last night. That certainly was … different." He sounded like he hadn't quite gotten over the shock, but he quickly added tones of decisiveness and optimism to his voice as he continued speaking. "Luckily, the handlers got our girl out of there *rápido* while the camera stayed on Carol, so no harm done. We here at the DNC sent a lovely bouquet of flowers to Carol, and we hope she feels better as soon as possible."

He paused a beat and when he began to speak again, he sounded perturbed. "Unfortunately, that wasn't the greatest visual to have associated with our candidate. And with Election Day just a couple weeks away, we can't afford any more screw-ups, or there won't be time to recover.

"And with time getting so tight," he continued, "we have news this morning that the polls are also extremely tight. As in, Clark-is-leading-by-seven-tight."

Gasps of astonishment were heard all around the room as well as over the call as participants world-wide took in the news.

Juan switched to a reassuring voice. "Okay, okay, I know it sounds like it can't be true, and I'm sure it's not. It's just what our internal polling is showing at the moment. I only mention it because I want to make sure everyone appreciates the seriousness of our position right now. We're gonna have to work even harder to make sure things go the way they're supposed to, that's all. No slacking!"

Voices sounded on the phone and in the room:

"Of course not!"

"We'll work as hard as we have to!"

"Just tell us what to do!"

"Good, that's what I wanna hear," came Juan's voice. "Now, there is a small, unanticipated problem. Some of you may have already noticed this, but it turns out that the enemy candidate is technically African-American and technically female." Angry murmuring broke out and Juan raised his voice to be heard over it. "I know, I know. I agree, she's not a real woman or a real African-American, but she does look the part enough to fool some people. So, we're going to have to come up with some new narratives, sort of custom-design them to take out this particular candidate."

"But racism and sexism narratives have always worked perfectly," protested Max. He adjusted his quirky, ironic dad glasses with one hand as he regarded the phone in the center of the table.

"Yeah, well, they just sound stupid now, okay? We can't use them." Juan was uncharacteristically blunt, and everyone around the table leaned back from the negativity.

Over the confusion, Rosemary brusquely said, "Don't keep us in suspense, Juan. What's the new message?"

There was a hollow pause before the DNC Chair spoke again. "Yeah, see, there's the issue. We kind of don't have one."

A new round of noises, now expressing fear and indecision, filled the air.

"Yeah, you know, we thought we had it all wrapped up against Nelson. We had a War on Women, and we had racism, sexism, Islamophobia … all the greatest hits. And we've been trying to keep rolling with that since Clark got the nomination, but it's just not as easy a sale."

A cynical, older sounding woman's voice lanced out of the speaker. "Excuse me, Juan?"

"Yes, who's this? Florence? Say who you are in case someone doesn't recognize your voice."

"Sure. This is Florence Houlihan, National Director of SPInstER. We're actually proceeding with the War on Women narrative. Ms. Clark is a notorious religious nut, and by that I mean that she went to Catholic school and apparently still attends church sometimes. And she is against a woman's Constitutional right to women's healthcare."

A chorus of angry exclamations rang out.

"Very good, Florence, very good. We should definitely make that an issue. She's a theo-fascist for sure. But we lean on that too hard, and the Jesus freaks come out to vote for her. We're gonna need more, people. We can't take any chances, with it being as close as it is. So, what we're gonna do today is open up the floor for suggestions. Let's all brainstorm some new angles together and see what sounds most promising, okay? Anyone who has a good idea, please introduce yourself and throw it out there, and we'll spitball it around, okay?"

After a brief pause, a nerdy sounding male voice came out of the speakers. "Um, hi, everyone. Can everyone hear me?"

"Yes," said Juan. "Who's this?"

"Oh, sorry. This is Jonathan Goober, up at MIT. I was thinking, we could take that raw polling data you have and analyze it. I've got colleagues in the atmospheric sciences department, and they could run that data through some of their climate modeling software and fix those numbers up. We could probably find a ten or twenty-point lead for Senator Harper, no problem."

"Good, good. I like that," said Juan.

"And this is Matt Sour over at NBSC," came another voice. "I think I can speak for all the media when I say: We'll report the shit out of those numbers!"

"Great! That should knock the wind out of Patty's sails. Good stuff, people, good stuff. See? This is already going in a great direction," said Juan. "Anyone else have an idea?"

"Hi, everyone. This is Dickie Gross over at Greenworld," came a soft, high-pitched feminine voice. "We were talking the other day about how many children the Clarks have, and how it's really irresponsible of them. We could go ahead and calculate the enormous carbon footprint all those children will have throughout their lifetimes, especially if they go ahead and have a lot of kids themselves. We'd be talking greenhouse gases in the mega-tons."

"Nice!" complimented Juan. "That makes for a powerful mental image. Run with that, Dickie."

"Hello, people. This is Marsha McNutty at the National Science Curriculum Council," came a didactic female voice. "Dickie, get those calculations over to me ASAP, and we'll incorporate them into every high school science class next week."

"Excellent, great idea," said Juan. "We are really cooking now. Okay, who's next?"

A voice like a crow cawing over a flattened squirrel on the side of the road came out of the speaker. "Hi, Juan, it's Gloria. Want me to start casting sexual harassment accusers?"

"Yeah, you know what? Go ahead and line up a dozen or so, Gloria. Hopefully we won't need them, but it's good to have them in our hip pocket if need be," agreed Juan.

And on it went, as right-thinking patriots from every sector of American life contributed ideas. Majedah listened with one ear as she scribbled in an open notebook in her lap. She had drawn a line down the center of a page and labeled one side, *Reasons why I should get Carol's job* and the other side, *Reasons why I won't get Carol's job.* The *Reasons why I should get Carol's job* side already had several weighty entries, such as: *Went to same Ivy League 7 Sisters school as Angela Harper*; *Pretty*; *Most intelligent journalist at 24/7*; *Feminist*; and *Sleeping with Spinner.*

Now the tip of her pen hung, poised at the top of the blank *Reasons why I won't get Carol's job* column, suspended by Majedah's reluctance to name her own shortcoming. At last, she forced herself to write the repugnant truth, angrily scrubbing the words onto the page: *I am Patty Clark's bitch.* A sole, bitter tear punctuated the unfortunate sentence as it plunked onto the page.

A new voice came over the speakers, masculine yet tempered by years of hormone therapy and vocal coaching to replicate a feminine timbre, too. "Hey, everyone, it's Delilah Wander, Director of the Harper campaign, for anyone who doesn't know." Everyone chuckled at the ridiculous thought. Majedah took time out from her self-pity to reflect on how conscientious her party was about appointing leaders who represented each of the major American identity groups. *We are such good people*, she thought to herself.

"We just got a massive new grant from the Flow Foundation," said Delilah, "and we're going to invest in some serious opposition research against Patty Clark."

There were murmurs of approval as the news sank in.

"Yeah," continued Delilah, "we've got some fantastic contacts working for us in various intelligence agencies, and they're reaching out to counterparts abroad to find dirt on Clark. We've already gathered some juicy tidbits, too," he teased.

Juan voiced what everyone thought. "Well, don't leave us hanging like that, Delilah. Anything you can share?"

"Let's just say that our foreign intelligence counterparts have come up with some of the most salacious options," Delilah gushed. "I don't want to give away too much, but how big a media splash would tales of Patty Clark paying for pedophile Cleveland steamer retro-Cold War collusion make?"

Now the meeting attendees could barely contain their excitement, and exclamations broke out around the room and over the phone.

"Oh, that would make a very big splash," confirmed Rosemary from her chair at the head of the conference table. "A very big splash indeed. We could all retire rich with material like that."

A wave of tittering and scattered cheers welled up until Juan cut it off with a serious note. "And it would do something crucial in this election cycle," he declared. "It would make enough bible-thumping, white nationalist Clark supporters stay home on Election Day." The room became silent as the strategy worked its way into everyone's consciousness. "Because make no mistake, folks, this race is much closer than it should be. Every single vote counts, including the ones we can demoralize and suppress. Whoever can come up with the best piece of dirt on Patty Clark is gonna be the hero of the election."

He paused to let the proclamation sink in. Then he closed with, "Okay, that's it for today, folks. Keep working hard, now—this is the home stretch."

The sounds of countless devices disconnecting pinged over the speakers and the 24/7 staffers began to gather up their things. Rosemary stopped them with one last instruction. "You heard the man, people. Get out there and dig, dig, dig that dirt!" Then she added something that coalesced and crystallized Majedah's machinations. "Whoever gets what we need to sink Patty Clark," said Rosemary, "can pretty much write their own ticket at this station."

MAJEDAH'S TRAVEL-FOR-RESEARCH REQUEST had been granted immediately and by that evening, she was knocking on the door of a small white house in the middle of a run-down block in Wycksburg. Her breath hung in a ghostly cloud as she glanced up and down the street, relieved to see that the neighborhood was quiet in the late October evening and she was apparently unobserved. Then the door opened, and a tall, stick-thin woman stood silhouetted against the interior light. "I was wondering when you'd show up," she said. She turned and gestured for Majedah to follow. "Close the door behind you."

"Thank you for inviting me in," said the journalist. She glanced about, using her finely honed reporter skills to take in information. The tiny foyer opened directly into a compact living room, which contained worn furnishings, a television, and books, toys, and dust on everything. Three children hovered nearby, focusing curious eyes upon the visitor.

Majedah's host turned to make sure she was following. The woman looked to be in her late fifties (though Majedah already knew she was only 47). Her skin was a prestigious deep brown shade, and her frizzy hair was subdued in a utilitarian non-style with multiple plastic clips. She wore a shabby fleece robe open over a faded hoodie, tired jeans, and dirty pink Croc knock-offs. "Come on into the kitchen where we can talk," she said over her shoulder as she led the way through a cluttered dining room. Majedah followed, trailed by the children.

The youngest, a boy who came up to Majedah's hip, caught at her sleeve and asked, "Are you the lady from television?"

Majedah looked down into large, dark eyes that could melt even the heart of a dedicated feminist like herself, and she exercised some rarely used facial muscles with a genuine smile. "I work for a television broadcast company, yes. What do you do?"

"I go to school," said the lad. "I'm in first grade."

"How clever of you," said Majedah. "Do you like going to school?"

"Yeah, it's okay," allowed the boy. "I got the highest score on the math quiz, and Missus Perry let me be in charge of feeding the fish all week," he reported with pride.

"Good job," said Majedah in an affectionate voice she hardly recognized as her own.

The party had arrived in a dingy kitchen with precisely the hideous cracked linoleum floor and Formica countertops Majedah had anticipated. She returned her gaze to the more pleasing tiny face by her side. "And do you help your mom here at home?"

"Most of the time, yes," replied the child. "Except when she's away in the hospital. Then I—"

"That's enough out of you, Jordy," his mother cut him off. "Eric," she directed the oldest child, "you take your brother and sister upstairs and finish your homework. Let me talk to the lady in peace."

"Yes, ma'am," said the older boy. "Come on, everyone," he told his siblings.

"Goodbye, TV lady," called Jordy, waving as he was shepherded from the room.

"Goodbye, Jordy," said Majedah. "It was nice to meet you."

"Nothing but trouble, those kids," grumbled their mother. She dropped gracelessly into a pitted chrome-framed vinyl chair and shoved another one towards Majedah. "Have a seat," she said.

Majedah, who had driven directly from the airport to the house, had hoped for an offer of coffee or water, at least. But after seeing the kitchen, she was just as glad to focus on the task at hand and do as the woman directed. Her hostess leaned back in her own chair, crossed her arms, and cocked her head to regard Majedah sidelong from beneath crafty, lowered lids. Majedah flashed her high-intensity charming smile and said, "Thanks for inviting me in, Alice. This must be such an exciting time for your whole family—"

"I suppose you came here looking for dirt on my sister," Alice cut her off.

Majedah paused to decide how to play it. Her heart pounded suddenly in her ears as the importance of getting this meeting just right struck her.

Now that they were sitting across from one another in the glare of the ceiling fixture, Majedah could see that Alice's skin was sallow and lined, and her hair was so dry it looked brittle. Her eyes were circled with dark skin and sunken deep above hollow cheeks. Majedah looked into them and saw the eyes of an addict: always hungry, always calculating. She decided on a direct course of action and said, "Yes, I did. Do you have anything for me?"

"Oh, baby, do I ever. I got just the thing'll sink that bitch in the shit she deserves."

Majedah fought to keep from falling into an ecstatic swoon and kept her eyes on Patty Clark's sister, who seemed happy to talk now that she had gotten started.

"Look at this place," the slovenly woman grumbled indignantly. "You ever see such a dump? How's this for treating her sister like garbage, huh? An' she live up in that great big mansion, with servants an' everything. *Staff.* Huh!"

Majedah shook her head sympathetically, and Alice went on.

"*Her* kids all live like little princes and princesses, while her niece an' nephews gotta live in this shithole, wearin' all hand-me-down clothes from their little shit *highnesses*, thank you very much."

"That's so cruel," Majedah empathized. In her head, she began to compose a headline: *Patty Clark's Niece and Nephews live in Squalor in Shadow of Billionaire's Mansion*. She would have to send a crew around to get footage of that little cherub, Jordy, with his great, dark eyes. She cautiously phrased a question to tease out some details. "So, you'd be willing to go on camera with me to discuss how your cold-hearted, wealthy sister turns her back on your family in your time of need?"

"What are you talking about?" snapped Alice. She looked at her guest as though she were an idiot.

I pissed her off! I'm going to lose the story! Majedah's scalp grew damp from a flash of panic.

"That ain't my dirt I got on Patty," said Alice. "That's just the way she *is*. That's just the reason I don't care who I sell my dirt to. She don't want to help me with all her money, then she can help me with someone else's money, that's how I see it."

"Oh, yes. Yes, of course." Majedah felt giddy being so close to the scoop that would sink the fascist candidate. Terrified of saying the wrong thing, she opened her mouth as though to speak and held out one hand, palm up. In as neutral a tone as she could muster, she prompted, "Sooooo..."

Alice picked up the cue. "So, you got money?" she asked.

"I can get you money," Majedah quickly assured her.

"That's good, because I got dirt," said Alice. She folded her arms and leaned back in her chair, waiting for her guest to make an opening bid.

Majedah's customary confidence faltered in the face of such high stakes, so she reminded herself that she was much smarter than Alice, and also that the woman clearly needed money and was ready to do business. Majedah wasn't going to show weakness by being the first one to make an offer, so she asked, "Just what kind of dirt are we talking?"

Alice's smile was sly. "Oh, this is very powerful dirt. Powerful enough to take out all those church people say they gonna vote for my sister. Uh uh, no sir, they not gonna vote for her once they hear what ol' Alice knows."

Majedah was now so desperate to know what the dirt was that she could barely remain seated. Her hands betrayed her and began drumming rapidly on the tabletop. Alice noticed the nervous action and smiled triumphantly. Majedah dropped her attempt at bargaining and blurted out, "Okay, just tell me what it is, Alice, so I can figure out how much it's worth."

Alice likewise ditched her coy demeanor and said, "It's three different times since her last baby was born, takin' that abortion pill."

Majedah involuntarily closed her eyes and drew in a deep breath through her nose in a spasm of ecstasy. When she exhaled and opened her eyes again, she was in an exalted state. She felt as though she and Alice, at this cheap kitchen table, in this shabby kitchen, in a low-class neighborhood of Wycksbug, were bathed in a shaft of divine light from a new star, so consequential to the future of humankind was this moment. Not to mention, it was also the key to Majedah achieving everything she wanted in life: fame, adulation, and the anchor seat of *An Hour of Your Time*.

Majedah reflected on what an ideal messenger Alice was for delivering this crucial story to the world: a close family member who was also a bitter, resentful borderline personality guided by the twin motivations of greed and revenge for perceived wrongs. "Alice, that is shocking news," Majedah began.

"It's also very valuable news," Alice reminded her.

"Yes, no doubt about it, very valuable news indeed," Majedah agreed.

"I bet Randi Madcow would think it was very valuable news, too. Maybe she'd think it was even more valuable than you do."

"Randi's network doesn't have the resources News 24/7 has," Majedah volleyed. Alice gave her a look that said she was listening. "News such as this must be released to the public in a very particular way, or it loses its value," Majedah explained. "News this powerful needs to be delivered by a witness who is willing to give her name and show her face. Quoting unnamed sources can only go so far, okay? To make this story stick and take out those values voters, we'd need you to go on the air, live, with me, to tell the American people the truth about your sister."

Alice only needed to think about it for a second. "I'll do it, but I need to get paid a *lot*," she said.

"Of course," Majedah answered quickly. "But just so we're clear, you understand we can't actually *pay* you to say something, right?"

"What? Then what are we even talking about?" Alice was instantly furious.

"It's unethical for a journalist to pay a witness to say something," Majedah explained. "But it's proper and common for media companies, as well as the opposing candidate's donors, to pay witnesses a *stipend* for their expenses and trouble."

Alice was soothed. "That's fine. You can call it pay or you can call it a stipend, long as I get my money."

Majedah nodded once. "Then I think we have an understanding. Now, about that stipend ..." She pulled a paper napkin from the cheap plastic holder on the table (and she was in such a state of journalistic intoxication that she failed to register the incongruity of a ready supply of napkins in an addict's house) and lay it flat in front of her. Then she took out a pen and wrote a number on the napkin. She pushed the napkin across the tabletop so Alice could see it.

The hard luck woman's eyes went wide when she saw the number and an avaricious grin spread across her face. She looked up at Majedah and nodded. "Oh, yes, missus news lady. I think we can work together just fine."

Chapter 24

DISCREET AND PROFESSIONAL, Majedah and Spinner never spoke to one another at the office. This was easily accomplished, as Majedah was still stationed in the Pool, while Richard Spinner's office was twelve stories above in the rarified uppermost echelons of the corporation. It was to this venerated space that Rosemary now led Majedah, only halting her double time march when she reached Spinner's executive assistant's desk. By way of greeting, Rosemary barked, "Is he in, Judy?"

"Uh oh, this looks important," observed the stunning brunette.

"The most important," Rosemary confirmed. Majedah stood just behind her, not speaking, simply letting everything happen.

Judy knocked on the massive double doors, cracked one open, and stuck her head in. "Mr. Spinner? Rosemary's here, and she says you're going to want to hear this ASAP. Okay?" There was a rumbling response, the executive assistant nodded once, then pulled the door wide and waved the two visitors in.

Majedah followed her Sherpa into the cavernous space and Judy pulled the door shut behind them. If Spinner was surprised to see his paramour in his chrome-and-leather furnished, window-walled aerie, he didn't show it. Without rising, he waved a hand at some chairs and said, "Come on in, ladies. Hope you don't mind me calling you 'ladies;' you never know these days. *Huh! Huh!*" As they sat, he cut to the chase. "So, what's the scoop?"

Rosemary leaned back in her chair, one foot propped on her opposite thigh and hands templed on her stomach, and announced, "Majedah found it."

"Found what?"

"The Dirt."

"Well, this is certainly good news, if it's as big as you say," Spinner allowed. "Are you going to tell me, or do I have to guess?"

"Majedah," said Rosemary, "you tracked it down; why don't you do the honors?"

"Happy to," said the brilliant young reporter. She looked directly at Spinner and announced, "Patty Clark is a hypocrite and a phony Christian."

"No shit, Sherlock. They all are. Tell me something I don't know," said the CEO. "You got specifics?"

Majedah told him what she had learned from Patty's sister.

The Great Man leaned back in his chair as he considered it from all angles. "Three times, you say?" he asked.

"Yes," Majedah confirmed.

"And how does—Alice is her name?—how does Alice know this?"

"Patty Clark told her herself. Alice says Patty could never have told her husband what she was doing, but she had to unburden herself to someone. They're sisters; sisters share everything," explained Majedah.

"Thank God women love to talk so much, right?" said Spinner. He thought another moment then asked, "Did you verify it?"

"I couldn't get anyone at Patty's doctor's office to talk, but I tracked down a pharmacist who confirmed that he filled the prescription two of the three times."

"Excellent. And these witnesses will go on the record?" Spinner folded his hands under his chin as he listened.

"Well, I'm still negotiating with them. As of now, Alice is 90% there. We talked some numbers, and she's almost ready to go on the air. The pharmacist says he prefers to remain an unnamed source for now."

The CEO nodded as he thought. He turned to the News Director. "Rosemary, what do you think? Would just the sister be enough to run with this story?"

"Are you kidding? Patty Clark's own sister turning her in for exercising her right to woman's healthcare even as she tries to deny that right to everyone else? The seriousness of what Patty Clark did, combined with the high drama of family betrayal, would make this biggest story of the century—maybe of all time!" gushed the usually businesslike director.

Spinner nodded again. "That's exactly what I was thinking. Okay, here's what we'll do." He turned to the reporter. "Majedah, you get back down to Wycksburg. We're going to need you to report live from the scene of the crime, as it were, and also be on-hand to keep nudging your informants. But we can run with unnamed sources for now. Let's get you reporting live from in front of Patty's campaign headquarters in primetime tonight." Then he focused on the News Director. "Rosemary, who's producing *An Hour of Your Time* right now, Sara?"

"Yes, Sara Murphy."

"Tell Sara to put Majedah in the first block tonight."

"Okay."

A tiny squeak of irrepressible excitement slipped past Majedah's lips, but in the throes of taking action, the executives didn't hear it.

"Get Majedah a location team and get them on the next plane to Wycksburg."

"You got it."

"And get the social media team on it now, so they can start leaking it onto the Internet."

"Of course," said Rosemary. "Anything else?"

"Yes," said Spinner. He looked from one to the other of his employees, his grin spreading wider by the second. "Put your seatbelts on. It's going to be a wild ride."

THE HASTILY CUT-TOGETHER new opening graphics for *An Hour of Your Time* didn't look half-bad. The bumper had been shortened from 15 seconds to 10, and it no longer featured any images of the already-forgotten Carol Crawford. Clips of major events and newsmakers' faces faded into one another until the video resolved into the familiar shot of the Freedom Tower and the percussive lettering that spelled out the show title (sans any host's name). Then News 24/7 daytime anchor Toffee Barbeaux appeared, seated behind a massive news desk, a panel of pundits off to the side and primed to start blathering.

"Good evening, I'm Toffee Barbeaux. Welcome to *An Hour of Your Time* where tonight, we have incredible breaking news," she said.

She was replaced by the flashing red screen and startling sound effect of the Breaking News indicator. When Toffee reappeared, she was on a split screen with Majedah. The reporter was standing in front of a large building in which numerous windows were aglow. For this momentous report, Majedah had chosen a tailored khaki trench coat with the waist cinched tight to show her slender figure, and her throat was wrapped in a raspberry Narla Veulvi pashmina. She looked serious and fabulous.

"Joining us tonight from Patty Clark's campaign headquarters is News 24/7 field reporter Majedah Cantalupi-Abromavich-Flügel-Van Der Hoven-Taj Mahal," read Toffee. "Majedah, we understand you've uncovered some shocking allegations against the Republican candidate for president. Can you tell us what you've learned?"

Majedah nodded as the split screen switched to being fully dedicated to her. The importance of the moment weighed upon the young journalist; in fact, she had spent the whole flight contemplating what the tone of her delivery should be. First, there was her righteous hatred for the Christo-fascist candidate, which she shared with all right-thinking people. Layered on top of that was her disgust with the woman, for her self-serving hypocrisy. But then, Majedah also supported and celebrated Patty's choice. She was conscious of her own journalistic reputation for being a sort of unofficial spokesperson for Patty Clark, which meant people could reasonably expect her to cheer Patty's decision to come to the side of Feminism and be redeemed. After considering all these things, Majedah had decided to go with a sympathetic and supportive tone underlain with the unspoken hard truth that the candidate's deeds, though righteous, were fatally flawed by hypocrisy.

She drew a breath and began her consequential report. "Good evening, Toffee. Yes, I can now reveal details of conversations I've had with multiple people who are close to Patty Clark. These sources confirm that, on three different occasions, Patty Clark availed herself of a woman's right to choose. Of course, that itself is not a problem. It's admirable, really; as you know, the Clarks already have an environmentally devastating five children. The problem is that Patty Clark has put herself forward as a Christian alternative for America and is on the record as saying she thinks abortion is, and I quote, 'wrong.'" Majedah's face disappeared momentarily but her voice continued over footage of the candidate's recent appearance at Freedom University, the noted Christian institute of higher education.

Then the screen split between Toffee and Majedah again. The anchor shook her head and tsk-tsk'ed. "That really is a problem, Majedah, as you say."

"That's right, Toffee. The question now becomes whether these same Christian 'values voters' will come out on Election Day to vote for Patty Clark, or if they will just stay home. In a country as divided as ours, this bombshell news could be the deciding factor over who goes to the White House in January." Her glossy black hair lifted and fluttered about her face in the chilly evening breeze. Behind her, Patty Clark's campaign headquarters lights shone defiantly.

"Majedah, what's the atmosphere like in Wycksburg right now?" queried Toffee.

"Well, as you can see, I'm standing in front of the Clark campaign's headquarters." The camera panned to the side so the building came into view. It hulked behind the reporter, solidly built of brown brick and steel and sporting a massive *Clark for America* banner above the central bank of doors that led inside. "And Toffee, I don't know if you can hear this or not," continued Majedah. The camera panned back to her. "But there's a loud sort of rushing sound all around here at the moment." She held the microphone away from herself and out to one side. Sure enough, it picked up the background noise.

"I do hear it," Toffee said. "It kind of sounds like a tornado—you know how people always say they sound like a freight train? Or a really high wind, like a hurricane rushing past. What is that?"

Majedah brought the mic back to herself. "That's the sound of the media descending on this location," she explained. "We really can't overemphasize the importance of this bombshell breaking news."

"Absolutely not," agreed Toffee. She smirked. "Looks like all our competitors are rushing to catch up with us."

Majedah allowed herself a triumphant chuckle. "Yes, it does, Toffee. But News 24/7 was here first, because we broke this story." She addressed her cameraman. "Dave, can you pan around and show the scene to our viewers?"

The broadcast went full screen again as the camera panned 180 degrees. Satellite trucks, SUV's, taxis and Ubers, and even bicycles screeched into view as far as the eye could see as a veritable army of reporters and journalists descended on the scene. Voices shouted instructions and pronounced breathless reporting, and fistfights broke out over prime locations. T-shirt vendors and food trucks jockeyed for position. A convoy of law enforcement vehicles streamed in, and dozens of cops in full riot gear deployed into the growing chaos.

"Wow, that is a lot of media attention," observed Toffee. "Has the Clark campaign addressed the situation yet? Have they at least issued a statement?"

"No, nothing at all," reported Majedah. She dropped the mic for a moment to elbow aside a pushy MSDNC correspondent who was trying to set up a report from inside her frame. Then a loud murmur sounded from the collective mob as, behind Majedah, a yellow rectangle of light opened in the building façade. The reporter quickly picked up her microphone and began to comment. "Toffee, it looks like someone is coming out of the building now. We got here first so we are in the best location to bring this development to our viewers. Stand by so we can see what's happening."

"We are absolutely standing by," Toffee assured her. "This is probably the biggest news story in the whole world right now; there's nothing more important for us to broadcast. We'll be with you the whole time, so our viewers don't miss a thing."

Majedah turned to watch as a phalanx of bodyguards emerged from the building. They cleared the space in front of the doors and placed barricades to secure a half circle. Then Vic Waveny appeared. He and another campaign worker carried a heavy wooden podium between them, which they set down almost directly in front of Majedah. Vic stationed himself behind it and looked up. Seeing Majedah, he gave a quick nod of recognition. He wore business clothes with his favorite western hat, but his customary jovial demeanor was gone, replaced by a downcast resolve. He looked like a man determined to perform his duties, no matter how distasteful those duties had become.

Majedah turned to the camera. "Toffee, as you can see, Vic Waveny is about to make a statement. He's the Press Secretary for the Clark campaign, so we can assume this will be an official statement."

Vic raised his eyes to survey the bloodthirsty media mosh pit that faced him, slowly swiveling his head from one side to the other as he took in the awesome scale of the moment. Then, without preamble or technical support, began to speak in his booming voice.

"G-g-g-g-g. G-g-g-g-g-g-uuuuuuuuuuu-guuuuu-guuuuuuuuuuuuuuuud.d.d. Good eee. Good EEEeeeeeeeee. …"

Majedah gestured furiously at her crew. "Reece, get the directional mike! Get the boom! Get what he's saying!" Producers all around scrambled to improvise tech that could capture the statement.

"Good eeeeeeeeeeee. Good eeeeeeeeeeeeeeeeee. Good eeeee-EEEEE-EEEEEEvening everywuh-wuh-wuh-wuh-one," said Vic. He paused to take a breath then continued. "B-b-b-b-b-b-b-bbbbbby-EEEEEEE n-n-n-n-n-n-NUH-NUH-NUHNUHHHHHHHHHH-now, y-y-y-y-y-y-y-y-y-y-y-y-yooooooooooo've huh-huh-hearrrrd…" In the glare of countless carbon arc lights, his face had already gone red, and sinews and veins stood pronounced on his straining neck.

Next to Majedah, Reece, the field producer, held out the boom until her arms shook with fatigue. As the official statement wore on, Dave took over while Reece tended the camera. All around Majedah, other remote broadcast crews were doing similar things, positioning themselves for the time it would take Vic to issue a statement. Every news station in America and many more around the world broadcast the unscheduled presser live so as not to risk missing a single syllable. No one even broke for a commercial.

It was nearly two a.m. when Vic finished delivering the official statement—that the campaign had no comment at this time—and by then, Patty Clark had vanished so completely that not even her husband or children knew where she had gone.

Chapter 25

"SO, IT LOOKS like the polls are just about tied now, even before we have to send the data to our statisticians for adjustment." Celebrity pollster Nina Mango's voice rang triumphantly from the ceiling speakers in the massive News 24/7 conference room.

There were sighs of relief all around. Juan Conquista spoke over the sound. "And Nina, would you go over the hypothetical ask as well?"

"Oh, yes, this is my favorite data point today," said the husky voiced statistician. "When we asked likely conservative voters if they believed the bombshell about Patty Clark inducing multiple incidents of constitutional women's health rights on herself, 56% said they were unsure. But when we asked them, if it turned out the allegations *are* true, whether that would affect their vote, a full 78% said they would stay home. 78%!"

"Hooray" cheered the professionals of all stripes who were gathered in conference rooms across the country and around the globe. From her seat at the enormous table, Majedah cheered along.

"78 percent? Sounds like 'game over' to me!" said Juan. "So that's it for now, people," he wrapped up the meeting. "Everyone should be focused on proving beyond a shadow of a doubt that

Patty Clark did this thing. We prove it, we win. We've got five days until Election Day. Can we do this?"

"*Si, se pueda*," chanted the team in unison, and everyone raised his/her/zis/myz/Zz/blue/equis/gander fist in the air. Across the table, Majedah caught Melissa's eye. The pool reporter gave her a questioning look, and Majedah nodded to indicate her raised hand. Melissa glanced at her own arm and realized she had forgotten to make a fist. Her raised arm was identical to everyone else's except that her fingers were straight, producing a perfect Third Reich salute. Lips rounded in an "oops" expression, Melissa quickly balled her hand into a fist to create the correct gesture of inclusivity and goodness. She shrugged her shoulders and mouthed "thank you." Majedah gave an approving nod and held her own fist straight out in the air.

Back in the Pool, Scout asked, "Majedah, when are you going to be doing your live interview with Alice Clarke?"

"Last I heard, it was going to be Monday night."

"Oh my god, on Election Day Eve!" exclaimed Mysty. "Are you going to do it in the eight o'clock hour?"

"I don't want to jinx it, but that's what Rosemary told me." Majedah was so excited she was barely able to control the pitch of her voice.

"That is so awesome," said Melissa. "Are you going to do it in the studio here?"

"Yes," chirped Majedah.

"Oh my god, that is so amazing," purred Mysty. "You get to interview someone really, really important, in studio, on Election Day Eve, while there's still no announced replacement for Carol. What great exposure. You are so lucky, Majedah."

"Luck had nothing to do with it," Majedah informed her. "It was hard work, intelligence, an elite education, and my natural gift for journalism." Her co-workers nodded their comprehension.

"I wonder where Patty Clark is right now," pondered Melissa.

"No one knows," Candy informed her. "Not even her family."

"I hope she's all right," Melissa speculated.

"I don't," snarled Mysty. "If it were up to her, people like me would be in death camps!"

"Yeah," Scout chimed in.

Chastened, Melissa concurred. "I guess, if Patty Clark kills herself, then Angela will definitely win, so that would be good."

And though the young reporters (along with every journalist and member of the media from every single outlet everywhere) spent the day working and surfing and prying and searching as hard as they could, no one could find a trace of the missing Republican presidential candidate. Finally, long after five o'clock had come and gone, Chester came through and told everyone to wrap it up for the day. "Everyone needs to get some rest so we can work harder tomorrow," he instructed them. "Let's all grab some supper first, though. Rosemary said we could expense it."

Majedah joined her colleagues at the Buzz for a vegan rice bowl and several pink martinis before taking a taxi to her Upper West Side building. She paid the driver and stepped onto the sidewalk, focusing on putting her wallet away and ignoring a scruffy woman who was panhandling passers-by. Majedah had almost made it to the front door when the bum stepped in front of her. "I'm sorry, I don't have any change," she began.

"Majedah, it's me," said the woman. She glanced around furtively before pulling down the scarf that covered her head and half her face.

Majedah gasped as she recognized the missing candidate. "Oh my god! What are you doing here?"

Patty Clark put a finger over her lips. "I have to talk to you," she said. She quickly rewound the scarf, but not before Majedah had gotten a good look at her face; Patty looked like hell. Her lips were cracked, her nose was red and raw, and her eyes were haunted. "Please," she said.

Now Majedah looked around to make sure they were unobserved. "Okay, sure. Come on inside. We can talk in my apartment."

"SHE REALLY DID that?" Richard Spinner's leather desk chair creaked as he leaned back against it, but his gaze was riveted on Majedah's face. "I'm honestly shocked, and you have no idea how hard it is to shock me. I'm not shocked that Clark had a bunch of abortions and lied about it—I always assumed she had—but I'm shocked that she came to you and admitted it."

Majedah had taken a gamble and jumped the entire chain of command that morning, preferring to bring her news directly to the ultimate decision maker. This was a once-in-a-lifetime opportunity, and she didn't trust anyone else to manage it for her. Now, as she registered the experienced older man's surprise, she was glad she had. "Well, as Patty herself put it, she has a history with me. She said I'm the one reporter who's always given her a fair shake and let her tell her side of the story," explained Majedah. "And she wants to tell her side of this story."

"Majedah, this is simply incredible," Spinner boomed. "In all my long and immensely consequential career, I don't think I've ever had as huge a blockbuster story as this dropped on my desk." He splayed a thick-fingered hand across his breastbone and clutched a handful of Egyptian cotton and loose skin. Then he laid his forearm on his desk and leaned forward to jab an index finger in Majedah's direction. "You get Patty Clark to come on the air live with you, Majedah, and I'll give you the whole *Hour of Your Time* slot on Monday night."

Majedah wished she were sophisticated enough to maintain a calm demeanor, but she wasn't. "The whole hour?" she squeaked. "On Election Day Eve?" She covered her mouth with her hands as her eyes went round and wide, dominating her face.

"That's right, kitten. We'll go back to the original in-studio interview format, and you can host the whole thing."

In bed that night, Majedah worked hard to turn the gears of Spinner's ancient machinery, fantasizing all the while about her triumphant turn as guest host of the most-watched news broadcast in the entire world. In her excitement, she tossed and turned for hours while Spinner snored beside her. Just before finally slipping off to sleep in the wee hours of the morning, she vowed to herself that she would land the interview, no matter what it took.

"I SPOKE DIRECTLY to Mr. Spinner himself and secured the most-high profile, highest rated time-slot there is for your interview." Majedah paused for dramatic effect before announcing her triumph: "We get the entire hour of *An Hour of Your Time* on Monday night, Election Day Eve. Just you and me."

Beside her, Patty Clark stared straight ahead. She wore a hoodie with the hood up, a military-style parka, jeans, and basketball shoes. The glossy, thick ringlets that Majedah remembered were tucked away and hidden. In the dim light, the fallen candidate almost looked like a hardened street person, a runaway teen who had learned to survive on her own. But up close, as Majedah was, Patty's eyes were disturbing in their intensity. "That's good," she said. She nodded a couple times, almost to herself, then her body went rigid as a new passion struck her. "There's just one condition, though." She turned her fevered gaze on Majedah. "I want Alice there."

"What, in the interview?" Majedah had almost forgotten about the unfortunate woman whose claims had brought down a mighty candidate. "Why would you want her there? I thought this was going to be your opportunity to tell America your side of the story."

"Oh, I'm going to tell my story—about how I trusted one person on this earth, the one person a woman should be able to trust: her sister. I'm going to tell about how I confided in *my sister* when my heart was breaking, and I had to make the hardest decisions of my life, and how she turned around and stabbed me in the back. And I want to look her in the eye while I'm telling it." She stared at the ground and gripped the edge of the seat on both sides of her with gloved hands. Then she spoke in a cold, controlled voice that made Majedah shiver. "Tell me … how much did she want for selling her sister out?"

Terrified of saying the wrong thing, Majedah hemmed and hawed. "Well, it hadn't been finalized. She was going to agree to show her face and tell her story in person, and we were in the process of negotiating—"

"Thirty pieces of silver," Patty spat. Then she gave a bitter laugh. "Blood is thicker than water, but I guess money's thickest of all." She shook her head then let it drop forward, her eyes closed. For a moment, Majedah thought she was going to cry. But then Patty drew a great breath through her nose, lifted her chin, and looked straight ahead again. "You get Alice there, I'll do it," she said.

"BY ALL MEANS, get the sister there," boomed Spinner. "Maybe they'll fight! *Huh! Huh!*" His expression became dead serious. "You get them to fight—live, on the air—and I'll make you the permanent anchor of *An Hour of Your Time*."

Sitting ramrod straight in the chair facing his desk, Majedah momentarily lost the ability to breathe.

"I'LL DO IT, but my *stipend* just got a lot more expensive," said Alice. She was in her favorite bargaining position, leaning back in one of her cheap kitchen chairs with her arms folded.

Majedah's mouth was dry from the extraordinary stress of negotiating the most anticipated journalistic interview in all of broadcast history. Her brain, overtaxed with incessantly playing out every possible angle and contingency, had finally stopped thinking altogether on the plane ride down to Wycksburg, and now Majedah was running on pure instinct. "That's not a problem," she said robotically. "We'll send a car for you at ten on Monday morning."

"And I get hair and makeup at your TV station?"

"I'll get you your own dressing room."

"And a stylist? I need wardrobe help."

"And a stylist."

"And I get to keep the clothes?"

Majedah never batted an eye. "You get to keep the clothes."

Alice thought for a moment, until it was plain that nothing else would occur to her. She smiled, leaned forward onto the tabletop, and held out her bony hand for a shake. "Deal," she said.

Chapter 26

THE DAY BEFORE the most obsessively, fanatically, hatefully anticipated presidential election in American history was ominously dark and chilly, even for November in Manhattan. Majedah had spent the first part of the previous night drinking hard in an attempt to quell her nerves, the second part vomiting from drinking too much (and nerves), and the third part recovering in a Xanax-induced semi-coma. She awoke after nine in the morning. But the rules for regular people were already losing their grip on Majedah, and she took her time.

Without giving her anxiety the chance to build again, Majedah washed down another Xanax with her green tea. She replied *Thanks!* to her mother's email, which wished her luck "dispatching the beast". She listened, tight lipped, to a voicemail from her father, telling her how proud he was, even though the topic was so sad, and wishing her great success. She dressed in warm leggings and an oversized hoodie and went for a run. She showered, dressed in a cashmere sweater, jeans, a leather jacket, and boots, and left the apartment.

In her mind, Majedah was already miles above the wannabes in the Pool, but as she had nowhere else to go (*yet*, she assured herself), she turned up at her loathed life preserver-shaped desk just as the others were talking about where to get lunch.

"Majedah!" they all exclaimed and quickly flocked around her to coo and babble.

"Don't stop talking on my account," she patronized them. "What's for lunch? I'm starving."

The passel of press settled on walking five blocks to Hillary's Hot n' Cold Buffet. "Let's all sit here and eat," suggested Scout.

"Great idea," Mysty seconded.

But Majedah knew everyone just wanted to hound her for details about her stupendously important interview that night. Plus, it was almost time for her to re-up her calming medication, so she said, "I'm just going to get mine to go and head back to the office."

Rather than criticizing or becoming peevish, her co-workers all accepted her decision without question.

"Of course, Majedah," said Melissa. "You probably need to start getting ready for your show tonight."

"Yes, that's right, I do," Majedah agreed.

"I'd already be in the stylist's chair, getting primped to perfection," sighed Mysty.

"Your day will come," Majedah said generously. Then she finished paying for her heirloom spelt and germ salad, gave a little wave with just her fingers, and left the eatery.

Majedah hurried down the sidewalk towards the security of her building. Her nerves were beginning to flare up again and her head started spinning, imaging all the things that could go wrong that night. The interview was simply too significant and too hyped, and Majedah had never faced anything that would be quite so universally and intensely scrutinized. Daunted, she pulled her leather jacket tighter around herself and shivered. A taxi blared its horn just as it zoomed past, and the young reporter jumped then stumbled in her high-heeled boots. Her lunch threatened to escape her grasp, and she had to dance and fumble for several steps to hold onto it. Flustered, she crossed the last street before her block just as cold, fat, wind-driven raindrops began to hammer into her face. "Oh, goddamn it!" Majedah fumed.

She could see the entrance halfway down the block and quickened her steps. As she eagerly approached the doors, she noticed a familiar-looking form between her and her goal, and her heart was suddenly pounding against the base of her throat. He spotted her and began to approach.

Majedah swallowed hard. "Oh, my god, Kevin, what are you doing here?" she moaned.

He had come to a halt in front of her, barring her way to the building. He loomed tall and tense. The besotted grin he had worn the last time he saw her was gone. His mouth was a grim line that pulled down at the corners and his eyes were bright with fury, or perhaps grief. He seemed not to notice the icy water plastering his hair to his head and running down his face like tears as he answered her question with another: "Is it true?"

"Is what true?" Majedah glanced wistfully past him towards her building before returning her attention to his laser-like stare. "About Patty Clark? Yes, it's true," she said impatiently. "Now, do you mind if I go inside? The rain is getting into my—"

"Not Patty," he cut her off. "You and Spinner. Is it true?"

"What? Where in the world did you hear that?" Majedah stalled. Shocked at how sorry she suddenly felt, she contemplated whether she could plausibly deny it.

But Kevin had discerned the truth in her reaction, and he began to hurl angry questions at her. "What is he, like, 50 years older than you? You know you could have lived two more of your lifetimes in the time he's been alive, right?"

Majedah's wounded pride piqued her. "I resent your ageist comments," she scolded.

Kevin was relentless. "What are you even planning to do with him?" he demanded. "Are you going to marry him?"

"What?"

"Have his babies?"

Majedah's stomach contracted at the thought, but she snapped, "That's none of your business, Kevin."

"Is he going to ask your father for your hand? You know he's older than your father, right?" Kevin's red eyes betrayed that at least some of the drops running down his face were tears. "Maybe he should ask your grandfather."

"Kevin, what has gotten into you? You need to stop!" Majedah moved to push past him but he stepped to the side, blocking her again. She glared into his face. "What are you even doing here?" she demanded.

"I just needed to see if it was true. I needed to hear it from you." Kevin's rage seemed to have spent itself, and now he just looked sad. In a calmer voice, he asked one last question: "Is this really what you want, Majedah?" His robin's egg eyes were locked on hers, searching for a sign one way or the other.

Majedah held his gaze, fighting against its compelling force. Then she looked away, past his shoulder, at the gleaming News 24/7 headquarters. Her gaze slid up, up, up the shining façade to the rarified upper stories where executives and celebrities ruled, and where there was a vacant office with an empty shelf that needed to be refilled with Golden Vulva Awards for Feminist Broadcasting.

When her eyes met his again, her face was resolute. She pronounced each word clearly and deliberately. "Yes, Kevin, this is what I want."

His posture remained straight and his chin up, but his eyes glinted, wounded as from a mighty blow. His voice now was so soft that she read his lips as much as heard him. "That's all I wanted to know." He reached to touch her cold face with one hand and leaned towards her. She felt his lips, wet with rain, place a kiss on her cheek; it was the tenderest kiss she had ever experienced, and the most pure. Then he straightened again, turned his back to her, and walked away.

Now fighting a cavernous ache in her soul that dwarfed her pre-show jitters, Majedah scurried into the warm, dry maw of the great global media headquarters, and the venerable building took her into its embrace.

THE AFTERNOON PASSED in a blur of meetings, fittings, stylings, and preparations. Majedah was instructed what to ask by executives and coached by producers on how to elicit responses. She was dressed and plucked and blow-dried. She was fed and watered. The heady rush of being pampered and catered to like the star she was on the verge of becoming almost made her forget the sight of Kevin's face.

At 6:43, Alice Clarke arrived and was installed in a comfortable lounge one floor below the main studio. Sara Murphy, the lead producer of *An Hour of Your Time*, escorted Majedah to greet her guest. Alice read the face of the check in the envelope Sara handed her, gave Majedah her canniest look, and asked for a glass of champagne. Majedah recalled Spinner's promise that, if she could get the sisters to fight, she could host *An Hour of Your Time* permanently, and she ordered the nearest assistant to bring Alice a bottle.

At 7:07, Patty Clark entered the News 24/7 building alone and was escorted to the main green room. Sara and Majedah went to see that she was settling in and had whatever she needed. They found the Republican candidate for president perched on the edge of an armchair. She had miraculously pulled herself together for the interview and looked both sympathetic and impressive in a warm white jacket over a matching sheath dress. But she was also bouncing a knee and nervously sipping a glass of seltzer water with a miserable expression on her face.

Majedah went to sit on the coffee table, facing her, and took her hand in both of hers. "How are you doing, Patty?" she asked in the most solicitous voice she could muster. (In fact, the scene with Kevin made it all too easy to empathize with the grief Patty must be feeling.)

The fast food magnate's amber eyes were large and shining, and tension pulled lines around her mouth. She returned Majedah's look gratefully and answered, "Actually? I'm scared to death, Majedah." She looked down at her lap. "I'm about to open up my deepest, darkest secrets to the entire world. I—I've never felt so vulnerable."

"Well, try not to be frightened, Patty. It will just be you and me and a couple technicians in the studio, so it will really feel small and intimate," Majedah reassured her.

Patty's eyes snapped back up. "And Alice, right?"

"Yes, Alice is already in the building."

"She better be," Patty snarled. "That's the only thing giving me courage to get through this—facing that two-faced bitch on live TV and calling her out for the faithless, self-serving junk whore she is."

A thrill ran through Majedah at the unraveling candidate's fightin' words. "Then hold on to that anger, Patty," she advised, squeezing the woman's hand in her own. "Feed it. Let it run through you."

Patty was nodding. "Yes, I think that would be best. It's making me braver."

"Good, good. Feel it, take ownership of it. ... Let it control you."

"Yes. Yes!" Patty growled low in her throat like an alley cat gearing up for a fight.

"Patty, your husband is here," interrupted Sara. The unflappable producer ignored Majedah's glare.

"Patty! My God, we've all been so worried." Norris Clark made a beeline for his wife.

Patty put down her seltzer water and jumped up to meet her husband's embrace with one of her own. "I'm so sorry, babe," she said into his chest. "I couldn't face you. I didn't know what to do."

"Damn it, Patty, don't you know that, whatever it is, we'll figure it out together?"

A hovering production assistant near Majedah said, "Aww," and a stylist sniffled loudly.

As she gazed at the reunited couple, Majedah had a baffling moment of doubt. The sight of husband and wife finding peace and comfort in one another's arms made her feel warm inside, made her eyes well up, and made her want to protect them and wish them well.

It made her long for such love and comfort herself.

It made her remember such a love had been offered to her only hours earlier, and she had thrown it away forever.

It made her insides twist into billows of envy and wrath. It made her want to scream. It made her yearn to take destructive action of nihilistic depth and depravity. It made her lust to destroy the Clarks utterly, completely, and immaculately.

When Sara told Majedah it was time for her to go get her makeup done, the soon-to-be-anchorwoman realized she had been staring at the Clarks like a madwoman and gripping the edges of the coffee table so forcefully that her nails had gouged tiny crescents out of the wood. She made herself smile and thank Sara. She stood gracefully, touched Patty on the shoulder, and told her she'd see her soon and not to worry, she'd do fine. She said a quick hello to Norris (who glared at her, clearly intent on holding a grudge because she hadn't called him to say she knew where Patty was) and followed Sara from the room.

A surreal trance-like state settled over Majedah as she sat in the makeup artist's chair for the final preparations. By the time she was led into the studio (the actual *An Hour of Your Time* studio, but with Carol Crawford's feminine renovations replaced with an understated, plain set) to take her place for the show, she had become preternaturally calm. Her microphone was attached, her nose was powdered, and she was left alone on the dove-gray linen sofa. She was a cobra, perfectly still and poised, beautiful and deadly, coiled in readiness to deal the fatal strike.

The camera lights went on. "Five, four," the producer counted down, using only her fingers for the final three digits.

And then the inaugural edition of *An Hour of Your Time with Majedah Cantalupi-Abromavich-Flügel-Van Der Hoven-Taj Mahal* went live.

Chapter 27

IN THE MASSIVE 24-7 conference room, the scene was reminiscent of the night of Carol Crawford's fateful interview with Senator Harper. Huge screens lined the walls, champagne flowed, and every News 24/7 employee who wasn't directly involved in producing the program was crammed into the space. The only difference was the mood in the room; instead of the euphoric jubilation inspired by Angela Harper's appearance, a red-tinged bloodlust sharpened the tone of the celebration. The staffers were here to see the enemy vanquished.

Dylan, the recently hired copywriter, couldn't suppress his anxiety. He had only been on the job a few days the last time everyone gathered in the conference room for a viewing party, and that had ended in disaster. "Do you think this will work?" he asked.

Chester gave him a confident look. "It already has worked," he declared. "Just by being here, Patty Clark has admitted that she partakes of women's health services, which she wants to deny to all other women. So, she's lost the women's vote. And she's also lost the religious fanatics' vote. She's done."

Dylan nodded in understanding and his tense posture relaxed visibly. "That's what I was thinking. So, this is really just for fun?"

"Yes. It's our victory lap." Chester licked the back of his hand and ran it over the crown of his head several times, smoothing his jet-black hair. "This is where we parade the body of our enemies' leader for them all to see and be completely demoralized, so they never, ever try to take power again."

Rosemary, who was passing by the men on her way to the catering table, commented, "If all goes well, Majedah will get Patty to cede the election tonight. We may not even need an Election Day this year."

A whoop rose up around her from everyone who had been in earshot of her comment.

"Rosemary, what's our viewing share?" asked Chester.

The director gave him a triumphant grin. She raised her voice to be heard over the exhilerated buzz and announced, "Attention, everyone! As of now, we can safely say that every television in America is tuned to us, and globally, four billion people are live-streaming us!"

The entire room said "Wow" in unison before breaking into rapacious cheering. On the multiple massive screens, the opening sequence of the breathlessly anticipated show began to play. In equis excitement, Mara leapt atop the long conference table and began to canter from one end to the other. "It's starting, it's starting!" equee whinnied. Then equee began to rear and pedal equis front hooves in the air.

Mysty, whose view of the nearest screen was blocked by equis antics, hissed, "Oh my god, Mara, *stop*."

"Really, Mara, do you always have to be such an asshole?" added Scout.

Mara went back down on all fours and glared at them. "Sorry that my excitement *bothers* you two so much," equee sneered before jumping off the far side of the table.

"Equee always has to overdo it," grumbled Scout. Mysty nodded in angry agreement.

Then all eyes were on the screens.

"Good evening and welcome to *An Hour of Your Time.* I'm Majedah Cantalupi-Abromavich-Flügel-Van Der Hoven-Taj Mahal, your host for the evening, and tonight, we at News 24/7 bring you a presentation of utmost importance as America makes up its mind."

Up on the top floor of the skyscraper, in an elegantly furnished lounge with two full walls of windows offering views of Manhattan and massive TV screens on the other two, another celebration was taking place. In the center of the room, a huge ice sculpture of the presidential seal presided over chilled shellfish, shrimp, caviar, crab, and lobster delicacies. Tuxedoed servers poured champagne for a hundred executives, stars, and guests, and there were linen-topped tables covered with bowls of strawberries and litchi fruit and platters of artisanal cheeses, bread crisps, and rare cured meats. Richard Spinner, dressed impeccably in white tie, nudged Angela Harper, pointed with his chin at a screen, and asked, "What do you think of our new girl, there?"

"You mean, your new *woman*?" she chided him with a wink. "Remember your words, Richard." The just-about-president-elect watched Majedah speak for a moment before nodding approvingly. "She's young, but she's smart and well-spoken."

"And she's a true believer," Spinner assured her.

"Well, then, if she can pull this off—and I dare say she can—she's got a future. After all, it's crucial to our future electoral strategy that we make women of color the face of our party." The senator squinted at the screen. "What is she, anyway? Mexican?"

"I'm not sure. Arab of some kind, I think."

"Oh, an Asian. Kinky. I like it." She bumped him playfully with her creaking hip and grinned. Spinner clinked his flute to hers and they toasted the evening.

In the studio, Majedah stood to greet her guest. She was

momentarily disoriented by how good Patty looked. The woman was here because she was broken and humiliated, so why was she standing so straight, with her head held high? Her shoulder-length halo of ringlets shone and bounced, and her eyes were bright and sharp. She strode purposefully towards Majedah, and the young anchorwoman had no time to shake off her misgivings before Patty had the audacity to embrace her and kiss her on the cheek, like they were at a cocktail party or something. Like they were equals.

Majedah recovered quickly and gestured for Patty to join her on the sofa. She quickly recalled her victorious mindset and began. "CEO Clark—Patty, if I may—"

"You may, Majedah," said Patty with a cheerful nod.

"Patty," continued Majedah. She concentrated on maintaining a tone that was partly sympathetic and partly righteous. "You've come to us tonight because you want to tell America something." She was relieved to see her guest's expression finally become contrite.

"Yes, that's true, Majedah. I've committed a sin, and I want to confess it to you, live, on the most-watched news channel in the world, so that I can put it into my own words. Because, as we all know, confession is good for the soul."

"Yes, that's true." Majedah would have agreed to anything to keep Patty Clark talking in this vein. She remembered her coaching and set the stage for the candidate's downfall. "And as you've just demonstrated, you are a practicing Christian. According to polls, America's "values voters" had planned on casting their votes for you. It must be very painful for you to have to admit that you've let them down like this."

Patty gave a maddeningly casual shrug. "Well, we Christians understand that no one is without sin. Or as you secular folk like to say, nobody's perfect."

"Yes, but, you must admit, we're talking about an extremely serious sin here. The worst kind, in fact."

"What's the worst kind of sin?" asked Patty.

"Why, murder, of course. Killing an innocent baby." Majedah paused uncertainly. *Did she just get me to refer to women's health rights as murder?* she wondered. Patty's knowing look and sidelong grin confirmed that this was exactly what had happened.

"Well, now, I don't know that I did anything that terrible," said the candidate.

In the conference room five stories below, the jubilant atmosphere had shifted subtly. The happy background buzz had grown completely silent as everyone stared at the screens uneasily.

"You know, Patty doesn't look as broken up as I expected her to." Dylan inadvertently voiced what everyone was thinking.

In the elite lounge above, the revelers continued eating, drinking, and talking, except for the few who were actually watching the interview. Among these was Richard Spinner. He elbowed a waiter out of the way and moved closer to one of the screens, so that no one could walk between it and him, until he was standing directly in front of it, head tilted back to see the entire image, his Pernod-Ricard Perrier-Jouet fizzing, neglected, in one hand.

Anger made Majedah's words come out clipped and harsh. "Yes, well, why don't you tell our audience exactly what it is you did, and they can make up their own minds about how serious it was."

"That's what I came here to do," confirmed Patty. "But this is America, and I have the right to face my accuser."

Majedah was so flustered she had forgotten about Alice, who was waiting off set. She faced the camera. "For our audience, let me explain that CEO Clark has requested that her sister, Alice, join us for this interview. Alice, as you know, is the brave citizen who first came forward with this important information about the Republican candidate for the presidency. So, we're going to bring her into the studio now to join us."

The two women stood and looked to one side. The broadcast cut to a shot of Alice Clark walking onto the set. The station stylists had found a sophisticated, saddle-colored suede pantsuit for Alice and piled her frizzy hair into a casual updo on top of her head. Her makeup was soft and natural, and the junkie actually looked fabulous.

Majedah's glance bounced from one sister to the other, watching for signs of rage that she could stoke into a physical altercation. Every employee in the conference room below held his breath. In the executive lounge above, Spinner clenched his fists and muttered, "Come on, come on," under his breath.

Patty stood with her hip cocked, feet planted firmly on the floor, and arms crossed over her chest. Her chin was pulled back, her mouth was a thin, tight line, and her brows were drawn down over narrowed eyes. Majedah rubbed her hands in anticipation and watched the candidate's sister approach.

From the moment she set foot in the room, Alice's gaze was locked with her sister's. Her entrance was slithery and slouchy, but her eyes were hard and her jaw was set.

Majedah could practically see searing bolts of negative energy shooting between the two women. Patty stood steady as a rock, wrath and betrayal carved into her expression. Alice crept towards her like the craven skank she was, a smirk pulling at her mouth even in the face of her sister's white-hot rage. The distance between them closed to 20 feet, then 15, then five. In the conference rooms and lounges of the building, in parties across America, and in every corner of the world, viewers held their breath as the impending contact came closer. Majedah felt like she was watching a flaming meteor of death crashing towards the earth and, fearing the impact, she discreetly stepped back several paces from Patty's side.

Never breaking eye contact, Alice sidled right up to Patty and came to a halt inches away from her. Then the women faced off, glaring into one another's eyes. The tension was so thick that Majedah thought she would scream. Along with the rest of the world, she was paralyzed, waiting to see what would happen next.

Patty flinched first. Her shoulders gave a sort of shudder and she made a snorting sound.

Then Alice made several more snorting sounds through her nose. Her shoulders rolled forward and seemed to convulse.

Suddenly both women were shaking with laughter, the kind of mirth that comes from deep within and involves the entire body. They collapsed into each other's arms and hugged one another, howling and cackling.

Majedah did not understand what was happening, but she knew it wasn't good. Cold panic swept over her as she watched the sisters, and the triumph she had been feeling fled in the face of a deadening numbness. At last, her journalist senses overrode her helplessness and commanded her, *Do something!* She glanced at the camera for reassurance then approached her guests. "Um, excuse me, ladies, but would you like to tell the rest of us what's going on?" she inquired in a snotty voice.

Patty and Alice both turned to face her, wiping their eyes and sniffling, Patty's arm over Alice's shoulders and Alice's around Patty's waist. "Whoo! Yes, sorry, of course," said the candidate. "I was just fixin' to make my confession now, if y'all are ready for it."

"Yes, we're ready," said Majedah coldly. "That's why we're here—so you can face your accuser and confess your sin." She hoped wildly that maybe it was still going to be okay.

Patty clasped both her hands in front of her and stood in a parody of contrition. She tucked in her chin, pouted out her lower lip, and looked up at Majedah from beneath thick lashes. "I, Patty Clark, confess that I have committed a sin," she pronounced. "The sin of lying."

Majedah was baffled. "Lying—?"

"To you!" Patty dissolved into another fit of hysteria, joined by her sister.

"Me too!" said Alice. They clung to one another as they roared and shook and doubled over.

Although Majedah still didn't understand what was going on, her gut told her it definitely wasn't going to be okay. A high-pitched ringing began to sound in her ears and her vision darkened, as though the lights had gone dim. She thought she could feel the building shake. Distraught, she looked at Sara for guidance, but the producer seemed as unnerved as she was.

Majedah faced the cackling sisters. "You lied? What did you lie about?"

"About inducing abortions," snorted Patty. "I never did any such thing. I'd never kill any of my babies. I love my babies."

"And I lied about being a greedy junkie," Alice chimed in.

"But I was in your house," Majedah argued. "I saw the wretched conditions you and your children live in."

"That's because she's too proud to take a single penny from her baby sister," explained Patty between fits of giggling. "She'll only take hand-me-down clothes from her kids' cousins, but that's it."

Majedah grasped for the last disappearing vestiges of the story she had broken. "But why is she so poor, then? Why doesn't she have a job? And her son even said she goes to the hospital sometimes. I saw scars from needle marks on her arms."

"I'm poor and I go to the hospital because I'm sick," said Alice. "I have severe Crohn's disease, and sometimes it flares up real bad."

"That's right," explained Patty. "She looks like death warmed over and she can't hold a job because she's sick, not because she's an addict ... something a real journalist could have figured out really easily—if she had tried," she added.

"B-but I did my research," Majedah insisted. "What about the pharmacist who filled your RU-486 prescriptions?"

The sisters looked at one another, and Alice answered first. "You must've talked to Howard Merkel." She held her hand level, just above her own head. "About this tall? Greasy brown hair and glasses?"

"Y—yes..."

"Yeah, he hates me," said Patty. "Not only that, he spends all his free time volunteering at the local Angela Harper-for-President office. A fact he talks about all the time on social media, if you had bothered to look."

"But ... but so what?" Majedah tried. "Just because he's a Democrat, doesn't mean you didn't get the prescription."

"It does mean that he's strongly biased against me and motivated to lie. And if you had looked into his background at all, you'd have learned he's known around town for gossiping, slander, vandalism, and he's also passed a few bad checks in the past. So, yeah, he's quite capable of lying. But you didn't look into his background, just like you didn't look into Alice's. These people said what you wanted to hear, and that was good enough for you," Patty finished archly.

The ringing in Majedah's ears grew louder and this time, she was certain she really did feel the building shake. Several small fragments of ceiling tile fell to the ground nearby, trailed by a plume of dust. Cameramen and techs exclaimed uneasily and looked at the ceiling. Majedah could think of nothing more to say. In a growing state of shock, she pulled her mic from her jacket, dropped it on the floor, and drifted off the set.

At that moment, an enraged Rosemary burst in. "Majedah!" she barked. "Spinner's office. Now!" She took Majedah's arm, twisted it painfully behind the fallen journalist's back, and frog marched her down the hall to the elevator.

In the conference room below, hysteria had broken out. Chairs and tables were overturned, LED screens were smashed, smoke and dust billowed, and shrieks rent the air. Poor Mara, terrified beyond all sense, galloped through the crowd until equee accidentally collided with Mysty's sizeable backside and crashed to a halt. Equee and mys tumbled to the ground, taking Scout with them. Candy, who stood nearby, pounded Zz fists into equee flanks and screamed, "Be careful! You could have hurt mir and zir!"

Angstrom caught sight of the melee and leapt to Mara's aid. "You've always been jealous of equis beauty," nut cried. Nut lifted a chair above gander head and brought it down on myz upraised arm.

"Argh!" mys screamed. Candy came to myz aid and lifted mys to myz feet. Zz tried to do the same for Scout, but ze was in a full-out battle with Mara. Ze pulled hanks of hair from equis shining silken mane, while equee battered zis with equis hooves. Angstrom tried to hit zis with gander chair too, but Candy came up behind 24 and ripped it from gander grasp, then rapped 24 soundly on gander head with it. Nut sank to the ground, and suddenly no particular pronoun could be applied to the unconscious camera operator.

With a guttural howl, Mohammed ran past them, seized all 6-feet, 6-inches of Chester Chen, hoisted him in the air over his head, and dashed from the room. Ululating madly, he ran up fourteen flights of stairs with the flailing producer held aloft. Then they burst out onto the roof. Without pause, Mohammed ran to the parapet, yelled "Allahu akbar!" and hurled the gangly producer over it. Then he leaned over the edge and watched eagerly as his offering plummeted towards the pavement.

Meanwhile, Rosemary had reached Spinner's office, where the mogul waited. She flung Majedah into the room and pulled the door shut violently behind her.

The young journalist stumbled then regained her footing. She straightened and looked up to see Spinner seething behind his desk and glaring at her. He was hyperventilating and his face was red with hot rage. Majedah could see actual steam lifting off the crown of his head. She swallowed drily, smiled, and said, "You wanted to see me?"

The meeting did not go well. Spinner called Majedah a traitor. He bellowed that, in one show, she had destroyed everything he had spent his entire life building. He called her a stupid cunt and an idiot and a silly little twat. He turned his desk over onto the floor. He threw an Emmy at her and it exploded against the wall next to her. With a shriek, Majedah escaped from the chamber and slammed the door shut behind her.

As she wandered forth, the building shuddered and plaster rained down. Majedah touched her face and her fingers came away red with blood from cuts made by the shattered Emmy. Panicked, drunken elites from the viewing party ran screaming in all directions, some of them careening into her in their terror. Majedah coughed from the dust and smoke as she stumbled zombie-like down the hall.

Something strange was happening. The horror of the destruction of her career and her industry was being overshadowed by something even more massive and more dreadful. The scales were falling from Majedah's eyes, and reality itself was sliding and shifting.

Nothing was reliably true anymore.

Things she had always known to be real turned out to be false: fake silhouettes constructed of meaningless words and cardboard taped together on a foundation of still more untruth. Now the narratives were coming apart and collapsing, leaving an alien, incomprehensible world in their place.

And as they fell, Majedah's entire identity fell with them. Things she had always believed about herself—her intelligence, her sophistication, even her essential goodness—were themselves constructs based on the shattered mirages that lay in pieces all around. Majedah stumbled over a spilled platter of caramelized onion and chèvre wontons as she grasped how very important it had been to her that the narratives were real. She held her head in her hands and clenched her eyes as revelations appeared to her in blinding flashes.

She was not oppressed and victimized because of her sex and ethnicity; in fact, she was extremely privileged, in the country and in the world.

"Ugh," Majedah groaned, grimacing against the pain in her mind.

Patty Clark wasn't an ignorant racist hillbilly; she was a role model who had outsmarted all the supposedly brilliant people in this tottering building.

Majedah came to the elevators, but the doors were stuck open and the alarm was ringing deafeningly. She stumbled over bodies and debris and pushed open the door to the stairwell, then began the long descent from the twentieth floor. Revelations continued to batter her.

People who admired Patty Clark weren't Klansmen and Nazis; they were self-reliant and just wanted to be left alone.

As she passed the floor where she used to work, the door burst open and a brawl spilled onto the landing. Majedah looked at her co-workers and, right before her eyes, they shifted into different creatures altogether than those she had known. Scout and Mysty weren't glamorous women of size; they were obese, sad men who were addicted to medication, cosmetic surgery, and therapy in a never-ending and doomed-to-fail attempt to love themselves. And Mara wasn't a beautiful golden palomino centauress, either; he was a tall, unhappy man with long, stringy, blond hair. His once luxurious tail was now revealed to her as a cheap blond hair extension from Duane Reade that he had pinned to the back of his pants, and his gleaming hooves were really just shiny black tap shoes.

Traditional, faithful lifestyles weren't oppressive and hateful; they were loving, healthy, and sane. It was her colleagues who were hate-filled and sick.

Majedah doubled over with psychic pain as she continued her descent to the lobby, through which she staggered. Fissures opened in the granite floor tiles while chunks of wood and plaster showered down. As she passed Essi Kunz's 12-foot-tall magenta vagina, the sculpture tottered off its plinth and crashed to the ground.

These artworks aren't important or noteworthy. In fact, they're not even art. They're just hideous and demoralizing.

Majedah emerged onto the plaza and limped forward. Fifty yards away, two strapping construction workers were walking up the sidewalk on their way to grab a late supper. One of them, Tony Fabrizio of Queens, was complaining to his companion, Richie Pendergast of Rockland County. "So, she says, 'That's it, Tony. We're through!' And she throws her drink in my lap and storms outta the place."

Richie shook his head sadly. "That's definitely on her, Tony. I wouldn't sweat it. Anyway, you're better off without that psycho."

"I know," Tony replied sadly. "But there goes another six months of my life, down the toilet. And now I'm alone again." He shook his handsome head of wavy dark hair and spread his hands in a supplicating gesture to the sky. "I mean, what's a guy gotta do to find someone, you know?"

As if in answer to his soulful question, a breathless Chester Chen fell gracefully into Tony's outstretched arms. The spindly producer and the beefy builder looked into one another's startled eyes and found love at last.

Up on the roof, Mohammed watched Chester's miraculous salvation with mounting fury. "What the—?" he fumed. Then he fell to his knees, fisted his hands in the air, and threw back his head. "Allahu akbarrrrr!" he howled at the sky as searing hot rage shot through his body, detonating the vest he had worn in hopes of getting near to the Republican candidate at some point that evening. The resulting explosion shook the city for blocks around and set off the collapse of the News 24/7 skyscraper in earnest.

Majedah limped off the plaza and headed uptown. Behind her, the global headquarters of the last of the great media broadcast companies collapsed under the weight of rampant bigotry and dishonesty and crumbled to the ground with a deafening roar and a rush of smoke and dust.

News 24/7 wasn't an enlightened global leader of news; in fact, it hadn't been for decades. Its ever-diminishing audience of clingers to a monolithic past had never admitted to themselves, as had everyone else, that there was a whole world of free-flowing information from unedited, first-hand accounts available on the internet. People now were free to program their own news streams and select their own sources.

I thought I was working towards becoming a cutting-edge news celebrity, but I was really fighting to be the best-known anachronism in a dying medium.

Majedah reeled through the chilly November night, passing through alleys and parks. Reality kept changing, morphing, shifting. It was becoming utterly unrecognizable, even though it had been right in front of her all this time. Her mind was not her own, and the epiphanic blows kept on coming.

Maybe my mother isn't actually a brilliant feminist scientist and businesswoman; maybe she's just a monster.

Most of all, the narrative that had been crucial to Majedah was that Patty Clark was a hypocrite who did what any rational, successful female would have done. No one was so good that she could have all those children and a red-blooded male husband and still be able to build an empire and run for president. *Even those hypocritical Christians sometimes choose not to be pregnant, right? It was the right thing for a woman to do.*

Except that maybe it wasn't, and Patty Clark had been true to her principles after all. She really was that good.

Which meant that Majedah wasn't.

Far from being the intelligent, educated, sophisticated, and moral super-citizen she had always presumed herself to be, Majedah was actually something else entirely. Names for what she really was swarmed her broken mind, and she waved her hands about her head in an attempt to shoo them away. But regret and self-loathing swelled within until Majedah no longer considered herself worth preserving. She staggered across the West Side Highway while cars swerved to avoid striking her; then she scrambled over a Jersey barrier and tumbled down an earthen embankment. Skinned, filthy, and numb, she hobbled beneath an overpass and into a hidden encampment.

"Hey, who's that?" came a rough voice.

Another answered, "Some fancy-ass bitch don't belong here."

In this place, through an interminable night of horrors, several more narratives met their demise. Majedah learned that not all people of color, undocumented immigrants, and homeless people were passive victims of society. In fact, some of them could be quite predatory. Some of them were perfectly capable of victimizing a helpless, traumatized woman in crisis, and of laughing while they did so.

In the gray dawn, when the revelry had spent itself and the abusers had crawled into their makeshift lairs for the day, Majedah lurched onward. Her good clothes had been taken from her, and she wrapped herself in a heavy old overcoat, malodorous and stiff with various dried substances. She traversed the wasteland beyond the highway, while sane, busy people rushed by without taking notice of yet another mentally ill indigent person.

A second night passed in much the same manner as the first, and daylight found the once-up-and-coming journalist slumped in a stupor, back against a concrete pylon, head lolling, and legs splayed out in front of her.

A tiny part of Majedah's brain that still functioned recognized the sounds of a large, expensive vehicle crunching to a stop on the gravel of the nearby service road. Footsteps approached and hands were laid upon her, and for the first time in two days, they were gentle. Majedah felt her head being lifted and her hair brushed back. A masculine voice she didn't recognize said, "Yeah, that's her."

Now a set of feminine footsteps advanced, and Majedah sensed that a woman was bending over her. She summoned the strength to crack open her swollen eyes and found herself looking into the keen amber eyes of the president-elect. "Majedah, baby, I'm sorry we had to put you through that," she said.

Surely, I'm delirious, thought Majedah. She let her eyes close and her head drop again. She heard the woman instruct the secret service agents to put her in the car. She felt hands lifting her, her feet dragging along the ground, and then she was laid on a warm, soft surface. It felt like absolute heaven, and Majedah succumbed to peaceful oblivion.

Chapter 28

A PRESENCE AT her side led her through the blackness. She floated weightless in the ether, turned, and looked down upon a dark planet. Covered in dull, gray plates, it spun in a frigid vacuum.

"Watch," said her companion. Majedah did, and the sphere wobbled unevenly on its axis, spinning ever faster. The hard, dark surface began to glow red, then white, from the speed.

"Oh no! What about the people?" Majedah gasped.

The molten surface began to lump up unevenly, becoming a lopsided mass that threatened to shake the planet out of its orbit entirely. Majedah could hardly watch, but then the suffocating tiles began to dislodge and lift off. Unburdened, the planet spun faster still, and the increase in speed flung off the last of the calcified, deadly mantle.

"Ah," breathed Majedah, as the sun rose over the equator, chasing away the darkness with brilliance and warmth. The planet, now spinning smoothly, was revealed as a vibrant blue and green earth, full of possibilities and delights. "It's so much nicer now."

"Now it's your turn." The presence turned on her instantaneously, tearing, digging, and shredding. Majedah screamed in agony as she felt hair, teeth and nails pulled out. Her skin was raked and rent and torn from her entirely.

"I wish there was another way, but the gentler persuasions had no effect on you," the being explained. And even as Majedah screamed, the torment somehow turned to rejuvenation. A dead, false shell had been peeled away and a clean, honest, natural Majedah had been reborn. She felt the smoothness of her face, the lustrous satin of her hair, and held her unlined hands out in front of her so she could see them. Then she gazed with wonder on the dark angel by her side, the one who had been sent to rebirth her as a clean, awakened, alive girl.

"I'm sorry I had to put you through that," said the angel.

Majedah awoke to see her mother standing over her. "Mom?" she said. "Where am I?"

"You're in the hospital, Majedah," Julia answered. Her eyes looked overly bright.

Majedah tried to lift her arms but they were so weak. She looked down her body to see an IV taped to the inside of each elbow. A crisp white blanket was pulled up to her chest and tucked in tight, making it hard to move. Exhausted, Majedah gave up the effort and closed her eyes briefly before reopening them. Her mother was still there, watching her face intently. She tried to remember how she had gotten there, but the only recent memory she could conjure was some bizarre dream about a space angel and a planet. "What happened?" she asked.

"What happened?" repeated Julia. "Oh, not much. The world ended, but no big deal." She gave a bitter laugh.

"What are you talking about?" Majedah squinted as she struggled to reorient herself.

"Why, your big interview, of course." Julia's voice was much too animated. Majedah groggily noticed that she sounded manic as she spoke. "You know, the interview where you made the greatest news organization ever to exist look like a bunch of idiots? The one where you let some ignorant hillbilly fry cook make fools of everyone?"

Majedah's brow furrowed as unpleasant memories began to come back.

Julia, watching her expression, nodded vigorously. "Rings a bell, does it? Now you remember how you were basically responsible for the upset election of the new Hitler? How you catapulted the wrong candidate into the White House? How you singlehandedly destroyed history?"

"What? Patty won?" Then Majedah's poor, fractured mind went white with terror as she saw Julia draw a large butcher's knife from her purse, grasp it with both hands, and raise it in the air over her bed.

"Mom! What are you doing?" squealed Majedah.

"I'm doing what I should have done twenty-five years ago; I'm aborting you, Majedah!"

Majedah screamed as the knife came down. Then the door burst open and suddenly a man was there, wrestling with Julia. "Let me go, you fascist," hissed the feminist scientist. But she was no match for Kevin's strength, and he soon disarmed her and pinned her arms behind her back.

The sounds of the scuffle had drawn in a hospital security officer. He took custody of the raving feminist from Kevin, then spoke into his walkie-talkie. Soon, two white-coated orderlies appeared with an enormous net, which they threw over Julia. She spat and yowled as they carried her from the room. "Lucky for you, there's an empty bed in the special wing," one of them told her. "You'll be good as new before you know it."

With the drama averted, the room was now empty except for patient and visitor. Kevin stood awkwardly against the wall as though afraid to get too close. "I'm sorry. I hope you don't mind me bursting in like that. I would have knocked first, but it seemed pressing that I enter at once," he babbled nervously. "Anyway, I know you're not interested. I'm not here to be a problem, I just wanted to make sure you were okay. I'll go now—"

"Kevin," Majedah interrupted him. "Come here, please."

"Well, okay, I mean, if you're up for it." He approached the bed cautiously, his face pink, until he stood beside her.

"Come closer," Majedah said weakly.

Kevin bent to be able to hear her better. Majedah reached up, pulled his face to hers, and locked her lips to his. The young engineer flailed his arms and grew redder still, but only for a moment. Then he surrendered to the most thrilling kiss he had ever experienced. When it finally ended, it left a crooked grin on his face. "So, I guess this means you're feeling better?" he ventured.

Majedah looked up into his honest, decent (and not to mention, rather good-looking) face and answered, "I've never felt better in my life."

OVER SIX YEARS had passed since the fall of the house of Spinner, and it turned out that a mere fry cook who had earned her degree from the School of Hard Knocks rather than the Ivy League actually had a lot of common sense and good ideas. America had shaken off her malaise and rediscovered herself as a nation of optimists and individuals, and times were booming.

It also turned out that petrochemical engineers were very well compensated. So much so, in fact, that Mandy McGuiness did not need to seek employment outside her home. And so it was that one afternoon, in the late stages of her fourth pregnancy, she took advantage of a moment's peace to enjoy a nap in a backyard chaise lounge. The sound of the backdoor slamming open awakened her. As her eyes flickered open, Mandy saw her mother leaning over her, a jeweler's loupe in one eye and a calculator in one hand as she fitted a set of calipers to Mandy's protruding midsection.

"Oh, Mom, really!" Mandy chided. "I thought we talked about this."

Kevin appeared, a chunky baby in one arm. "I'll take that," he said, plucking the measuring device from his mother-in-law's hands.

"I was just looking," protested the white-haired grandmother. "Looks like another nine-pounder is in the works!" She smiled dotingly.

"Grandma, come push me on the swings," demanded a small, freckly boy with russet curls and robin's egg blue eyes.

"Me too! Me too!" pouted his black-haired younger sister. She jumped and grabbed for her grandmother's hand.

"Okay, okay." Julia took the chubby baby from his father and followed the older siblings across the emerald lawn to the swing set.

Kevin pulled a lawn chair close to his reposing wife and sat. He took her hand in his and stroked it fondly as they watched their children play. "Did you have a nice nap?" he asked.

"Yes, I did. Thanks for an hour of peace and quiet." Mandy's stomach rumbled. "Hmm, looks like it will be a perfect evening for grilling out," she commented.

"Sure does."

Mandy let her gaze run over the pleasing contours of her husband's face, then across the yard at her growing family. A feeling of profound peace and joy, which seemed to accompany her most of the time these days, washed over her now. She felt an acute sense of belonging: to this man, to this family, to this place, to the bright, good earth on which they existed, and to the One who had put them all here. She closed her eyes in silent gratitude.

After all, she figured, her life was pretty good.

Fin

About The Author

Ms. Boule thanks everyone who has provided moral support, feedback, advice, and encouragement in the creation of this satire. She is grateful for her friends in the literary world who laugh along with her as SJW insanity rages in all directions. May we never lose our sense of humor.

Ms. Boule entertains correspondence at
DeploraBoule@gmail.com.

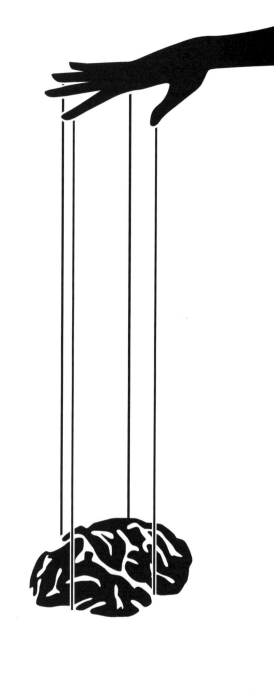

Made in the USA
San Bernardino, CA
12 December 2019